"The entire series is simply elegant."
—Lisa Gardner, #1 *New York Times* bestselling author of *Before She Disappeared*

"Thoroughly enjoyable . . . moody and atmospheric, exposing the dark underside of Regency London."
—Deanna Raybourn, *New York Times* bestselling author of *An Unexpected Peril*

"This riveting historical tale of tragedy and triumph, with its sly nods to Jane Austen and her characters, will enthrall you!"
—Sabrina Jeffries, *New York Times* bestselling author of *The Bachelor*

"Filled with suspense, intrigue, and plot twists galore."
—Victoria Thompson, *USA Today* bestselling author of the Gaslight Mysteries

"Harris is a master of the genre." —*The Historical Novels Review*

"Harris melds mystery and history as seamlessly as she integrates developments in her lead's personal life into the plot."
—*Publishers Weekly* (starred review)

"With such well-developed characters, intriguing plotlines, graceful prose, and keen sense of time and place based on solid research, this is historical mystery at its best." —*Booklist* (starred review)

"Perfect reading. . . . Harris crafts her story with the threat of danger, hints of humor, vivid sex scenes, and a conclusion that will make your pulse race. Impressive." —*The New Orleans Times-Picayune*

WHAT THE DEVIL KNOWS

A Sebastian St. Cyr Mystery

C. S. HARRIS

BERKLEY
New York

BERKLEY
An imprint of Penguin Random House LLC
penguinrandomhouse.com

Copyright © 2021 by The Two Talers, LLC
Excerpt from *When Blood Lies* copyright © 2022 by The Two Talers, LLC

Map of London courtesy the Lionel Pincus and Princess Firyal Map Division,
The New York Public Library / New York Public Library Digital Collections

ISBN: 9780593102688

The Library of Congress has catalogued the
Berkley hardcover edition of this book as follows:

Names: Harris, C. S., author.
Title: What the devil knows : a Sebastian St. Cyr mystery / C. S. Harris.
Description: New York : Berkley, [2021] | Series: A Sebastian St. Cyr mystery
Identifiers: LCCN 2020030401 (print) | LCCN 2020030402 (ebook) |
ISBN 9780593102664 (hardcover) | ISBN 9780593102671 (ebook)
Subjects: GSAFD: Mystery fiction.
Classification: LCC PS3566.R5877 W4733 2021 (print) |
LCC PS3566.R5877 (ebook) | DDC 813/.54--dc23
LC record available at https://lccn.loc.gov/2020030401
LC ebook record available at https://lccn.loc.gov/2020030402

Berkley hardcover edition / April 2021
Berkley trade paperback edition / March 2022

Printed in the United States of America

For our little tuxedo girl, Nora,
June 2000 to January 2020

Más sabe el diablo por viejo que por diablo:
"Most of what the devil knows is due to the fact
that he's old rather than because he's the devil."

—OLD SPANISH SAYING

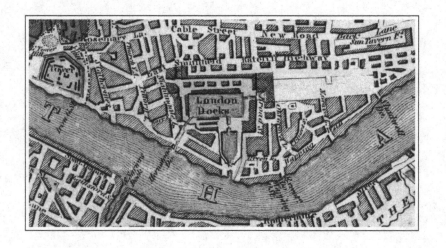

WHAT THE DEVIL KNOWS

WHAT THE DEVIL KNOW 5,7

Chapter 1

Saturday, 8 October 1814

Molly Maguire hated the fog. Hated the way it reeked of coal smoke and tore at her throat. Hated the way the damp, suffocating blanket could turn even the most familiar lane into something ghostly and strange.

It was always worse at night, when the temperature plummeted and folks lit their fires. That's when the mist would drift up from the docks, swallowing the dark hulls and tall masts of the big ships at anchor out on the river and creeping along the mean streets and foul alleyways of the part of East London known as Wapping. Sometimes Molly would dream of a different life, the life she'd once known, when cold, wet nights were spent safe and dry in a warm, gently lit cottage. But that life belonged to the past. In this life Molly walked the streets at night.

She'd been on her own since before she turned thirteen, and she told herself she should be used to it by now. Yet after three years, she still shrank from servicing men with foul breath and rough hands and urgent, rutting manparts. It didn't hurt anymore like it had at first, at least not usually. But Molly still hated it even more than she hated the fog.

The bell in the clock tower of St. George's-in-the-East struck midnight, the dull clangs sounding oddly loud in the dense fog. If business had been good, Molly would have given up and gone back to the small, wretched room she shared with five other girls. But she was desperate for money. It might be Saturday night, but the fog had driven most potential customers off the streets. She'd had a couple of drunken seamen who took turns on her, one right after the other, then demanded a discount. But even they weren't as bad as the fat old magistrate who'd pinned her against one of the looming towers of St. George's.

A man like him, he could've bought himself a fine piece of Haymarket ware and tumbled her in the back room of a Covent Garden coffeehouse. Instead he'd picked up a cheap little Wapping doxy and taken her up against the soot-stained old stones of the church, his big hands tearing at her bodice and painfully squeezing her breasts as he thrust into her hard enough to make her wince. She could still smell the stink of his spilled snuff and fine brandy clinging to her. And when it was all over and she'd asked for her money, he'd laughed at her.

"I don't pay whores," he said, buttoning his flap over his ponderous gut.

"Wha-aat?" she'd wailed. "What you think? That I did this because I—"

He backhanded her across the mouth, splitting her lip against her teeth. "Consider yourself fortunate that I've decided not to have you committed."

"Fat old wagtail," Molly muttered now to herself. It felt good, saying it out loud, so she said it again. "Fat old wagtail. Should've lifted his bloody watch, that's what I should've done. He owed me, he—"

She broke off as a dark, bulky shadow emerged from the fog swirling up near the corner. Probably old Ben Carter, she thought. She'd already tangled with the watchman once tonight and was in no mood to deal with him again. The black mouth of a noisome alley yawned beside her, and she ducked into it, gagging as the stench of rotting fish heads, rancid cabbage leaves, and what smelled like raw entrails enveloped her. She had her head turned, looking anxiously over her shoulder for the watchman, when her foot caught on something and she pitched forward.

"Mother Mary and all the saints," she swore softly as she came down on what felt like a big overstuffed sack. Her outflung hands slid over warm, smooth cloth and something else. Something wet and sticky.

Rearing back with a gasp, she stared down at the man before her, at the familiar greatcoat with silver buttons, at the hideous yawning wound in that fat neck, at the fine once-white cravat now soaked dark with blood. More blood matted his bushy gray hair and swooping side-whiskers. She sucked in a quick breath and smelled him, smelled the brandy and the snuff and the blood.

A scream rose in her throat, but she choked it back. In her mind she was screaming, screaming over and over again, her heart pounding in her chest. She heard the sound of heavy approaching footsteps and threw a panicked glance back at the mouth of the alley in time to see Watchman Ben pass with his lantern.

"Twelve o'clock on a foggy night and all is well," he called.

She pushed to her feet, ready to run as soon as the watchman was safely gone. Then her gaze fell on the body before her, on the gold watch and chain spilling from that blood-splattered silk waistcoat, and she hesitated.

Molly might be a whore, but she'd never been a thief. Still, the man did owe her, didn't he?

She told herself he owed her.

Chapter 2

$\mathscr{T}$he Frenchman was nervous.

Small, lithe, and dark-haired, with a hawklike nose and hooded, nervous eyes, he stood beside the fire crackling on the hearth of Sebastian's library, hands stretched out to the blaze. The morning had dawned cold and gloomy, the sky leaden, the city wrapped in mist. "They're watching me," said the man, his French low and quick. "Even here in London, I've been followed."

Sebastian St. Cyr, Viscount Devlin, heir to the powerful Earl of Hendon, stood with his hips resting against the edge of his heavy, dark oak desk, his arms crossed at his chest and his gaze on the man who'd been on his payroll for the last five months. "Do you know why?"

"Who can say? When the Bourbons drove into Paris, they claimed the past would be forgotten. They spoke of healing wounds and uniting all Frenchmen together again." The man's lips pulled away from his teeth into a rictus of a smile. "They lied. Louis himself might mean well, but his brother and niece are vicious snakes. They're beginning to move against anyone they consider their enemies, bringing back the Jesuits, strengthening the power of the church. . . . There have already been deaths. There will be more. I'm not going back."

"Where will you go?"

"Louisiana, perhaps. I hear they speak French there." The man, whose name was Labourne, rolled his shoulders in a Gallic shrug. "I'm sorry I do not have more to report."

Sebastian nodded, swallowing his disappointment and frustration. It had been more than twenty years since the sun-spangled summer morning when his mother, Sophia, the beautiful, gay, scandalous Countess of Hendon, had sailed away from Brighton, never to be seen again; three years since he'd discovered she hadn't drowned that day, as he'd always been told. At first, war with France made tracing her difficult. But with the abdication of Napoléon, Sebastian had assumed the task would become easier.

He'd been wrong.

"Can you recommend someone who could take up where you left off?"

Labourne frowned thoughtfully at the nearby wall of leather-bound books. "There are one or two who might be willing. When I have spoken to them, I will send you their names."

Sebastian pushed away from the desk. "Thank you."

He was standing at the library window and watching the Frenchman stride swiftly down the wet street when Hero came to rest her hand on the small of his back.

"I'm sorry," she said softly.

He turned to take her in his arms, holding her close, breathing in the sweet familiar scent of her. She was a tall woman, nearly as tall as he, dark-haired and Junoesque in build, brilliant and strong, and he loved her and their son with a ferocity that filled his life with joy and, sometimes, terror.

After a moment, he drew a deep breath and said, "Do you think I'm wrong to keep trying to find her?"

Hero lifted her head from his shoulder to meet his gaze. "No."

"She obviously doesn't want to be found."

"Perhaps not. But she owes you answers."

"Does she?"

"I think so, yes." She paused, and he expected her to say, *I just hope you're ready for whatever answers she might have to give.* But all she said was, "The man has no idea where she might be?"

"He says she was in Paris, then traveled to Vienna. It was when he followed her to Vienna that he realized he was being followed himself."

"By agents working for the Bourbons?"

"He thought so, and I'm inclined to believe him."

"But . . . why? Because of what he used to do in the past, or because of what he was doing for you now?"

"I'm not sure." Sebastian glanced down the street again. The Frenchman was gone, swallowed up by the mist. "Her presence in Vienna is . . . puzzling." In the wake of Napoléon's defeat, the representatives of Europe's leading states were gathering in the Austrian capital, intent on hammering out a long-term peace plan and rebuilding the world's power structure. The city was crowded with an influx of powerful Englishmen and their hangers-on; it struck him as the last place to appeal to the errant wife of the Earl of Hendon.

"I assume she no longer calls herself Lady Hendon?"

"No. *Dama* Cappello."

"Cappello? Why?"

"Labourne didn't know."

A hackney coach drawn by a big, rawboned bay appeared out of the fog, and they watched together as the ancient vehicle drew up before their steps with a rattle of trace chains.

"Who's that?" asked Hero as a beefy, bushy-browed man in a brown corduroy coat swung open the carriage door and hopped down.

Sebastian felt a sense of foreboding settle upon him. "One of Sir Henry's constables. Something must have happened."

Chapter 3

*Y*ou'd think an East End magistrate'd have more sense than t' go wandering around someplace like Wapping in a stinkin' fog."

This piece of worldly wisdom came from Tom, the small, sharp-faced young tiger who perched at the rear of Sebastian's curricle as he drove east through the City. Once, Tom had been a pickpocket. But after serving as Sebastian's groom for more than three years, the lad had ambitions of someday becoming a Bow Street Runner.

Sebastian guided his chestnuts around a plodding brewer's wagon, then said, "It is rather curious, I'll admit."

"It's bleedin' harebrained, that's what it is."

Sebastian ducked his head and smiled.

They drove up the rain-drenched expanse of the Strand at a spanking pace, then passed through Temple Bar, that ancient division between Westminster and the City of London itself. By now the fog had mostly cleared, with only stray wisps still hovering over the river and clinging to the city's countless belching chimneys. The farther east they traveled, the older, narrower, and more decrepit the houses became, the more ragged the men, women, and wretched children on the streets, the more foul the air. By the time they reached Wapping, they were in an area dominated by the ships rocking at anchor in the Pool of London, by vast docks and looming brick warehouses. This was a district of sailors' victuallers and boat and mast makers, of endless taverns, rowdy seamen, thieves, and whores.

Turning into Nightingale Lane, Sebastian drew up near a shuttered apothecary shop. He could hear the cry of seagulls and the flapping of furled sails from the ships tied up in the nearby basin; smell the reek of tar and resin and dead fish that hung heavy in the air. "That wind has a cold bite to it," he told the boy. "Best walk 'em."

Tom scrambled forward to take the reins. "Aye, gov'nor."

"And keep your ears open. You might hear something useful."

Tom grinned. "I kin do that, too, yer lordship."

Hopping down to the wet, worn cobblestones, Sebastian turned toward a group of somber men huddled in conversation at the mouth of a nearby alley. At his approach, one of the men stepped away from the others and said, "Lord Devlin. My apologies for bringing you out on such a miserable morning."

His name was Sir Henry Lovejoy, and he was one of Bow Street Public Office's three stipendiary magistrates. Small and slightly built, he had a balding head, pinched, unsmiling features, and a serious demeanor. Once, Lovejoy had been a moderately successful merchant. But the tragic death of his wife and daughter some years before had shifted the trajectory of his life, leading him to adopt a severe religious belief and devote himself to public service.

Sebastian had known the dour little magistrate since those dark days when the Viscount had been on the run from a false accusation of murder, and Lovejoy assigned the task of bringing him to justice. Since that time, the two men had cooperated in solving a number of murders, for Sebastian's access to and knowledge of the rarefied world of the Haut Ton made him an invaluable ally when it came to cases involving either the nobility or the royal family. This death was decidedly different, although Sebastian suspected he understood only too well why Lovejoy had reached out to him.

"It's certainly bracing," said Sebastian, walking up to him. Then his gaze went beyond the Bow Street magistrate to the bloody ruin of a man lying farther into the alley, and he whispered, "Good God."

Stout and gray whiskered, the man was sprawled on his back, his heavy arms flung wide at his sides, his legs splayed. What had once been a white cravat was now soaked dark with the blood that had gushed from the gaping slash across his throat and the shattered, sickening pulp that had been the side of his head. The grimy brick walls of the narrow alley were splattered with gore and what Sebastian realized with a twist of his gut must be brain matter. He'd spent six years at war as a cavalry officer, but the sight of violent death still bothered Sebastian, and he suspected it always would.

"Ghastly, isn't it?" said Lovejoy.

Sebastian studied the dead man's full-cheeked, gape-mouthed face; the vacant, staring eyes; the open, buttonless greatcoat; the striped waistcoat; the old-fashioned breeches. Below that, the man's feet were completely bare.

"Someone's helped themselves to his shoes and stockings, I see."

"And his hat, buttons, purse, and watch," said Lovejoy. "I can easily imagine footpads bashing in his head. But why would they bother slitting his throat, as well?"

"It does seem rather excessive."

Lovejoy squinted up at the seagulls wheeling noisily overhead. "I'm told that ten days ago, a seaman by the name of Hugo Reeves was killed not far from here in Five Pipes Fields in Shadwell. His head was smashed in just like this, his throat cut so viciously his head was half off. No one thought much of it at the time. The streets near the docks are always dangerous, although the brutality of the attack was seen as unusual even for around here. But after this . . ."

His voice trailed away, his nostrils flaring as he sucked in a deep breath. "You can imagine what people are now saying."

Sebastian met his troubled gaze. "They're saying it's like the Ratcliffe Highway murders."

Lovejoy pressed his lips together and nodded.

Less than three years before, in December 1811, the East End of London had been terrorized by two horrific sets of murders. First, on 7 December, four members of a family—a twenty-four-year-old linen draper, his young wife, their three-month-old baby, and a fourteen-year-old apprentice—were found with their heads bashed in and their throats slashed. No explanation for the carnage was ever found. Then, just twelve days later, while the city was still reeling from the first attack, the killer struck again at the King's Arms on nearby New Gravel Lane, butchering the fifty-six-year-old publican, his wife, and their maidservant.

Within days of the second murders, a suspect was arrested. But before he could be brought to trial, the man was found hanging in his cell in Coldbath Fields Prison. The authorities immediately declared the case closed. There were whispers, of course: suggestions that the magistrates were too eager to blame the killings on a conveniently dead man. But the ugly, senseless murders ceased. And so with the passage of time, the panic and whispers died down.

"Do you think it's possible?" said Sebastian, his gaze on the stiffening dead man before them. "That this could be the work of the same killer, I mean."

Lovejoy hunched his shoulders against a cold gust of wind. "It always seemed to me that there were certain . . . anomalies in the official version of events. When the murders ceased, I assumed I must be wrong. But now . . ."

Sebastian hunkered down beside the blood-drenched corpse. Despite the cold, the coppery-sweet smell of spilled blood and raw flesh was strong—the stench of death. He had to stop himself from cupping his hand over his nose and mouth. "You say he's a magistrate?"

Lovejoy nodded. "Sir Edwin Pym, of the public office in Shadwell High Street."

Yanking off his glove, Sebastian touched the back of his hand to the dead man's cheek. "He's stone cold. But then, the night was cold. Any idea when he was last seen?"

"According to his housekeeper, he went out last night around ten. She was expecting him back before midnight, but obviously he never returned."

"Does she know where he was going?"

"She claims she does not."

Sebastian glanced over at him. "You say that as if you don't believe her."

A quiver of revulsion passed over Lovejoy's features. "I'm told Pym had a habit of trolling for harlots at night—the younger the better."

"Lovely." Sebastian pushed to his feet, his gaze taking in a nearby pile of smashed hogsheads, a row of overflowing dustbins, the slick gleam of a mound of rotting fish heads. "The alley's been searched?"

"In a preliminary fashion. I'll have the lads tear it completely apart once we've moved the body, but I'll be surprised if they find anything."

Sebastian brought his gaze back to the bloody, shattered ruin of the dead magistrate's head. "What would do that, do you think?"

"An iron bar? A large hammer? I've sent for a shell to have him carried to Gibson. Perhaps he can tell us."

"If anyone can," said Sebastian. A former army surgeon who now made his home in Tower Hill, Paul Gibson could read the secrets a dead body had to tell better than anyone Sebastian had ever known. "The Ratcliffe Highway murderer used a maul, didn't he?"

"For the first set of killings, yes. A seaman's maul. Although I believe there was some confusion as to what he used to cut his victims' throats."

Sebastian studied the gaping wound in the dead man's neck. "This looks like it was done with a sharp razor, but I could be wrong."

Lovejoy started to say something, then paused.

"What?" prompted Sebastian.

Lovejoy cleared his throat. "It may mean nothing, but Sir Edwin Pym was one of the leading magistrates involved in the investigation of the Ratcliffe Highway murders."

Sebastian looked over at him. "And the other victim you mentioned—Reeves? Was he involved in any way?"

"Not that I'm aware. But then, I was at Queen Square Public Office at the time, so my knowledge of the inquiries is limited to what I read in the papers like everyone else."

Sebastian glanced toward the group of men still standing near the mouth of the alley, silently watching them. He recognized the constable who'd been sent to fetch him and a couple of Lovejoy's other lads, but the rest were undoubtedly local. "There are plenty of magistrates in the East End. Why were you brought into this?"

Lovejoy looked vaguely uncomfortable. "Lord Sidmouth has asked me to take over the investigation of the murders." As Home Secretary, Henry Addington, Viscount Sidmouth, was officially in charge of all the stipendiary magistrates of the metropolis's nine public offices. "I'm to report back to him as soon as I leave here."

"An unenviable interview."

Lovejoy pushed out a harsh breath. "Indeed. I'm told the Home Office is most anxious to prevent a resurgence of the panic that gripped the entire city in December of 1811."

"Bit hard to do, once word of this spreads beyond Wapping—as you know it will, soon enough." Sebastian found his gaze drifting back to the dead man's bare feet, now a bluish white. "What do you think? Did the killer strip him of his boots and valuables? Or did someone else come along later and help himself to the easy pickings?"

"The latter scenario, surely? We'll be watching all the pawnshops, of course—although even if some of the stolen items turn up, I doubt it'll tell us much about the murder itself."

Sebastian nodded. "You mentioned Pym's housekeeper. What about his family?"

"He lived alone. His wife died some years ago, and his only daughter is married and lives in Stepney. I'm told there's a son, as well, but he's a sea captain with the East India Company."

"You said the man killed last week was a seaman?"

"A ship's carpenter, yes."

"The man blamed for the Ratcliffe Highway murders was also a seaman, was he not?"

"He was, yes. But then, most people around here are connected in some way to the maritime trade."

"Given the three-year gap between these new murders and what happened in 1811, it's possible we're dealing with a seafaring man—a killer who sailed away three years ago and is now back."

"How perfectly ghastly to think about. But why would such a man go after an unknown sailor and a Shadwell magistrate?"

"You assume this murderer has a logical reason for what he does." Sebastian let his gaze drift over the gore-splattered wall beside them and felt a new ripple of disquiet sluice through him. "If I had to guess, I'd say it's more likely that whoever did this simply enjoys killing."

Chapter 4

"Is it true, what folks are sayin'?" asked Tom when Sebastian walked back to the curricle some minutes later. "That the Ratcliffe Highway murderer is alive and that 'e's at it again?"

Sebastian leapt up to the carriage's high seat to take the reins. "It's either him or a copyist who wants us to think the murders are all the work of the same killer."

Tom scrambled back to his perch. "Why would somebody want that?"

"To frighten people, perhaps."

"Well, I'd say folks around 'ere is mighty scared, no doubt about that. Didn't 'ear nobody talkin' about nothin' else."

"Can't say I blame them," said Sebastian, giving his horses the office to start.

He went first to Sir Edwin Pym's impressive eighteenth-century brick house on Wellclose Square, one of the few affluent areas in Wapping.

The dead magistrate's housekeeper was a dour-faced older woman with iron gray hair, a sparse bosom, and a steely demeanor that gave no quarter. Mrs. Tyndale was her name, and she insisted once again that she had no idea where her master had gone the previous night or why. Nor had she any idea who might have wanted to kill him.

"A God-fearing man, he was," she said, staring at Sebastian as if daring him to contradict her. "God-fearing and righteous."

A God-fearing, righteous man with a taste for abusing very young prostitutes, thought Sebastian. But there was no point in saying it.

Leaving Lovejoy's constables to search the dead man's house, Sebastian turned his horses toward the home of Pym's daughter. But first he made a stop at the ancient Roman road now known as Ratcliffe Highway.

Stretching east from the old City of London, the highway ran parallel to the river Thames to form the unofficial northern boundary of Wapping. Shadwell lay to the east and Tower Hill to the west, with Whitechapel to the north. It was a dangerous area of seedy lodging houses, looming warehouses, and rough men.

With the mist blowing cold against his face, he drew up opposite Number Twenty-nine Ratcliffe Highway. The building's narrow, ordinary-looking ground floor was now a chandler's shop. But three years ago it had been the premises of linen draper Timothy Marr and his young wife, Celia.

Sebastian studied the shop's neatly painted green door and wide bay window. They said Marr and his young family had lived in the house only eight months before dying there so hideously. The man had sailed on the East Indiaman the *Dover Castle* before marrying and settling down with his new wife and child to become a respectable shopkeeper. He'd taken on two apprentices, a fourteen-year-old shop boy named James Gowan and a thirteen-year-old servant girl, Margaret Jewell.

Did you know you were in danger? Sebastian wondered, staring across the cart- and wagon-choked street at the simple brick building. *Did you know someone was watching you, waiting for the chance to strike?*

According to all reports, the answer was no.

It had been a Saturday in early December. Timothy Marr had his shop open late that night, for this was a working-class neighborhood, and workingmen and -women could do their shopping only after a long day of labor. Tradesmen around Wapping and Shadwell tended to stay open up to midnight on Saturdays, the day working folk received their wages. In fact, Marr kept his linen draper's open so late that he decided to send little Margaret out for oysters.

But the child found it difficult to fulfill her errand, so that it was past twelve by the time she made it back to Number Twenty-nine. She was probably afraid she'd be in trouble for taking so long. Instead, her tardiness saved her life.

Arriving back at the linen draper's, she tried the front door, only to find it locked. Puzzled, she rang the bell and banged the knocker and then, with growing consternation, called to a passing watchman for help. The racket attracted the attention of the pawnbroker next door, who volunteered to climb over the fence between the two shops' rear yards and investigate.

What he found would no doubt haunt him forever.

The young apprentice, James Gowan, lay just inside the open back door to the shop, his face smashed, his brains spilling out of his shattered skull. Beyond him sprawled the broken, bloody remains of Celia Marr and her husband, Timothy Marr. In the kitchen below, their infant son still lay in his cradle, his skull crushed and his throat cut so savagely that the tiny body was nearly decapitated.

The killings were both brutal and senseless. Nothing of such hideous ferocity had happened in London in anyone's memory. A paralyzing terror gripped the city as residents rushed to buy guns, knives, sickles, hammers—anything with which they might defend themselves against such a dangerous killer.

And then it happened again less than two weeks later. At a tavern called the King's Arms just a short distance away in New Gravel Lane, the publican, his wife, and their maidservant were all slashed and beaten to death.

Sebastian lifted his gaze to the sashed windows of the living quarters above the shop and found his thoughts drifting to his own wife and baby son. Hero and Simon were his world, and the fear of somehow losing them haunted his days and nights. He thought about setting up a business and living in a house that had witnessed such a horrible tragedy, and knew he couldn't do it.

He supposed it was possible that the similarities between the two recent killings and the three-year-old murders were entirely coincidental. It was also possible that the new murders were the work of a copyist, someone deliberately modeling his acts on the sensational murders of the past. Or the man responsible for the Ratcliffe Highway killings might not have been the poor sod who'd hanged himself in his cell at Clerkenwell gaol three years ago, but someone else entirely. Someone who was once again active.

As he watched a young apprentice of fifteen or sixteen open the chandler's front door to peer apprehensively about, Sebastian realized he didn't find any of those three possibilities reassuring.

Sir Edwin Pym's daughter lived in a respectable but modest-sized terrace house on a quiet street in Stepney.

Her name was Katie Ingram, and unlike her father, she was petite and very fair-haired, with a small pointed chin, a shy demeanor, and large sad eyes. But if she'd been crying, it didn't show.

She received Sebastian in a modest-sized, simply furnished parlor and was obviously embarrassed to be found wearing a gaily sprigged muslin gown. "I haven't had a chance to assemble proper mourning clothes yet," she said, her hands coming up to slide self-consciously over the upper arms of her long pintucked sleeves.

"Thank you for agreeing to see me at such a time," he said, taking the seat she indicated near the fire. "I know this must be difficult for you."

She settled in the chair opposite him. "Bow Street sent word that you were wanting to ask me some questions, but I don't know how much help I can be. My father and I . . . we haven't spoken to each other in a long time."

"When did you last see him?"

"Well, I *saw* him in Wapping High Street a few months ago. But I haven't actually spoken to him in years." She paused, her gaze on his face. "Does that shock you?"

"No."

She didn't look as if she believed him. "My father didn't approve of my choice of husband, you see. When I turned twenty-one and married Andrew against Papa's express wishes, he said I was dead to him and swore he'd never speak to me again. And he never did."

Sebastian tried to imagine himself cutting off all contact with Simon for such a reason, and couldn't. "I understand you have a brother."

"Yes, Steven. He's the captain of an East Indiaman."

"Did your father speak to him?"

"When Steven was in London, yes. But he's not here at the moment. They sailed six—no, seven months ago now."

"Do you mind telling me the name of his ship?"

"It's the *Lady Perry.* Why?"

"I was wondering if there might be some connection between your family and a seaman who was killed last week. Reeves was his name, Hugo Reeves."

"If there is, I'm not aware of it." She shifted her gaze to the fire, her lips parting as she drew a shaky breath. "They're saying his throat was slit and his head bashed in, like those people killed three years ago on Ratcliffe Highway."

"Yes. I'm sorry."

"I don't understand. The man responsible for those killings is dead."

"So the authorities believe, yes."

A boy's shout, followed by a chorus of children's laughter, drew Sebastian's attention to the windows overlooking the rear gardens, although from this angle he couldn't see anyone on the terrace below. He said, "You've children?"

She smiled. "Yes. Two boys and a girl."

"Did Sir Edwin keep in touch with them?"

She shook her head, her smile fading. "You didn't know my father, did you?"

"No, I didn't."

"He was . . . an unpleasant man. Angry and unforgiving when crossed, endlessly vindictive, scornful of anyone weaker than he, and governed always—*always*—by avarice and greed."

"Do you know of anyone who might have wanted to kill him?"

"Specifically? No. But I suspect the number of those who will truly mourn him is small."

He could see the children now—a sturdy fair-haired boy of perhaps eight, a younger, darker girl, and another even younger boy. And he wondered how any man could have such fine grandchildren and deliberately stay away from them in a fit of pique.

Aloud, he said, "Did you know any of the people who were killed on Ratcliffe Highway and New Gravel Lane three years ago?"

"No, my lord."

"Did your father?"

"I can't say for certain, but I don't believe so, no."

"Do you know if he had other suspects at the time besides the man who killed himself in prison?"

"I remember hearing they'd detained a number of different men, but I don't know if any of them were seriously considered suspects." She started to say something else, then hesitated.

"What is it?" he asked, watching her.

She thrust up from her seat to go stand at the window with her gaze on the children below. "This is going to sound ridiculously fanciful, but . . ."

"Yes?" he prompted again when her voice trailed off.

"I think—no, I *know* someone has been watching us. Not simply watching us, but following us."

Sebastian felt a chill pass over him. "You've seen this person?"

"Not well enough to describe him. He's usually little more than a dark shape that melts into the night, or a shadow that's there and then gone. But I've felt his presence at other times, even when I couldn't see him." The color in her cheeks darkened. "As I said, I know it sounds fanciful."

"How long has this been going on?"

"For a week, at least. Perhaps more."

"Given what happened to your father, I don't see how anyone could doubt you."

From the garden came the little girl's voice, chanting, *"One for sorrow, two for joy . . ."*

Katie Ingram kept her gaze on the children below. "I've been thinking about those families that were killed—about that poor little baby, beaten to death in his cradle with his mother and father lying dead upstairs." She swallowed. "My husband is a captain on a coal rig that runs back and forth between Newcastle and London. He won't be home for at least another ten days, and I . . . I'm frightened."

"Three for a girl, four for a boy . . ."

Sebastian said, "If you'd like, I could speak to Bow Street about having someone assigned to watch the house."

Her lips parted. "Would they do that, you think?"

"Five for silver, six for gold. Seven for a secret, never to be told . . ."

"I think so, yes."

"Oh, thank you. Thank you so much," she said, just as the other two children chimed in on the counting rhyme, their voices rising in a triumphant crescendo.

"Eight for a wish, nine for a kiss.

"Ten for the bird you must not miss."

Chapter 5

Charles, Lord Jarvis, stood at the window of his chambers in Carlton House, his gaze on the wet, crowded forecourt below.

A second cousin to mad old King George III, Jarvis was widely acknowledged as the real power behind the fragile regency of the Prince of Wales, the King's vain, lazy, self-indulgent son. A large, imposing man with piercing gray eyes, Jarvis had a strong aquiline nose and an unexpectedly winning—and very deceptive—smile. He was not smiling now. The dispatches from the peace conference gathering in Vienna looked promising, but the last thing they needed as they set about putting the world back together after the defeat of that Corsican upstart was to have some ridiculous mass hysteria sweep the capital. If—

"Beg your pardon, my lord," said his clerk, clearing his throat, "the Home Secretary has arrived."

"It's about time," snapped Jarvis, turning from the window as Henry Addington, Lord Sidmouth, came in on a swift step.

The clerk bowed discreetly and withdrew.

The Home Secretary paused just inside the doorway, his hat in his hands. "My apologies for keeping you waiting, my lord." He bowed low, the thin, overlong graying dark hair that fringed his balding pate falling forward into his face so that he had to sweep it back as he straightened. "But I thought it best to confer with Sir Henry Lovejoy of Bow Street before—"

Jarvis waved aside his apology with an impatient hand. "What the devil is going on?"

Sidmouth swallowed. In addition to being Home Secretary, he was both a former prime minister and a former speaker of the house, while Jarvis held no official portfolio in the government. But with the exception of the Prince Regent himself, there was no more influential man in all of Britain than Jarvis. Brilliant, utterly ruthless, and in command of a web of spies and informants that gave him a well-earned reputation for being eerily omniscient, he could destroy Sidmouth with a snap of his fingers—and wouldn't hesitate to do so if he considered it best for either Britain or the monarchy.

"I'm afraid it's difficult to say at this point, my lord. Pym's death does indeed mirror those of the Ratcliffe Highway murders of three years ago, as well as that of a seaman killed last week. But I'm told nothing's been discovered so far to suggest these new deaths have anything to do with those of the past."

"But they could conceivably be the work of the same man?"

The Home Secretary's small eyes widened. "Oh, surely not, my lord. I mean, the scoundrel they had in prison hanged himself! Why would a man do that if he weren't guilty?"

"You don't have much of an imagination, do you, Sidmouth?"

The Home Secretary's gaze drifted away. "I take it you're referring to these rumors—the idea that Williams didn't actually hang himself but was in fact murdered in his cell? Surely no one would believe such a thing, my lord."

"You'd be amazed what people believe."

The Home Secretary shifted uncomfortably.

Jarvis went to stand behind his delicate French desk, the fingers of one hand tapping impatiently on the sheaf of reports he'd been reading. "These rumors—and the ridiculous terror accompanying them—must be squashed immediately. Do you understand me? Immediately."

The Home Secretary paled. "I understand, my lord."

"I trust that you do. The last thing the Regent needs at the moment is something like this."

There was no need to expand upon the reasons why this moment was so sensitive. After decades of war with France and—off and on— much of the rest of Europe, Britain was finally at peace. But the long-yearned-for cessation of hostilities was proving in some ways to be as unsettling and disruptive as war. The streets were filled with hungry, ragged ex-soldiers and sailors unable to find work. Wages were collaps-ing and prices spiraling out of control. There was agitation against the government's plan to impose the so-called Corn Laws, an import tax to protect wheat-growing British landowners, which would drive the cost of bread beyond the reach of the poor. And of course Ireland was, as al-ways, hovering on the brink of revolt. The last thing they needed was a string of grisly murders terrifying the already restive population.

"Next time I see you," said Jarvis, "I expect to hear that this wretched episode is behind us."

"Yes, my lord," said Sidmouth, and bowed himself out.

Chapter 6

Why would the same killer strike both a prosperous magistrate and a common sailor? Even if the murders were completely random, the disparity in the victims would be odd. And Sebastian found it difficult to conceive of a meaningful link between the two dead men.

He spent the next several hours down by the docks, talking to various weathered men of the sea, looking for anyone who had known Hugo Reeves. The picture that emerged was of a seaman in his early thirties, of medium height and build, described as a hard-drinking gambler and—according to one old salt Sebastian found nursing a glass of rum in a tavern near Hermitage Basin—"more'n a bit on the ugly side."

"What do you mean by that?" asked Sebastian.

The aging seaman—a gray-whiskered Cornishman named Jago Stark— looked at Sebastian over the rim of his glass. "Means I wouldn't have wanted to turn me back on the bastard, that's what it means."

"Who do you think killed him?"

The older man grunted and took a deep drink of his rum. "Somebody doin' the world a favor."

"Do you know if Reeves had any dealing with Sir Edwin Pym?"

"Who?"

"Sir Edwin Pym, one of the Shadwell magistrates. He was killed last night."

"Well, I wouldn't be surprised if Reeves was hauled before the beaks more'n a time or two."

"What about Timothy Marr, the Ratcliffe Highway linen draper who was murdered three years ago? Could Reeves have known him?"

"Why would he?"

"Marr sailed on the *Dover Castle*. Did Reeves?"

"Don't think so." Stark fixed Sebastian with a long, steady gaze. "Why you askin' all these questions?"

"Just trying to figure out if there could be a connection between the murders."

The seaman shook his head. "People die around here all the time."

"Do you know where Reeves was staying when he was killed?"

"Think maybe it was the Copper Kettle, but I could be wrong. He was the kind of man you stayed away from, if you're smart."

Sebastian tried the Copper Kettle, but the one-legged, gnarled old innkeeper turned his head, spat, and said he'd never let that bugger anywhere near his place. It took a while, but Sebastian finally traced the dead seaman to a mean lodging house on Globe Street.

"Aye, 'e was 'ere," said the slatternly landlady, who sat smoking a clay pipe on a three-legged stool just inside the open front door of her squalid establishment.

"What can you tell me about him?" said Sebastian.

The landlady stared up at him with narrowed, suspicious eyes. "Wot's there t' tell? 'E was a seafarin' man. Liked t' drink, gamble, fight, and tup women. Guess 'e finally tangled with somebody meaner'n 'im who beat 'is 'ead in."

A drizzle had begun to fall, buffeted by the wind coming off the river, and Sebastian could feel the mist billowing in through the open door. "Do you know if he ever had any dealings with Sir Edwin Pym?"

The lodging-house keeper gave a breathy chuckle that showed her toothless gums. "Can't see that sailor 'avin' anythin' t' do wit anybody who's a 'sir.'"

"Can you think of anyone who might have wanted to kill him?"

"Anybody what served on a ship wit 'im, maybe? How'm I t' know?"

"Any of his mates around?"

She sucked on her pipe. "Nah. There were a couple, but they sailed on the *Gosforth* a few days ago."

Sebastian stared out at the rain, frustratingly aware of the fact that he was getting nowhere. He touched his hand to his hat and said, "Thank you," just as the rain began to come down harder.

Before heading back to Mayfair, Sebastian stopped by a coffeehouse in Westminster frequented by ex-cavalrymen.

He found two men there he both knew and respected, and who were at loose ends since the cessation of the war with France. Desperate for any kind of work they could find, they were more than happy to agree to spend the next week or so watching Katie Ingram's house from dusk to dawn. He'd thought about asking Lovejoy to assign a couple of his men to the task, but the Bow Street Runners were doubtless already stretched thin in the race to catch the new East End killer. And truth be told, Sebastian felt more comfortable giving the assignment to men he knew and trusted.

"Who're we watchin' for, exactly?" asked the tall Scotsman named Campbell.

"Anyone who intends the woman or her children harm," said Sebastian.

The Scotsman nodded. "Reckon we can do that, Cap'n."

After that, Sebastian drove back to Stepney to introduce the men to Sir Edwin Pym's daughter and assure her that they would be guarding her house every night. She looked at him with solemn, knowing eyes that glittered with gratitude.

But she was too frightened to risk losing the protection she so desperately needed by inquiring too closely into its origins.

By the time he drew up outside his own bow-windowed town house in Brook Street, it was pouring, with water shooting off the eaves in a dull roar and running deep in the gutters.

"Baby 'em," he told Tom, handing his tiger the chestnuts' reins. "They've earned it. I'll probably be going to Tower Hill later, but if this weather keeps up, I'm taking the damned carriage."

With a laugh, Tom wiped his wet face and moved up to the high seat.

Sebastian hopped down to the pavement, then paused to look back at his tiger through the driving rain. "When you were listening to the gossip in Wapping, did you by chance hear anyone voice their opinion of Sir Edwin Pym?"

"Oh, aye. Right unpopular 'e was, from the sound o' things. They mighta been scared o' the way he was killed, but I'd say more'n a few of 'em are right glad he's dead, however it came about."

Sebastian thought about the dead man's dry-eyed daughter, and nodded. "That sounds about right."

Chapter 7

*H*ero Devlin sat in one of the upholstered chairs beside the drawing room fire. Dressed in a long-sleeved afternoon gown of soft midnight blue wool made high at the neck and embellished with champagne-colored satin rosettes, she had a serviceable notebook balanced on one knee while her young son played on the hearthrug nearby. She was trying to compose a list of questions for the new article she was writing on the miserable fate of London's many orphans, but her thoughts kept straying.

Her series of articles for the *Morning Chronicle* had been enraging her father, Lord Jarvis, for nearly two years now. But while Jarvis terrified virtually everyone from royal dukes to field marshals, his wrath had little effect on his daughter, who was every bit as strong-willed and determined as he—and in some ways nearly as ruthless. Lately it had occurred to her that she was far more like her father than she cared to admit, but she had never decided if that was a good or a bad thing.

She glanced over at Simon, who sat with his legs sprawled out before him, his attention all for the enormous long-haired black cat he was carefully petting with a splayed hand. The cat feigned indifference bordering on disdain, but the truth was that the little boy was its special person.

At twenty months, Simon Alistair St. Cyr was unusually tall, like both his father and his mother, with Devlin's lean build, nearly black hair, and strange yellow eyes. But his winsome smile was that of his maternal grandfather, and as she watched him, Hero found herself wondering just how much of each of his four very different grandparents swirled around within this little boy: Jarvis, so brilliant, hard, and merciless; the scandalous Lady Hendon, so beautiful and so outrageous; Hero's own gentle mother, dead now for over a year; and that other grandfather, the shadowy figure who remained a mystery to them all. The man who had fathered Devlin on another man's wife before disappearing without a trace.

It was the most urgent of the many questions Devlin wanted to ask his mother: *Who is my father?* But Hero was becoming increasingly afraid he might never get the chance to ask it—that he might live the rest of his life never knowing, always wondering.

The front door opened below, and she watched Simon's head lift as a step sounded on the stairs. Then Devlin appeared in the doorway. He'd taken off his wet, many-caped driving coat and tall hat, but rain still glistened on his lean cheeks and flecked his high black boots.

"Papa," cried the little boy, disturbing the cat as he pushed to his feet and ran across the room.

Reaching down, Devlin grasped the baby around his sturdy waist and raised him high. Simon squealed with delight, and Devlin hugged the child so close that the boy squirmed to get down. It was the only indication Devlin gave as to just how deeply what he'd seen that morning had disturbed him. But Hero knew him; knew how much each brush with murder and the violent emotions swirling around it always cost him.

"I wasn't expecting you back so soon," she said.

He set Simon on his feet. "The rain drove me back, although I'll need to go out again to talk to Gibson. Hopefully his autopsy will turn up something, because at the moment we've nothing to go on. Absolutely nothing."

"Was it as bad as Sir Henry's note this morning made it sound?"

Devlin went to pour himself a glass of wine. "If anything, it was worse. I'm afraid it makes grim hearing."

"Tell me anyway."

"You're certain?"

"Yes."

He took her at her word and did, keeping his voice low so the boy wouldn't hear.

"Good heavens," she said softly when he had finished. "You think these new killings are related in some way to the Ratcliffe Highway murders?"

"It's difficult to avoid leaping to that conclusion, isn't it? Although that doesn't necessarily mean it's true." He took a slow sip of his wine and came to stand with his back to the fire, his gaze on Simon, who was now playing with a wooden toy horse and cart. "I thought you had an interview with the director of some workhouse today?"

"He's sent word that he'll be unable to meet with me."

"That's unfortunate."

She set aside her notebook. "If I didn't know better, I'd suspect Jarvis of having directed one of his henchmen to put a spoke in my wheel."

"Would he do that?"

"Of course he would."

Devlin met her gaze and smiled. Then the smile faded. "How much do you know about the events surrounding the Ratcliffe Highway murders?"

"I know what was in the papers. Why?"

"I didn't pay much attention."

"As I recall, the killings occurred at the time you were trying to drink yourself to death."

He gave a soft laugh and took another sip of his wine. "Something like that. Do you remember if there were other suspects besides that fellow who hanged himself? What was his name?"

"John Williams." She rose from the chair to go hunker down on the rug beside Simon, the hem of her gown trailing across the carpet as she reached to show him how to reattach his horse to the cart. "And there were dozens of other men detained. I always thought that was part of the problem. They were hauling in every Irish, Greek, or Portuguese sailor unlucky enough to catch their attention for some reason. And then after the second set of killings, when they settled on John Williams, they simply ignored the fact that two sets of bloody footprints had been found leading away from the house on Ratcliffe Highway."

"So Williams could have had an accomplice."

"He could have. Or he might not have had anything to do with the murders at all. At the time I thought the evidence against him rather unconvincing. But then he hanged himself in his cell, and the killings ceased, so I assumed they'd settled on the right man after all."

"Sir Henry said much the same thing."

She looked up at him. "Really? I'm surprised. I thought Sir Henry had an unwavering confidence in the English system of justice."

"Perhaps he simply likes to project that impression."

"I believe Pym was—" She broke off as someone knocked loudly at the front door below.

They heard the door open, then a man's gruff voice asking for Lord Devlin, followed by the soothing responses of their majordomo, Morey. A moment later, Morey appeared in the drawing room doorway.

"A Mr. Nathan Cockerwell to see you, my lord," said the majordomo with a bow. "Says he's a Middlesex magistrate here to speak to you about this morning's unpleasantness. I've taken the liberty of having him wait in the library."

"I'll be right down," said Devlin, his gaze going to meet Hero's.

Chapter 8

The East End magistrate was a fat-faced, rotund little man somewhere in his late fifties or sixties, with a bulbous red nose, a full-lipped mouth, and an old-fashioned powdered wig. The style of his clothing dated to the same period as the wig, his frock coat long and square-tailed, his breeches buckled beneath the knees over sagging clocked stockings.

"So you're Devlin, are you?" he said gruffly when Sebastian walked into the library.

"I am, yes. How do you do, Mr.—?"

"Cockerwell. Nathan Cockerwell, JP for Middlesex." He gave a short, jerky bow. "I hear Bow Street has asked for your help with the investigation into this morning's killing."

"That's right."

Cockerwell pursed his lips. "Damned impudent of Sir Henry, if you ask me."

Sebastian walked to a nearby tray that held glasses and a carafe of brandy. "May I offer you a drink?"

Cockerwell hesitated, then swiped a hand across his mouth. "Don't mind if I do. Bit nippy out there today."

Sebastian poured the man a glass. "Did you know Sir Edwin well?"

"Known the man more'n fifty years, we grew up together. Pym was a Middlesex justice of the peace himself before being appointed to the Shadwell office, and of course we've both been churchwardens at St. George's forever."

Sebastian nodded. The municipal system of Greater London was hopelessly antiquated, fragmented, and confused. Outside of the area within the narrow confines of the old City of London, most of the sprawling metropolis's government was still in the hands of the vestries of each individual Middlesex parish.

Known as "vestries" because they'd grown out of the ecclesiastical system and because their members had originally met in the vestry of their parish church, the vestries were composed of all men in a parish who paid a certain monthly tax. It was the vestries that appointed the various parish officials such as the parish constables and night watchmen. But it was the Middlesex County magistrates or justices of the peace who did things like license pubs and who had the power of summary judgment.

In an attempt to create some kind of unity and cohesion across the metropolis, Parliament had passed the Middlesex Justices Act of 1792, establishing seven new public offices modeled on the original Bow Street office. Each public office had three stipendiary magistrates directly appointed by the Home Secretary, plus eight professional constables who were coming more and more to be known as "police." But both the vestries and the Middlesex justices still retained most of their old powers, and none of it was coordinated in any way.

Sebastian held out the glass. "Was Pym at Shadwell at the time of the Ratcliffe Highway murders?"

The East End magistrate took the brandy and drank deeply before answering. "Oh, aye. Played an important role in helping nab that scoundrel Williams. As did I, if I do say so myself."

"You still think John Williams was the Ratcliffe Highway murderer?" asked Sebastian, pouring himself a glass.

"Of course he was. Never any doubt in my mind." The magistrate took another slurping swallow. "Just like I know who murdered Sir Edwin last night."

"Oh? Who's that?"

"Seamus Faddy, that's who!"

Sebastian replaced the stopper in the carafe and turned to face his guest. "And what makes you suspect this Mr. Faddy?"

"Had a set-to with Sir Edwin just this past week, he did. On Monday."

"About what?"

"About a gentleman's purse what went missing in the High Street."

"And that's enough to convince you of the man's guilt?"

"If you know Faddy, it is. The lad was born to hang."

"Have you picked him up for questioning?"

"As soon as we find him, we will. He knows we're after him, the little bugger." Cockerwell drained his glass and smacked his lips. "So you see, Sir Henry had no need to go involving you in any of this. We can take care of our own affairs, thank you very much."

"I've no doubt that you can," said Sebastian, smiling. "More brandy?"

"Perhaps a tad, thank you."

Sebastian refilled the man's glass. "Do you know of anyone else who might have had reason to kill Pym?"

Cockerwell threw back his head and laughed. "Oh, aye, there's a slew of 'em, all right. Although most of 'em are in Botany Bay—or St. George's poor hole." He winked. "If you know what I mean."

"Even dead men have relatives."

Cockerwell's grin faded and he punched the air between them with one meaty finger. "I'm tellin' you, it's Seamus Faddy done for Pym. You mark my words. We'll get him soon enough."

Sebastian took a slow sip of his own brandy. "Did this Mr. Faddy have a quarrel with Hugo Reeves?"

"Who?"

"Hugo Reeves. The seaman who was found ten days ago with his head bashed in and his throat slit."

"Oh, him. I wouldn't know. I take it you're thinking the two murders are connected?"

"You don't?"

"Nah. Seamen are always indulging in fisticuffs, my lord. That brawl obviously got more'n a bit out of hand, that's all. You don't want to be listenin' to a bunch of silly, scared fishwives and barmaids who've nothin' better to do than stand around on street corners, telling tall tales and frightenin' each other out of what few wits they have by trying to connect things that have nothing to do with each other."

"You're not worried?"

"Me? Why would I be?"

"Because you and Sir Edwin both investigated the Ratcliffe Highway murders and put John Williams in gaol."

Cockerwell's heavy jaw sagged. "What are you suggesting, my lord? That a dead man's ghost might be after us?" He laughed again. "Buried him at the crossroads with a stake through his heart, we did. That ghost ain't walkin', let alone killing nobody."

It was the traditional retribution meted out to those found guilty of having committed the grave sin of self-murder. Ineligible for burial in hallowed ground, the bodies of suicides were dumped into small, narrow graves dug at a crossroads, with a stake driven through the heart to keep the dead's wicked soul from wandering. It had always struck Sebastian as a treatment more calculated to produce the unquiet dead than anything else. But then, he didn't believe in ghosts—at least, not that sort.

"What about the other suspects in the Ratcliffe Highway killings?"

"Weren't none to speak of," said Cockerwell.

"Really? I thought dozens were hauled in for questioning."

"Well, at first, maybe. But Williams did it, my lord. Never any doubt of that." He said it proudly, as if such certainty were proof of his brilliance and competence rather than a sign of dangerous closed-mindedness.

"What about the two sets of bloody footprints that were found leading away from the Marrs' house?"

Cockerwell waved one thick hand through the air in a dismissive gesture. "Nah, it was Williams, all right. The murder weapon was his."

"The maul? It was?"

"Well, it belonged to one of his mates."

"Oh? And who was that?"

"Some fellow was out to sea at the time."

"Without his maul?"

"Well, obviously." The beefy magistrate drained his glass and set it aside. "You don't wanna go making something complicated out of this, my lord. Wapping ain't Mayfair. We've got us some bad elements, but we know who they are, and we can take care of 'em ourselves. Ain't nothin' for a fine lord such as yourself to be botherin' with."

"I see. Well, thank you."

Cockerwell winked again. "Glad we got that straight."

Sebastian was at the window of his library watching the East End magistrate stride away with his head down, a faint smile curling his fleshy lips, when Hero came to stand beside him.

"How much did you hear?" asked Sebastian, setting his brandy aside largely untouched.

"Enough to know that if I were Mr. Seamus Faddy, I'd be worried."

"I wonder if Calhoun knows where the lad might have gone to ground."

Hero laughed. "If he's a thief, Calhoun knows him."

Chapter 9

*I*n a profession filled with fussy, painfully correct gentlemen's gentlemen, Jules Calhoun was an outlier.

His unflappable disposition and unsurpassed skills with brush, needle, and iron made him invaluable to a nobleman whose pursuit of murderers could at times wreak havoc on his wardrobe. But it was Calhoun's unusual background and connections that marked him as unique, for he'd grown up in a series of notorious flash houses in the worst back alleys and stews of London.

"Seamus Faddy?" said Calhoun when Sebastian found the valet blacking a pair of boots. He was a slim, lithe man in his thirties with straight flaxen hair, a high forehead, and the kind of even features and cheerful disposition that made him a favorite with the housemaids. "Aye, I know him, my lord. What's he done now?"

"Butchered Sir Edwin Pym, according to one of Pym's fellow magistrates."

Calhoun studied the toe of the half-polished boot in his hands, as if considering this. "Seamus? I doubt it, my lord. Although there's no denying he has a temper, and Pym was one ugly customer, so I suppose it's possible."

"Faddy's a pickpocket?"

"Not anymore, my lord. He started out that way as a wee tyke, but I've heard he's moved on to higher pursuits these days."

"Meaning he's now a second-story dancer?"

"Something like that," said the valet with a laugh, reaching for a clean cloth. "He's a likable lad, but volatile. Definitely volatile."

"Tell me about him."

"Well, if I remember correctly, his mother died young, and then his da was stabbed to death when the lad was maybe eight or nine."

"So he grew up on the streets?"

"For a time. Then m'mother gave him a room with some other lads she took in."

"And he repaid her handsomely, I presume."

A gleam of amusement shone in the valet's soft blue eyes. "M'mother's got a tender heart, for all she tries not to show it. But she's a shrewd businesswoman when all's said and done."

It wasn't uncommon for proprietors of the lowest sort of lodging houses and taverns to take in street children and act as fences for whatever they stole. The moralists called them "nurseries of crime" for a good reason—although those same moralists seemed oddly disinclined to do anything themselves to prevent the city's many orphaned children from starving to death in the streets.

"So how old is he now?" asked Sebastian.

"Seventeen, maybe eighteen."

"What's his quarrel with Pym?"

"That I don't know, my lord."

"I'd like to talk to him, if you can find him."

"He's been out on his own for a few years, but I think m'mother keeps in touch with him."

"You can tell her I've no intention of handing him over to the magistrates, if she's worried about that."

"I reckon she's taken your lordship's measure by now."

Sebastian watched Calhoun pick up the second boot. "If Seamus grew up in one of your mother's flash houses around Smithfield, what's he doing down in Wapping?"

"I think he was originally from the Tower Hamlets and has drifted back that way lately."

"Richer pickings."

"True enough," said Calhoun. Most of the inhabitants of Wapping and Shadwell were wretchedly poor, but the cargoes aboard the ships in the Pool and stored in the area's vast warehouses were a frequent target for thieves.

"Given that he's moved on to more sophisticated forms of thieving, seems odd for Pym to have accused the lad of reverting to picking pockets."

"'Tis a bit, no doubt."

"Perhaps your mother would be willing to offer a theory about that."

Calhoun laughed again. "I can ask, my lord."

The rain was still coming down hard when Sebastian left in his town carriage for Paul Gibson's surgery in Tower Hill.

Once, Gibson had been a surgeon with His Majesty's Twenty-fifth Light Dragoons. Then a French cannonball tore off the Irishman's left leg below the knee, leaving him racked with the kind of pain that can lead a man to seek relief in the sweet, deadly embrace of poppies. In the end he'd left the army and come here, to London, to teach anatomy at the hospitals of St. Thomas's and St. Bartholomew's and to open a small surgery in a timeworn Tudor-era house practically within the shadows of the Tower of London. This was one of the oldest surviving sections of the city, a warren of ancient stone houses, cobbled lanes, and narrow courts that had clustered around the medieval castle since the days of the Normans.

Avoiding the house itself, Sebastian took the narrow side passage to where a rickety gate set into a high wall gave access to the rear yard. At the base of the yard lay the old stone outbuilding where Gibson performed his official autopsies—a single-roomed structure that also served as the site of the surreptitious dissections Gibson regularly practiced on cadavers filched from area churchyards by crews of motley grave robbers, euphemistically known as "resurrection men." Gibson was one of their best customers.

Until recently, the yard stretching from the house to the low outbuilding had been a neglected jumble of weeds and rubble and dark secrets. But it was slowly being transformed into a garden, thanks to the mysterious Frenchwoman who shared Gibson's house—but not his name.

The door to the high-windowed building stood open to the rain, and Sebastian could hear Gibson warbling a favorite old Irish rebel song as he worked:

We bravely fought and conquered
At Ross and Wexford town;
And if we failed to keep them,
'Twas drink that brought us—

He broke off as Sebastian came to stand in the doorway, the rain running off his high crowned hat and dripping from the shoulder capes of his greatcoat.

"Ah, there you are, me lad," said Gibson, exaggerating his brogue as he set aside some nasty-looking instrument with a clatter. The rain drummed on the roof, splashed in the puddles in the garden outside. "Wasn't sure I'd be seeing you in this weather."

The day was so gloomy that Gibson had lit the lantern that hung suspended from a chain over the stone slab in the center of the room. Sebastian took a swift, cursory look at the naked, bloody cadaver bathed in the lantern's golden light, then glanced away. "Can you tell us anything yet?"

Gibson reached for a rag to wipe his gore-covered hands. "Not a lot, I'm afraid." The surgeon was of medium height and leaner than he should be thanks to his increasing opium addiction. At thirty-four, he was only a couple of years older than Sebastian, but his once-black hair was already heavily laced with silver, his gray-green eyes sunken, the lines on his face dug deep by years of pain. The two men had been friends for nearly ten years, since the days when both wore the King's colors and fought the King's wars from Italy and Portugal to the New World. When the surgeons cut off the mangled remnants of Gibson's lower leg in a blood-soaked tent somewhere in Portugal, Sebastian had been there, helping to hold his friend down as he screamed and screamed.

"Can you at least tell me what he was hit with?" said Sebastian.

"Something heavy."

"Well, hell."

Gibson's eyes narrowed with a smile that faded quickly. "Crushed the back and left side of his cranium, plus his temporal bone."

"So he was hit more than once?"

"Oh, yes. A good four or five times, I'd say. I suspect the blow to the back of the head knocked him down; then your assailant hit him a few more times for good measure once he was on the ground."

"And the wound to his throat?"

"That came next. Believe it or not, he was still alive when it was cut."

"Jesus. How is that even possible?"

"Some people are hard to kill."

Sebastian forced himself to take another look at the dead magistrate's face. Sir Edwin Pym had been a fleshy man, with full cheeks and bushy silver side-whiskers, caked now with dried blood. His gray eyes were open and staring, his mouth sagging, the cut across his fat neck raw and gaping.

"What was used to slit his throat?"

"Don't see how it could've been anything other than a very sharp razor."

"Not a knife?"

"I doubt it. The cut's too clean."

"He's sliced from ear to ear."

"Pretty much, yes."

Sebastian turned to stare out at the rain-beaten garden with its stone-lined paths and a towering ancient chestnut whose leaves were turning a glowing amber with the coming of winter. It was one thing to kill a man, but to slash and repeatedly batter a living, breathing being with such bloody abandon suggested a level of savagery—or fury—that was difficult to think about.

Gibson said, "I hear people are panicking, buying blunderbusses and rattles, convinced it's the Ratcliffe Highway murderer come back to kill us all."

Sebastian shifted to meet his friend's troubled gaze. "You didn't happen to attend either of the inquests three years ago, did you?"

Gibson shook his head. "No. But I read the accounts in the papers. This sounds like what I remember of the surgeon's reports."

"Any chance we could be dealing with the same killer?"

Gibson's eyes widened. "I suppose so, but . . . Surely that isn't possible, is it?"

"Probably not." Sebastian let his gaze drift around the dank, stone-walled room. "Did you perform the autopsy on the seaman who was butchered the same way ten days ago?"

"No. But I can find out who did, if you'd like."

Sebastian nodded. "It might help." His gaze settled on the dead magistrate's neatly folded clothes resting on one of the long shelves across the back of the room. "I assume his pockets were empty?"

"Oh, yes. Someone picked him clean. But whether or not it was the killer, there's no way to tell." He hesitated a moment, then said, "I did notice one thing that may be relevant."

"Oh? What's that?"

"I think yon magistrate was tupping a woman right before he was killed."

"I won't ask how you know that."

Gibson swiped a hand down over his beard-stubbled face. "No, don't."

Sebastian found himself suddenly repulsed by the dead man's large, bulging white belly and flaccid sex. "Sir Henry said the old bastard had a reputation for picking up doxies, the younger the better. It's possible that's how the killer lured him into that alley—with a girl."

"Could be. Except why not kill him right away? Why let him do the deed first?"

"You have a point there. So maybe he wasn't lured. Maybe he was in the alley with the girl when the killer came upon them."

"If so, then what happened to the girl?"

The rain beat harder on the roof, nearly drowning out the rattle of a cart's iron-banded wheels thumping over the cobbles of the distant lane. Sebastian drew the cold, damp air deep into his lungs and shook his head. "Good question."

Chapter 10

*F*or reasons he couldn't quite explain, Sebastian found himself standing with his shoulders hunched against the rain, his gaze once again on the chandler's shop that now occupied Number Twenty-nine Ratcliffe Highway.

It was the vicious slaying of Timothy and Celia Marr's tiny fourteen-week-old baby boy, he decided, that made the Ratcliffe Highway murders so inexplicable. There was a certain brutal logic in a thief deciding to kill his victims in order to avoid being recognized and possibly hanged. But the gruesome slaughter of a helpless babe made no sense. It whispered of the kind of evil that lay beyond the bounds of normal human comprehension, of a man who took a sick delight in killing even the innocent, simply for the sake of killing. And that, combined with the scale and brutality of the other deaths, made these murders singularly horrific and profoundly disturbing.

He stared at the house, only dimly aware of the workmen and shawl-huddled women pushing past him, of the carts and wagons rattling up and down the wet street, of the brown-and-black dog nosing rubbish in the flowing gutter. He knew he could be wrong. Knew the deaths of Sir Edwin Pym and that obscure ship's carpenter might have nothing to do with the dreadful series of murders that had terrified London three years before. But he found that difficult to believe. The strange manner of the killings was too similar . . . and Katie Ingram's report of someone stalking her and her children too ominous.

According to the 1811 reports, after thirteen-year-old Margaret Jewell, the neighboring pawnbroker, and the night watchman burst into Timothy Marr's shop that December night to discover the horror within, they sent word to the nearest public office, which happened to be the Thames River Police Office in Wapping High Street. The policeman who responded was the first official at the scene. He immediately searched the premises, took possession of the bloody murder weapon he found there, and organized a search of the neighborhood.

All of which made him someone Sebastian needed to talk to.

The Thames River Police Office was not one of the municipal public offices set up in 1792. Established by a separate statute eight years later, the River Police were entrusted with the prevention and detection of crimes on the river. In addition to forty-three watermen, they also employed five land constables. But the constables were supposed to deal only with matters related to the river. Thus the river policeman who responded to that frantic message on the night of the Marr murders was technically acting outside his jurisdiction. And when Sebastian stopped by the police headquarters near the Wapping New Stairs, he discovered that the man involved had left the service.

"Is he still alive?" Sebastian asked the clerk behind the counter.

"Oh, yes, my lord. He's set up as a slopseller in Wapping Street, down by the corner of Brewhouse Lane. Horton is his name. Charlie Horton."

Charlie Horton's slopshop lay near the docks, in an area dominated by timber yards and cooperages and the government's massive Gun Wharf. A slopshop sold hammocks and ready-made clothes to seafaring men, mainly flannel shirts, canvas trousers, and warm peacoats. It was closed for the Sabbath, but Horton himself opened the door to Sebastian's knock.

The former river policeman looked to be somewhere in his late forties or early fifties. He was still upright and strong, with the craggy, sun-darkened face of a man who'd spent his youth at sea. His thick, short-cropped hair was iron gray, his eyes the color of the river on a sunny day, his hands big and blunt-fingered. When Sebastian introduced himself and explained the reason for his visit, Horton fixed him with a steady gaze and said with a lingering Scottish burr, "Yer wantin' me to tell ye about what I found that night? Ain't a pleasant thing to be rememberin'."

"I understand. But I'd appreciate anything you can tell me."

Horton swiped a hand across his face and looked away, so that for a moment Sebastian thought the man intended to refuse him. Then he nodded to the dark-haired, half-grown lad playing with a small white dog near the fire. "Caleb, tell yer granny his lordship and me've gone for a walk, would ye?"

"Your son?" asked Sebastian as the two men left the shop and turned to walk along the rows of ramshackle businesses and warehouses fronting the river. For the moment the rain had stopped, but the flagstones were wet, and the eaves of the ancient buildings lining the narrow, winding lane dripped. The scents of tobacco and spices, rum and hides and coffee—all the cargoes of the world brought here to the docks of London—hung heavy in the damp air.

"Aye, my lord. He still has bad dreams from hearin' me talk about them murders. Don't want him to have to listen to it all again. He's scared enough as it is with these new killings."

"You think the recent deaths are related to what happened three years ago?"

Horton threw Sebastian a look he couldn't quite read. "Reckon you must at least suspect it, my lord, else you wouldn't be here talkin' to me, now, would ye?"

Sebastian nodded. "Do you believe John Williams was really the Ratcliffe Highway murderer?"

Horton stared out at the forest of masts filling the river. "Maybe. Or I guess I should say maybe he was one of 'em. Never did see how it could've been just one man done the killing. Even if we hadn't found two sets of bloody footprints leading away from the back of the Marrs' house, how could one man beat to death three people in one room? You answer me that. Surely one of the three would've run, especially the woman. If nothin' else, she'd have run to try to save her babe, wouldn't she? I mean, what mother wouldn't? Instead, she was found still in the shop, lyin' just a few feet from the lad."

"The apprentice?"

"Aye. James Gowan was his name. From the looks of things, he'd just put up the shutters but hadn't had time to put the pin in 'em. I think the killers must've been watchin' from the shadows outside, and as soon as the shutters went up, they followed the lad inside, locked the door behind 'em, and started killin'."

"The shop door was locked from the inside?"

"Aye. That's why the pawnbroker from next door had to go over the back fence to try to get in. Found the back door standin' open, he did."

"Where was Timothy Marr?"

"Behind the counter. He may've been there when the killers broke in, or he may've gone back there after somethin' he could use as a weapon. But there wasn't nothin' in his hands. People say the family must've been killed as part of a robbery gone wrong, but that don't make sense. Marr had five pounds in his pocket, and there was more money in the till. None of it was taken."

"The killer—or killers—could have been interrupted by the girl coming back and knocking on the door."

"Oh, aye. Sure enough, she said she heard footsteps, so there's no doubt the killers was still there when she came back. But you'll never convince me they was there to rob Marr. Why kill that wee babe in its cradle? What robber takes the time to bash in a baby's skull and slit its throat, but don't bother to first scoop up the money he's supposedly come to steal?"

A seagull screeched overhead, and Horton glanced up, his eyes narrowing as he stared at the heavy gray skies. "Long as I live," he said quietly, "I'm never gonna forget the sight of that blood-soaked cradle."

Sebastian said, "Where did you find the ship's maul?"

"That was upstairs, in the Marrs' bedroom. Leanin' against a chair by the bed, it was. And get this: there was more'n a hundred and fifty pounds in the drawer of a chest right beside it, untouched."

"The maul was the only weapon you found?"

"Aye."

"So if there were two killers, one of them took his weapon away with him."

"Aye, I suppose he must've."

"There's no doubt the maul was the murder weapon?"

"Oh, no doubt at all. Drippin' with blood and all covered in hair and flesh, it was. A real mess." Horton paused, then said, "There was a rippin' chisel found lyin' on the counter downstairs, but it was completely clean—not a trace of blood on it."

"A ripping chisel?"

"Aye. Big iron thing nearly two feet long. We never could figure out exactly what it was doin' there, or why Marr didn't pick it up and use it to try to defend himself."

"Perhaps he tried. Perhaps he was reaching for it when the killers knocked him down."

"Aye. That could be it."

"What about the blade that was used to slit the victims' throats? Was that found?"

"Not then, no. A month or so later, they found a knife they thought might've been the one used, but I never believed it. And only Celia Marr's throat was slit, by the way—hers and the wee babe's."

"Neither Marr nor his apprentice had his throat cut?"

"No. 'Twas only at the second set of killings, the ones at the King's Arms, where everybody's throat was slit."

"Were you called to the scene of the second set of killings?"

"No, thank God." They'd reached the wharves along the Thames now, near where the worn stones of a set of watermen's steps led down to the gray, wind-whipped river. Horton stared out over the water, his face contorting with remembered horror. "Once was enough. I never want to see something like that again."

Sebastian watched a waterman ferrying a passenger across the ship-filled river. The splash of the oars was lost in the whistling of the wind through the ships' rigging and the thump of the mighty hulls against the wooden wharves. "Tell me about the two sets of bloody footsteps that were found leading away from the Marrs' shop."

Horton hunched his shoulders against the cold wind gusting up off the river. "A fellow who lived across the street—an old seaman by the name of Douglas—noticed 'em while I was still searchin' the upstairs. After the magistrates settled on Williams as the killer, they tried to say we was confused, that the men searchin' the house must've got blood on their boots and made the prints themselves by just milling about, but that ain't the way it was. As soon as Douglas spotted the footprints, he kept everyone away until I come back downstairs. Then him and me followed 'em. Went down the yard and over the fence to an empty house that faced onto Pennington Street in the back. I reckon that's how the killers got away. Some men was seen runnin' down Pennington Street right before the hue and cry was raised."

"How many men?"

"A fellow who claimed to have seen them said there must've been ten or twelve. I never believed that, but there was three men seen hangin' around outside the Marrs' shop right before the murders."

"Three?"

"Aye. A tall, brawny fellow in a Flushing coat, a smaller cove in a torn blue jacket, and a third man that nobody could seem to describe."

"But you only saw two sets of bloody footprints leading away from the house?"

Horton nodded. "Aye. Never could figure that out, unless the men seen in the street earlier had nothin' to do with the killin'."

"Or the third man could have been posted as a lookout in front and didn't get blood on his shoes."

"There is that. Blood and sawdust, it was."

"Sawdust?"

"Aye. Marr was havin' a carpenter do some work on his shop. You know that wide, fancy bay window you see there today? He'd just had that put in. Front of the shop used to be all brick."

"That might explain the ripping chisel you were talking about."

Horton nodded. "I remember there was somethin' about one of the fellows who was doin' the work complainin' that his rippin' chisel was missing, but I don't recall it all exactly. Like I said, it was more'n a bit confusin'."

"Did you come up with any suspects besides Williams?"

Horton huffed a rough laugh. "Must've been fifty or more taken into custody by one public office or the other. When I got back to the River Police, they had three Greek sailors who'd been hauled in for somethin' else, and for a time they was thinkin' maybe they was the killers."

"Why?"

"One of 'em had blood splattered on his clothes. Only, it turned out they had solid alibis, and the truth is, whoever did those killings would've had a lot more than a few blood splatters on 'em; they'd have been soaked in gore."

"Who else was questioned?"

Horton frowned with the effort of thought. "Well, let's see. There was a bunch of Irish and Portuguese sailors. Anyone with bloodstains on his clothes or who was found wearin' a Flushing coat got hauled in. Someone said they thought a one-eyed man'd done it, so for a time anyone missin' an eye—particularly if he was Irish or Portuguese—was in trouble. They even remanded into custody a servant girl who'd been dismissed by Mrs. Marr six months before."

"A girl?"

"Aye. Thought it was batty, meself. Weren't no way that little slip of a girl could've swung that big, heavy maul, let alone used it to kill three people before one of 'em overpowered her. They also looked real hard at Marr's brother. They kept him locked up for days."

"Why?"

"Seems the two'd had a big row. But in the end they let him go."

"Was there anyone in particular that you yourself suspected?"

Horton stared off down the river toward the Isle of Dogs, his lips pressing together in a tight line.

"So there was someone," said Sebastian when the man remained silent.

The ex-policeman let out a heavy breath. "Aye, my lord. Two of 'em, to be honest. One was a fellow by the name of Hart—Cornelius Hart. He was workin' for the carpenter put in that bay window for Marr. But the fellow's dead now; died late last summer."

"And the other?"

"Ablass. Billy Ablass."

"Who is he?"

"A sailor—call him Long Billy, they do, on account of him being so big and tall. He was the only man whose name came up in connection with both the Marrs and the killings at the King's Arms. He was a shipmate of Williams's, and a mean, all-around nasty son of a bitch in general. Led a mutiny on a ship they was on—the *Roxburgh Castle*, it was. Bow Street was lookin' at him even after Williams was found hanged, but then it was all dropped at the insistence of the Home Office."

"Why?"

"Because they had a dead man they could blame, and they wanted everything to quiet down so's people would forget about it and quit frettin'."

"Do you know if this Ablass is still around?"

"Aye. Heard just the other day he's back in London."

"He's been gone?"

Horton nodded. "Sailed on an East Indiaman not long after the 1811 murders."

Sebastian felt a gust of wind lift the spray from the tops of the choppy waves on the river and throw it against his face. "Did Ablass have a motive for the killings?"

Horton shook his head. "Nothin' more than theft—the same motive they gave for Williams doin' it."

"Was either man a known thief?"

"No, my lord."

"Exactly why was Williams brought in for questioning in the first place?"

"Someone laid information against him a few days after the King's Arms murders."

"Who?"

"Nobody ever said."

"Odd."

Horton brought his gaze back to Sebastian's face. The wind off the river flapped the tails of his worn corduroy coat and fluttered the brim of his hat. "Aye, my lord, that it is."

Chapter 11

By the time Sebastian traced Billy Ablass to an inn on Pope's Hill in Shadwell, the light was fading from the overcast, rainy day and a mist was beginning to drift up from the docks and warehouses that lined the Thames.

The Three Moons was a surprisingly respectable brick inn built late in the last century, with symmetrical white-painted sash windows and a decorative pediment over the central front door. Inside Sebastian found a taproom filled with laughing, drinking, shouting men, the air heavy with the smell of ale and tobacco smoke and the fire crackling cheerfully on the hearth. The young woman behind the counter was washing tankards in a tin tub. But she reached for a cloth to dry her hands as she watched Sebastian cross the ancient flagged floor toward her, her green eyes narrow and thoughtful and decidedly unwelcoming.

She was tall and comely, with thick, warm brown hair and pale ivory skin. Her gown was of forest green wool with a white fichu at the neck, and she had the easy, self-assured manner of a woman who has long known men and how to handle them.

"You lost or something, your lordship?" she said mockingly as he drew nearer.

He paused before her, one hand resting on the gleaming counter between them. "Hopefully not. I'm looking for Billy Ablass."

She held herself very still. "Why? What's he done?"

"Nothing to my knowledge. Has he been staying here long?"

"Since his ship docked a few months ago." She curled her widespread hands around the edge of the counter and leaned into them. "Now that I've answered your question, seems only polite for you to answer mine: What would a fine gentleman such as yourself be wanting with the likes of Billy Ablass?"

"I'm looking into the death of Sir Edwin Pym."

She straightened abruptly and drew back, her arms falling to her sides. "You don't look like a Bow Street Runner."

Sebastian took a card from his pocket and laid it on the counter. "I'm not. The name's Devlin."

She picked up the card to study it. *"Viscount Devlin,"* she read. "So you actually are a lord." She raised her gaze to his face. "What makes you think Ablass has anything to do with what happened to Pym?"

"I don't know that he does."

"And yet here you are."

Sebastian shifted to let his gaze drift around the room. The inn lay on the ridge overlooking the former marshland that now formed the riverfront, so the men here were more likely to be timber-yard workers, tradesmen, and shopkeepers than seamen. "Was Ablass staying at the Three Moons when he was in London three years ago?"

"I wouldn't know. I wasn't here then." She set the card back down before him, then stared at it a moment, as if considering the implications of his question. "You're thinking they're linked, aren't you? These new killings and the Ratcliffe Highway murders of three years ago."

"I think it's possible, yes. Is Ablass here?"

"Now? No. He went off this afternoon, and I haven't seen him since."

"What's he like?"

She lifted one shoulder in a shrug. "He's a sailor. He likes to drink, fight, gamble, and tumble women. They're all much the same. They get off their ships at the end of a long voyage flush with their wages, spend like there's no tomorrow, then head back out to sea in a few months when they're broke."

"He's from London?"

"He claims he's from Danzig."

The word "claims" didn't escape him. "Was he here last night?"

"Reckon he came in sometime after midnight."

"You saw him?"

"Briefly. Why?"

Sebastian looked into the woman's moss green eyes and found himself reluctant to explain the reasoning behind his question. Whoever bashed in Sir Edwin's skull and slit his throat in that noisome alley must have been covered in blood. If Ablass was indeed the killer, then she couldn't have helped but notice—unless of course he'd taken off his bloodstained coat and gloves and washed at a pump somewhere before walking into the Three Moons.

He said, "Do you remember the night Hugo Reeves was killed?"

"Vaguely. It's been more'n a week. Why?"

"Was Billy Ablass here that night?"

"Sorry. I don't recall."

He wasn't convinced she was telling the truth. "Did you know Reeves?"

"I'd seen him around. He used to come in here sometimes."

"Did he know Ablass?"

She shrugged. "They may've been shipmates once."

"On his last voyage?"

"Reckon you'd have to ask Ablass that."

"When was the last time you saw them together?"

"Reeves and Ablass? You think I remember?"

"I think you do."

She met his gaze, then looked away. "Could've been a few days before Reeves was killed. They got into a brawl over something, but—" She broke off as the street door behind him opened with a jangle of the bell and a gust of cold air that flickered the rushlights in their holders. Something passed over her features—something Sebastian couldn't quite read. "That's him."

Turning, Sebastian watched a big man in a rough coat, seamen's trousers, and nailed boots cross the taproom toward them. He was as tall as Sebastian and broader through the shoulders, with long legs, a muscular, beefy build, and wild black hair. His beard was full and as dark as his hair, his small brown eyes set close, his nose prominent enough to rival that of the Duke of Wellington. He walked right up to Sebastian, hands curling into fists at his sides.

"You the rotter what's been askin' after me around town?" he demanded, his chin jutting out aggressively as he took up a wide-legged stance. The accent sounded a lot more like Kent than Danzig.

Claims, indeed, thought Sebastian. He leaned back against the counter, his own hands dangling loose. "You're Billy Ablass?"

"I am. Who the bloody hell are ye?"

"The name's Devlin."

It meant nothing to the big seaman. "What ye want wit me?"

"I'm looking into the death of Sir Edwin Pym."

The man's nostrils flared. "I ain't got nothing t' do wit that."

"Where were you last night?"

"Here—not that it's any of yer bloody business."

"I understand you came in after twelve. But Pym could easily have been murdered before that."

"Not by me!"

"You were held for questioning after the Ratcliffe Highway and King's Arms murders, weren't you?"

"So? I wasn't never charged with nothin'."

"But you were questioned. Why?"

"Because somebody don't like me. That's the way it goes, ye know?"

"You were shipmates with John Williams?"

"Aye. On the *Roxburgh Castle*. What's that got t' do wit anything?"

"And you knew Hugo Reeves?"

"Ain't like I was best mates with either of 'em, if that's what yer sayin'."

"Do you think Williams was the Ratcliffe Highway killer?"

Ablass snorted. "Course he was. Everybody said so."

"So who do you think killed Sir Edwin Pym?"

The abrupt shift in topic back to the present seemed to momentarily confuse him. "How'm I t' know?"

"What about Hugo Reeves? Who do you think killed him?"

"How the blazes would I know how the fool come t' get his head bashed in?"

"So you weren't good mates with Reeves, either?"

"Said that, didn't I?"

"Where were you that night?"

"The night Reeves was killed? Ye think I can remember? I reckon I was here, but I couldn't swear t' it."

"And last night?"

"I told ye, I was out drinkin'. Stopped in the Jolly Roger and Pewter Pot and maybe a few other places I don't remember too well."

"By yourself?"

"Wit different mates. Why?"

"I'm thinking they could vouch for your movements."

Ablass leaned into Sebastian, his big head thrust forward. "Ye know what I'm thinkin'? I'm thinkin' I done answered all the questions I'm gonna answer." Then he turned and pushed through the inner door that led to the stairs.

Sebastian was aware of the woman behind the counter watching him. She said quietly, "He's a dangerous man; you know that, don't you?"

"He does seem to have gone out of his way to leave me with that impression."

She stared at him, her eyes half-hidden by her lowered lashes, and he couldn't begin to guess what she was thinking. She said, "What's it to a fine gentleman such as yourself, anyway, if somebody slits the throats of a common seaman and a corrupt East End magistrate?"

"Was Pym corrupt?"

"Of course he was. They most all are, around here. And you didn't answer my question."

He wasn't sure how to explain to her the disquiet that drove him, the certainty that this brutal string of killings wasn't over. Or the way he was haunted by three children chanting, *Ten for the bird you must not miss.*

"It isn't just about them," he finally said. "It's about . . . all of us."

Her troubled gaze met his, and what he saw there told him that she understood.

Outside the Three Moons, the mist was thicker, the normal crowds of carousing sailors and workmen thinned by the rain and the creeping fog and the threat of bloody murder.

Sebastian hunched his shoulders against the cold, damp wind gusting up from the river as he walked down the hill to the stables where he'd left his carriage. He could smell the sea in the air, the tang of brine mingling with the reek of tar and the scent of fresh lumber from a nearby timber yard. He could hear the wind whistling through the rigging of the ships hidden in the mist, hear the click of his own bootheels on the wet cobblestones and something else—

The rush of footsteps coming up behind him, fast.

Chapter 12

Sebastian whipped around, yanking his knife from the sheath in his boot as he settled into a fighter's stance.

"Want something, gentlemen?" he said, the honed steel blade catching the light from the oil lamp on the corner of a nearby shop as he held the knife before him.

The two men stopped their forward rush, their chests jerking with their labored breathing, their eyes narrowed and watchful and glittering with animosity. One was of medium height and slim, with a long pale face and rusty hair that hung over the collar of his rough dark coat. His companion was a shorter, darker, meatier man in seamen's trousers and a peacoat, his face hidden by the kerchief he'd drawn up over his nose and mouth.

It was the shorter man who spoke, his chin jutting up. "Wot makes ye think we was wantin' something?"

Sebastian shifted so that his back was to the shop's brick wall. "Just out for a stroll, are we?"

"Ain't no law agin that, now, is there?"

Sebastian nodded toward the short length of pipe the man held at his side. "And the pipe?"

The man brought it up, the corners of his dark eyes crinkling as if with amusement. "Wot? This? This is fer protection. It can be dangerous around here, ye know. Yer lordship ought to remember that, before ye go wanderin' around these parts. Ain't safe fer a fine gentleman such as yerself."

"Is that the message you were sent to deliver?"

The two men exchanged glances. "That's jist the way it is," said the taller man, his voice thick with a Glaswegian burr. "Givin' ye a friendly warning, we is."

"You're most generous." Sebastian held himself utterly still, his senses alive to the furtive sounds of the mist-filled night around him, the distant screech of a fiddle, a woman's low laugh, the slop of the tide against the hulls of ships whose outlines were lost in the swirling white.

The Glaswegian held a chunk of what looked like brick in his hand. He brought it up now, his lips pulling back into a hard smile that showed broken brown teeth. "Spent ten years before the mast, I did, servin' under popinjays such as yerself. Always struttin' about, they was, thinkin' they's better'n us, treatin' us worse'n a man oughta treat a dog. Treatin' us like we was nothin'. That's what ye think, ain't it? That we're *nothin'*."

Sebastian was watching the men's hands. He didn't think they were stupid enough to rush someone with a knife, but there was a palpable wave of hatred roiling off them. Whether the men had been sent after Sebastian by someone or had simply marked him as an easy target, they seemed reluctant to back off even though the dynamics of the confrontation had shifted against them.

And then he saw the Glaswegian's eyes narrow and knew even before the man drew back his arm that he was going to pitch the brick at Sebastian's head.

Sebastian ducked easily, bringing up his knife just as Peacoat came at him.

"You stupid son of a bitch," swore Sebastian, one jagged end of the heavy iron pipe raking across the side of his head as he flung up an arm to knock the worst of the blow away.

The attacker's heavy peacoat stopped some of Sebastian's knife thrust, but not all of it. He saw the man's eyes flare with surprise; heard the painful expulsion of his breath as Sebastian yanked his bloodstained blade free, ready to strike again.

"Danny!" cried the Glaswegian, catching his friend as he staggered back. For one icy moment, the seaman's gaze met Sebastian's. "He dies, I kill ye. Ye hear me? I'll kill ye."

"Get him help quick enough and he won't die," said Sebastian.

The Glaswegian held Sebastian's gaze a moment longer. Then he melted away into the mist, half propping up, half carrying his friend.

"Damn," said Sebastian, swiping a sleeve across his bloody forehead as he leaned back against the rough brick wall beside him. *Damn, damn, damn.*

"Maybe you simply looked like a rich, easy target for a couple of local footpads," said Hero, watching Sebastian hold a damp cloth to the side of his face.

The dressing room was lit by the soft golden glow of a brace of candles, the house quiet around them, the mist outside thick even this far from the river. "Maybe." He dipped the cloth into the basin of warm water on his washstand, then squeezed it out again, the trickle sounding loud in the stillness of the night. "Either that or someone sent them to try to scare me off."

"From looking into what happened to Sir Edwin Pym, you mean? Or from poking into the old Ratcliffe Highway murders?"

"I'm not sure."

"You're certain one of them wasn't Ablass?"

Sebastian shook his head. "Ablass is a big man, whereas the Glaswegian was of average size and his companion even shorter."

"They could have been his mates."

"True. But then, why wasn't he with them? Ablass doesn't strike me as the kind to send other people to fight his battles." He dabbed at the bloody graze again, his eyes on his reflection in the mirror. "Everything I'm hearing about the Ratcliffe Highway murders makes me think that the official explanations given at the time were wrong. From what Charlie Horton told me, it sounds as if robbery couldn't have been the motive—at least not with the Marrs."

"What other motive could there have been?"

"Revenge, perhaps? I can't think of any other reason for killing a tiny babe. Either revenge or a pure, sick lust for murder."

"God help us," she whispered.

He took one last dab at the cut, then turned from the washstand. "Sir Henry was planning to review the evidence accumulated by the Shadwell Public Office after the 1811 murders, so maybe he's found something that will help make sense of this."

"What kind of human being could bash someone's head to a bloody pulp and then slit their throat?"

"One who is utterly and completely without conscience, or very, very angry." He carefully dried his face with the towel, then set it aside. "Do you have any interviews planned for tomorrow?"

She nodded. "I'm meeting the director of the Foundling Hospital at eleven." She tipped her head to one side, her gaze on his face. "Why? I don't think anyone would describe Bloomsbury as dangerous territory, if that's why you asked."

"No. But it might be a good idea to take a couple of footmen with you, just in case."

He thought she might be annoyed with him for worrying about her, even though she knew he admired what she did and would never try to stand in her way. But she only smiled and said, "I'll be fine. I promise."

He grunted and reached to pull her into his arms.

Chapter 13

*A*ll the depositions of evidence taken before the Shadwell magistrates at the time of the 1811 murders have disappeared—as have the records of Williams's pretrial hearing," said Sir Henry Lovejoy the next morning when he and Sebastian met in a coffeehouse overlooking the crowded, noisy chaos of Covent Garden Market.

Sebastian paused with his steaming coffee raised halfway to his lips. "How can that be?"

"The Home Secretary ordered them sent to his office in January of 1812. According to Sidmouth's clerk, everything was returned to Shadwell the following month, but the clerk at the Shadwell office insists they were never received."

"And no one followed up on it?"

Lovejoy shook his head. "The Shadwell clerk says they assumed the Home Office had decided to keep them—which frankly beggars belief. I understand that at one point the Home Secretary asked Aaron Graham, one of Bow Street's former magistrates, to handle the investigation.

But his health has been failing for several years now and he's currently taking the waters in Bath. I've written to ask his thoughts on all this, although it's doubtful I'll receive an answer. He's quite aged, and I'm told he's not well at all."

"There must be someone who remembers."

Lovejoy took a tentative sip of his hot chocolate. "Well, there are detailed newspaper accounts of both the investigations and the hearings, which I've been reading. No doubt they contain a number of inaccuracies, but I suppose they're better than nothing."

"Any reference in the reports to Hugo Reeves?"

"Nothing I've found so far. Why?"

"I'm told he was seen arguing a few weeks ago with a seaman named Billy Ablass."

Lovejoy's eyes widened at the name. "Interesting. Ablass is mentioned in the newspaper reports as one of the suspects in the Ratcliffe Highway killings, although he was eventually released."

"I couldn't find many willing to admit they knew Reeves, but it doesn't sound as if he was particularly well liked."

The magistrate took another sip of his chocolate. "I'll have the lads look into him more. To be frank, everything I'm reading simply reinforces my previous suspicion that the case against John Williams was staggeringly weak. The man returned late to his lodgings on the night of the King's Arms murders—as he was evidently wont to do most nights. He was friends with the publican and his wife, and acknowledged drinking there that night—but presumably the same could be said of any number of men. And his laundress reported that he'd had blood on one of his shirts around the time the Marrs were killed. He claimed the blood was from a fight—which was a favorite pastime of his, according to his laundress. And the blood was described as 'splatters' around the collar—nothing like what one would expect to find on the clothes of the perpetrator of such a massacre."

"That's all they had on him?"

"Essentially. Oh, and he had money in his pocket when he was taken up for questioning, whereas he'd earlier told people he was running low on funds. However, since he'd just pawned some of his clothes and had two pawn tickets to back up the claim, that really shouldn't have been seen as incriminating. He reportedly had a reputation as a natty dresser."

"Was there anything besides the blood-splattered shirt to link him to the first set of murders?"

"Not initially. But then the bloody maul found in the house on Ratcliffe Highway was traced to a seaman who'd left his tool chest at a mean hostelry called the Pear Tree."

"And?"

"Williams was staying at the Pear Tree."

"That's more damning."

"It was certainly seen to be. But then, any number of other men also frequented the Pear Tree and its taproom, so it wasn't nearly as inculpatory as everyone seemed inclined to believe."

"And then he was found dead?"

"Yes. On the very morning he was scheduled to appear for his pretrial hearing."

"I thought you said there was a hearing."

"There was. They held it anyway."

"With the man dead?"

"Yes. They found him guilty."

Sebastian stared out the coffeehouse's foggy front window at the crowded, noisy piazza beyond. "And then they announced that the case was closed?"

"Essentially, yes. What I found particularly troubling is that there was a witness to the King's Arms killings."

"There was?"

Lovejoy nodded. "A young journeyman who kept a room in one of the inn's garrets. He heard strange noises and shouts from below, and crept downstairs to see what was happening."

"He saw the killings?"

"Not exactly. But he did see the murderer standing over one of the bodies—a large, dark-haired man in a Flushing coat."

"What did Williams look like? I don't think I've heard anyone say."

"He was said to be small and slender, with golden hair."

"Bloody hell. And yet they still pegged him as the killer?"

Lovejoy sighed. "At one point the lodger was himself taken into custody as a suspect—despite the fact he was so terrified he leapt nearly naked from the window of an upstairs room."

"Who was he?"

"A man named Turner. Jake Turner."

Chapter 14

*J*ake Turner was now a journeyman wheelwright employed by a large company on Wapping High Street.

A slim young man of medium height with soft brown hair and a sensitive face, he was not at all anxious to talk about the King's Arms. But the company's owner, who held a lucrative contract with His Majesty's government, had no desire to anger a viscount who was both the son of the Chancellor of the Exchequer and a son-in-law to the King's powerful cousin Lord Jarvis.

"Go on wit ye, lad," said the company's gruff, gray-whiskered, rotund owner. "Don't want to keep his lordship waiting. Take all the time ye need wit him, yer lordship; never ye fear. All the time ye want."

Jake Turner pulled off his leather apron and reluctantly tossed it aside.

They sat at the stairs near Execution Dock, with the wind off the river buffeting their faces and the air fresh in their lungs. "I don't like thinkin' about them days," said Turner, his jaw set hard as he stared out over the choppy water.

"Understandable." Sebastian studied the younger man's tense profile. "How old were you?"

"Just turned twenty-one, my lord. I'd finished my apprenticeship earlier that year and had only been at the King's Arms seven or eight months."

"Can you think of any reason why someone might have wanted to kill the publican and his family?"

"No. Old John and Mrs. Elizabeth were good people. They kept a respectable house—no cockfights or gambling or cock-and-hen dances at the King's Arms, the way you see at other taverns around here. They always locked up at eleven o'clock sharp—well, unless a friend happened to come by lookin' for a pot of ale. That's what happened the night of the killings, you know. A constable who lived a couple houses down stopped in for a beer."

"What time was that?"

"Maybe ten to eleven. There wasn't anybody still in the taproom by then, so he and Old John sat in the kitchen by the fire for a minute and talked. Some big fellow with dark hair had been seen hanging around the outside of the house, and with what'd happened to the Marrs on everyone's mind, Old John was worried. Then the constable went off home with his beer and I went to bed." Turner sucked in a deep breath that shuddered his chest. "It was a few minutes later I heard the front door bang open."

"It wasn't locked by then?"

"I guess not. Must've been just on eleven."

"Then what?"

"I heard loud thumps and shouting and screaming, and then suddenly it went completely quiet. I . . . I'm afraid it took me a minute to screw up my courage and go downstairs to see what had happened."

"That must have taken courage, indeed."

Turner glanced over at him, his eyes wide in a pale face. "You're the only person I've ever heard say that. Most folks think I'm a coward because I didn't rush down there to try and save them."

"I suspect all you'd have succeeded in doing would have been to get yourself killed."

"I'm not sure that makes it any better."

"Discretion is the better part of valor, remember?"

A ghost of a smile touched the younger man's face, then faded. "I've never been as scared in my life as I was creeping down those steps. The door to the kitchen was ajar, and when I got to the bottom of the stairs, I could see a man standing with his back to me. He was leaning over"—Turner had to pause and swallow again before he could go on—"over one of the bodies. There was blood . . . splattered everywhere. You wouldn't believe the blood. For a moment all I could do was just stand there and stare. Then he straightened and put his hand up, like this—" Turner touched his chest. "Like he was putting something in the inner pocket of his coat."

"What did he look like?"

"He was big. Must've been six feet tall, at least. He had on a dark Flushing coat that hung all the way down to his heels, and I think he had dark hair, but he was wearing a hat, so maybe I'm wrong. I was so shocked, I couldn't move—couldn't do anything. Then he started to turn, so I flattened back against the wall and ran up the stairs again as quiet as I could."

"He didn't see you?"

"I don't think so. He didn't come after me."

"Was he alone?"

"I don't know, my lord. He was the only one I saw, but I couldn't see the whole kitchen from where I was."

"What did you do then?"

"I thought about hiding under my bed. But I realized he'd surely find me there if he came looking. So I tore the sheets off the mattress, tied them together, and tied one end to a bedpost. Then I climbed out the window. The sheets weren't long enough, but there was a night watchman passing below, and he caught me when I dropped."

"Then what happened?"

Turner scrubbed his hands down over his face. "I wasn't wearing much—just my nightcap and a shirt. I think I must've been half-crazy with fear. I started screaming about how there was a murderer loose in the house. The watchman swung his rattle and shouted 'Murder! Murder!' and people came pouring out of the neighboring houses. I figure whoever was in the house must've heard the racket and run out the back while the men were still trying to break down the tavern's front door."

"It was locked?"

"Aye. The killer must've locked it behind him when he first went in. A couple of men also broke open the front cellar flap, figuring they could get in that way. That's where Old John was, you know—in the cellar. Lying headfirst on the stairs where he'd fallen."

"Did you see him?"

Turner nodded, his lips pressed together and his eyes wide. "His throat was slit from ear to ear so bad the blood was running down the steps. You could hear it dripping."

My God, thought Sebastian. "And his wife?"

"She was in the middle of the kitchen, not too far from Bridget—Bridget was their maidservant, you see. She was by the hearth."

"Do you know what was used to kill them?"

The younger man nodded. "A big iron crowbar. It was still lying beside Mrs. Elizabeth." He swallowed. "I remember I was standing there, just staring at it, when someone sang out, saying the back window was open and there was blood all over the sill. So a bunch of the men from the neighborhood who'd gathered in the house went pouring out the back door, thinkin' they could maybe catch the killer."

"Did they see anyone?"

"No, my lord. And then they hauled me off to the watchhouse, so I've no idea what happened after that. They let me go the next day, but there's still lots of folks who look at me sideways, thinkin' I must've had somethin' to do with the killings after all."

"Do you know if anything was stolen from the house?"

"They say Old John's silver watch was missing. I know he had it on that night because I remember seeing him play with the chain while he was sitting by the fire. At first people were thinkin' that's what I must've seen the man in the Flushing coat put in his pocket. But Old John was lying on the cellar stairs, so it must've been Mrs. Elizabeth I seen that big fellow standing over, which means it couldn't have been the watch."

"So what do you think he was putting in his pocket?"

"I reckon it must've been his knife. I think he must've been leaning over her, slittin' her throat."

"Their throats were all slit?"

Turner nodded, his cheeks now pale. "And their heads bashed in. I've never seen so much blood in my life." He glanced over at Sebastian. "You think there's some kinda link between what happened then and these new killings, don't you?"

"Do you?"

"Seems like there must be."

"Did you think John Williams was the Ratcliffe Highway killer?"

"Good Lord, no."

The vehemence of his reply took Sebastian by surprise. "Why not?"

"I knew Williams—knew him well. He was a good friend of Mrs. Elizabeth, so he was at the King's Arms all the time. She mothered him; that's the way she was—she liked mothering the lads. I guess she must've had children of her own once, but by then she only had a little grand-daughter that I knew of. There's no way Williams could have been the man I saw standing over Mrs. Elizabeth's body—I'd have recognized him. And even if I hadn't, Williams was short and slight and fair-haired, whereas the man I saw was big and tall and dark. Apart from which, Williams couldn't have done something like that. He wasn't like that at all."

"Oh? What was he like?"

"He was a friendly, happy-go-lucky fellow, and a real natty dresser. That's what he spent his money on—clothes. Clothes and going to the cock-and-hen clubs. The girls all liked him. He dressed fine and always treated them well, and he was educated, too. He was always reading all sorts of books."

"I thought he was a seaman."

"He was. Never made much sense to me. I figure there must've been some secret in his past he was hiding, but he wasn't a killer. No one'll ever convince me of that." Turner was silent for a moment, his troubled gaze on a tall ship making its way up the river, its sails fluttering in the gusty breeze. "I reckon that's why folks was so mad at me, and why a heap of 'em still are— 'cause they wanted me to say it was Williams I saw that night, and I wouldn't do it."

Sebastian studied the younger man's drawn face. He might have survived the attack on the King's Arms, but that savage December night had shattered his life in ways Sebastian suspected Turner would never recover from. After six years at war, Sebastian knew only too well that those who witness such bloody carnage are never quite the same again. And on top of the sights and sounds and paralyzing fear of that night, Turner was also living with the shame of being labeled a coward. That, plus the never-ending animosity he'd earned by refusing to put his neighbors' lingering fears to rest and name a dead man a killer.

"Who do you think the murderer was?"

Something leapt in the young man's eyes, something that looked very much like fear. "I don't know."

"No idea?"

"No. None." He stood up abruptly and looked back toward the workshop. "I know Mr. Cook said I could be gone as long as I like, but I really should be getting back, my lord. I got work I gotta finish."

"Do you know a man named Billy Ablass?"

Turner sucked in a quick breath. "I know who he is. Why?"

"Could he have been the man you saw that night? He's big, isn't he?"

He threw another yearning look at the workshop. "I don't know. I'm sorry, my lord, but I must get back."

Then he brushed past Sebastian and walked rapidly away, his head down and his arms wrapped around his waist as if he were desperately trying to hold himself together.

Hold on to the tattered remnants of his sanity.

The tavern once known as the King's Arms stood just a few hundred yards from Ratcliffe Highway. It was a tall, narrow brick building flanked by lower, meaner houses. At some point in the last three years someone had changed its name to the Queen's Head. But when Sebastian reined in his curricle across the street and gazed up at the garret window from which the young journeyman lodger had made his escape on that blood-soaked night three years before, he found himself wondering how much business the public house did these days. A palpable aura of horror clung to the place; it seemed unlikely to attract anyone eager to drown his sorrows in liquid good cheer.

The narrow road known as New Gravel Lane marked the boundary between St. Paul's Parish to the east and St. George's Parish to the west. It was one of the things that had hampered the investigations into the two sets of 1811 killings, for despite their proximity, the murders had taken place in two different parishes. Thus, two vestries were involved, and both had jealously guarded their ancient prerogatives, each printing their own handbills announcing a reward and refusing to share information with either the neighboring parish or the Thames Police. Then the Thames police were ordered by the Home Office to stop operating outside their jurisdiction, while the magistrates at the Shadwell Public Office essentially sat back and waited for information to be brought to them.

And it occurred to Sebastian now as he stared up at the facade of that death-haunted house that something similar was playing out again. The seaman Hugo Reeves had been butchered in Five Pipes Field in St. Paul's Parish, while Sir Edwin Pym was murdered in an alley off Nightingale Lane in St. George's Parish. A coincidence? Or a deliberate, clever use of London's archaic system to keep the authorities divided?

"My lord!"

Sebastian was gathering his reins when he heard a boy's shout.

"Lord Devlin!"

Turning, he saw a half-grown lad pelting down the lane toward him, one elbow cocked skyward to clap a hand on his hat and keep it from flying off as he dodged workmen and stray dogs and women with shopping baskets. In his other fist, he clutched what looked like a sealed missive.

"Message for ye from Bow Street," said the boy, gasping for breath as he skidded to a halt beside the curricle. "I like t've never found you, m'lord!"

"From Sir Henry?" said Sebastian, recognizing the magistrate's hand as he reached to take the message the boy was holding up.

"Aye. They found another dead body, my lord!"

Sebastian broke the seal and skimmed Lovejoy's terse message.

The dead man was Nathan Cockerwell.

Chapter 15

Jesus," said Sebastian on a harsh exhalation of breath.

He stood with Sir Henry Lovejoy at the entrance to a short dead-end alley just off Cinnamon Street near the river. The surrounding brick walls were black with soot, the stench of urine and rotting produce eye watering. Seagulls circled, screeching overhead, and he could hear the hulls of the ships knocking against the wharves with the inrushing tide.

Nathan Cockerwell lay sprawled on his back half-buried beneath a pile of rubbish at the end of the alley, his arms stiff at his sides, one leg bent at an awkward angle. His blood-soaked powdered wig lay beside his smashed nearly bald head. His face was a shattered mess, his eyes wide and staring, his head tilted back, and his mouth agape. The slit across his throat was deep enough to cut to the bone.

"Who found him?" asked Sebastian, his gaze drifting around the noisome, squalid space.

Lovejoy held a handkerchief to his nose. "A rag-and-bone man looking for something to pick up."

"I'm surprised he didn't simply strip the body and go on his way."

Sebastian forced himself to walk forward, his gaze on the muck-smeared cobblestones around the dead magistrate's head. "I don't think he was killed here," he said, eyeing the collapsed pile of refuse and the surrounding brick walls. "There isn't enough blood."

Lovejoy came to stand beside him. "I suppose that makes sense. Who in their right mind would go wandering down a dark alley with a butcher on the loose?"

"When did he go missing?"

"Last night, although the servants didn't inform his wife until this morning. I gather she makes it a practice of retiring early and does not like to be disturbed."

"Whereas Mr. Nathan Cockerwell obviously did not make it a habit of retiring early. Do you know if he shared his colleague's taste for young prostitutes?"

Lovejoy cleared his throat. "I believe Cockerwell's passion was for dogfights."

"Sounds like a pleasant chap." They watched a fly crawl out of the dead man's open mouth, and Sebastian swallowed, hard. "Is his wife able to talk, or has she drugged herself into oblivion with laudanum?"

"As a matter of fact, she's asked to speak to you."

Sebastian looked over at him. "She has?"

Lovejoy nodded. "Cockerwell seems to have told her you're assisting Bow Street's investigation of the recent murders."

"He told me to my face that I was wasting my time."

"Yes, she said that. It's part of why she wants to talk to you."

The Middlesex magistrate's impressive town house lay in Princess Square, not far from Pym's house in Wellclose Square. Most magistrates were wealthy enough to live comfortably, although not extravagantly. But Nathan Cockerwell's house—a late eighteenth-century brick pile with private stables and an extensive garden—oozed extravagance.

"Gor," said Tom as Sebastian reined in his horses at the corner. "That's 'is 'ouse?"

Sebastian handed the reins to the boy and jumped down. "Suggestive, isn't it?"

Cockerwell's newly bereaved widow received Sebastian in a grand parlor crowded with rosewood furniture, massive oil paintings in gilded frames, and a collection of Chinese porcelains that would have delighted the Prince Regent. She looked much the same age as her late husband, stout and gray-haired, with a slablike face, a small nose, and small pale eyes. Like Sir Edwin Pym's daughter, Mrs. Cockerwell did not appear to have shed any recent tears. But unlike Katie Ingram, the magistrate's widow obviously possessed a good supply of mourning clothes. She was decked out in a heavy black bombazine gown, a black cap, black gloves, and a black handkerchief she clutched theatrically in one hand. The other hand was fisted around a bottle of smelling salts.

"Lord Devlin," she said faintly when he bowed before her. "So good of you to come. I fear you find me quite unable to stand." Both her accent and her diction were noticeably better than her late husband's. She waved the black handkerchief toward a nearby chair. "Do, pray, be seated."

"Thank you." He adjusted the long tails of his coat as he sat. "Please accept my condolences on the loss of your husband."

She tilted her head back against her chair and closed her eyes. "You're too kind."

He found himself hesitating. "I could come back another day if you find it too distressing to speak to me n—"

Her eyes popped open. "No. No, what must be done, must be done." She struggled to sit up straighter. "Mr. Cockerwell was telling me you've agreed to assist Bow Street in their investigation into the death of Sir Edwin."

"I have, yes. Although he seemed to think my involvement unnecessary."

She waved the handkerchief again, this time in a dismissive gesture. "Mr. Cockerwell was always an independent-minded man."

"I understand he knew Sir Edwin Pym quite well."

"Oh, yes. Knew each other from the time they were lads, they did. Started as bricklayers together."

Sebastian blinked. "I hadn't realized that."

"And both were churchwardens for St. George's, of course. My father—he was the rector at St. George's back then—thought I was mad, wanting to marry my Nathan. But I knew he'd go far."

"And so he has," said Sebastian, his gaze drifting around the over-stuffed, expensively furnished room. *Or rather, he did go far until someone bashed in his head and dumped his body in a back alley.*

He was wondering how to approach the questions he'd come to ask when she forestalled him by saying bluntly, "I know who killed him. Know who killed them both."

"Oh?"

"It's that new vicar at St. George's. York is his name, Reverend Marcus York."

"The reverend quarreled with Mr. Cockerwell?"

"Oh, yes, quarreled with them both—Sir Edwin, too."

"Over what?

The handkerchief fluttered. "Everything!"

"Could you perhaps be more specific?"

A spurt of annoyance flared in her beady eyes. "The control of the vestry. The poor rate. The workhouse . . . There was very little that horrible man didn't gripe about. It's been going on for years."

"I thought you said Reverend York was new at St. George's."

"That's right. He only arrived ten years ago."

Only.

"I see. And has the reverend had much interaction lately with either Mr. Cockerwell or Sir Edwin?"

"Yes, of course. York was pinching at poor Mr. Cockerwell again just last week."

"About what?"

"Mr. Cockerwell never said. But I've no doubt you can discover it easily enough. You're supposed to be good at that sort of thing. Or so Mr. Cockerwell said."

"When he was complaining about my involvement in the investigation of the recent deaths?"

"That's right." She fixed him with a fierce stare. "You will look into it, won't you?"

"Oh, yes." He suspected she was far more interested in exacting revenge against a longtime enemy than in actually finding her husband's killer, but the "new" vicar of St. George's certainly sounded like someone Sebastian needed to talk to.

"Good." She leaned back in her chair again, her eyes sinking half-closed. As far as she was concerned, she had accomplished what she'd set out to do. He was now being dismissed. "If you would be so kind as to ring the bell to have Jenny show you out?"

Sebastian rose to his feet. "Of course. Thank you for seeing me at what I know must be a difficult time for you."

She gave a regal nod. "He's a beastly man, that reverend. It's past time he got what was coming to him."

"No doubt," said Sebastian, and left her there, a faint smile on her full, self-satisfied face.

Chapter 16

*H*ero arrived at the Bloomsbury Foundling Hospital shortly before eleven. A sprawling three-story-high redbrick complex that lay just to the north of Guilford Street, it was a "hospital" only in the word's old-fashioned meaning of a charitable institution offering "hospitality" to the indigent. Its existence was a testament to the humanity and hard work of an eighteenth-century sea captain named Thomas Coram.

Coram had been so horrified by the number of dead and dying infants he saw abandoned in the streets of London that he decided to do something about it. Petitioning the King for a charter, he immediately ran into headwinds from conservative moralists who believed that rescuing foundlings would serve only to encourage sin and debauchery. But he eventually managed to round up several dozen prominent aristocratic ladies and their lords who agreed to lend their respectability to his venture. For a time the Foundling Hospital thrived as *the* fashionable philanthropy, with everyone from Hogarth to Handel helping raise funds for its endowment.

Lending one's name to the cause was still relatively fashionable—the Prince of Wales himself had recently served in the (purely honorary) position of president of the board of governors. But generous donations were somewhat less forthcoming.

"I wish we could do more," said the Reverend Reginald Kay, the hospital's plump, white-haired little chaplain, who—with an eye to a possible generous donation—had enthusiastically agreed to escort Hero around the famous chapel and elegant administrative rooms. "But the need is so great and our resources are so small."

"How many foundlings do you take in every year?" asked Hero, their footsteps on the wooden floorboards echoing as they walked the length of the institution's impressive gallery of paintings and statues, all donated by various artists and patrons. It was from this gallery that the Royal Academy of Arts had been born.

"None, actually."

She drew up before Raphael's *Massacre of the Innocents* and swung to face him. "What?"

"When the institution first opened, they hung a basket outside the gates with a little bell attached, where desperate women could leave their infants. But they were quickly deluged with hundreds and hundreds of babies. The governors frantically applied to Parliament for funds, but by the terms of the grant they received, they were required to take every infant that was offered." He shook his head. "It was madness."

"How many babies are we talking about?"

"Fifteen thousand in four years."

"Good heavens," whispered Hero.

Kay nodded. "It was hopeless. They had to change the rules. Now infants may only be presented by their mothers at certain prescribed times, and the mothers must prove to the satisfaction of the directors that they were of good character before they, er, fell into misfortune."

"So the babies you take in aren't technically foundlings?"

"Not anymore. Their mothers are always known."

"And can the mothers ever get their children back?"

"They can, yes, if their circumstances change. A careful record is made at the time the infant is surrendered. And the mothers typically leave some token with their babes—a locket, perhaps, or a marked coin. Sometimes it's only a piece of ribbon or cloth, or a verse written on a scrap of paper. We've quite a collection, I'm afraid. They're heartbreaking."

"How many of the women manage to reclaim their children?"

"Some have," he said, his face tensing at if to hold back a flood of unwanted emotions. "But not many."

"And how many infants do you take in every year?"

"As many as we can. The children are sent to foster mothers in the country until the age of four, but we have space for only six hundred children here. After they return from the country, they stay with us until they're between twelve and sixteen years of age, so . . ." His voice trailed away.

"So less than a hundred a year," said Hero.

"Oh, yes."

"And the thousands of foundlings you no longer take in? What happens to them?"

Kay spread his hands wide in a helpless gesture. "The various parishes deal as best they can. Not all of the baby farms are bad." He paused a moment, then added, "Just most of them."

There was a late eighteenth-century act of Parliament that required all parish children under the age of four to be raised in country houses situated at least three miles from London. The thinking behind the law was good—that such infants would be more likely to survive in a healthy rural environment. In practice, the parish workhouses signed contracts with "baby farms" that were seldom if ever inspected and regularly killed most of their charges.

And no one cared.

"Of course, the foundlings are only part of the problem," said Kay as they moved on to stand before a bust of Marcus Aurelius. "The number of children orphaned in the city every year is shocking. I've heard that one out of every three London children will lose at least one parent before they reach the age of eighteen."

Hero glanced out the window at the long covered walkways that fronted each dormitory wing. The arcades were decorative, but they also served a purpose, for they were used as rope walks. It was here that the orphaned boys were put to work at a young age making rope to help support the facility. "And how many lose both parents?"

He shook his head. "That I don't know. But in the truly wretched areas such as St. Giles, Bethnal Green, or Wapping, it must be nearly one out of four, surely? How can any city handle a problem of that magnitude?"

"I've heard the major cities on the Continent have systems in place."

"Do they? I wonder how successful they are at keeping their children alive."

"I don't know," said Hero. "I understand the survival rate for children in the various parish workhouses is shocking, but I've never heard just how shocking."

The reverend sighed and looked away, his face solemn as he stared at Hogarth's depiction of Moses brought to the Pharaoh's daughter. "A survival rate of ten percent is considered average, but for some it's more like five percent."

"Dear God."

"If they're old enough, most orphans would rather take their chances on the streets—and, to be honest, they're probably more likely to survive there. Of course, the boys typically end up becoming thieves, while the girls—" He broke off and cleared his throat. "Well, the less said about that, the better."

Hero found her gaze drawn again to the scene outside the window, where the rows of little boys worked to braid rope, their hands red with the combination of biting cold and rough, scratchy rope fibers. In the course of researching various articles on the city's laboring poor, she'd interviewed dozens of orphans who were eking out wretched existences as street sellers, crossing sweeps, and ballad singers. Some she'd quietly helped find respectable employment or, for the really small ones, foster homes. But she knew the number whose lives she'd touched was woefully small, and the size of the problem suddenly struck her as insurmountable.

In some ways the lives of the Foundling Hospital's children were pitiable. Abandoned as infants by desperate mothers unable to care for them, they were raised as babies and toddlers in country foster homes before being subjected to the rigorous discipline of an institution and then apprenticed out somewhere between the ages of twelve and sixteen. But in truth, these were the lucky ones.

They weren't dead.

Chapter 17

S t. George's-in-the-East lay just to the north of Ratcliffe Highway, on that ancient ridge overlooking what had once been marshland but was now the teeming, squalid morass of Wapping and its docklands. The church had been built early in the eighteenth century in an Italian Renaissance style with Byzantine flourishes. But its once-white stones were now black with soot, its distinctive pepper-pot towers crumbling from lack of maintenance. The churchyard stretched away to the east, long and narrow and filled to overflowing, for this was a poor area where people lived hard and died young.

"I've been here ten years," the Reverend Marcus York told Sebastian as the two men walked the gravel paths of the churchyard, the hem of the reverend's black cassock swishing against the long grass that choked the tightly packed tombs and endless lichen-covered headstones around them. The sky above was gray, the cold wind filling the air with yellow and brown leaves spinning down from a nearby row of linden trees. "Ten years. And people like Mrs. Cockerwell still—" He broke off and pressed his lips together lightly. "I shan't say more. The poor woman's only just lost her husband."

"So tell me about him," said Sebastian. "But please don't censor your words simply because he's dead. I won't be able to understand how he came to die if I'm only given a false impression of the man he was."

The Reverend York swung to face him, his pale blue eyes widening, his homely features tense and twitching. He was an extraordinarily tall, thin man somewhere in his thirties, with a long neck, limp nondescript brown hair, and a bony face. "You're serious?"

"Very. How else am I to understand what's happening around here?"

The reverend drew a deep breath, then nodded and continued walking, his gaze fixed straight ahead, his brows drawn as if he found the license to speak ill of the dead profoundly troubling. "Very well, if you insist. The truth is, Nathan Cockerwell was a corrupt, conscienceless thief who bled this poor parish of every groat he could—and then some."

Sebastian blinked. "And Pym?"

"Was much the same."

"Both men began as bricklayers?"

"Not really. Their fathers were bricklayers who somehow managed to acquire enough capital to finance the building of a block of cheap, poorly constructed houses. From there they spread their influence and control until they eventually came to own a great deal of real estate in the area. I can't say for certain, since I wasn't here at the time, but from what I've heard, I think one could safely surmise that both men shared their sons' bare-knuckle ruthlessness and utter lack of scruples. We had someone similar in the Wolds when I was growing up."

"You're originally from Lincolnshire?"

"I am, yes. My father has the living at Maplethorpe. Pym was always telling me to go back there and take what he called my 'quaint antiquated notions' with me."

"And which of your antiquated notions did he find most objection-able?"

"It's difficult to say. Perhaps my conviction that churchwardens shouldn't treat the Poor Fund as their own private purse? Or that taxes should be assessed fairly rather than lightened as a reward for one's cronies and made ruinously onerous for one's enemies?"

"Pym and Cockerwell did that?"

"That and more. The East End is a cesspool of corruption, the magnitude of which I suspect most would find difficult to believe."

"So exactly which of his sins drove you to quarrel with Cockerwell last week?"

The reverend looked away, a faint flush creeping up to color his thin, sunken cheeks. "Heard about that, did you?"

"Yes."

York sighed. "I fear there is a long-standing corrupt alliance between the Middlesex justices of the peace and some of the city's richest, most powerful brewers. The county magistrates issue the publicans' licenses every September at the Brewster Sessions. And if a publican won't pay a bribe and commit to exclusively carrying the right beers, the justices refuse to grant or renew his license. Last September's Sessions was particularly venal, and I objected. Vociferously."

"And that led to a heated argument?"

"I fear most of my disagreements with Cockerwell were heated. He was a choleric gentleman, and I . . . I can become passionate when the powerful use their positions to destroy good, simple men."

"Cockerwell and Pym did that?"

"Constantly. I've lost count of the number of tradesmen forced to sell out and move because their taxes were unfairly leveled at ruinous rates, or the publicans who've been thrown into debt when their license renewals were unfairly rejected."

"Anyone recently?"

"Oh, yes. Cockerwell and I crossed words over a family that lost their house after the justices took away their license and refused to renew it. Ryker was the man's name. Ian Ryker."

"Are they still around?"

"Sorry, no."

"Did you by any chance know the seaman who was killed ten days ago? Hugo Reeves?"

The reverend shook his head. "I know he was born and raised in the parish, but I never actually saw him until the day I buried him."

"Did you ever hear of any connection between Reeves and the two magistrates?"

"No. I don't see how there could be one, surely?"

"Who do you think killed them?"

"I don't know. Believe me, I wish I could be of more help to you. I've a wife and seven children, and I find these renewed killings beyond terrifying. Everyone is buying cutlasses and blunderbusses, but somehow it doesn't seem quite right for a man of God to do the same."

"Do you think there's a connection between the new murders and what happened three years ago?"

"Well, there must be, surely?" The vicar nodded to a tall monument of gray stone that stood near the apse of the church and was only beginning to weather with the passage of the years. "I buried them, you know—the Marrs, I mean. The husband in one coffin, the wife and her babe in another. Who would do that? Who would slaughter a poor, defenseless child and his mother?"

"Did you know them?"

"The Marrs? Oh, yes. They came to services regularly every Sunday. I baptized—" He broke off and had to swallow before he could continue. "I baptized little Timothy. And then three months later, I buried him."

"The other victims—the ones from the King's Arms—were buried at St. Paul's?"

York nodded. "Yes. It was their parish."

"Did you know John Williams, the man accused of killing them?"

"No. Only what I read in the papers." A bleak, haunted look came over his expressive face. "After the Marrs were killed, their bodies were laid on their beds and the house opened up so that everyone in the neighborhood could see them." He swallowed. "The blood wasn't even washed from their wounds."

"You saw them?"

He nodded. "It was a hideous sight. Afterwards I wondered why I went—why any of us went. I suppose many were attracted by the spectacle—the same compulsion that draws people to hangings and cockfights and bull-baitings. But that's not why I went."

"So why did you go?"

"I think it was because a part of me didn't want to believe the horror of what people were saying had happened." He looked vaguely discomfited. "I suppose, like so many clergymen, I have a tendency toward naïveté. I like to believe the best of Our Lord's creatures. I mean, I knew such dreadful things happen in time of war. But here? In London? On a calm December night?" He shook his head. "Until I saw that poor, savagely murdered family with my own eyes, I somehow couldn't accept it as real." He paused. "And now it's happening again."

"You don't have any idea at all who could be doing this?"

"No. Pym and Cockerwell were evil men, but the violence of the attacks upon them . . . It's beyond shocking."

"This publican you were telling me about—Ian Ryker. Was he originally from Wapping?"

"I believe so. The son was a rifleman newly returned from the wars. He actually threatened Cockerwell and Pym at the Sessions."

"He did?"

"Oh, yes, quite explicitly. Then he turned and strode from the Sessions House before the magistrates collected their wits enough to order him taken up. He's said to have left the area, but I don't know where he's gone.

You don't—" His eyes widened. "Good heavens, you can't think he's the one doing this?"

"Probably not," said Sebastian, his gaze drawn again to the three-year-old stone monument near the church's east end, its base half-buried beneath a pile of windblown dead leaves.

Chapter 18

Grace Calhoun's Red Lion Inn lay in a decrepit back alley not far from the vast, death-haunted market of Smithfield. Every week great herds of bawling cattle, sheep, and goats were driven to Smithfield through the streets of London to be slaughtered. Two hundred years before, in the days of the Tudors, Bloody Queen Mary had used the conveniently open space to burn Protestants to save their souls, and her sister, Elizabeth, had in turn used it to burn an even greater number of Catholics, because that's what royals did with people they hated.

Dusk was gathering by the time Sebastian walked into the ancient inn's smoky taproom. The trestle tables and old-fashioned booths were crowded with the usual assortment of thieves, pickpockets, highwaymen, and whores, for the Red Lion had a well-earned reputation as one of the worst flash houses in London. It was here that Jules Calhoun had come of age, and here that his mother still spent much of her time.

"She's back there," growled the beefy man behind the bar, jerking his head toward a small cabinet tucked beneath the rickety stairs leading to the second story. "If'n that's why yer here."

"It is. Thank you."

The barman grunted and turned away.

Sebastian found Grace Calhoun looking over an assortment of pewter tankards and other items scattered across a small table in front of her.
She was a tall woman, still slender and attractive, with thick dark hair
only lightly touched by gray and cold, shrewd eyes that narrowed at his
approach.

"Told Jules I'd send word when I heard from Seamus Faddy," she said
when Sebastian came to stand in the doorway. "And I ain't."

"This isn't about Faddy."

"No?"

Sebastian shook his head. "I'm hearing talk about the magistrates
who sit on the Middlesex licensing committee—that they regularly de-
mand bribes and force publicans to commit to only selling beer from
their favored breweries. You know anything about that?"

Grace twitched one shoulder and set aside the tankard she'd been
inspecting. "There's a reason most of my houses have all been in the
City. This business is hard enough without havin' t' deal with a bunch of
corrupt old Middlesex wankers in wigs."

"So it's true?"

She huffed a scornful laugh. "Find that hard to believe, do ye, yer
lordship?"

"Which breweries are we talking about?"

"The Black Eagle is probably the worst of them, and Meux and Company. Used t' be most public houses brewed their own beer. But these
days the big breweries've made it too hard for us t' get the ingredients."
She picked up a silver pocket watch with an ornately carved case. "Of
course, bribin' corrupt magistrates is only one of the ways breweries
control publicans. They've others."

"Such as?"

She turned the watch in her hand, studying it. "Well, there's loan-

ties. Brewers are rich, while the sort o' folks who keep taverns aren't. So the breweries lend money to publicans lookin' to buy a house or havin' a run o' bad luck."

"And in exchange the publicans commit to buying only from that brewery?"

"Clever, huh?"

"What happens if a publican reneges on the deal?"

"I knew a tavern owner in St. Giles tried that. Meux sent twenty draymen with horsewhips to change his mind."

"I assume it worked?"

A lock of hair fell onto her forehead, and her gaze met his as she brought up a hand to push it back with her curled wrist. "What do you think?"

He watched her move on to an enameled snuffbox. He seriously doubted this assortment of disparate objects had been legally assembled, but all he said was, "You ever hear of a Wapping publican named Ian Ryker?"

"Why you wantin' to know?"

"I understand he tangled with Nathan Cockerwell at the last Brewster Sessions."

She shook her head. "The Ian Ryker I knew is dead."

"Since when?"

"Last summer. He had a son, though, also named Ian. He was with the army in Spain, but he's back now."

"Any idea where I might find him?"

"Last I heard, he'd taken up with the woman who now owns the Black Devil in Bishopsgate." She paused, and for a moment he found it hard to breathe as she looked up, her face carefully wiped clean of anything he might have read there as she met his gaze. He thought she might say something more.

But she didn't.

The Black Devil was a half-timbered, picturesque Tudor relic with diamond-paned windows and a high gabled roof that lay to the east of Smithfield in an old part of the city that had somehow escaped the ravages of the Great Fire of 1666. Once it had belonged to an ex-rifleman named Jamie Knox, a man who looked enough like Sebastian that the two could have been brothers.

Or half brothers.

The true nature of the connection between Sebastian and the mysterious tavern owner remained unknown. Sebastian was the Earl of Hendon's heir, but he was not, in truth, Hendon's son. His true sire remained unknown, as did Knox's. Knox's mother had been a Shropshire barmaid who'd claimed her baby's father could be one of three men: a Romany stable hand, an unidentified English lord, or a similarly unidentified Welsh cavalry officer. The two men's eerie resemblance had alternately intrigued, baffled, and troubled both for over a year. And then one dark, rain-blown night, a bullet meant for Sebastian had slammed into Knox's chest, and Sebastian had been left to wonder if he'd just lost a half brother he didn't even know he had.

The Black Devil backed onto the elm-shaded medieval churchyard of St. Helen's, Bishopsgate. It was there beside the ancient wall that divided the crowded burial ground from the tavern's courtyard that Sebastian went to stand with his hat in one hand.

Over the last eighteen months, the earth had settled and the grass grown over Jamie Knox's grave. It was hard to think of him lying down there. Hard to think of the vital, enigmatic man he'd once been reduced to bones and dust. Sebastian drew a deep breath and felt an ache pull across his chest, felt the damp wind cold against his face. He should have been the one to die that night. The killer had come for him, but seen Knox and mistaken the ex-rifleman for Sebastian. He was still struggling to come to terms with the quirk of fate that had allowed him to live by killing Knox instead. The man who'd fired that bullet was dead, yet the sense of regret, of an obligation unfulfilled, remained. But then, how can you ever recompense the man who died in your place?

Sebastian found the Black Devil filled with hard-drinking, boisterous tradesmen, apprentices, and shopkeepers, for this was a working section of the city. The taproom's floor was of uneven flagstones, the ceiling low with heavy oak beams, the wainscoted walls blackened by centuries of smoke from the wide stone hearth.

At his entrance, the dark-haired young woman behind the bar froze in the act of filling a tankard, the light from the rushes flaring golden across her pretty face as she watched him walk toward her.

"Ye ain't wanted here," she said.

Her name was Pippa, and it occurred to Sebastian as he studied her almond-shaped brown eyes and small chin that she'd always simply been "Pippa," that he'd never heard her last name. All he knew about her was that she'd given birth to Knox's son, and with his dying breath Knox had regretted not marrying her, for he'd understood only too well what it was like to grow up the bastard son of a barmaid.

Sebastian paused with one hand resting on the ancient bar's scarred surface. "I'm looking for a man named Ian Ryker."

"Why? You ain't nothin' but trouble. Jamie never listened t' me when I told him that, and look what happened t' him. He'd still be alive, if'n it wasn't for you."

"Is Ryker here?"

She met his gaze and deliberately held it, the full breasts above the low-cut bodice of her shabby red gown lifting as she sucked in a quick breath. "No."

"He can either have a conversation with me or he can deal with Bow Street. I would advise him to choose the former rather than the latter."

Sebastian heard a step, and a man came to stand in the doorway behind her. He looked to be somewhere in his thirties, with flaxen hair and pale blue eyes and a hard, sun-darkened face.

"Why?" said the man, leaning one shoulder against the door casing in a pose that was calculated to look casual but was not. "Who'er you?"

"It's Devlin," Pippa said quietly in a way that told Sebastian they'd discussed him before.

The man stayed where he was. He was tall, nearly as tall as Sebastian, his face harshly planed, his mouth thin and tight-lipped. Sebastian had been around enough soldiers in his day to recognize one when he saw him. "Why you want t' talk t' me?"

"I think you know."

Ryker hesitated, then nodded and pushed away from the doorframe. "Bring us a couple o' bitters, would ye, Pippa?"

They sat in the small office that had once belonged to Jamie Knox. It was a sparsely furnished space with a simple table, a couple of straight-backed chairs, and a window that overlooked the inn's yard and the churchyard beyond it. *Pippa doesn't like the view,* Sebastian remembered Knox telling him once. Sebastian thought she must hate it now that Knox himself lay buried there. And he found he had to work at not resenting this fair-haired stranger for being here, in Knox's place, while Knox himself was simply . . . dead.

"What regiment were you with?" Sebastian asked as the two men sat at the table, the tankards of ale between them.

"The Ninety-fifth," said Ryker. It was a rifle regiment, Knox's old regiment. "And you?"

"The Twenty-fifth."

Ryker nodded and took a sip of his ale.

Sebastian said, "How long have you been back?"

"A few months. But I reckon you knew that."

"I take it Pippa told you about me?"

"Aye. Said you looked enough like Knox t' be his own brother. I didn't believe it when she said it, but it's sure enough true. She says she never knew how that came about."

"No one does."

"I reckon somebody knows." Ryker took another sip of his beer. "I hear you're lookin' into what happened to them two magistrates in Wapping."

"Where'd you hear that?"

"I still got friends over there."

"Your father had a public house in the area?"

"Aye. The Green Man, on Rope Walk Lane."

"Why did he lose his license?"

Ryker leaned back in his chair. "Because he was tired of havin' to pay the Black Eagle's inflated prices, plus bribes to Cockerwell and his mates."

"I'm told he died last summer, before the Middlesex Brewster Sessions."

"Aye."

"He lost the license before it came up for renewal?"

"Aye."

"So why were you at the sessions?"

A smile curled the rifleman's hard mouth. "Seemed a good opportunity to tell that lot what I thought of 'em."

"I hear you threatened Nathan Cockerwell."

The fanlike creases beside the man's blue eyes deepened. "Nah. I just told him one of these days someone was gonna cut out his guts and feed 'em to the crows. Didn't say I was gonna do it."

"So where were you last night?"

The amusement slid into something brittle and dangerous. "Here. Why ye askin'?"

"Because someone didn't exactly cut out his guts, but they did do a pretty good job of nearly taking off his head."

"Good. But it weren't me. If it'd been me, I'd have made him suffer first. Some men don't deserve to die quick."

Sebastian took a measured swallow of his ale. "Any idea who did do it?"

Ryker shook his head. "Those bastards must've ruined dozens—no, make that hundreds of men and women over the years. Good luck to whichever one finally paid a couple of 'em back."

"You think that's why Pym and Cockerwell were killed? Because they were corrupt?"

"Why else?"

"You don't think it could have something to do with the Ratcliffe Highway murders?"

"I don't know nothin' about them. I was in Spain when that happened."

"Did you know any of the people killed?"

"Not really."

"You didn't know the publican of the King's Arms?" Wapping might be crowded with public houses, but surely the son of a man with a tavern in Rope Walk Lane would have known the longtime owners of the King's Arms.

Ryker gave a dismissive twitch of one shoulder. "I knew who he was. That's all."

"Who do you think killed him?"

"Somebody wanted him dead, I reckon."

A young child's laughter rang out in the taproom, followed by a low-voiced warning from Pippa. Sebastian said, "Whose beer did the King's Arms sell?"

The rifleman's lips pulled back in a smile that showed his teeth. "I'm not one as could tell ye that. Ye might try askin' out at the Black Eagle. I reckon Sampson Buxton-Collins might know."

A rush of small, quick feet sounded; then a ball rolled through the doorway to the office, chased by a sturdy lad of about three. He was tall and lean, with dark hair and yellow eyes. And even though Sebastian had seen the boy before, the sight of him still hit Sebastian's gut and took his breath. The child looked enough like Simon that the little boys could be brothers.

Or first cousins.

"What the bloody hell ye doin' in here?" growled Ryker, his face darkening. "Ye know ye ain't allowed in here."

The boy, his own face now tight and solemn, grabbed the ball and retreated backward out of the room in a way that told Sebastian all he needed to know about this man and the way he treated his predecessor's young son. As soon as the child reached the doorway, he turned and fled.

"Bloody little bastard," growled Ryker.

And Sebastian found himself wondering, *To whom did Knox bequeath his tavern?* To Pippa? Or to his infant son?

Sebastian suspected it was the latter. And that was worrisome.

Chapter 19

"A in't seen nor heard nothin', Captain," said Adam Campbell, one of the veterans keeping a watch on the daughter of Sir Edwin Pym.

Sebastian had swung by Stepney to check on the men, to reassure himself that the evil stalking the streets of the East End had not touched this frightened woman and her three children. He'd found the tall Scotsman standing across the street from Katie Ingram's modest town house, his battered old shako pulled low over his eyes, the collar of his coat turned against the cold and damp. The mist was coming up again, drifting in dirty white patches that slid across the haloed sickle moon hanging overhead.

"Max's watchin' the back o' the house," said Campbell. "He says he ain't seen nothin', neither. Maybe us bein' here is enough to scare away whoever's been troublin' her."

"Perhaps," said Sebastian.

He was aware of the curtain shifting at a window of the house across the way and glanced up to see the silhouette of a woman standing there looking out at the darkness, doubtless drawn by the sound of hushed male voices and perhaps frightened by the sight of shadowy figures half-hidden by mist. He told himself today's killings were different from those that took place around Ratcliffe Highway three years ago. Today's killer was targeting men, not entire families, and he was killing his victims in the street rather than attacking them in their homes at night.

And yet Sebastian wasn't convinced that was as significant as one might assume. An open draper's shop and an empty pub on the verge of closing for the night were far easier to invade than a crowded lodging house down by the docks or the homes of wealthy men such as Pym and Cockerwell, with their locked doors and multiple servants. What did that mean for someone like Katie Ingram, a woman alone in a small house with just three young children and a couple of maidservants?

He heard the front door open and saw her step outside. She now wore the mourning clothes society demanded of a woman in her position, her newly dyed black muslin gown dull and dark in the night, the shawl around her thin shoulders also black.

"It's Devlin, Mrs. Ingram," he said, raising his voice and touching his hand to his hat as he walked across the street toward her. "I'm sorry if I alarmed you. I was only checking on the men."

She shook her head. "I knew it was you." She hesitated, then drew a deep breath and said, "I heard about Nathan Cockerwell. I never liked the man, but to die in such a way . . ." Her voice trailed off, and she drew her shawl tighter around her shoulders. "I'm frightened."

He knew he should say something like *Don't be.* It was the standard response, after all. But he saw no reason to either ridicule her fears or diminish the very real danger she faced. "These are good men," he said instead. "And Bow Street is sparing no effort to catch whoever is doing this."

"I know," she said, giving a jerky little nod, her fingers showing white where they clutched her shawl. "Thank you. Thank you for everything you're doing."

And yet the fear in her eyes remained, stark and haunting.

That night, Sebastian dreamt of a tall, shadowy man with yellow eyes that seemed to burn out of the darkness, and of a beloved golden-haired woman whose laughter brought an ache to his chest and made him cry out.

"It's just a dream," Hero whispered, her breath soft against his cheek.

He opened his eyes with a gasp. For a moment his world spun around in a whirl of confusion, then settled into a familiar view of blue silk bed hangings lit by the red glow from the fire banked on the hearth. He drew another shuddering breath, then gathered her to him, her body settling warm and solid against his.

"Why does it matter to me so much?" he asked, pressing a kiss to her forehead. "Why can't I let it go?"

After he said it, he realized there was no reason for her to understand what he was talking about. But she did.

"I suspect it's because you feel it goes to the core of who you are. I was thinking the other day, we aren't our parents and grandparents, and yet their abilities and failings, virtues and faults, do seem to intertwine within us. And knowing them helps us to better understand ourselves."

"Does it?" He speared his hand through her heavy dark hair, drawing it back from her face. "I sometimes wonder how well I ever knew my mother. I was eleven years old when she ran off to Italy with her latest lover and Hendon told me she'd died. I knew the face of the gentle, laughing woman she showed me, but there was so much else there I either didn't see or didn't understand—that I still don't understand."

Hero slid her hand in a soft caress across his chest. "Perhaps we can never entirely understand those we love—or ourselves, for that matter. But that doesn't mean your need to hear her explanation for what she did—or to learn the identity of the man who is your father—is either a mistake or futile."

He held her to him, listened to the wind throwing a light rain against the windowpanes and the howl of a lonely dog somewhere in the night.

"I saw Jamie Knox's son this evening," he said after a moment. "He looks enough like Simon to be his brother."

"And now he's growing up with a man who could be a brutal killer," said Hero. "How did Pippa ever meet him?"

"Ryker? I suspect he presented himself as an old friend of Jamie Knox. They were in the same rifle regiment."

"Do you think he's behind the new killings in the East End?"

"I think he could be. I suspect he's more than capable of the kind of slaughter I saw in those two alleys."

"I'm worried about that little boy."

"So am I," Sebastian admitted. "But I don't see what we can do about it. He's with his mother."

It was inescapably true. And yet that cold reality brought him neither comfort nor absolution.

Chapter 20

*T*he next morning dawned clear and brisk, with small puffy white clouds that floated high in a deep blue sky.

Sebastian walked the gravel paths of what was left of Henry VIII's ancient Privy Garden. With him was the man known to the world as his father—the man Sebastian himself had believed to be his father until a series of shattering revelations that came close to destroying him. The resultant estrangement between the two men had been bitter and painful. But they were slowly working their way toward forging a new relationship based on mutual respect, an old affection, and some uncomfortable truths.

Now nearing seventy, Alistair St. Cyr, the Fifth Earl of Hendon, was a stout man with a barrel chest, thinning white hair, and a blunt, heavy-featured face. As Chancellor of the Exchequer under a succession of prime ministers, he was both powerful and knowledgeable. He was also one of the few men in the Kingdom with the courage to occasionally stand against Jarvis.

"Yes, I've heard tales of the shocking corruption amongst the Middlesex magistrates and some of the East End vestries," said Hendon when Sebastian asked him about it. "There was an MP from Devon who made a push recently to set up a select committee to investigate it all, but Sidmouth managed to get it shut down."

"Sidmouth? Why?"

"Largely, I suspect, because the only thing more important to the Home Secretary than hanging Luddites is suppressing dissent and calls for reform."

"He can't do both? Try to drag us back to feudal times *and* do something about the rampant corruption in the East End at the same time?"

Hendon stared off across the parterres of tidy plantings toward the row of linden trees lining Whitehall, his jaw working back and forth in that way he had when thoughtful—or troubled.

"What?" said Sebastian.

"I don't know for certain, but . . ."

"Yes?"

"I've long suspected that Jarvis and Sidmouth use East End publicans to spy on the area's workers. Back in the early days of the French Revolution, they yanked the license of any publican who allowed radicals or reformers to meet in their taverns. But then they stopped—at least for the most part. It still happens occasionally, but I've come to the conclusion that's only when a publican refuses to spy for the government."

"How diabolically clever," said Sebastian. Taverns were basically the only place common folk had to meet, discuss politics, and organize, and they'd played an important role in the foundation of the corresponding societies that had sprung up across England in the 1790s. Anyone anxious to keep an eye on discontent would be hard put to find better-placed spies than the publicans of working-class taverns.

Hendon drew a deep breath, then let it out slowly. "Yes. Although I suppose it's necessary if we're not to see a guillotine set up in King's Cross."

"Because calls for true representative government and tax reform are a sure road to an English Reign of Terror? You don't think the suppression of people's rights might well prove far more dangerous in the long run? Particularly when they're starving?"

Hendon twisted his head around to stare at him. "Good God, Devlin. You sound like Thomas Paine!"

Sebastian smiled. "Hardly. I'm not at all fond of violent revolution."

"I should hope not." Hendon drew his chin back against his chest. "Some years ago, Parliament voted thousands of pounds for the relief of the poor in the East End. It was supposed to be administered by the various parishes' vestries, but it's my understanding much of it simply disappeared into the pockets of certain churchwardens—Cockerwell and Pym being foremost amongst them."

"Bloody hell. What kind of men line their own pockets by allowing poor women and children to starve to death?"

"Particularly heartless, venal ones," said Hendon. His eyes narrowed. "You've involved yourself in these recent ghastly murders, haven't you? In *Wapping* of all places, Devlin?"

"You think I should only investigate murders that occur in Mayfair?"

"No, I think you should leave such activities to the magistrates and constables. That's what we pay them to do!"

It was an argument they'd had so many times over the past three and a half years that Sebastian simply smiled and shook his head. "You're acquainted with Sampson Buxton-Collins, are you not? The man now running the Black Eagle Brewery?"

"I am. Why do you ask?"

"Tell me about him."

Hendon's frown deepened. "The family's origins are decidedly common—I believe the grandfather made his fortune in tobacco before moving into banking. They've deep pockets—very deep pockets indeed. He's closely related to the Barclay, Lloyd, and Gurney banking dynasties."

"He's a Quaker?" The Quakers had long dominated England's banking segment, largely because they were once seen as particularly honest—a reputation they were rapidly losing.

"He is, yes."

"What do you think of him?"

"Frankly, I find him both arrogant and unscrupulous."

"Unscrupulous? In what way?"

"Well, for one thing, he has the clerk of the Shadwell Public Office on his payroll."

"That's allowed?"

"Evidently so—at least in the East End. If you had any sense, you'd stay far, far away from that lot."

"You have reason to believe they're dangerous?"

Hendon grunted. "Powerful men who believe their wealth is threatened generally are dangerous."

"Careful, or you're liable to start sounding like Paine yourself."

Hendon's eyes bulged as he sucked in a quick gasp of air.

But Sebastian only laughed.

The Black Eagle Brewery lay on Brick Lane, at the point where Spitalfields shaded into Bethnal Green.

Once an area known for the graceful country retreats of merchants and noblemen, for spreading market gardens and the cottages of prosperous Huguenot silk weavers, Bethnal Green was now the wretched home of starving, out-of-work journeymen with idle looms, Jewish and Irish refugees, and more than one notorious insane asylum.

Sampson Buxton-Collins—said to be one of the wealthiest men in

England—divided his time between his recently purchased estate in Hertfordshire and the Georgian-style redbrick mansion that one of his predecessors had erected next to the sprawling brewery complex. He received Sebastian in an elegantly wainscoted room with a mammoth crystal chandelier and a towering, gilt-framed van Dyck over the marble fireplace.

"You find me shockingly busy, of course," said Buxton-Collins with the hearty, patently insincere, jovial manner often affected by large, overbearing men. "But never too busy for the son and heir of the Earl of Hendon, eh?"

In his mid-forties, Buxton-Collins was a mountain of a man with a head of curly fair hair, a strong nose and chin, and the cold, alert eyes of a raptor. Despite his size, he had a reputation as an avid sportsman and something of a dandy. He was dressed in yellow pantaloons, glossy black boots, a double-breasted navy blue coat, and an elaborately tied cravat with a jeweled quizzing glass hanging from a silk riband around his neck.

"I appreciate your taking time out of your busy schedule to meet with me," said Sebastian.

"No worries, no worries! I was just about to go for a gander around the brewery. Try to do it every day. Important to keep an eye on things, eh?"

"I understand."

"Good, good, then you'll not mind walking with me while we speak."

They crossed a vast paved entrance court surrounded by towering redbrick buildings and crowded with sweating, shouting men and snorting teams of shires hitched to wagons piled high with oaken kegs, barley, or coal. The cold air was heavy with the pungent smell of fermenting beer, fresh manure, steam, and raw lumber from a new warehouse going up nearby.

"We didn't have steam power until I put it in myself in 1805, can you believe it?" Buxton-Collins said proudly, shouting to be heard over the roar of the machinery from the enginehouse. "And this we only just put in—" An eye-watering stench boiled out at them as he flung open the door to a cavernous room filled with clanging machinery. "Mechanical mashers! Amazing, isn't it? Until this year, all we had was a crew of sturdy Irishmen with long oars and mashing forks." He let go of the door to brace his hands against the sides of his enormous belly as he laughed. "Like something out of the Middle Ages, it was."

"You produce mainly—what? Porter?"

"Mostly, yes. That's what people want these days. Has to be aged for two years, which is good for us. There's not many can afford to tie up their capital in a big vat for two years. Come look at this." He led the way to a newly built vat house filled with dozens and dozens of enormous vats set up on thick iron pillars. The air was so heavy with the smell of oak and fermenting beer that Sebastian imagined a man could get light-headed simply by breathing in there for too long. "The biggest vats hold almost two thousand barrels. Impressive, eh?"

"Very." Sebastian let his head fall back as he stared up at the vats' massive wooden staves and thick iron hoops. "As long as one of them doesn't break."

Buxton-Collins laughed so hard he started wheezing. "Oh, no fear of that, believe me."

"How many public houses do you supply?" Sebastian asked as they turned to walk along the nearest row.

"Close to a thousand, I'd say. About five hundred we simply supply, maybe two hundred we own outright, and then another three hundred or so we finance."

"And the ones you own or finance are all required to sell only your beer?"

The brewer winked. "What do you think?"

"I've heard that if a publican in the Tower Hamlets won't agree to sell only your beer, the magistrates won't give him a license."

The good-natured, indulgent smile slid off the brewer's fat face. "Not sure who told you that, but there's not a bloody word of truth to it. You hear me? Not a bloody word."

Sebastian let his gaze drift over the vats towering above them. "You knew Sir Edwin Pym and Nathan Cockerwell, I assume?"

"Oh, aye. Terrible business, what happened to them. Terrible." Buxton-Collins heaved a heavy sigh. "People are saying we will be forced to follow the lead of the French and establish a proper police force. Although to be honest, I can't help thinking it might be better to see four or five individuals get their throats slit every year rather than subject Englishmen to that kind of control."

"As long as one of those slit throats isn't yours?"

He laughed. "True, true."

"Who do you think killed them?"

"Pym and Cockerwell? Oh, footpads. No doubt about it."

"You think so?"

"But of course. Who else could it be?"

"Do you remember a Wapping publican named Ian Ryker? He kept the Green Man on Rope Walk Lane."

"Ryker?" Buxton-Collins pursed his lips in an exaggerated pantomime of remembrance. "Can't say I do."

"Cockerwell revoked his license last summer after Ryker refused to sell only your beer."

"Did he?" Buxton-Collins cast him an amused sideways glance. "I hope you don't think I deal with such matters personally?"

"No, I don't suppose you do."

The brewer pushed open a door that led back out to the court. "You're thinking Ryker might be behind these savage killings?"

"No, he couldn't be; he died last summer."

"So you're wondering if perhaps there's someone with a similar grudge? If you like, I could ask my agents if there've been any other cases."

"Yes, that might help," said Sebastian.

"Always happy to be of assistance," said Buxton-Collins, standing in the weak morning sunshine with his folded hands resting above his large belly. His face creased into a smile that looked surprisingly jolly as long as one didn't notice his eyes.

Chapter 21

$\mathcal{P}$aul Gibson was elbow-deep in the chest cavity of the pale, eviscerated corpse laid out on his stone slab when Sebastian came to stand in the outbuilding's open doorway.

The day might have been clear, but it was still cold enough that the surgeon had a brazier burning beside him. Unless he was dissecting a cadaver filched from one of the local churchyards, Gibson usually did keep the building's door open, for the high-ceilinged room always reeked of death.

Sebastian glanced at what the surgeon was doing to Nathan Cockerwell's insides and then looked pointedly at the far wall. "Anything interesting?"

"Not really." Gibson set aside some dripping organ Sebastian made no effort to identify, then reached for a rag to wipe the dead magistrate's body fluids from his hands and arms. "The bones of his face and head are too shattered for me to be able to tell what he was hit with. His throat was slit quickly and deeply, most likely with a very sharp razor. Beyond that, all I can say is that you're probably looking for the same man who killed Pym—but then, I assume you've already figured that out for yourself."

"Nothing to tell us where he'd been or what he was doing before he was killed?"

Gibson tossed the rag aside. "Only that he'd been drinking to excess on top of a fish dinner, which he'd also eaten to excess. Judging from the condition of his heart and liver, I'd say he regularly did both."

"So he was foxed?"

"Let's just say he wasn't sober—which presumably made him easier to kill."

"But no indication of where that might have happened?"

"That he was killed? None whatsoever." Gibson limped from behind the table, his face tightening with pain as his weight came down on his peg leg. "I talked to Walt Salter, by the way—he's the surgeon who performed the postmortem on the ship's carpenter who was killed a couple of weeks ago."

"And?"

"He said the wounds on Hugo Reeves's body reminded him of the victims of the Ratcliffe Highway murders—and he should know, seeing as how he did the autopsies on all seven victims."

Sebastian blew out a long, troubled breath. "Coincidence seems increasingly unlikely, although we could be dealing with a copyist."

"Could be," Gibson agreed. "But if we're not, that means the authorities hounded an innocent man into killing himself three years ago."

"Either that or John Williams had a partner who's still alive—and still killing. Did this Salter do the postmortem on Williams's body?"

"No, that would have been done by the prison surgeon." Gibson scraped a palm across his beard-stubbled chin. "Do I take it you're thinking Williams might have had a bit of help hanging himself?"

Sebastian met the Irishman's troubled gaze. "I think it's a distinct possibility, wouldn't you say?"

"I still have the lads looking into Hugo Reeves," said Lovejoy when Sebastian stopped by his office in Bow Street. The magistrate's office was small and lined with bookcases crammed with well-worn books and volumes of scientific journals, for new discoveries in everything from electricity to botany were Lovejoy's secret passion. He sat behind his plain, serviceable desk, the wig of his office still on his head from a recent hearing, his spectacles pushed down to the end of his nose. "But so far, I can't say they've found anything of interest. We're also looking into the voyage of that ship you said both Williams and Ablass were on—the *Roxburgh Castle*. The Admiralty hasn't been able to locate the manifest of the 1810–1811 voyage, so we don't know yet if Reeves was on it, as well. It seems there was a mutiny on the ship that year, which might explain the missing manifest—it's been filed someplace else."

Sebastian nodded. "I'm told Ablass was the ringleader."

"Was he? Interesting."

"Do you know if there were any similar killings between the time of the Ratcliffe Highway murders and Reeves's death?" said Sebastian.

"No. None. We're quite certain of that." The magistrate paused to open one of the deep drawers in his desk. "I think you might find this interesting, though." He leaned over, then straightened to lay a big, heavy hammer on the desktop with a thud.

Sebastian stared at the worn, heavy shipwright's maul and felt his breath catch. "Is that it?"

"It is. The Shadwell Public Office sent it to Bow Street after Williams was buried."

Reaching down, Lovejoy came up with a long iron crowbar that he set beside the maul, then a heavy ripping chisel. "Sobering, is it not?"

Sebastian reached for the maul. "It is indeed." The hammer was massive, with a wooden handle and a hefty iron head made thick at one end for driving nails, and narrow at the other for setting the nailheads below the surface of ships' timbers. The pointed tip bore a small chip. He turned the maul in his hands and traced what looked like the initials "IP" crudely punched into the head. "What a ghastly relic."

Lovejoy nodded. "There's also this," he said, holding out a skillfully rendered drawing of a man's profile. "Thomas Lawrence himself sketched Williams after his death."

"Good heavens." Sebastian set aside the maul to reach for the print. Lawrence had chosen to draw Williams as if he were still alive and sitting up, his eyes open, his mouth closed. The face was obviously young, with a straight nose, full lips, and high cheekbones. The hair was curly and was drawn darker than Sebastian had expected, the ears small and low, the forehead sloping. Williams's shirt was open, and around his neck, high up under his chin, Lawrence had drawn the twisted handkerchief that had killed the man.

"When did he draw this?" asked Sebastian.

"I'm not certain why or when Lawrence was given access to the body, but he was."

Sebastian was silent for a moment. "It doesn't look like the face of a man who could commit such horrible murders."

"No. But then, what would such a man look like?"

Sebastian found he could not tear his gaze away from that sensitive, doomed face. *What were you really like?* he wondered, tracing the handsome, delicate features. *Did you do it?*

Did you?

According to Lovejoy, the man known to the world as the Ratcliffe Highway murderer had rented a room at an inn called the Pear Tree.

Crowding together two and more to a room, eating in their lodging house's big kitchen, and washing at the pump in the yard, seamen had a habit of returning to the same lodgings year after year, whenever they were in London between voyages. Sebastian figured if anyone could tell him about the man who had died so mysteriously in Coldbath Fields Prison three years before, it was the proprietor of his lodging house.

The Pear Tree turned out to be a decrepit two-story inn with a low-pitched roof and grimy windows on a narrow cobbled alley near the docks in Old Wapping. Its taproom was a stark, ugly cave with a low, water-stained ceiling and a sawdust-covered floor that reeked of spilled beer, sweat, and the vague hint of stale vomit. It was early enough in the day when Sebastian arrived that there were only a few rough seamen lolling in the taproom, most of them looking hungover from the night before.

"'E ain't 'ere," said the bent, gray-bearded old man behind the bar when Sebastian asked for the publican. "The missus is in the kitchen, though, if'n ye was wantin' t' talk t' 'er."

"Please."

The old man stared at Sebastian a moment, then hobbled out from behind the bar to lead the way to a steamy, greasy kitchen that smelled of cooked cabbage and kippers. The room was empty except for a stout woman in a wooden chair beside the fire who sat with one gouty foot propped up on a stool before her. She said her name was Sarah Vermilloe, and she looked to be somewhere between fifty and seventy, with frizzy, fading red hair, a plain, lumpy face, and an enormous shelflike bosom. She was wearing a clean, starched white cap and a brown stuff gown made in the style of twenty years before, and her speech was markedly better than her surroundings might have suggested.

"Course I remember John Williams," she said as Sebastian settled on a bench beside the nearest trestle table. She was knitting a gray sock, her needles clicking at lightning speed. "Lovely young man, he was. Just lovely. And only twenty-seven when he died, poor lad."

The *poor lad* combined with the *lovely young man* suggested that Mrs. Vermilloe's attitude toward her late lodger was far more charitable than one might have expected, given that the world considered him guilty of butchering seven people, including a fourteen-year-old boy and a help-less babe. Sebastian said, "How well did you know him?"

She tugged at her yarn, loosening a length from the ball she kept in a basket by her foot. "Came here whenever he was ashore, he did. Called this his home away from the sea."

"And how long had he been coming here?"

"Must've been nine or ten years. As soon as he got off a ship, he'd come and give me his earnings to keep for him as his banker. Made me promise to only give him so much a week."

"He did?"

Her eyes were dark and small and nearly lashless, and the skin be-side them tightened when she smiled. "You look surprised. But that's what the lads do—leastways, the smart ones."

"And John Williams was smart?"

"Oh, yes; quite superior in every way, he was." The knitting needles stilled as she leaned forward and dropped her voice in the manner of one imparting a secret. "Always figured there was a story there somewhere, if you know what I mean? You don't see many seamen as fastidious as he, or who can read and write such a fine hand."

"What kind of a story?" Jake Turner had said something similar, Sebastian remembered. Not quite in the same words, but similar.

"I just figured there was something in his past he was runnin' from and didn't want nobody to know about. My Robert called him fop-pish and prissy, but I do like a young man who takes pains with his ap-pearance. That's what he spent his money on, you know—clothes. And then he'd run low on funds and have to pawn some of them. Quite the natty dresser, he was. Always 'bang up to the mark,' as the nobs say. And a most pleasing countenance, he had. My Robert likes to say his face was feminine and weak, but I never thought so."

Sebastian was beginning to suspect that the absent Mr. Robert Vermilloe had not been nearly as fond of their dashing young lodger as his wife had been. "I'm told he was a big, tall fellow," said Sebastian, who'd been told no such thing.

"Oh, no; don't know where you might have heard that, my lord. Not much taller than me, he was, and slight. Very slightly built."

Sebastian tried to envision a small, slightly built young man swinging a heavy ship's maul and single-handedly wreaking the kind of bloody carnage Horton and Turner had described, and decided it was unlikely.

"Are any of his mates still around?"

She gave her yarn another tug. "Don't know as he had any to speak of. He shared a room with a couple other men, but I wouldn't have called them his mates. And I'm afraid Jack Harrison was killed last summer and the other's off to sea at the moment, if you was wantin' to speak to them. The thing is, most of his friends were girls. Real popular with the ladies, he was—in a friendly way, I mean. Liked to go to the cock-and-hen clubs and have a good time drinking and dancing and singing. You know how young people do go on."

The cock-and-hen clubs were public houses where men and women could meet and dance. Many of the women who frequented them were prostitutes, which was why the moralists were always tut-tutting and preaching against them. But then, the moralists were against any activity for what they called the "lower orders" that didn't involve hard work or prayer.

Sebastian said, "Do you think he killed all those people three years ago?"

Her hands stilled at their task, then sank to her lap. She was silent a moment, obviously choosing her words carefully.

"No," she said at last. "I never did believe it. They tied me all up in knots at that hearing they held, twisting things around and getting me to say things I never intended. But the truth is, I never had a more conscientious, good-humored, pleasant lodger than Johnny Williams. Yes, he'd get into fights when the other men'd make fun of him. But there wasn't a mean bone in his body. Why would he suddenly do something like that? Not once, but twice?"

"Why did the other men tease him?"

"Because of his clothes and his ways and all." She looked troubled. "You know what I mean?"

Sebastian suspected he did. "You said he had lady friends; can you name any of them?"

"Not right off the top of my head. But maybe if I think on it some."

"Thank you," said Sebastian, pushing to his feet. "I'd appreciate it."

She looked up at him, her knitting lying idle in her lap, her lumpy, plain features twisted with grief for the handsome, gay young man who'd once befriended her. "I never thought he killed himself, either. Why would he do that? It makes no sense. He hadn't even been committed for trial yet. Why would he give up hope?"

It was a question for which Sebastian had no answer. He said, "Where exactly did they bury him?"

"At the crossing of Cannon Street Road and that new lane—Cable, I think they're calling it now." Setting aside her knitting, she heaved to her feet and padded across the kitchen to a dresser, where she rummaged around in a drawer for a moment before coming up with a folded, tattered newspaper clipping. "Don't know why I saved it," she said, handing it to him. "Except that to be throwing it away seemed like denying what they'd done to the poor lad."

Sebastian opened the clipping carefully, for the paper was brittle, the creased folds easy to tear. It was the *Times*'s account of John Williams's burial procession. "If Williams didn't kill himself, then who do you think did?"

He saw the leap of fear in her eyes, quickly hidden as her gaze slid away from his. She picked up her knitting. "Oh, I never gave no thought to that," she said.

And though he continued to press her, she refused to be drawn any further.

Chapter 22

$\mathcal{S}$ebastian stood at the intersection of Cannon Street Road and Cable Lane, his back to a tavern called the Crown and Dolphin, his gaze on the press of costermongers and coal heavers, draymen and staggering, hungover sailors passing back and forth in the crossing before him. The air was heavy with the smell of manure and coal smoke, ale and roasting meat and the ever-present brine from the tide rolling in to slosh against the wharves at the base of the hill. Ironbound wheels rattled over uneven cobbles; children shouted and laughed; dogs barked; women called to one another. All seemed oblivious to the moldering bones of the disgraced man who lay a scant four feet below them, his body awkwardly contorted into the deliberately small space dug for him, a stake driven through his heart. But then, why wouldn't they be? There was nothing to indicate that a twenty-seven-year-old seaman had been dumped into a shallow hole dug here at the center of the crossroads, with unslaked lime thrown in on top of him before the dirt and cobbles were quickly replaced.

It was as if he had never been. All that remained was the memory and lingering horror of what he'd supposedly done.

The discovery of John Williams's silent, hanging corpse in a prison cell in Clerkenwell had infuriated London. He'd not only "cheated the gallows," as the saying went; he'd also cheated the people, who were always eager for a gruesome display of public vengeance dressed up as justice.

And so the Home Office had devised an alternative spectacle. On New Year's Eve 1811, a rough, angled platform was fixed atop a cart, and John Williams's limp body tied to it. His "murderous implements"—the ship's maul from the Marrs' shop, the iron crowbar from the King's Arms, and the ripping chisel (which hadn't actually been used to kill anyone)— were displayed around him, along with the sharpened stake that would be driven through his heart. And then, in what was described as a "salutary example to the lower orders," the dead man was paraded through the streets.

Accompanied by a phalanx of public officials and constables with drawn cutlasses, the cart had rolled past the Marrs' linen shop on Ratcliffe Highway, down Old Gravel Lane to Cinnamon Street and Pear Tree Alley, then up New Gravel Lane to the King's Arms before coming here, to the crossroads.

The young seaman with the handsome, weak face hadn't been convicted of anything. Yet by his supposed suicide, he was seen as having branded himself as the killer. According to the *Times* article now in Sebastian's pocket—Mrs. Vermilloe had insisted he take it away with him—the thousands of Londoners who'd gathered to watch the ceremonial degradation had been unexpectedly solemn and silent. But when the stake was driven through the dead man's heart, a cheer went up. By both his death and the final ignominy of his unhallowed burial, John Williams freed the people of London from the fears with which they had lived for weeks—the fear of sudden, hideous, blood-splattered death, and the fear that comes from any raw, inescapable reminder of the secret evil that can lurk within our fellow men.

Sebastian acknowledged that it was possible John Williams really was the Ratcliffe Highway murderer—or at least one of them. It was possible the slightly built young man with the mysterious past, a handsome but weak face, and a taste for fine clothes had picked up a heavy maul and crowbar and for some unknown, unimaginable reason used them to slaughter seven men, women, and children.

It was possible. But Sebastian doubted it. And if Williams was innocent of the hideous crimes for which he'd been blamed, then that opened up the possibility that eight people had been murdered in that cold December of 1811: four at the Marrs' shop, three at the King's Arms.

And one in a solitary cell in Coldbath Fields Prison.

Chapter 23

$\mathcal{S}$ebastian drew up in front of his house in Brook Street to find a man leaning against the iron railing at the top of the area steps, one elbow looped around a finial and the brim of his slouch hat tipped rakishly over one eye.

He was young, no more than eighteen or nineteen, with overlong, somewhat ragged black hair, quick green eyes, and a wide leprechaun face that looked as if it was made for carefree smiles but was currently scowling. His pantaloons were a shocking shade of yellow, his waistcoat striped black and white, his coat black, and he had a black kerchief knotted jauntily around his neck. The clothes were not well tailored, but neither were they shabby.

"You know that cove?" asked Tom, eyeing the man.

"No. But I think I know who he is." Sebastian handed the tiger his reins. "Stable 'em."

Tom cast the man another suspicious glance. "Aye, gov'nor."

The young man made no attempt to alter his posture as Sebastian hopped to the ground. "Yer 'is nibs, are ye?"

"I suppose that depends on which 'nibs' you're looking for," said Sebastian, walking up to him, the high wheels of the curricle rattling over the cobbles as Tom urged the chestnuts toward the stables. "I'm Devlin. I take it you're Seamus Faddy?"

The young man sniffed, his gaze assessing Sebastian from his high-crowned beaver hat and caped driving coat to his glossy Hessians. "Grace Calhoun says yer wantin' t' talk t' me." Mr. Seamus Faddy was obviously not happy to be where he was. But there were few in Grace's orbit with the courage to say no to her.

"Did she tell you why?"

"She reckons ye think I know somethin' about that Shadwell magistrate gettin' 'is head bashed in last week. But I don't."

Sebastian was aware of an elderly woman in a purple velvet pelisse and ostrich-plumed hat coming toward them on the flagway, a small fluffy white dog tucked up under one arm and a frown on her face as she stared at the vision in black and yellow. He considered suggesting they continue their conversation in his library, then thought better of it.

"Let's go for a walk, shall we?"

Seamus pushed away from the railing. "What's the matter? Afraid I might prig some o' yer precious geegaws if ye was t' let me into yer house?"

"Something like that," said Sebastian.

The lad huffed a scornful breath as they turned toward the leafy square just visible up the street. "Nah. Grace made me promise t' keep me daddles to meself."

"I'll have to remember to thank her for that."

"Huh," huffed the lad again. He was quite short—nearly a foot shorter than Sebastian—and slender. But there was a wiry strength about him that Sebastian imagined would be quite capable of swinging a heavy maul at a despised magistrate's head. Would he have been able to do the same three years ago?

Unlikely.

"I didn't have nothin' t' do with what 'appened t' Pym," Seamus Faddy was saying. "Not a blessed thing."

"Where were you that Saturday night?"

"Me? Spent the evenin' with some old friends up in Clerkenwell, I did. Not claimin' I wouldn't 'ave liked to bash in 'is 'ead, because I would. Only it weren't me as done fer 'im."

"Any idea who did?"

"Nope. And that's the gospel truth." Seamus laid a splayed hand across his chest and cast angelic eyes heavenward. "I swear."

"Right," said Sebastian.

The lad laughed. "Not sayin' I'd tell ye if'n I did know, mind ye. But the fact is, I don't."

"Did Grace Calhoun also make you promise to tell me the truth?"

"I told her I'd try. Cain't ask for more'n that."

At least the lad was honest in that respect, thought Sebastian. "I understand you've abandoned your former career as a pickpocket."

"That's right. Moved up in the world, I have."

"So why did Sir Edwin Pym accuse you of lifting a gentleman's purse on Wapping High Street a week ago Monday?"

Seamus Faddy's eyes narrowed in a way that made him look less like a leprechaun and more like a gargoyle. "Weren't just anybody's purse; 'twas 'is *own* purse 'e accused me o' liftin'. Said I was cheatin' 'im of 'is proper cut, and if I didn't pay up, 'e was gonna see me dance the hempen jig. So me, I says, 'Ye can't prove I done nothin' without hangin' a noose around yer own fat neck.' And that's when 'e sets up the screech that I'd prigged 'is purse. So I ran."

It took Sebastian a moment to decipher this. "Are you telling me Sir Edwin Pym was taking a cut of whatever you stole from the shipping and warehouses along the river?"

Seamus Faddy wrinkled his nose, his gaze on a heavily laden coal wagon plodding toward them in the street. "The word Pym used was a 'tithe.' Like 'e was the bloody Church of England and we was 'is congregation or somethin'."

"'We'?" said Sebastian.

"Me and me lads. Got me a crew, I do."

Moved up in the world, indeed, thought Sebastian. It took intelligence, cunning, and ruthlessness to command a gang of thieves on the riverfront, especially at such a young age. A man like that would surely be more than capable of slitting a hated enemy's throat. Aloud, he said, "And Nathan Cockerwell? Did he share in Pym's 'tithes'?"

"Nah. Although from what I'm 'earin', he and Pym was runnin' some other rigs together."

"Such as?"

Seamus cast him a look dripping with scorn. "Ye don't know much, do ye?"

"Sadly, no."

Seamus Faddy laid a finger beside his nose and winked. "Ask the vicar. Reckon he could tell ye. Or any publican in the Tower Hamlets, when it comes down to it."

"You ever hear of a former rifleman and publican named Ian Ryker?"

Seamus let his gaze drift over the upper windows of the house beside them with the kind of appraising gleam calculated to strike fear into any homeowner. Then he said, "Ryker?" with an airy tone that was more than a bit telling.

"So you do know him."

"Let's just say I heard some talk."

"What kind of talk?"

"Heard 'e tangled with Pym o'er somethin'. Don't ask me what."

"When did this happen?"

"Last week sometime. Over by the basin, it was."

"And how did you come to hear about it?"

"I hear things. Keep me ears open, I do. It's necessary fer me business."

"No doubt. And did you hear the outcome of this, er, entanglement?"

"Oh, aye. Ryker threatened to cut out Pym's gizzard, while Pym swore 'e was gonna send Ryker to the same place as 'is da."

"Ian Ryker's father is dead."

"Yeah, I kinda figured that. Might be worth yer while t' find out how he died, don't ye reckon?"

Sebastian studied the young thief's gleaming dark green eyes and faintly malicious smile. "I 'reckon' you might be right."

Chapter 24

"Do you think any of what Seamus Faddy told you is true?" asked Hero.

They had wrapped Simon up in a warm coat, hat, and mittens, and were taking him for a walk around Grosvenor Square. The sun was still shining, but high clouds were beginning to gather and the chill in the air was becoming more pronounced.

Sebastian watched as Simon braced his legs far apart and carefully bent to pick up a feather, which he placed in the basket whose handle he carried clutched in one fist. This was a "treasure-gathering" expedition, and the basket was already filled with a collection of pretty leaves, acorns, interesting rocks, and bits of moss.

"I believe the part about Sir Edwin Pym demanding a 'tithe' from the gangs that plague shipping on the river. It fits with everything else I'm hearing about the man, and it explains the strange pickpocketing accusation. As for the rest? Who knows? Seamus isn't being honest about something—although, as far as I'm aware, he didn't have a motive to go after either Cockerwell or that seaman who was killed last month."

"As far as you're aware," said Hero.

"True."

"And the information about Ryker?"

"Seems as if it would be worth investigating further. I've been wondering why Grace Calhoun gave me Ryker's whereabouts so easily. She always has her own reasons for being helpful."

Hero intervened to stop Simon from adding a fat beetle to his basket. "I keep thinking about what the landlady at the Pear Tree said about John Williams—about the kind of man he was. Do you think she could be that mistaken in his character?"

Sebastian squinted up at the weak, hazy sun. "I honestly don't know. We like to think we can recognize the instincts of a brutal killer when they lurk within our fellow men. But there is a kind of murderer who learns young to hide his true nature behind an outward semblance of normalcy. Was that John Williams? I've no idea."

She looked over at him. "Yet you doubt his guilt."

"It's his suicide that bothers me as much as anything. He hadn't even been committed to trial yet; he was only facing his pretrial hearing, and the evidence against him was damnably weak."

"If his guilt was weighing heavily on his mind . . ."

Sebastian shook his head. "The kind of man who could brutally slaughter two entire families—including women and children—wouldn't feel guilt. I can understand a man wanting to save himself the humiliation of a public hanging, but Williams wasn't there yet."

A red squirrel ran across their path to dash up the trunk of a nearby oak tree. Simon shrieked with delight and darted after it.

"Oh, no, you don't," said Hero with a laugh, catching the little boy around the waist to swing him up into her arms, the basket thumping against her hip. To Sebastian, she said, "You think Williams was murdered, too?"

"I think it's certainly possible."

"By whom?"

Sebastian remained silent, his gaze following the progress of the squirrel as it ran chattering into the highest branches overhead.

"Jarvis," she said, her voice tight. "You think Jarvis had him killed."

He wanted to deny it, but couldn't. "Possibly. Or the Home Secretary at the time."

She stared off across the square as Simon squirmed to get down. "Yes, I can see them deciding to quickly eliminate Williams in order to calm the public's fears. But . . . the killings did cease."

Sebastian took Simon from her arms and swung the little boy up onto his shoulders. "They did, which certainly makes John Williams's guilt seem more likely. Except . . ."

Hero caught Simon's basket before it fell. "Except?"

"The general assumption is that Williams had no motive for the killings beyond either theft or an act of mindless brutality. It's one of the things that made the murders both so shocking and so frightening, because everyone in London feared they might become the killer's next victims."

"Yes," said Hero.

"But what if the killer did have a motive—only no one discovered it? And he quit killing when he'd achieved his purpose?"

"And now he has a reason to start up again?"

"Him, or someone who is copying him," said Sebastian as they turned their steps toward home.

Hero glanced over at him. "That's the problem, isn't it? You don't know which you're dealing with. A vicious, murderous seaman who sailed away three years ago but is now back? A madman copying the Ratcliffe Highway killer for the sick, twisted delight it brings him? Or someone else, someone with a very real purpose we can't begin to understand." She stared down the street to where a rag-and-bone man was talking to a cook standing at the top of her household's area steps.

"What?" Sebastian asked, watching her.

"I've been thinking about what Lovejoy told you—about how Pym liked to pick up young prostitutes, and how Gibson said he'd probably been with a girl right before he was killed."

"Yes," said Sebastian, not following her line of thought.

"I could try talking to some of the young girls on the streets of Wapping as part of my research into the city's foundlings and orphans. They might be able to tell me something."

"I can't see the *Morning Chronicle* publishing an article about child prostitutes on the streets of London."

She made a face. "I won't be able to say what they're doing, of course, except in the most euphemistic of language imaginable. But they might know something, and I doubt any of them have willingly spoken to the men Sir Henry sent to comb the neighborhood."

"That's certainly true." They'd paused beside the house steps, and he reached out to touch her cheek with the back of one hand. "But you will be careful."

"Will the presence of my coachmen and two footmen, plus a primed pistol in my reticule, reassure you?"

No, he thought. But he didn't say it.

That evening Sebastian attended the funeral of Sir Edwin Pym.

It wasn't the "done thing" amongst the aristocracy for ladies to attend funeral services, but that restriction obviously did not hold in the East End. The nave of St. George's-in-the-East was crowded with an impressive showing of Middlesex magistrates, prosperous area merchants, and other dignitaries, many with their wives. Standing at the back of the church, breathing in incense and cold stone and a bouquet of clashing perfumes and pungent body odors, Sebastian let his gaze drift over the assembled mourners. And he found himself thinking, *Any one of them. Any one of them could be the killer.* Men who live lives of greed and corruption make many, many enemies, and Sebastian knew he had only begun to scratch the surface in identifying them.

He shifted his attention to the figure before the altar. Attired for the occasion in his best vestments, the Reverend Marcus York wore a sorrowful expression that gave no indication of the fact that he was officiating at the funeral of a man he had detested. A good priest had to also be a good actor, and Sebastian told himself he would be wise to remember that.

It had not been his intention to approach Katie Ingram at her father's funeral. But after the brief graveside service, as the mourners were streaming back across the churchyard toward their carriages, and the last of the light was fading from the cloudy sky, she walked up to him. She wore a black wool spencer over a black bombazine mourning gown, with black gloves and a veiled black hat, and she looked so small, fragile, and vulnerable that it touched his heart.

"Thank you for coming, my lord," she said. "You needn't have done so."

He found himself hesitating. *What do you say to a woman at the funeral of a father she hasn't spoken to in ten years?* He finally settled on, "An impressive gathering."

She let her gaze drift over the departing mourners. "Yes. Father would have been pleased. Although I can't help but wonder how many of them are delighted to be here." A stricken look came over her face. "That was a horrible thing for me to say, wasn't it?"

He found himself smiling. "Understandable, under the circumstances."

She gave him a wry, trembling smile in return. "I overheard more than one wife observing to her husband that the funeral was shockingly plain and rushed. I know I should care, but I don't. I just wanted to get it over with."

The funeral *had* been rushed. Pym's inquest had been held only that morning, with the predictable verdict of murder by person or persons unknown. A "proper" funeral typically took at least a week to organize and involved a far more lavish display of crepe and black plumes and various other expensive trappings.

"If Steven had been here," she was saying, "he would have been horrified. But he's not here, so . . ."

Her voice trailed away, a bleak expression stealing over her drawn features, and Sebastian said, "How have you been? Honestly?"

She took a deep breath and let it out. "Honestly? I won't deny I'm frightened. And that I'm not sleeping well, even with the two guards you've so generously provided."

"They tell me they haven't seen anyone watching the house."

"No, nor have I." She glanced down, and he saw that her hands were clenched together tightly against the midriff of her mourning gown. "You haven't . . . You aren't any closer to finding out who's doing this?"

"No. I'm sorry."

She pressed her lips into a tight line and nodded. "I'd like to think it's over."

"Perhaps it is," he said. But he knew from the haunted look in her eyes that she didn't believe it any more than he did.

Chapter 25

*T*he Regent has received a promising report from the men he has following Princess Caroline," said Jarvis, smiling faintly as he leaned back in his chair and took a sip of his tea. "Promising, and deliciously compromising."

He was seated at his breakfast table in the company of Mrs. Victoria Hart-Davis, the pretty young widowed cousin of his late wife. She'd been living in his Berkeley Square town house since the death of Lady Jarvis over a year before. Some tongues had wagged, of course, although the arrangement was perfectly respectable, given that the Dowager Lady Jarvis also resided in the house. True, his aged mother seldom left her room these days. But Jarvis had never been the kind of man to allow such considerations to get in the way of what he wanted.

"Oh? And what is our dear Princess of Wales doing now?" asked Victoria, also smiling. She had the kind of heartbreakingly lovely face that made men think of rose petals and kittens and everything soft and gentle.

Jarvis knew better.

"Seems our dear Princess Caroline has taken up with a handsome but decidedly lowborn Italian fellow a dozen years or so her junior. Shocking, is it not? Whoever would have imagined she might do such a thing if she were allowed to leave England?"

Victoria laughed out loud. "Who, indeed? Perhaps the Prince will finally be able to get his divorce after all."

"If not now, then soon. She's been gone just over two months and she's already scandalized half of Europe." He paused at the sound of the front door opening and a familiar voice speaking to Grisham, his butler. A moment later Hero entered the room.

"Papa," she said, jerking off her fine emerald kid gloves as she came to kiss his cheek. She'd finally put off the mourning she'd worn for her mother for so long and was dressed in a frogged spencer of emerald velvet over a cream walking dress embroidered around the hem with a garland of leaves. An emerald cocked hat with a jaunty cream ostrich plume sat at an angle on her head. "And Cousin Victoria," she added, going to kiss her cheek, as well.

"Darling," said Victoria, reaching out to take Hero's hand and hold it fondly for a moment. "Do sit down, won't you? Have you breakfasted? I can ring for a—"

"Thank you, but no. I don't mean to trouble you, and I shan't interrupt you for long." She gently disengaged her hand and turned to fix Jarvis with a steady gaze. "I had a question I wanted to ask Papa."

"Oh? Shall I leave?" said Victoria.

"Only if you wish," said Jarvis, his gaze holding Hero's. "Do I take it this involves Devlin's latest start in—what is it? Wapping of all places?"

"It does, actually."

"I figured as much. And?"

"Did you order John Williams killed in his prison cell?"

"Who?"

"John Williams. The man held responsible for the Ratcliffe Highway murders three years ago. He was found hanging in his cell. Did you have him killed?"

"I did not." He let his gaze rove assessingly over his tall, dark-haired daughter. Her looks had improved since marriage, but it was still a pity she took after him rather than her mother and pretty little cousin. "Do you doubt me?"

She hesitated a moment, then shook her head. "No. I can't think of any reason for you to lie."

"Thank you," he said dryly, setting his teacup aside. "There's no denying the man's death was fortuitous. And the murders did cease abruptly, so perhaps the bungling magistrates of the East End did somehow manage by sheer chance to nab the right man. But did someone kill him? I neither know nor care."

"What about the Home Secretary at the time? Could he have ordered it?"

Jarvis huffed a low laugh. "Do you seriously think he'd have dared make such a move without my approval?"

"No," she said, considering this. "I suppose not."

"Are you certain you won't sit and have a cup of tea?" said Victoria. "I could ring for a fresh pot."

Hero glanced at her cousin. "No, thank you. And my apologies again for interrupting your breakfast."

"When are you going to tell her?" asked Victoria after Hero had gone.

"Soon," said Jarvis, and reached out to take her hand.

Chapter 26

Tan Ryker was in the yard of the Black Devil, supervising the unloading of casks from a high-sided brewer's wagon, when Sebastian came to stand in the archway. The morning sky was becoming increasingly overcast, the temperature falling, the centuries-old cobbled space filled with the shouts of men and the clatter of horses' hooves and the smell of aged oak and ale.

The tavern had been built on ancient foundations, with narrow Roman brickwork at the base of the old wall separating its yard from the burial ground of the medieval church to its rear. According to Jamie Knox, there was a Roman mosaic in the Black Devil's cellar, although Sebastian himself had never seen it. And he found it unsettling to be thinking about Knox now, while watching Ryker treat the tavern as his own.

Ryker was obviously aware of Sebastian's silent presence, and after a moment he left the men toiling up and down the cellar steps to come plant himself several feet in front of Sebastian. "I take it yer here fer a reason?"

Sebastian kept his gaze on the publican's sharp, bladed face. "You didn't tell me you had a quarrel with Pym as well as Cockerwell."

Sebastian watched as the publican considered denying it, then pressed his lips into a tight, angry line and said, "What of it, then?"

"Care to tell me what the disagreement was about?"

"What d'ye think? Pym and Cockerwell and the rest of that lot on the licensing committee cheated the publicans of the Tower Hamlets fer years. Pym might've moved on to the Shadwell Public Office, but he still had his finger in every crooked game around."

"You know anything about the government forcing publicans to spy on radicals and reformers in the Tower Hamlets?"

Ryker's face twisted into a sneer. "They say yer married to the daughter o' Lord Jarvis himself. Maybe ye ought t' be askin' his lordship 'bout that. I reckon he could tell ye more'n a simple Bishopsgate tavern keeper."

"In other words, you do know about it."

Ryker huffed a harsh laugh. "Think there's a publican in the East End who don't?"

"How did your father die?"

Ryker sucked in a quick breath at the sudden shift in topic. "What the bloody hell business is it of yers?"

"Is that why you were threatening Pym? Because of your father?"

"Don't know who ye been talkin' to, but I wasn't threatenin' him. He was threatenin' me."

"Why?"

"He was always threatenin' people—anybody and everybody. He even threatened the vicar of St. George's himself. Who goes after a bloody vicar?"

"Pym threatened Reverend York?"

"Aye."

"When was this?"

"Musta been last summer sometime."

"Over what?"

"Why don't ye ask the reverend? I got ale t' see stowed." And with that, he turned and walked away, his back straight, his head held high, his animosity like a humming presence in the ancient courtyard.

"Sidmouth called me into the Home Office again yesterday evening," said Lovejoy as he and Sebastian walked along the terrace of Somerset House.

Once this was the site of a grand riverside Renaissance palace of the same name, home to the brothers, widows, and uncles of kings. But in the eighteenth century, as complaints arose about the lack of any grand public buildings in London, the old Tudor edifice had been torn down and a massive Georgian quadrangle constructed in its place to house a variety of public offices and learned societies. Like the old palace, the new building stood right on the Thames; from the terrace, they could see the wind whipping spray from the tops of the whitecaps, smell the fish and brine in the air.

"And?" asked Sebastian, looking out over the river. There were no ships here above the narrow arches of London Bridge, only barges and watermen and the old horse ferry up at Mill Bank, scheduled to soon be replaced by a new bridge.

"He wanted to know when the palace could expect someone to be remanded into custody. I told him I understand people are frightened, but we're doing the best we can."

"Somehow I doubt that appeased him."

"Unfortunately, no. He's coming under considerable pressure from above."

"If he'd done something to rein in the East End magistrates' corruption, he might not have found himself in this position."

Lovejoy looked over at him. "You think that's what's behind these killings? Corruption?"

"I think it's likely, yes." He told Lovejoy, briefly, of the sordid relationship between the Middlesex magistrates and the brewers, and of Seamus Faddy's allegations against Pym—although he kept Faddy's name to himself.

"Merciful heavens," said Lovejoy when he had finished. "I knew it was bad, but I had no idea it was as bad as all that. It makes it difficult to believe the current choice of victims is as random as it was in 1811."

"If the 1811 victims were indeed chosen at random," said Sebastian.

Lovejoy stared at him. "You think they weren't? But . . . there was never any connection found between them."

"No, there wasn't. But there's a lot about the events of three years ago that doesn't add up."

"True." The magistrate turned his head as a seagull came in to land on the parapet beside them, the wind off the river ruffling the bird's feathers. "We've checked with all the ironmongers in the area, on the off chance someone might have found the murder weapons and then sold them; we've scoured the pawnshops looking for Pym's watch and buttons; and we've interviewed hundreds of Wapping inhabitants and street sellers, hoping one of them might have seen or heard something. And yet so far we've learned nothing. The public offices at both Shadwell and Whitechapel have hauled in scores of men who were either seen in the area around the time of the killings or suspected of having blood on their clothes—particularly if they're Irish, Greek, or Portuguese. But they haven't found anything, either."

"It's exactly what happened three years ago, isn't it? Every foreigner is suspect simply by virtue of being foreign—as if Englishmen don't kill."

The magistrate's head tipped back, his eyes narrowing as he watched the seagull take flight. "Well, they don't normally kill like this." He paused, then added, "Thank God."

※

Sebastian found the Reverend Marcus York down on his hands and knees in the vestry of St. George's-in-the-East, a broomstick clutched in one fist, his head tilted sideways as he swept the brush end beneath a battered old chest.

"Lord Devlin!" said the reverend, scrambling to his feet when he became aware of Sebastian's presence. "I was just trying to retrieve a button that rolled beneath the chest."

"Don't let me interrupt."

"No, no, quite all right." He whacked with both hands at the gray smudges of dust that showed on the knees and hem of his black cassock. "I fear the attempt is in vain." He looked up. "How may I help you, my lord?"

"I was wondering if you've heard anything that might shed light on the recent killings." Sebastian watched the reverend's face go slack-jawed with concern and added, "Please understand that I'm not asking you to betray anything said to you in confidence."

York stooped to pick up the broom he'd left lying on the floor and propped it in a nearby corner. "That would indeed be improper. But the truth is, I've heard nothing. Nothing at all."

Sebastian studied the reverend's long, bony face. "I'm told Sir Edwin Pym threatened you last summer. What was that about?"

The reverend grimaced as the two men turned to walk along the church's side aisle, their footsteps echoing hollowly in the vaulted nave. The air was heavy with the scent of candle wax, old incense, and the boiled linseed oil someone had recently used on the church's Dutch oak pulpit and doors.

"I take it the incident did occur?" said Sebastian when York remained silent.

The reverend let out his breath in a pained sigh. "It did, yes. Pym heard I'd been speaking to a member of Parliament from Devon."

"You mean, the MP who was interested in investigating corruption in the East End?"

York glanced over at Sebastian. "You're familiar with him?"

"Only by repute."

"Yes, well, somehow or another, Pym got wind of our conversation. Suggested I might want to reconsider working with the man—'if you know what's good for you' is the way he put it. Not an explicit threat, but after ten years, I know only too well what happens to those who make the mistake of crossing men such as Sir Edwin."

"Oh? What does happen to them?"

"Tax increases. Ruinous lawsuits. Carefully engineered bankruptcies."

"The sudden arrival of a score of draymen with horsewhips?"

York cast him a sideways glance. "Heard about that, did you? I've often thought Horton got off lucky, simply losing his position with the River Police."

Sebastian drew up beside one of the church's stout Doric columns and swung to face him. "You mean Charlie Horton? He tangled with Pym?"

The reverend nodded, his face solemn. "Pym and Cockerwell were furious with him for questioning their identification of John Williams as the Ratcliffe Highway murderer. I don't know how they engineered his dismissal, but they did."

"Tell me about the MP from Devon who was pushing for an investigation of corruption in the East End," said Sebastian as a patter of rain sounded above. "Why did he back off?"

York looked at him with wide, bleak eyes. "He didn't. He died."

"Of what?"

"The coroner's jury found that he drowned. Accidentally."

"In the Thames?"

"Yes."

"Convenient."

"I suppose that's one word for it."

"And the publican you were telling me about before—Ian Ryker. How did he die?"

York let his head fall back, the big, homely features of his face tight with strain as he stared up at the ceiling's ornate plasterwork. "They said he fell down drunk and broke his skull. I suppose it's possible, but . . ."

"But?" prompted Sebastian when the vicar lapsed into silence.

"Ian Ryker might have been a publican, but he was a sober man. I never heard of him drinking to excess."

"The incident occurred after he lost the license for his tavern?"

"It did, yes. There was speculation that he must have been drowning his sorrows over his misfortunes, but I never believed it."

"How well did you know the son—the younger Ian Ryker?"

"Not well. He took the King's shilling a few months after I arrived."

"And returned last summer?"

"Yes. In June, I believe."

"Was this before or after the father died?"

"Shortly after. He tried to get his father's license renewed for himself at the Brewster Sessions in September, but they turned him down."

It was not quite the story Ryker had told, Sebastian noted. "They turned him down because of his father?"

"Perhaps. Although if truth be told, I think they were afraid of the son and wanted him to move on—which he did, when he lost his father's tavern."

"They were afraid of him? Why? Because he was a rifleman?"

"That, plus he had a reputation for ruthlessness in his regiment—a ruthlessness not always directed at only the French."

Sebastian studied the vicar's half-averted profile. "You've heard something, have you?"

"What? Me? No, oh no." The vicar drew his watch from his pocket. "Goodness, look at the time. You must excuse me, my lord. I've a sick parishioner I promised to visit this afternoon. His daughters are afraid he'll not survive the night."

"Of course," said Sebastian. "Thank you for your time, Reverend."

"Always happy to help in any way I can," said the vicar, blinking rapidly, his face still turned away, his mouth working silently as if fighting to hold back a torrent of betraying words that could spill forth at any moment.

Chapter 27

Charlie Horton was up on a ladder at the rear of his slopshop, digging through a box on a high shelf, when Sebastian came to stand with his arms crossed at his chest and his head tilted back so he could look up at the former Thames River policeman.

"I'm hearing that Pym and Cockerwell are the reason you're no longer with the Thames River Police," said Sebastian. "Is that true?"

Horton went very still, one hand curling around the edge of the box, his entire body visibly tensing as he balanced on the ladder. After a moment, he said, "And now you're thinking maybe I'm the one who killed them? Is that it?"

"No. But I am wondering why you didn't mention it."

Horton shifted his big hands to the ladder's sides. "Ashamed, I suppose."

"Why? Did you do something wrong?"

"I didn't think so at the time. Just spoke my mind. But I should've known better." The skin beside his eyes tightened with what looked like amusement tinged with a note of self-mockery. "I've learned to be a wee bit more careful."

"You told me the other day that if John Williams really was the Ratcliffe Highway killer, then you thought he couldn't have done it alone—that he must have had help."

Horton climbed slowly down the ladder, then paused at its base, his hands still gripping one of the rungs. "Yes. Although like I said, I'm still of two minds as to whether he was guilty at all. The only things linking him to the killings were his friendship with the King's Arms publican and his wife, and the fact that the blood-soaked maul that was used to kill the Marrs came from the Pear Tree."

"How did you know where the maul came from?"

Horton shook his head. "I can't take credit for that. The night of the killings, I took the maul back to the Thames Police offices, and that's where it stayed. Nobody washed it, and it was so covered in blood and hair that it was nearly two weeks before anybody noticed there were initials punched into the iron head: a 'P' with what looked like an 'I' before it."

Sebastian nodded. "Sir Henry showed me the maul. So what was the connection to the Pear Tree?"

"Seems the initials were supposed to be 'JP,' for a German sailor named Johann Peterson who'd left a chest of tools at the Pear Tree when he went to sea."

"Why didn't this Peterson take his tools with him?"

"Damned if I know. Makes no sense, does it?"

"So who identified the maul as being from the Pear Tree?"

Horton turned and began straightening a pile of rough shirts on a nearby shelf. "That was Robert Vermilloe, the Pear Tree's publican. As soon as we discovered the initials, the Thames River Police printed up a handbill describing the maul and offering a reward for information. Between the initials and a chip it had out of the point, it was pretty distinctive. I guess Vermilloe must've heard about it, because one of the Shadwell magistrates hustled to take the maul to Newgate and show it to him."

"Newgate? Vermilloe was in Newgate? Why?"

"He'd been in prison for something like seven weeks at that point. For debt—twenty pounds, I think it was."

It was a hefty sum; a housemaid in a good establishment typically only made fifteen pounds a year. "Who was this debt to?"

"I'm not sure I ever knew, my lord."

"And when the magistrate took the maul to Newgate, Vermilloe was able to identify it?"

"Oh, aye. Collected a good-sized chunk of the reward money, he did."

"And no one found that a bit suspect?"

Horton shrugged his shoulders. "Some did—especially when his wife insisted she couldn't identify the maul."

"She did?"

"Aye. But then their eleven-year-old nephew piped up and said he was sure the maul had come out of Peterson's chest. Seems he and his little brother used to play with it when they were at the Pear Tree."

"Doesn't sound as if the Vermilloes took very good care of the tools Mr. Peterson entrusted to them."

"Thought the same, I did. Vermilloe always struck me as a slippery fellow. But I was inclined to believe the lad. I mean, a child wouldn't lie about something like that, would he? The maul must've come from the Pear Tree, and it was the main thing had people convinced John Williams must be the killer."

"How many people besides Williams, Vermilloe, and his young nephews had access to the seaman's tool chest?"

Horton gave a rude snort. "Just about anybody came through the inn, from the sounds of it. And get this: While the boy identified the maul as the one he and his brother had played with, he also testified that it'd gone missing a week or two before the Marrs were killed."

"He was certain of that?"

"Aye. It was another thing that never made sense to me—that Williams would take the maul and hide it someplace a week or more before he planned to use it. I mean, he *lived* at the Pear Tree; why'd he need t' take it ahead of time? And where was he gonna hide it? In the room he shared with two other sailors—neither of whom could exactly be described as his mates?"

Sebastian stared out the shop's front window at the dark clouds roiling and bunching overhead. "How long after Vermilloe identified the maul did Williams die? Do you remember?"

"Oh, aye, on account of it bein' Christmastime. The magistrate took the maul to Newgate on Christmas Eve."

"And when was Williams found hanging?"

"Two days later, on Boxing Day. People said that's why he killed himself, because he figured the jig was up once they knew where the maul was from. But I didn't see it that way, myself. I mean, anybody coulda taken that maul—anybody."

"So why do you think Pym and Cockerwell were so intent on blaming Williams?"

"I don't know," said Horton with a roll of his shoulders. "Maybe because of the kind of man he was."

"Meaning what?"

Horton kept his attention on the shirts he was folding. "He might've been a seaman, but he wasn't exactly what you'd call a *masculine* man, if you get my drift?"

After talking to Mrs. Vermilloe, Sebastian rather thought he did. "What do you know about his background?"

"Nothing. Absolutely nothing. I've no idea where he came from. Some said he was Scottish; others said he was Irish, although he didn't sound either one to me. There was even talk at the time that Williams wasn't his real name. All I know is he had no relatives that I ever heard of. Certainly no one ever stepped forward."

"Under the circumstances, that's not surprising, is it?"

"I suppose not."

"You think that's why Pym and Cockerwell were so intent on identifying him as the Ratcliffe Highway murderer? Because he seemed friend-less? And because they thought him . . . not masculine?"

"Well, that and because somebody informed on him. But like I said before, I never knew who that was. I think Williams was just an easy sus-pect, and then after he killed himself, they thought it made them look good to have caught the killer everyone was after. They was baskin' in all that glory, and the last thing they wanted was for me to come along and say, 'Now, hold on a minute.' So they tried to get me to shut up. And because they were both vindictive bastards, they then got me fired." Horton gave up trying to straighten the pile and turned to face Sebas-tian. "That's all there is to it."

"Where were you on the nights Pym and Cockerwell died?"

Something flared in the ex-policeman's dark, narrowed eyes. "You are thinking I did it, aren't ye? You're thinkin' I been carryin' a grudge against Pym and Cockerwell these last three years, and it ate at me till I finally decided to pay them back. Then why am I botherin' to make it look like the Ratcliffe Highway murderer done it? Hmm? You tell me that?"

"To make people question the magistrates' haste in naming John Williams the sole killer, perhaps?"

Horton opened his mouth to say something, then pressed his lips together and shook his head.

"Where were you on the nights they died?" Sebastian asked again.

"In bed, asleep. But I've no way of provin' it, if that was gonna be your next question. Don't even have a wife t' vouch for me. She died two years ago."

'I'm sorry," said Sebastian.

But Horton only stared back at him, his face held tight and his dark eyes glittering with anger and resentment and what looked very much like fear.

Chapter 28

The girl said her name was Eliza Jones and that she was eighteen years old.

Hero didn't believe the age and doubted the name. She'd found the girl lounging outside one of the cock-and-hen clubs on Old Gravel Lane, the flounce of her tawdry yellow gown hiked up high enough to show a stretch of bare leg, a bored moue on her lips as she called out to likely customers.

At first the girl sneered when Hero walked up and explained why she wanted to interview her. But the promise of a couple of shillings sharpened Eliza's interest and made her considerably more cooperative.

"I been on the streets two—no, must be prit' near three years now," said Eliza. She was a small, skinny thing with limp flaxen hair, a sharp face, and enormous blue eyes shadowed with a worldly wisdom that Hero knew she herself couldn't begin to guess at.

"Where were you before that?" asked Hero.

The girl wrinkled her nose and sniffed. "Bethnal Green workhouse."

"You were there with your parents?"

"Nah. Lost me da when I was a little nipper, and m'mother died a few years after that. Had an aunt kept me and my little sister for a while, but then she got herself a new husband, and he didn't like havin' t' feed us, so she turned us over to the parish."

The girl swiped the back of a balled-up fist against her runny nose, and Hero handed over her handkerchief.

"Thank you kindly," said the girl, blowing her nose hard.

"So you were fifteen when you left the workhouse?"

The girl shook her head. "Ran away when I was thirteen." She'd obviously forgotten she'd just claimed to be eighteen.

"And your little sister?"

"She died the first winter we was in the workhouse."

"I'm sorry," said Hero.

The girl shrugged and dabbed at her nose again.

"Why did you run away?"

Eliza looked at Hero as if she were daft. "You ever been in a workhouse?"

"No."

"They get you up before dawn, give you a pint of thin porridge for breakfast, then make you work all day pickin' oakum. If you complain that you're hungry, or cold, or that your hands are so raw they're bleedin' and you can't work no more, they beat you with a stick and shove you in a dark hole and leave you there for days and days without anything to eat or drink." She stared off into the distance, her face stark, her throat working as she swallowed. "I think that was the worst part, that dark hole."

"But at least you were safe."

Eliza wiped her nose with Hero's silk handkerchief again. "You mean from other coves besides the schoolmaster and whoever else decided t' have a go at me? There was this girl brought into the workhouse—Rose was her name. She said that on the streets, men'd pay me to do what I was being forced to do for the schoolmaster for free. So when she made up her mind to run away, I went with her."

Hero stared at the young girl's pale, wan face. She knew she shouldn't be shocked by the girl's story, but she still was. The city's workhouses were almost uniformly hideous. The law required them to provide their occupants with a specified amount of food and drink and work them only so many hours a day. But the parishes frequently let their contracts to unscrupulous men who simply pocketed the majority of the funds meant for the poor, turned a blind eye to the sexual exploitation of the houses' women and children, and worked the residents to death.

Hero glanced down at the list of questions she'd prepared and drew a deep breath. "How much do you make a day on the street?"

"Enough t' get by. Got me a room with some other doxies. Sometimes a customer'll get a bit rough, but at least nobody's stickin' me in some dark hole." The girl shivered, and her eyes took on a glassy, haunted look of gut-wrenching terror. "I think I'd die if I ever had to go through that again."

Hero hesitated and found she had to force herself to ask the next question. "I've heard that one or two of the magistrates around here like to pick up girls from the streets—especially the young ones."

Eliza's face suddenly went utterly blank. "I don't know nothin' about that."

"What about the magistrate who was killed the other day—Sir Edwin Pym? You know anything about him?"

"No."

"Who do you think killed him?"

The girl balled Hero's handkerchief up in her fist. "I dunno. And as long as whoever's doin' it keeps killin' magistrates and leaves us doxies alone, I don't rightly care, neither."

"You haven't heard any talk?"

"About the killings, you mean? People talk about 'em all the time. But ain't nobody knows who's doin' it."

"Would you leave the streets if you could? Not for the poorhouse, but to work in a factory or perhaps in domestic service."

The girl laughed. "Ain't nobody gonna hire me."

"But if someone would? Would you do it?"

Eliza wrinkled her nose. "Nah. Heard about a girl fell into a hot vat of soap in a factory and was killed. And one o' the girls I know—Martha is her name. She used t' be a scullery maid. She had t' scrub pots all day till her hands bled, and sleep on the floor in the kitchen. They never gave her enough t' eat, so's she had t' steal food, and the cook was always beatin' her. Why would I want that?"

"It's not always like that."

"Ain't it? I like goin' t' the cock-and-hen clubs, and dancin' with the sailors, and havin' me some fun. I ain't lookin' t' change nothin'."

There were so many questions Hero wanted to ask, about how the girl kept from making babies, and what she'd do if she did make one, or where she saw her life in ten or twenty years. But the *Chronicle* would never publish any of that, so what was the point? To satisfy Hero's curiosity? To somehow reassure her that the girl's life wasn't as bad as Hero feared it must be?

You can't save them all, Devlin had told her once when she'd found herself overwhelmed by the tales of hardship and sorrow she heard from people on the streets. *All you can do is tell their stories to others, in the hopes of prodding society into changing.*

No, she couldn't save them all, she thought as she handed Eliza her shillings and told her to keep the handkerchief. And the truth was, they didn't all want to be saved.

Chapter 29

$\mathcal{R}$obert Vermilloe was behind the bar pouring a couple of pints of bitter when Sebastian walked into the Pear Tree's taproom.

The publican was a short man somewhere in his fifties, built thin and hard and wiry, with sparse, straight gray hair and protuberant light gray eyes. At the sight of Sebastian, he flexed his lips back from his teeth in the manner of a man confronting a difficult problem he wasn't quite sure how to deal with.

"Heard you was askin' for me," he said, casting Sebastian a swift sideways look before returning his attention to the tankards.

Sebastian paused at the bar, his glance taking in the barrels piled up along the back wall. "You know who I am?"

"Reckon there ain't likely to be two different nobs wanderin' into the Pear Tree two days in a row, now, is there?" Vermilloe carried the tankards to a couple of seamen sitting at a table beside the grimy front window, then came back to pick up a ragged towel and wipe at what he'd spilled. "Hear you're wantin' to know about that Ratcliffe Highway killer."

"You think John Williams was the murderer?"

"Course he was. The Crown gave out over five hundred pounds to people for helpin' catch him. Wouldn't have done that if he weren't the real killer, now, would they?"

"A reasonable deduction, I suppose. I assume your share was handsome?"

Vermilloe gave a sly smile and wet his dry, chapped lips. "The biggest, it was. If I hadn't identified the maul and crowbar, they'd have never known Williams was the one."

"You recognized the crowbar, as well?" said Sebastian.

"Aye. The slimy bastard used old Peterson's maul to kill the Marrs, and his crowbar at the King's Arms."

"So the crowbar came from Johann Peterson's tool chest, as well?"

"Sure did."

"It was marked with his initials?" Sebastian didn't recall seeing them. The smile tightened. "No."

"So how did you recognize it?"

"Just did, that's all."

"I'm told your wife didn't recognize the tools."

"She's a woman; what's she know of such things?" The innkeeper's lips twisted into a sneer. "Plus, she fair doted on that foppish cub. A real Squire of Alsatia, he was, spendin' all his blunt on clothes and prancin' around like he was somethin' he wasn't. Insinuating, he was. Liked to pretend he was a gentleman." Vermilloe snorted. "As if a gentleman'd be stayin' at a place like the Pear Tree and bustin' his arse as a common seaman."

"I understand you were in prison for debt at the time of the killings."

Vermilloe's tongue darted out to wet his lips again. "So?"

"Who was the debt to?"

Vermilloe sniffed. "Don't see how that's any of your business."

Sebastian let his gaze drift around the small, squalid taproom. "I suppose I could ask Bow Street to send a couple of their Runners around, if you'd prefer to speak to them."

No innkeeper wanted a Bow Street Runner poking around his tavern and looking into the origins of the rum in his cellars. Vermilloe's eyes narrowed down to mean, angry slits. "Ran a bit behind on my payments to Buxton-Collins, I did. That's all."

"Your porter comes from the Black Eagle?"

"What if it does?"

Rather than answer, Sebastian said, "Did you see John Williams the night of the King's Arms murders?"

"No. Come in late that night, he did. Real late. It's one of the reasons they knew he was the killer."

"How late?"

"Must've been close on one o'clock."

"That's late, indeed," said Sebastian. According to the young journeyman lodger who'd survived the murders, the killer had fled the King's Arms no later than ten or fifteen minutes after eleven. It was at most a five-minute walk from the King's Arms to the Pear Tree. So if Williams was the killer, where had he spent the intervening hour and forty-five minutes?

"Did he say where he'd been?"

"Claimed he'd been out drinkin', then gone to see some herbwoman about a wound on his leg wasn't healing right."

"A wound from what?"

"I don't know." His voice was growing testy. Aggrieved. "How would I know?"

"Did the herbwoman not vouch for him?"

"Don't know as anyone asked her."

"They didn't?"

Vermilloe tossed his towel aside and settled his hands on his hips. "It's because of these new killings you're here, ain't it? You're thinking Williams must not've been the Ratcliffe Highway killer after all."

"You don't?"

Vermilloe snorted. "Don't know who's behind these new killings, but whoever's doing it, you can be sure it's just some joker tryin' to make folks think he's the Ratcliffe Highway killer. That's all."

"And why would someone want to do that?"

Vermilloe twitched one narrow shoulder. "Reckon he's got his reasons, whoever he is."

Sebastian studied the man's thin, angry face. "I take it you've been paying Pym and Cockerwell a bribe to renew your license every year?"

He watched Vermilloe's face cloud with the wary expression of a man who realizes too late he's lost control of a conversation that's suddenly veered into dangerous territory. "What? No. I don't know what you're talking about."

"Right. Just like you never agreed to report your customers' disgruntled political talk back to the Home Office."

A venomous flare of anger showed in the publican's fishlike gray eyes before being quickly hidden by lowered lids. "Don't know who's been telling you this nonsense. I'm just a simple Wapping innkeeper, doin' my best to get by."

"Who do you think would want to kill Pym and Cockerwell?"

"Told you, I don't know."

"Take a guess."

"Don't know nothin' about it."

"What about Hugo Reeves, the seaman who was killed a few weeks ago? Did you know him?"

"Reckon I seen him around a bit. He come in here a few times."

"Any idea why someone would want to kill him?"

"Nah. Just got in a fight with the wrong sailor, from the sound of things." A raucous outburst of laughter drew his attention to the seamen by the window. "You don't know nothin' about what it's like around here. Nothin'!"

"Then tell me," said Sebastian.

But Vermilloe simply shook his head, his lips pressed together tight, his nostrils flaring with his shallow, rapid breaths.

The mist was rolling in again by the time Sebastian left the Pear Tree. He'd told Tom to wait with the curricle near a watering fountain on the corner of Cinnamon and King Edward streets, but he hadn't expected the fog to roll in this early.

Sebastian's hearing and eyesight were both abnormally acute. But the fog wrapped him in a gray, impenetrable shroud, dampening sounds and cloaking the presence of danger. He was aware of the rasp of his own breathing, of every nerve tingling as he walked down the cobbled street toward the corner. Then the dark outlines of his curricle came into view, the chestnuts throwing their heads and stamping their feet in agitation.

But the curricle's high seat was empty.

Chapter 30

Sebastian drew up abruptly, one hand slipping into his pocket, his fingers curling around the handle of the small double-barreled flintlock pistol he'd taken to carrying since that first night in Wapping. He watched as two men with cudgels stepped forward to range themselves one on either side of the horses. Then a gust of wind eddied the mist, showing him a third man standing against the grimy brick wall of a nearby sailmaker's shop. He had a knife in one hand, his other hand wrapped around Tom's upper arm. The boy stood rigid, his eyes open and blinking rapidly, his hands tied behind his back and a gag pulled tight across his mouth.

"Been waitin' fer ye, we have," said one of the men near the horses' heads. He wore seamen's trousers and a dark coat with a kerchief pulled over his lower face. But Sebastian recognized his light gray eyes, rusty hair, and voice. It was the Glaswegian from outside the Three Moons.

The other two men were larger, meatier, and totally unfamiliar.

"Have another message to deliver, do you?" said Sebastian.

The Glaswegian shook his head and brought up his cudgel to smack it against his left palm. "Reckon we're through talkin'."

It's a truism in combat that you always deal with the most immediate threat first, and in Sebastian's way of thinking, that meant the man with the knife holding Tom. He was no more than ten feet away, and Sebastian had a clear shot. He drew the flintlock from his greatcoat pocket, thumbed back the hammer, and pulled the trigger.

The night exploded in flame and smoke. The man went down, leaving a bloody smear on the wall where his head had been.

"Oye!" yelped one of the men by the horses.

Pulling back the second hammer, Sebastian pivoted and shot the larger of the two remaining men.

The Glaswegian charged. "You bloody bastard," he snarled, swinging his cudgel like a cricket bat at Sebastian's head.

Rather than try to duck, Sebastian stepped inside the man's swing and plowed into him. They went down together hard, Sebastian on top, the breath leaving the other man's chest in a whoosh as his back smacked against the cobbles.

"Who sent you?" Sebastian demanded, dropping the empty pistol to grab the man by the coat, pick his shoulders up off the ground, and slam him down again. "Who sent you, damn your eyes?"

The man gasped for breath, his mouth puckering, his eyes bulging.

Sebastian picked him up and slammed him down again. *"Who sent you?"*

"The Eagle!" said the man with a pained gasp. "Somebody from the Black Eagle."

Sebastian picked him up again. "Buxton-Collins?"

The man's face went gray as he fought for air. "Don't . . . know."

"Was it Buxton-Collins?" Sebastian slammed him down again and saw the man's eyes roll back in his head as he went limp.

One of the chestnuts whinnied in alarm, its white-socked legs dancing as the second man Sebastian had shot staggered up again, cudgel in hand.

Sebastian rolled, scraping the side of his face on the edge of the granite kerb as he snatched up the Glaswegian's cudgel and sprang to his feet.

The two men faced each other across a distance of five or six feet, the mist wafting between them. Both were breathing heavily, the big man bleeding freely from a wound to his upper left arm.

"You've already been shot, and at least one of your friends is dead," said Sebastian. "Give it up. Your odds of getting out of this alive aren't good anymore."

The big man's gaze slid sideways to the Glaswegian's limp, silent form. For a moment he hesitated. Then he threw down his cudgel and ran, his feet slipping and sliding over the damp cobbles as he disappeared into the fog.

Yanking his knife from his boot, Sebastian bent to check the man in the gutter. The Glaswegian was unconscious, but he wasn't dead.

The man by the wall didn't have much of his head left.

"You all right, Tom?" said Sebastian, going to slice the cords binding the boy's hands behind his back and yank the gag from his mouth.

"Aye," said the tiger, bringing up a shaky hand to swipe at his dry lips. "I'm that sorry, gov'nor. They was on me afore I even knew what was happening."

Sebastian put one hand on the boy's shoulder and held him tight. "Not your fault, lad. Not your fault."

Alive to the possibility that the surviving attacker could return at any moment with reinforcement, Sebastian left the Glaswegian and his dead friend lying in Cinnamon Street and drove straight to the public office in Shadwell. By the time he returned with a couple of constables, both the Glaswegian and the dead man were gone.

"Well, hell," said Sebastian, wiping a crooked elbow against something warm and wet running down the side of his face. Except for the blood splatter on the brick wall of the nearby sailmaker's shop and the slouch hat left lying upside down in the gutter, there was no sign that the attack had ever occurred.

Chapter 31

The windows of Sampson Buxton-Collins's Bethnal Green mansion were ablaze with a warm golden light that spilled out into the night, along with a roar of men's and women's voices mingled with genteel laughter and the delicate strains of Haydn played by a string quartet.

"Looks like 'e's 'avin' 'isself a party," said Tom as Sebastian drew up well back from the line of elegant carriages disgorging silk-top-hatted gentlemen and richly gowned ladies dripping with diamonds, emeralds, and rubies that glittered in the lamplight. The mist was thinner here away from the river, the cold air pungent with the scent of fermenting beer from the dark, looming mass of the brewery complex nearby.

Sebastian handed his reins to the tiger. "It does, doesn't it?"

"Yer still goin' in there?" said Tom, scrambling forward to the high seat.

Sebastian hopped down. "Why? You think I'm not dressed for the occasion?"

Tom cast a critical eye over his employer. "The shoulder seam o' yer coat is split, ye've manure smeared all over yer breeches, and the side o' yer face is bleedin'."

Sebastian swiped at the blood trickling down his cheek. "So it is."

Sebastian might have been wearing doeskin breeches and Hessians rather than the elegant evening dress of the brewer's other guests, but Buxton-Collins's butler recognized the Viscount from his previous visit. And no mere servant was going to turn away the son of the Chancellor of the Exchequer, even if he was bleeding.

As Sebastian pushed his way through the house's hot, overcrowded reception rooms, he recognized the Lord Mayor of London, several wealthy rival brewers, including Whitbread and Meux, and enough Quaker bankers to finance another twenty years of war with Europe. A half-dozen directors of the East India Company, numerous prominent members of Parliament, and an impressive showing of cabinet ministers were also in attendance. This was a very different gathering from what one might have found at a typical ball in Mayfair. There was definitely some overlap, but the emphasis here was not on landed estates or ancient lineage and grand titles, but on money and power.

The house's large, magnificently paneled eighteenth-century dining room, frequently used for meetings of the brewing company's board, had been emptied of its furniture and was now a ballroom filled with music and laughter. The air fairly crackled with an unmistakably mercenary atmosphere as the mothers of young unmarried women scouted the gathering for prospective rich sons-in-law.

Buxton-Collins was on the far side of the room, deep in conversation with Lord Sidmouth. The brewer's gaze met Sebastian's over the heads of the glittering crowd; then he murmured something to his companion and crossed to where Sebastian stood near the door, waiting for him.

"Lord Devlin," said the brewer with an assumption of hearty good cheer belied by the brittle animosity in his eyes. "How kind of you to surprise us by dropping in on our little gathering." His hand came up to slide along the black satin riband around his neck and lift his quizzing glass to his right eye. "Merciful heavens. Have you suffered some accident? If you'd like, I could call my—"

"That's quite all right," said Sebastian, dabbing at the blood trickling down his face again. "I'm not staying. I simply wanted to let you know that I received your message."

Buxton-Collins raised one eyebrow in a pantomime of confusion. "My message?"

"The one delivered by the three men who jumped me near Pear Tree Alley this evening."

"Have you been set upon? Goodness gracious. I do hope—"

"I'm fine, thank you, although Calhoun will no doubt despair of the effects of the incident on my coat and breeches. And two of the men you sent are damaged badly enough that I suspect it will be a while before they're able to report back on the success of their mission. The third is dead."

Buxton-Collins held himself very still, his normally booming voice lowered to a lethal hiss. "If you've been set upon by ruffians who told you they were in my employ, I am sorry, but I had nothing to do with this misadventure. And I resent both the suggestion that I would resort to such vulgar tactics and the implication that I might have reason to do so."

"You and I both know your reasons," said Sebastian, his body thrumming with anger and the lingering remnants of the bloodlust that had come close to swallowing him in the lane in Old Wapping. "You have a reputation as a smart man, Buxton-Collins, but what you did tonight showed a distinct lack of understanding of whom you're dealing with."

The faux-jovial facade was gone, leaving the big man's face white with anger, his nostrils pinched. "I say, if you think—"

"I came here for one reason and one reason only," said Sebastian, stopping him. "And that's to tell you this: Send someone at me again and you'll regret it."

"You can't just throw something like that in a man's face and leave," sputtered Buxton-Collins as Sebastian turned to go.

But Sebastian kept going, the elegantly dressed, overfed crowd parting before him like a school of fish clearing the way for a dark predator.

Thursday, 13 October

The fire on the hearth burned with a steady red glow and a cheerful crackle that sounded unnaturally loud in the stillness of the predawn hours. Dressed in clean buckskin breeches and a linen shirt open at the neck, Sebastian stood with one hand braced against his library's mantel, a glass of brandy cradled in the other as he stared down at the dancing flames.

The problem with murder victims as corrupt and loathsome as Sir Edwin Pym and Nathan Cockerwell, he decided, was that they left behind too many enemies with a good reason to kill them. Ian Ryker. Charlie Horton. Seamus Faddy, the Reverend York . . . the list was nearly endless. Add in the strange similarities between these new deaths and the infamous Ratcliffe Highway murders of three years ago, and the result was a giant muddle that seemed to keep getting worse instead of better.

Was John Williams the Ratcliffe Highway killer? One of two killers, the second of which was still out there? Or was Williams the innocent victim of authorities rushing to quiet a hysterical populace? Sebastian had his suspicions, but he also knew those suspicions could be wrong. And what did it all mean when it came to understanding the new murders? Was today's killer Williams's surviving partner? A copyist?

Neither?

He blew out a long, frustrated breath and took a deep swallow of his brandy. He was going in too many directions at once and he knew it. The problem was, he couldn't begin to decide where he should be focusing. And he felt a growing concern that his obsession with the past might be blinding him to something he should be seeing in the present.

A light step sounded on the stairs, a swish of silk, and Hero came to stand beside him. "Can't sleep?" she said, slipping her arms around his waist.

He drew her close and buried his face in the warm tumble of her rich dark hair. "I keep trying to decide if the Ratcliffe Highway killings are the key to what's happening today, or a dangerous distraction."

"I don't think you can call them a distraction," she said. "If justice was not served three years ago, then I'd say the deaths of the seven men, women, and children killed that December are as worthy of investigation as the murders of the corrupt East End magistrates killed this week."

He drew a deep breath. "If it weren't for the threat to Katie Ingram and her children, I'd be tempted to say they are more so."

She shifted her head so she could look at him. "The threat against Katie Ingram echoes what happened to the Marr family, but does it fit with the deaths of her father and Cockerwell?"

"It does if the motive behind the killings is revenge."

"For their corruption, you mean? For the deaths of three years ago? Or both?"

"I don't know. I don't know, and I don't know how to find out, and it's driving me mad."

"Sleep might help," she said softly.

He met her gaze and smiled.

Chapter 32

*L*ater that morning, Sebastian was drawing on his driving gloves as he came down his front steps when a familiar highbred team and black town coach swept around the corner from Bond Street to rein in behind Sebastian's waiting curricle. The sky was overcast, the pavement wet from last night's rain, the air cold and heavy with coal smoke. For a moment Sebastian's gaze met Tom's. Then Sebastian paused at the base of the steps while his father-in-law's footman leapt to fling open the crested carriage door.

"I take it you heard about last night?" said Sebastian, walking up to the carriage.

"I have no intention of discussing this in the street," hissed Jarvis. "Climb up."

"You could come in and have a cup of tea. I've no doubt Hero—"

"*Goddamn you.* Climb up."

Sebastian leapt up to settle on the facing seat and study his father-in-law across the icy distance that separated them. "I've no doubt you sympathize with Buxton-Collins's attempt to have me quietly dispatched in some back alley, but surely you understand why I might object?"

"He says he had nothing to do with that."

"Do you seriously expect me to believe he'd admit it?"

Jarvis's nostrils flared. "You created a spectacle in front of virtually everyone of importance both in the City and in government."

"Somehow I suspect most of Buxton-Collins's guests already knew exactly what he's like, and they don't care. All they care about is making money and keeping the lower orders in their 'place.'"

"Men such as Buxton-Collins are of vital importance to the security of the Kingdom."

"Because his family of bankers lends the money for the King's wars? Or because he and his mates on the Middlesex licensing committee help force East End publicans to spy on ordinary Englishmen?"

"What do you think kept us from going the way of France twenty-five years ago?"

Sebastian gave the King's cousin a slow smile. "The Glorious Revolution of 1688."

Jarvis swiped one big hand through the air between them. "Enough of this. You cause more harm than you know with this interference."

"Oh? Care to explain?"

Jarvis drew an enameled snuffbox from his pocket and flipped it open. "The people don't care who killed those Middlesex magistrates. They simply want to feel safe."

"You think they'll feel safe if the Crown hangs some hapless stooge and then the killings start all over again? Somehow, I doubt it."

Jarvis raised a pinch between thumb and forefinger, and sniffed. "I wonder, have you looked into the vicar of St. George's?"

Sebastian watched his father-in-law close his snuffbox and tuck it away. "The Reverend York? What about him?"

"I think you might find his career up at Cambridge most . . ." Jarvis paused as if deciding on the exact word, then settled on, ". . . instructive."

Sebastian studied the brilliant gray eyes and arrogant aquiline nose that were so much like Hero's. "Did you have John Williams killed three years ago?"

"I already told Hero that I did not."

"So you did." Sebastian pushed to his feet.

"I'm serious about Buxton-Collins," said Jarvis.

Sebastian hopped down to the street, then paused to look back at him. "So am I."

Sebastian spent the next several hours talking to men who'd been up at Cambridge twenty years before. He knew he was being manipulated by his Machiavellian father-in-law; he just couldn't quite figure out to what end. By the time he pulled up before the soot-stained classical facade of St. George's-in-the-East, dark clouds were pressing low on the city. But the rain still held off.

"I don't expect you'll have any trouble around here at this time of day," said Sebastian, handing Tom the reins. "But if you see anyone you think looks suspicious, just walk the chestnuts up and down the street. And don't hesitate to yell your head off if you must."

"I won't let 'em get me again, gov'nor," said the tiger, his jaw set hard as he scrambled forward to the high seat.

The Reverend Marcus York was in the churchyard watching his sexton dig a long trench beside one of the brick walls when Sebastian walked up to him.

"Lord Devlin," said the vicar, wiping his hands on his cassock. A pile of bones lay at his feet, and Sebastian realized that York was collecting the remains as they were flung up by the sexton's shovel. "We're just opening a new poor hole. They fill up quickly around here, I'm afraid."

"I'm not surprised," said Sebastian as the sexton paused to pick up a brown-stained, grinning skull and add it to the pile. "Was the seaman who was murdered several weeks ago—Hugo Reeves—buried in your poor hole?"

"He was, yes," said the reverend as they turned to walk away from the workman. "I try to say a few prayers over each of them, and I know we're all equal in our good Lord's eyes. But I can't help but feel a pang of sympathy for those condemned to such an anonymous end."

"Well, at least they're far from alone."

"True, true," said the reverend.

"Did any of Reeves's family or friends attend his burial?"

"I believe there were two or three seamen came."

"Anyone you recognized?"

"No. Sorry."

Sebastian stared off across the churchyard. He was aware of the long grass between the tombs rippling with the wind and of the heavy smell of damp stone and earth hanging in the cold air as he chose his words carefully. "Someone suggested I look into your time at Cambridge."

The reverend drew up short, his eyes glazing with the look of a man confronted with a past he had long tried to forget. "And did you?"

"I did, yes."

York turned his face into the wind, his rusty black cassock flapping around his legs. "That was a long time ago."

"It was."

"I didn't kill anyone."

"No. But I gather it wasn't for lack of trying."

"No," said the reverend on a pained gust of air. "I was a hotheaded young man, quick to take offense, arrogant in my righteousness, and a slave to my angry impulses. But I'm not that way anymore; I've learned to fight with words, not my fists." He looked over at Sebastian, the wind blowing the reverend's long, lanky hair into his face. "I have not struck a man in anger in eighteen years. I swear."

"Where were you on the nights Pym and Cockerwell were killed?"

"Visiting parishioners. I'm afraid there's been much sickness in Wapping this autumn. The cold has come so early, and people don't have enough to eat."

"Were you with one family? Or visiting several each night?"

"Oh, several, I'm afraid. So I've no real alibi, if that's what you're asking." The sound of a shovel scraping against bone carried across the churchyard, and he glanced toward the sexton, his strained features held tight. "I'm sorry, but I must get back."

"I understand," said Sebastian.

The reverend nodded and walked away quickly, his elbows bent, his hands thrust up into the sleeves of his cassock.

Sebastian didn't want to believe this passionate, caring man of God was a brutal killer. If the victims had been anyone besides Pym and Cockerwell, he probably wouldn't have believed it. But the targets of the much younger Marcus York's righteous anger in Cambridge had all been wealthy, abusive, bullying men—the kind of men who forced themselves on housemaids and beat their horses half to death and cheated the poor because they knew they could get away with it.

Sebastian watched as the reverend took up his position at the side of the poor hole again and stooped to collect a long bone thrown up by the sexton's shovel. Could a priest like that be driven to kill a couple of grasping, venal magistrates?

As he turned to leave, Sebastian wasn't convinced the answer was no.

Chapter 33

It wasn't until he was approaching the apse of the church that Sebastian realized someone was standing there, beside the distinctive tall gray stone monument he'd noticed before.

The man had his hat in his hands, his head bowed. He was a slim young man, probably somewhere in his twenties, his clothes those of a shopkeeper or a clerk. His windblown hair was light brown, his features even, his eyes squeezed shut as if he was in prayer. Then he must have heard Sebastian's boots crunch on the gravel path, because he opened his eyes and whirled around.

"I beg your pardon," said Sebastian. "I didn't mean to startle you."

The man swallowed hard and nodded, one hand coming up to swipe across his eyes.

"Did you know the Marrs?" asked Sebastian, his gaze going beyond the man to the tombstone inscribed *Sacred to the memory of Mr. Timothy Marr* . . .

The man nodded again. "He was my only brother."

"I'm sorry." Sebastian studied the younger man's tensely held features. So this was the brother who was remanded into custody after

Timothy Marr's death, the man whose last words to his brother were hurled in anger. "You're a linen draper, as well?"

He shook his head. "I keep our father's haberdashery." He sucked in a deep, ragged breath, his gaze returning to the tall monument. "I can't believe it's happening again."

"The killings, you mean?"

"Yes. *Oh, God!*" The words sounded torn from a hurting place deep within him, and he pressed his lips together as if to hold back more.

"Do you think it was really John Williams who killed your brother and the others?"

"It's what they said, right? And then the man killed himself and it never happened again, so I always figured it must be true. But now—" He broke off, his voice cracking.

"Was Timothy your older brother, or younger?"

"Older. But he ran off to sea. Our father never forgave him for it and left everything to me when he died. That's what the lawsuit was for, you know. Tim was furious when he came home and found out."

"Your brother sued you?"

The younger Marr gave a ragged laugh. "Over our father's shop. It's why they thought I might've killed him. As if I would."

Sebastian's image of Timothy Marr as a hardworking young linen draper and tender family man tilted slightly. "Did you know John Williams?"

"No, not at all."

"Did your brother?"

"I don't think so. I mean, no one ever said they knew each other. There was some talk that they'd sailed together once, but I don't think that was true."

"Before Williams hanged himself, who did you think killed your brother?"

Marr gazed off across the overgrown, rain-dampened churchyard. "I don't know. Some of the seamen they were looking into at the time seemed more likely to me. Real scrubs and shag-bags, they were."

"Such as?"

"Well, there was that big, mean-looking fellow. I can't remember his name, but I saw him the other day with one of those magistrates who was killed."

"You mean Billy Ablass?"

"That's it. Long Billy, they call him."

"Which magistrate did you see him with?"

The question came out sharper than Sebastian had intended, and he saw Marr's eyes widen. "Sir Edwin Pym, it was. Down by the Sun Tavern rope walk. I remember it because it struck me as queer, seeing them together. They were arguing about something. I couldn't tell you what, but it is odd, don't you think? To see them together, talking like they knew each other? And then just a few days later, Pym ends up murdered the same way as Timothy and all the others."

"Have you told anyone else about this?"

"No. Why?"

"Good," said Sebastian, meeting the younger man's gaze and holding it. "For your own sake, don't."

An unfamiliar lad was behind the bar at the Three Moons when Sebastian pushed open the door to the taproom. The lad was young, probably no more than fifteen or sixteen, tall, and slim, with long arms and legs he hadn't quite grown into yet. His hair was lighter than that of the young woman Sebastian had seen here before, but he had the same ivory skin, straight nose, and mossy green eyes, and so great was the resemblance between them that Sebastian had little doubt they were siblings.

"He ain't here," said the boy, throwing a hostile glance over one shoulder at Sebastian. It was midafternoon now; the taproom rang with men calling for ale, and the boy was busy filling tankards.

"How do you know who I'm looking for?" asked Sebastian.

The boy let out his breath in a scornful huff. "Hannah told me 'bout you."

"Hannah?"

"My sister."

Sebastian had seen the names painted on the sign above the inn's door: HANNAH AND CHRISTOPHER BISHOP, PROPRIETORS. "You two own the place together?"

The boy gave an adolescent shrug. "Have since our mum died last year."

"But you weren't here three years ago at the time of the Ratcliffe Highway killings?"

"I was. Hannah wasn't."

Sebastian studied Christopher Bishop's half-averted profile. "So was Billy Ablass living here at the time?"

The boy picked up two fistfuls of tankards. "No," he said, and headed toward a table by the door.

Sebastian waited until he came back. "Do you know where Ablass is?"

"Right now? No."

"Think your sister might?"

The boy stared at him, his thoughts impossible to read. "Ask her yourself. She's in the kitchen."

"Thank you."

Christopher Bishop grunted and turned away.

She was sitting on the floor in a corner of the bright, well-tended kitchen, a basket of fluffy gray-and-white kittens beside her, her head bowed over one she held in her lap. Her face was relaxed, a soft smile curling her lips. Then she looked up and saw him, and the smile faded to be replaced by something wary and closed.

"Lord Devlin," she said. "Somehow I suspected we'd be seeing you again."

He paused beside the window overlooking the inn's small flagstone yard. "Because you suspect Billy Ablass?"

"I didn't say that."

"No?"

"No."

"So tell me this: Did you ever see Ablass with Sir Edwin Pym?"

"With Pym? Good heavens, no. Why?"

"They were seen arguing just a few days before Pym was killed."

"They were?" A frown creased her forehead. "Well, if you're looking to me to explain it, I can't."

Sebastian let his gaze wander around the tiled kitchen with its large new stove, its rows of gleaming copper pots, its well-scrubbed table. "This is a nice inn. A man like Ablass seems . . . out of place here."

One of the kittens was struggling to escape from the basket, and she reached out a hand to capture it and put it back, her face thoughtful, as if she was trying to decide how to answer him. "This isn't Mayfair, my lord. We try to appeal to a better sort of customer, but it's a rough neighborhood and some of the men who come in can be trouble. Sometimes a man like Long Billy Ablass can be handy to have around."

"I'd think Ablass himself could be trouble."

"He knows to take it elsewhere."

He studied her half-averted face. He had the feeling she wasn't being entirely honest with him, but he couldn't begin to guess why or how. He said, "Do you pay the Middlesex licensing committee a bribe every year?"

He thought she might be offended by the blunt question. Instead she sucked in a quick breath, then gave a startled laugh. "Name me a publican around here who doesn't."

"Seems to me that might aggravate someone enough to want to kill."

She looked him evenly in the eyes. "Only someone who got into this business without knowing what's what. It's been like this since before my father built this inn almost thirty years ago. I grew up thinking that's just what publicans do—bribe magistrates."

It occurred to Sebastian that Ian Ryker had grown up in his father's tavern and yet still carried a hefty load of animosity toward the local magistrates. But then, they'd yanked the senior Ryker's license—and very likely murdered him, as well.

He said, "Did you know a publican named Ryker? Used to keep the Green Man on Rope Walk Lane."

"Ian Ryker? Yes. Why? He's dead now."

"Do you know his son, also named Ian?"

Her eyes went away from him again. "I know him. He's not around anymore."

"That's because he's taken up with a woman who owns a tavern in Bishopsgate."

"Has he? Well, then, good." The vehemence in her voice surprised him. "He can stay up there. We don't need his kind around here."

"Why's that?"

"He had a wife once. Only, she died. He claimed she fell down the stairs." Hannah Bishop paused, her chest shuddering as she drew a deep breath. "She didn't fall down the stairs."

Sebastian watched her features flatten beneath an onslaught of suppressed emotions. And he found himself thinking about Jamie Knox's little boy, his ball gripped tightly in his hands as he backed stony-faced away from the man who'd taken his father's place.

Chapter 34

That afternoon, Hero spent more time than she'd have believed possible trying to convince any of the heartbreakingly young girls on the streets of Wapping to talk to her. It took over an hour, but she finally found one, named Letitia Simmons, who at first refused to talk to her, then changed her mind and said she'd do it—but for five shillings instead of two—and three up front.

"This'll pay me rent for a week, it will," said Letitia, tucking the coins into the cleavage of her ample bosom. She was a pretty, strapping young girl of perhaps seventeen, black haired and black eyed, with rosy cheeks and a rosebud mouth and a way of throwing back her head when she laughed—which was often. She was a revelation to Hero. Hero had interviewed a number of such women several years before, when she was researching the economic origins of the city's exploding prostitute population. But she had never met a light-skirt like Letitia.

"Been on me own since I was fourteen," said the girl without the least bit of shame or self-consciousness.

They were sitting on a low wall down near the basin, Hero with her notebook balanced on her knee, the seagulls wheeling overhead and the breeze off the river smelling of fish and tar. "Is that when you lost your parents?"

Letitia shook her head. "Nah. Me mum died when I was seven, and they hanged me da when I was eleven."

Hero almost dropped her notebook and had to scramble to catch it. "Your father was hanged?"

"Aye. For counterfeiting. That's when they stuck me in the work-house."

"And you ran away?"

"Nah. It weren't so bad. I mean, they was all a bunch of pudding-faced bleaters, and the endless Bible readings was a real snore. There was this chaplain who was always takin' me aside and prayin' over me, warnin' me about the temptations of sin and the dangers of hellfire, and all the while he's doin' it, he's squeezin' me arm or me knee and smilin' like he just won the lottery or somethin'." She gave a derisive snort. "Dirty old wanker. But at least he never did nothin' else, which is more'n can be said for the turnkeys in Newgate—the nasty, rotten buggers."

"You were in Newgate?"

Letitia sniffed. "Quodded fer three months, I was."

Hero had to work to keep her reaction off her face. "So why did you leave the workhouse?"

"They apprenticed me to a bakery over in Brompton. You know, by the barracks?"

"Yes," said Hero, who thought she knew where this was going.

"At first it was real nice. All I had t' do was mind the shop and serve the people what come in. There was heaps of soldiers around all the time, and they liked me a lot. We was always laughin' and talkin', and there was this one sergeant—Miles—he was real sweet. Used to buy me hair ribbons and bits of lace and stuff. So when his regiment was sent to Dover, I went with him."

"You ran away from your apprenticeship?"

Letitia wrinkled her nose and shrugged. "The baker's wife, Mrs. Bieber, was real mean t' me. She was always smackin' me and tellin' me I was gonna go t' hell. Like that was gonna make me wanna stay with her rather than go with Miles."

"So then what happened?"

"I had a gay ole time in Dover. Made lots of friends down there. Only, Miles got a bit jealous and started smacking me around. So I left and come back up to London."

Hero blinked. "Why Wapping?"

Again that twitch of the shoulders. "It's where we lived before me mum died. Been here about six months now, but I ain't sure how much longer I'm gonna stay. They say Portsmouth is a grand place to work."

Hero asked her next question as casually as she could. "I hear that some of the magistrates around here like to pick up girls off the streets— especially very young girls."

"Oh, aye, real beard splitters, some of 'em are."

"Beard splitters?" said Hero, not understanding.

Letitia laughed so hard she rocked back on the wall. "That's what we call a cove what likes t' go with strumpets."

"Oh," said Hero, annoyed to feel herself coloring.

"That wanker what got killed last week was the worst."

"You mean Sir Edwin Pym?"

"Aye. Real rough, he was, always squeezin' yer diddeys and rubbin' his tallwag and barbels against you like he was a mangy dog with an itch to scratch."

This time Hero stopped herself from asking for translations, although she did write the unfamiliar terms down in her notebook.

"I learned real quick to run when I seen him comin'," Letitia was saying. "He was always treatin' girls like they was three-penny stand-ups and then payin' em nothin'. Did it t' one of the girls I room with the very night he was killed."

"Oh?" said Hero, barely daring to breathe. "Would she be willing to talk to me, do you think?"

Letitia opened her mouth to say something, then closed it as a look of instinctive wariness settled over her features. "Why?"

"It's just that I'm having such a hard time finding girls who are willing to talk to me. I'll pay her, of course—and you, too, if you can convince her to meet with me. Maybe bring her here tomorrow afternoon?"

"I dunno," said Letitia, slowly. "She's real skittish. She ain't like me."

"I'll pay you five more shillings if you can convince her to come."

Letitia licked her lips. "I'll sure enough try."

"Good. We can meet here tomorrow afternoon at, say, two o'clock?"

Letitia gave her a sly sideways look. "Maybe give me a shilling now so's I can show Molly you're good fer it?"

Hero gave her the shilling, then wrote in her notebook, *Molly*.

Chapter 35

$\mathcal{S}$ebastian arrived back at Brook Street that afternoon to find Hero in a chair by the nursery fire with Simon perched on her knee while she read him a book.

"Papa!" called Simon, looking up. "We readin' *book!*"

Sebastian paused in the doorway and smiled. "I see that."

"All done now," said the boy, scooting off Hero's lap to go plop down beside his box of tin soldiers.

"Sorry," said Sebastian.

Hero laughed. "It's not your fault. He was already getting restless."

"How long did he last?"

"At least ten minutes. I think that's a record. He can't sit still very long."

"Unless he's doing something he shouldn't."

"Oh, but that's different."

He came to warm himself in front of the fire. "How was your latest venture to Wapping?"

"Potentially fruitful," she said, and told him of her conversation with Letitia.

"Do you think this Molly will show?" he asked when she had finished.

"I don't know. But I suspect Letitia will do everything within her power to get the girl there and earn her shillings." She set the book she was still holding aside. "I wonder how many young doxies named Molly there are in Wapping."

"Probably quite a few."

Hero sighed. "I suspect you're right."

They watched Simon aim his toy cannon at a line of soldiers, then go, *"Boom!"* and knock them all down. *Where the devil did he learn that?* thought Sebastian. Then he looked up to see that the expression on Hero's face had shifted, and said, "What is it?"

She sighed. "I received a note a short while ago from Jarvis asking that I come to Berkeley Square tomorrow at five for a visit." A faint gleam of amusement showed in her eyes. "You are not invited."

"Oh?"

She pushed up from the chair and went to stand beside the window overlooking the street. The nursery was at the very top of the house, tucked up under the roof. "It's been a year now since my mother died, and—" She hesitated, then swung to face him. "I have the most lowering suspicion that he plans to tell me he's decided to marry Cousin Victoria."

Sebastian considered a range of possible responses to that statement and finally settled on a craven "You do?"

She put a hand up to her forehead. "The thing is, she's never been anything except warm and friendly to me, and yet . . ."

"You don't like her."

Hero gave him a quavering smile. "She's beyond brilliant; she's lived the most amazing life, traveled everywhere, been widowed twice. Sometimes I think I'm being unfair, that I simply don't want her to take my mother's place—and I don't. But the truth is . . . she's a female version of Jarvis, except worse. There is nothing she says or does that's not carefully calculated. How can someone be like that? *All the time?"*

"You don't think Jarvis knows that about her?"

Hero looked at him with wide, hurting eyes. "I suppose he does. No one's more astute than he. And yet . . . he is a man, and she is so very beautiful."

"He's still Jarvis."

"I suppose. Hopefully if that's what this visit is about, I'll somehow manage to convincingly wish them both happy." She glanced out the window, her attention caught by something in the street below. "There's the most reprehensible-looking fellow loitering by our area steps. Big and tall, with a long black beard and a nose to rival that of Wellington himself."

Sebastian went to stand beside her, his jaw tightening as he stared down at the man now mounting the front steps. "That's Long Billy Ablass."

Sebastian's majordomo, Morey, had refused to allow the burly seaman to come any farther into the house than two steps past the front door.

"Wot's this trumped-up jackanapes here think, hmmm?" demanded Ablass when Sebastian walked down the stairs to the entry hall. "Think I'm here to murder every last one of ye in yer beds? If'n I was, I wouldn't be comin' in the front door in the bloody daytime, the bleedin' fool."

Morey executed a dignified bow and withdrew.

"Why are you here?" Sebastian asked the tall, beefy seaman. His hair was sticking out at wild angles, his eyes bloodshot, his beard matted.

"I 'ear ye been askin' about me agin. It ain't good fer me reputation, ye know? Got folks whisperin' about me behind me back, it does."

"Oh? And what are they saying?"

"That I must be the new Wappin' killer, that's wot they're sayin'—and maybe the old one, too."

"Interesting."

"Interestin'! Ye think it's interestin'? Why I oughta—"

"*Don't*," said Sebastian icily when the man raised his fists and took a hasty step forward.

Ablass drew up, his throat working as he lowered his hands to his sides.

Sebastian said, "You were seen arguing with Sir Edwin Pym just a few days before he was killed. What was that about?"

"Arguin'? I don't know wot yer talkin' about."

"Yes, you do."

Ablass's lips parted in a sly grin. "Wot would me and some high-and-mighty magistrate be doin', havin' words?"

"I can think of several explanations."

The smile faded.

Sebastian said, "Where were you living at the time of the Ratcliffe Highway murders?"

"Wot? Ye think I can remember?"

"I think you can."

The man pointed one long, bony finger at Sebastian. "Ain't nobody gonna pin these new killings on me. Ye hear? I got nothin' to do with them dead magistrates."

"Just like you had nothing to do with Hugo Reeves or the original Ratcliffe Highway murders?"

"That's right!"

"Tell me this: Did you ever drink at the Pear Tree?"

Ablass pinched his lower lip between a grimy thumb and forefinger and pulled it down. "Sometimes. Why?"

"So you would have had access to Johann Peterson's chest of tools?"

Ablass took a step back. "Oh no. Ye ain't gonna try t' hang that around me neck again. The man what done those killings is dead."

Sebastian kept his gaze on the other man's face. "You knew John Williams, didn't you?"

Ablass started to deny it, then must have remembered he'd already admitted they'd been shipmates. "Aye, we was on the *Roxburgh Castle* together. Why?"

"Where was he originally from?"

"I dunno. If he ever said, I don't remember it. Why would I?"

"He never talked about home?"

Ablass shrugged. "Just t' say he'd run away t' sea as soon as he could."

"Did he say why?"

"Nothin' I remember."

"Did you know Timothy Marr?"

Ablass stared back at him, eyes half-hidden by lowered lashes. "No. Why would I?"

"He was a sailor before he opened his linen draper's, wasn't he?"

Ablass's lips curled into a sneer. "He weren't a sailor—didn't sail before the mast like the rest o' us. The captain's own personal servant, he was. You think he's gonna consort with the likes o' us?"

"So you did know him."

Ablass sniffed. "Knowed who he was."

"And the King's Arms? Did you ever drink there?"

"Reckon I may've, once or twice, but what of it? Two weeks they kept me locked up in Clerkenwell after Johnny hanged hisself—"

Johnny, noted Sebastian as the man raged on.

"Two weeks," Ablass was saying, "with leg-irons festerin' on me like I was a bloody thief or something. But they never found nothin' would stick, and you ain't gonna, neither. And ye keep tryin', yer gonna have cause t' regret it, if'n ye get me drift."

"Are you threatening me?" said Sebastian.

"Take it how ye will," growled Ablass, and turned to wrench open the door and stomp down the front steps.

"Charming fellow," said Hero, coming down the stairs.

"Isn't he?"

"I can see someone like that beating a man's head to a pulp and then slitting his throat."

Sebastian took a deep breath and let it out slowly. "So can I."

Chapter 36

That night Sebastian dreamt he heard a baby screaming in terror at the top of an endless flight of dark, twisting stairs. He raced up and up, feet pounding on worn bare wooden steps, breath rasping in his throat, his heart squeezing, squeezing.

"Simon," he cried. *"Simon!"*

He recognized the gaily sprigged wallpaper at the top of the stairs, the comfortable armchair drawn up before the crackling fire, the familiar array of blocks and tin soldiers. But when he reached the nursery, he found only an empty room.

And a small, gently rocking cradle drenched in blood.

He awoke with a start, heart pounding in his ears, throat dry and sore. Thrusting up, he swung his legs over the side of the bed and sat there, his body tingling. He was aware of Hero sleeping peacefully beside him and knew the urge to climb up to the nursery, to check on Simon and reassure himself the child was still there, safe. He told himself he would alarm Simon's nurse, Claire, unnecessarily, perhaps even wake the boy. And yet he wondered how he could ever get back to sleep without knowing.

He realized he was shivering, both in reaction to the dream and from the icy bite of the night air on his bare skin. Pushing to his feet, he went to throw more coal on the fire. It was when he was standing beside the hearth, his gaze on the flames licking at the new fuel, that he heard a faint, distant *snap, snap.*

He raised his head. His hearing, like his vision, had always been unusually acute. The sound had come from downstairs, he was certain. A moment later he heard a dull scraping noise, then the creak of a floorboard beneath stealthy footsteps.

He normally kept his small double-barreled pistol locked in his desk in the library. But for the past several nights, haunting thoughts of the old Ratcliffe Highway murders had driven him to bring the weapon, loaded and primed, to bed with him. Moving swiftly, he drew the pistol from its drawer, then placed his fingers over Hero's mouth and said quietly, "Don't be afraid."

Her eyes went wide, and he immediately withdrew his hand. "Someone's downstairs," he whispered, pressing the flintlock into her hand. "I want you to take this, go upstairs, and stay with Simon and Claire. I'm going to try to stop them down here, but if they get past me, I need you to protect Simon."

"Who—?" she started to say, but he was already moving.

Taking the heavy iron poker from beside the hearth, he crept down the corridor toward the back of the house. The footsteps were now coming from inside the servants' stair. Two men, he decided, perhaps three. Climbing fast.

The lingering terror of his dream rode him. He was breathing so heavily he was shaking, his naked body covered in a cold sweat. As he neared the door to the back stairs, it occurred to him that the men could simply keep going on up to the nursery. In his mind he was screaming, *Simon! Hero!* Then the green-baize-covered door from the servants' stair flew open, and a brawny, dark-haired man carrying a cudgel and wearing a rough seaman's coat stepped into the corridor.

Sebastian had planned to swing the heavy iron bar at the man's head like a club, but the angle was wrong. All he could do was shift his grip on the poker and ram the thick pointed tip like a sword into the man's chest.

It made an obscene popping sound, the man's blood spraying across Sebastian's face and body in a hot wet arc. He saw the man's eyes roll back in his head and tried to yank out the poker before the man fell. But the hook protruding some inches from the poker's tip must have caught on the man's ribs. He collapsed heavily, yanking the poker from Sebastian's grip just as a second man in pale canvas seamen's trousers and a black coat leapt over the body of the first and came at Sebastian with what looked like a fat butcher's knife gripped in his fist.

Sebastian kicked him in the face. But he was barefoot, and though the man staggered back, he recovered quickly. With an angry roar, he charged again, his big head lowered like a rampaging bull.

The force of his rush bowled Sebastian over. He went down hard, the man on top of him, Sebastian scrambling to wrap his fists around the man's knife hand and twist it back. He heard bone snap, heard the knife clatter to the floor as the man reared back with a howl. Gritting his teeth, Sebastian grabbed the knife and slashed it across the intruder's neck just as a third man came barreling through the narrow service door.

"Bloody hell," swore Sebastian, shoving the dying knifeman to one side. The new assailant yanked the bloody poker from the first dead man's chest and came at Sebastian with a snarl, a club in one hand and the poker in the other.

Sebastian still had the second man's knife, but it was too awkward and sticky with blood to throw. He lunged sideways to where the first man's fallen cudgel had rolled, just as the corridor exploded in flame and smoke.

The force of the pistol shot slammed the third man back against the wall. He wavered there for a moment, eyes going wide, blood pouring from his mouth as his jaw sagged. Then he slid down the wall to the floor, leaving a dark smear of red on the wainscoting behind him.

A sudden ringing silence descended on the night. His breath coming in great gasps, Sebastian turned to see Hero standing at the base of the stairs coming down from the nursery, his pistol still extended in her steady grip.

He was shaking more than she was.

"I hid Claire and Simon in a cupboard," she said, thumbing back the second hammer. "But I thought you might need some help."

Sebastian pushed to his feet. "Thank you." The urge to go to her, to take her in his arms and hold her close, was strong. But he went first to check all three men and make certain they were dead. He expected one of the intruders to be Long Billy Ablass, but all three were unknown to him.

"Are they dead?" asked Hero.

"Yes."

"Good." She lowered the pistol and came forward in a rush to wrap her arms around his waist and press her now trembling body against his.

Hero argued against it, but in the end Devlin convinced her to let the constables think he had killed all three attackers. She knew their world as well as he, knew that her controversial articles and other activities already skated close to the edge of what was considered acceptable for a woman of her station. She had killed before, and many of those who knew it already looked askance at her for it. As much as it angered and frustrated her, she had no desire to face social ostracism.

After the bodies had been removed, the constables seen off the premises, and Simon and Claire and the servants comforted and sent back to bed, she and Devlin sat together beside their bedroom fire, both too wound up to sleep.

"Who do you think sent them?" she asked after a time.

Devlin stared into the fire for a moment, the golden light glazing his prominent high cheekbones. "If I had to guess, I'd say Sampson Buxton-

Collins. Who else mixed up in all this has the financial resources to hire three men? But I could be wrong. Hell, it could be Seamus Faddy for all I know. He did say he has a crew."

She rolled her head against the back of the overstuffed chair to look over at him. "Why would Seamus Faddy be trying to kill you?"

"I've no idea. I don't think it likely, but I have to acknowledge it as a possibility."

She was silent for a moment, listening to the crackle of the fire and watching the flames leap. "Why would Buxton-Collins kill Pym and Cockerwell? They were his allies."

Devlin took a slow sip of the brandy he'd poured himself. "I don't know that he did. But it's possible he's afraid I'm on the verge of uncovering something else—something he'd kill to keep hidden."

"Such as? You already know about his cozy arrangement with the Middlesex licensing committee. And Jarvis and a succession of Home Secretaries have obviously been winking at it for years."

He gave a faint shake of his head. "I thought at first that we were looking for someone who enjoys killing for the sake of killing. But I think now that I was wrong. I think there's a pattern here and a reason. I'm convinced it's tied in to what happened three years ago. But I'm only seeing the hazy outlines of it, and I can't begin to grasp it."

He drained his glass and set it aside, then came to settle on the carpet at her feet and take her hands in his. "I'm so sorry. I never meant to bring danger to our house. I'm thinking perhaps it's wrong, what I do. That I shouldn't—"

She loosed a hand from his grip to touch his lips, then slide her fingertips down his neck in a light caress. "No. Dante assigned the hottest circle of hell to those who do nothing in the face of evil. Life shouldn't be about pursuing pleasure or being safe, being comfortable. It's about helping others, and reaching for what's right, and trying to make this a better world. That's what you do. It's a part of why I love you, and I won't have you give it all up out of some mistaken belief in what you owe me."

"If anything ever happened to you or Simon, I could never forgive myself."

"And I could never forgive myself if I let you change because of us."

He caught her hand again, his gaze holding hers, his yellow eyes shimmering in the firelight as he pressed a kiss to her palm. "God, how I love you."

Chapter 37

Friday, 14 October

arvis was drinking a morning pot of ale in solitary splendor at his breakfast table when he heard someone ringing a peal at the distant front door. There was a quick step in the entry hall and the voice of his butler, Grisham, raised in protest. Then the dining room door crashed open and Devlin stood on the threshold, his caped greatcoat hanging open, his driving whip gripped in one hand, and his face tight with rage.

"Unorthodox," said Jarvis, taking a slow sip of his ale. "I take it you haven't come to join me for breakfast?"

"You bloody son of a bitch," swore the Viscount. "Three men broke into my house last night with cudgels and knives."

Jarvis's hand spasmed around his tankard, but he kept all betraying traces of emotion from his face. "Hero . . . ?"

"She and Simon are fine. The men are dead."

Jarvis felt his breath ease out in a ragged sigh.

"Who sent them?" demanded Devlin, his hand tightening around his whip. "You know."

"You can't seriously believe that."

"I think you have a damned good idea."

Jarvis set aside his tankard with a thump. "This is your fault. You are the one meddling in affairs that do not concern you, drawing dangerous men into my daughter's life and—"

"*My fault?* You bloody bastard. If anything happens to my family—"

Jarvis pushed back his chair with a loud scrape and surged to his feet. "In case you have forgotten, your 'family' consists of my daughter and grandson."

"So why the hell won't you tell me who sent those men?"

"I don't know, damn you!"

The Viscount's lips curled into a hard, tight smile. "And yet you flatter yourself on knowing everything."

"Get out. Get out of my house."

Devlin nodded. "I've said what I came to say. We both know where we stand."

Then he turned on his heel and left.

Chapter 38

ampson Buxton-Collins was coming out of a coffeehouse across from the Bank of England when Sebastian intercepted him on the pavement.

"Lord Devlin," said the brewer, drawing up short. Today the big man was wearing fawn-colored pantaloons and a blue-and-white-striped silk waistcoat beneath a blue coat with large silver buttons. An extravagantly tall beaver hat topped his carefully arranged locks, and a silver-headed ebony walking stick dangled from one hand. "I heard about the attack on your house. Shocking business; beyond shocking. I do hope dear Lady Devlin suffered no ill effects from such an alarming incident."

Sebastian kept his voice low and even. "If I find you had anything—anything at all—to do with what happened last night, I swear to God I will destroy you."

The rich brewer's normally ruddy face went white with rage. He held himself stiffly, his nostrils flaring, the hand holding his walking stick coming up to point a finger at Sebastian. "You dare? You dare to threaten me? *Me?*"

Sebastian met the big man's glittering, blazing gaze and smiled. "Only you know if you have something to fear."

"The housebreakers' use of cudgels and knives suggests they could be the same men who were behind the recent East End murders," said Sir Henry Lovejoy later that morning as he and Sebastian walked down Bow Street toward the river. The day was cloudy but warmer, the rattle of a passing bricklayer's dray sending up a pair of pigeons to flap their wings in alarm.

"Perhaps," said Sebastian. "Or perhaps whoever sent them simply wants us to think that."

Lovejoy looked thoughtful for a moment. "Yes, I can see that. Unfortunately, we've only been able to identify one of them so far—a ne'er-do-well from Bethnal Green named Jud Piper."

"Bethnal Green? Does he have any known connections to Sampson Buxton-Collins?"

Lovejoy stared at him. "Buxton-Collins? You can't be serious."

"I wish I weren't."

"Oh, dear. I'll tell the lads to make some inquiries." The magistrate hesitated, then cleared his throat and said, "I do hope Lady Devlin was not too terribly distressed by last night's dreadful incident."

"No," said Sebastian baldly.

"Good, good." Lovejoy cleared his throat again. He'd never been able to disguise the fact that Hero made him uncomfortable. But then, Hero disconcerted most men. "You've heard that Ian Ryker was remanded into custody by the Shadwell Public Office this morning?"

"Ryker? Why?"

"Seems he was lying when he claimed he never left the Black Devil on the night of Sir Edwin Pym's murder. Two people have now sworn to seeing him in Wapping that night."

"Where are they holding him?"

"In Coldbath Fields Prison."

They called it "the English Bastille"—except that the original Bastille Saint-Antoine of Paris was considerably more comfortable than Cold-bath Fields Prison.

Standing in a broad green field of lazily grazing white sheep on the outskirts of Clerkenwell, the prison dated back to the first days of the seventeenth century. Rebuilt in the eighteenth century, it was a severe, grim place used primarily for political prisoners, vagrants, debtors, prisoners awaiting trial or interrogation, and those with short sentences. Men, women, and children were herded in together in open yards or crammed into small, dark, unheated cells that flooded when it rained. Provided with only foul water and stale bread, they were beaten with sticks or knotted ropes if they complained. An inquiry into the prison's wretched conditions and high death rate some dozen years before had ended with the prison governor successfully bankrupting one of the disappointed reformers by suing him for libel.

Sebastian could feel the place's miasma of fear, despair, and rot pressing in on him as he followed a turnkey down a long gallery of endless putrid cells to a small waiting room with a high barred window. The room was damp and icy cold and furnished with only a crude table and stools. The turnkey left him there some five minutes before returning with the publican Ian Ryker.

The man's clothes were torn, disheveled, and dirty, his eyes glittering with silent rage, his face mottled with bruises that suggested he had not surrendered peacefully to the constables. He was ironed on his right leg, and the chain clinked as he drew to a halt and brought up a hand to scrape across his beard-stubbled face. "If I'd known your lordship was comin' for a visit, I'd have shaved and asked me valet to lay out a change of clean clothes."

"Good God," said Sebastian.

Ryker tilted back his head, his eyes hooded as he continued to hold Sebastian's gaze. "You think I look bad, you ought to see the sorry bastards who've been in here a while."

"Why did you lie about where you were that night?"

Ryker shrugged and went to stand with his shoulders propped against the far wall, his arms crossed at his chest. "Didn't expect nobody t' know better."

"Now they think you did it," said Sebastian. *And perhaps with good reason.*

"Yeah, well, I'm workin' on that."

Sebastian studied the man's narrowed bloodshot eyes. "Three men broke into my house last night armed with knives and cudgels. You know anything about that?"

The publican's face remained admirably blank. "No. Why would I?"

"You haven't heard any talk?"

"Not sure who you think I consort with, but I don't normally number housebreakers and murderers amongst me mates."

"Ever hear of a man from Bethnal Green named Jud Piper?"

"Who?"

"Jud Piper."

"No. He one o' 'em?"

"Yes."

Ryker shook his head. "Sounds like you riled somebody up real good."

"Apparently."

He brought up a hand to rub the back of his neck, his eyes taking on a speculative gleam. "I was talkin' to a cuffin out in the yard a bit ago. He'd heard what I was thrown in here for and made it a point to come over and see me for himself. Seems he was here the night John Williams is supposed to 've hanged himself. Had the cell right next t' him."

"And?"

The rifleman gave Sebastian a slow, malevolent smile. "Let's just say you might want to talk to him. Flood is his name. Wendell Flood."

Wendell Flood was a small, spry old man with wispy white hair and the kind of wrinkled, desiccated face that one could not imagine had ever been young.

When the turnkey brought him to the room at Sebastian's request, the old man hopped up on the edge of the table and sat there like a scruffy bird perched on a fence rail. His clothes were a tattered collection of rags and patches topped by an incongruously fine green coat.

"I'm told you were in the cell next to John Williams back in December of 1811," said Sebastian.

Flood curled his hands around the edge of the table and leaned back, his speculative gaze on Sebastian's face. "Aye, that I was. Call 'em the 'reexamination cells,' they do. They're isolation cells, ye see. Use 'em for those they've hauled in for questionin' and want to question again."

"And why were you in there?"

The corners of the old man's eyes crinkled with a secret smile. "Don't rightly remember. I been in there off and on a fair number of times o'er the years. It's hard to keep 'em separate in me head. Gettin' old, ye know."

Sebastian suspected Flood remembered very well, but he didn't press the point. "Did you ever see Williams?"

"Oh, aye. We're mostly locked up in the cells only at night, ye know."

"How did he seem? Was he worried about his coming hearing, do you think? Cast down about it?"

"Nah. If anything, I'd say he was chipper. A real likable lad, he was. Said he reckoned he had nothin' t' worry about, because he hadn't done nothin'. Said he figured the saddle'd be put on the right horse soon enough."

"That's what he said? He used those exact words?"

"Yup. Last time I talked to him."

"Did you hear anything the night he hanged himself?"

Flood sniffed. "They asked me that at the inquest, and I told 'em I woke up at three and heard chains rattling. Nothin' else."

"How did you know it was three o'clock?"

"The church bells was strikin'."

"And that's all you heard? The church bells and chains rattling?"

Wendell Flood gave him a long, steady look. "Ye don't have t' be in here long t' know not t' pay too much attention to the things you hear."

The man's meaning was more than clear. Sebastian met his gaze and held it. "When did they find his body? Do you know?"

"Oh, aye. It was early the next morning. The turnkey—Beckett was his name, Joseph Beckett—he come into me cell and asked me and this other cove t' help him cut the poor lad down."

"So you saw Williams when he was still hanging?"

Flood nodded. "There's an iron rod runs across the top of all the cells, up near the ceiling. We use it t' hang our clothes and straw pallets from. That's what he was tied to."

"By a rope?"

"No, 'twas his own handkerchief." For the first time Flood looked away and swallowed, his features pinched. "He didn't die easy, the poor lad. Fought it hard, he did. His mouth was open and his eyes was bulging, and his arms was all bruised."

"Bruised?"

Flood brought his gaze back to Sebastian's face. "Aye."

"How far off the ground are these iron rails?"

"Six feet two inches. I know exactly because they asked the turnkey about it at the inquest."

"And how tall was Williams?"

"He was a middlin' man, maybe five-eight."

Sebastian was beginning to feel the cold and despair of this place curl itself around his belly. "Are there beds in the reexamination cells?"

"Nah. Just straw mats on the ground."

"A chair?"

Flood gave a scornful laugh. "There's a bucket t' use as a chamber pot. That's it."

"And had Williams used the bucket to stand on?"

"Nope. It was still over in the corner."

"So a man who'd somehow managed to stand on the floor and tie himself to that bar could simply have untied himself if he changed his mind and decided he didn't want to die?"

"Of course he could've."

"Were you there when they handed down the verdict at the inquest?"

"Aye. Called it self-murder, they did. Said those who had him in custody were in no way t' blame for what happened to him. That's what they said, at any rate. But when they brought in those other two coves and locked them in the reexamination cells, they posted a guard in there with 'em all the time to make sure that nothin' happened to *them*."

"What other two coves?"

"A tall, meaty sailor they called Long Billy, and a shorter cove by the name of Cornelius Hart."

"Hart?"

"That's right. Heard he was found dead a couple of months ago. Makes ye think, don't it?" He cocked his head to one side, his eyes alive with all that he'd carefully left unsaid. "Well, don't it?"

Chapter 39

*B*efore he left Coldbath Fields Prison, Sebastian asked to see the turnkey Joseph Beckett.

"I'm afraid that's impossible, my lord," said the plump, fussy clerk to whom Sebastian addressed this request. "He's dead."

"When did he die?"

The clerk peered at him over the upper rims of the silver-framed spectacles he wore pushed down on the end of his nose. "Must be two— no, nearly three years ago now. He was found one morning down by St. John's Gate with the knife still sticking out of him."

"He was murdered?"

"Well, that was the general consensus, yes," said the clerk with a high-pitched titter. "Men don't usually stick knives in their own backs, now, do they?"

Sebastian's next stop was the Mount Pleasant cottage of the prison surgeon, a man named Thomas Webb. Mr. Webb was not at home, but a helpful butcher's boy passing in the street suggested Sebastian try the Blue Dog on Clerkenwell Green.

"Spends most o' his days and nights there," said the boy. "Whenever he's not at the prison. Says tobacco smoke is the only thing'll get the prison stink out o' his nose." The boy flashed Sebastian a cagey grin and winked. "Leastways, that's what he says."

"You want me to tell you about my postmortem examination of John Williams?" said Webb when Sebastian found him in the Blue Dog's smoky taproom. The prison surgeon was a sallow-faced man somewhere in his forties or fifties, his shoulders rounded and slumped, his once dark hair heavily laced with silver. A general air of untidiness hovered about him; his hair was greasy and overlong, his old-fashioned black coat in want of a good brushing, his waistcoat straining over a bulging stomach and stained with what looked like egg. He sat at a table in the center of the room, a tankard of ale before him and a lit cheroot dangling from one corner of his mouth.

"If you don't mind," said Sebastian, settling in the chair opposite him.

Webb took a long, slow drag of his cheroot, his eyes narrowing against the curling smoke. "What on earth for?"

"It's been suggested his death might have some bearing on certain events of today."

The surgeon exhaled a long stream of blue smoke. "Don't see how it could, but very well. What do you want to know?"

"What time was it when you saw Williams?"

"Must've been around nine in the morning or thereabouts."

"Was he still hanging?"

"Oh, no. The turnkey and a couple of the other prisoners had already cut him down and laid him on his bed."

"His 'bed' being a straw pallet?"

"That's right."

"How long do you think he'd been dead?"

"Hours. He was stone-cold. But then, it was late December, and there's no heat in the prison, you know."

"Must be miserable in the winter."

"Oh, yes. The deaths always soar at that time of year."

"And how did Williams die?"

"Hanged himself, of course. It was more than obvious. You could see the mark the handkerchief had left all around his neck, and there was a deep impression from the knot, just here—" The surgeon turned his head and pressed his fingertips up under his right ear.

"The impression from the handkerchief went straight across his neck?"

"It did." Webb reached for his tankard and drank deeply, draining it; then he looked at Sebastian expectantly.

Sebastian signaled the barmaid. "The mark wasn't V-shaped or angled in any way?"

"No. But that doesn't mean anything."

"Was the hyoid bone broken?"

Webb stared at him. "How would I know? I *looked* at the man; I didn't *dissect* him, for heaven's sake."

Sebastian waited while the barmaid placed a couple tankards on the table between them, then said, "According to one of the prisoners who helped cut Williams down, his arms were bruised."

Webb took a drink from the new tankard, then swiped the back of one hand across his wet mouth. "It's not uncommon to see postmortem staining on the arms and legs of those who've been hanged. The uneducated might mistake such discoloration for bruising, but it's not. John Williams hanged himself; there was never any doubt in my mind."

"So he had discoloration on his legs, as well?"

"I've no idea. I didn't remove his clothing. Why would I? It was obvious how he'd died."

"He was still dressed?"

"Except for his boots and his coat, yes. He must have taken them off when he laid down to sleep . . . before he decided to kill himself, I suppose."

Sebastian watched the surgeon take another long drag on his cheroot. "How often do prisoners hang themselves from the iron rail in those cells?"

"I've seen it once or twice over the years," said Webb, the smoke leaking out of the sides of his mouth as he spoke. "Must admit I didn't expect it that time, though."

"Oh? Why's that?"

"I saw Williams when he was brought in. Quite cheerful he was, and confident of being released as soon as he was given a fair hearing—rather naively, I thought." The surgeon shook his head, tsked, and reached for his ale again. "The melancholia must have come upon him suddenly during the night. Prisons can be unpleasant places after dark."

"I'm told the prison governor ordered a watch kept on two other men who were later held there for questioning about the Ratcliffe Highway murders."

Webb shook his head. "It wasn't the prison keeper who did that. The order came from Bow Street magistrate Aaron Graham."

"It did?"

"Mmm."

"Do you know why?"

The surgeon took a final drag on his cheroot, dropped it to the flagstone floor, and ground it beneath his heel. "That's a question you'd need to ask of Bow Street."

Sebastian sat beside the river Thames, not far from the end of Old Gravel Lane, where a set of watermen's stairs led down to what they called Execution Dock. It wasn't exactly a dock, but it was definitely a place of execution.

It was here that the Admiralty hanged those convicted of piracy or murder on the high seas. The gibbet was placed out in the river below the low-tide mark, where the Admiralty's jurisdiction began. They always used a shortened rope to make certain the condemned men strangled to death slowly, thus making their end as painful as possible. Already that year, six men—including a fourteen-year-old boy—had been led here by a pompous procession headed by the marshal carrying a silver oar, the symbol of the Admiralty's authority. Afterward, when it was all over, the bodies were chained at the low-water mark and left there for days, until three tides had washed over them.

Sebastian lifted his face to the cool wind blowing off the water and breathed in the smell of rope and tar and exotic spices carried from the rows of ships rocking at anchor in the middle of the river or knocking against the wharves. The Crown was big on ceremonial processions for those they were about to kill or those they had killed. He thought of John Williams, still ironed at the ankle, his three-day-old corpse paraded through the streets of Wapping and Shadwell before being ignominiously dumped into a narrow hole. Had he been guilty of the horrible crimes that would forever be attributed to him? Or was he simply another victim, a convenient scapegoat? Sebastian was coming more and more to believe the latter. And he was increasingly convinced that the explanation for today's deaths lay buried in the murky events of that cold December.

Sir Henry Lovejoy had sent another message to Aaron Graham, the aged magistrate now taking the waters in Bath. But it was doubtful the old man was in any shape to remember what he'd known—or suspected—about John Williams's death in Coldbath Fields Prison, or why he had ordered a watch kept on the two suspects who'd been committed to the same prison for reexamination.

Sebastian pushed to his feet, his gaze on a skiff heading out to a towering East Indiaman, his heart heavy with the knowledge of what he was about to do. There was one person he hadn't spoken to yet, someone who probably knew more about the murder of the Marr family than anyone. He'd thus far avoided questioning Margaret Jewell, the servant girl who'd been just thirteen when her life dissolved into a nightmare. And though he was still reluctant to ask her to relive that awful night, he knew he had to do it.

Chapter 40

*S*he called herself Meg now, as a way of differentiating herself from the child she'd been—the child who cheerfully set off one cold December night to buy oysters and came back to a blood-splattered horror.

"Must you speak to her about that night, your lordship?" said Mrs. Jane Maple, the chandler's widow to whom Margaret Jewell was now apprenticed. She was a middle-aged, kindly-looking woman with full cheeks and a massive bosom, and her face fell when Sebastian explained why he'd walked into her shop. "It's dreadfully hard on her anytime it comes up."

"I understand," said Sebastian. "I truly am sorry. But it's important that I hear what she has to say."

The woman sighed. He could tell it went sorely against the grain with her, and if he'd been anyone but who he was, she'd probably have told him no. But who was she, a simple Wapping tradesman's widow, to say no to the son and heir of the Earl of Hendon?

At fifteen, Meg Jewell was a thin, wan thing with dull brown hair and a pale, plain face.

She huddled in a wooden chair beside Mrs. Maple's kitchen fire, her head bowed, her hands turning over and over in her lap as she threaded a white handkerchief through her bony fingers. She looked so forlorn that Sebastian came close to telling her he was sorry and walking away without asking her anything. But the thought of Katie Ingram and her three young children and the very real danger they faced drove him on.

"Can you tell me about that night, Meg?" Sebastian said gently. "I know you don't like to think about it, but it's important."

She lifted her head and looked at him, her breath coming hard and fast enough to jerk her narrow chest.

He said, "What time was it when you left the shop?"

She swallowed, her voice a thin, quiet reed. "A bit before midnight, my lord. Mr. Marr, he gave me a pound note and told me to go buy some oysters for supper. Mrs. Marr had never been well since her confinement, you see, and he thought maybe the oysters would be good for her."

"A pound note would buy a lot of oysters," said Sebastian. At a penny a dozen, oysters were a staple for the poor.

"Oh, it wasn't all for oysters, my lord," she said quickly. "He wanted me to go pay the baker's bill, too."

"What were the Marrs doing when you left?"

"Mrs. Marr was downstairs in the kitchen with Timmy, and Mr. Marr and James—that's James Gowan—they were in the shop folding up lengths of cloth and getting ready to close. We were all tired. We'd been open since eight that morning."

"That's a long day."

She nodded. "It didn't help to have that carpenter come by, troubling Mr. Marr about the ripping chisel that had gone missing. He wanted us to look for it again, so we did. Looked all over, but we never found it."

Sebastian thought about the clean ripping chisel that had been found on the shop's counter amidst the carnage of that night. Had Marr or his shop-boy somehow found it after Margaret left for oysters? Was that why it was simply lying there?

"What was he like as a master?" Sebastian asked. "Mr. Marr, I mean."

She stared at him for a moment in silence, then said, "He was always most agreeable with the customers."

The phrasing struck him as telling. "What about with you and the shop-boy?"

Meg dropped her gaze to her lap again. "He could be . . . impatient sometimes. He had what he called 'ambitions,' and he was always talking about how he expected us to work as hard as he did. He'd just spent all that money taking down the old brick shop front and putting in that big new window so's folks could see his bolts of cloth and everything better. Mrs. Marr said he was a bit anxious about it because it cost so much— that that's why he was always wanting things done *just so*."

In other words, thought Sebastian, he was an impatient, demanding taskmaster pushing hard to get ahead in the world. The kind of man who would sue his own brother over their father's will.

"What time did you come back with the oysters?"

Meg shook her head. "I couldn't find any oysters, my lord. The stall he sent me to was closed. So I went to John's Hill to pay the baker's bill, only he was closed, too. It was past midnight by then and everything was closing. I tried another oyster stall that was closed, so I gave up and went back to the shop."

It struck Sebastian as odd that Marr had sent the young girl out so late when he must have known everything was closing. Had the linen draper not realized the time? Or had he wanted her out of the way for some reason?

"I was afraid he'd be mad at me," Meg was saying. "But when I got back to the shop, all the lights were out, the shutter was up on the front window, and the door was locked."

"What did you do?"

"I thought at first they must've forgot I was out, so I rang the bell. It was late and the streets were getting empty, and I was so cold and scared. I couldn't understand why they wouldn't come and let me in. So I pulled the bell harder and banged on the door, and that's when . . ." Her voice faltered, and she swallowed hard.

"That's when what, Meg?"

She sucked in a quick breath. "That's when I heard footsteps comin' down the stairs. I thought they were finally coming to let me in. Only, then I heard the baby cry out—just once. It was a funny, sharp cry that broke off sudden-like. And after that, I didn't hear anything."

Sebastian felt a chill run up his spine as the significance of what she was saying struck him. "You heard the footsteps coming *down* the stairs?"

She looked at him uncertainly, as if wondering why he had questioned that. "Yes."

"And then you heard the baby cry out?"

"Yes."

"And then what did you hear?"

"Nothing. It was eerie quiet. I was so scared I was shaking. I tried hollering and banging the knocker as hard as I could. I even kicked the door, but nobody came." Her voice cracked, then fell to a whisper. "I reckon they were all dead by then."

She was crying freely now, great, body-racking sobs that tore through her thin frame. Unwilling to push her, Sebastian waited.

She brought up her handkerchief to wipe her eyes and nose. "It was nearly half an hour later that the watchman finally came by, and then Mr. Murphy from next door came out to help. That's when—that's when we found them." She looked up at Sebastian with watery, pleading eyes, her voice a torn whisper. "You ain't gonna make me tell you any more, are you, my lord?"

"No," said Sebastian, feeling hollowed out by what he'd just heard and hating himself for what he'd put her through. "No, I'm not. I'm sorry for asking you to go through it all again. Thank you."

Chapter 41

*C*harlie Horton was sweeping the pavement in front of his slopshop when Sebastian turned his horses into Brewhouse Lane. The sky above was white with high clouds, the light flat, the narrow cobbled street crowded with rattling drays and carts, the air ringing with the hoarse shouts of lumpers and draymen and the whistling of the wind through the rigging of the ships lying at anchor out in the Thames.

At the curricle's approach, the former river policeman looked up, his hands tightening around the handle of his broom, his face unreadable as he watched Sebastian rein in.

"Go ahead and walk 'em," Sebastian told Tom as the boy scrambled forward to take the reins. "I could be a while."

"Aye, gov'nor."

Horton watched Sebastian hop down and walk toward him. "Heard what happened to you last night. You're lucky you're still alive."

"How did you come to hear about it?"

"Still got friends in some of the public offices." Horton's eyes narrowed as he studied Sebastian's face. "Looks like they got you a bit."

Sebastian had to stop himself from reaching up to touch the back of his hand to his cheek. "That's from a few days ago, actually. I seem to be making some people more than a bit nervous. You wouldn't have any idea who, would you?"

Horton shook his head. "I might be inclined to suspect Pym or Cockerwell if they weren't dead."

Sebastian glanced toward the open door to the slopshop, where the boy, Caleb, hovered, and said to Horton, "Walk with me a ways?"

Horton nodded and handed the broom to his son. "Finish up here, would you, lad?"

"I was up at Coldbath Fields Prison this morning," said Sebastian as they turned to walk down the street, past a string of low, grimy brick buildings housing everything from sailors' victuallers and sailmakers to squalid lodgings and pawnshops. "I wanted to talk to the turnkey who was in charge of John Williams the night he supposedly hanged himself. Only when I asked, they said the man was murdered just a few weeks after Williams was found dead."

Horton nodded, his features grim. "It's one of the reasons I worried the lad might not have killed himself. Always figured that turnkey could've let a couple of men into the cell and turned his back while they strangled him. And then they killed the turnkey so's he couldn't rat them out."

"Who would have the ability to do something like that?"

Horton looked over to give him a tight smile. "Anyone with money. Or power."

"Well, that narrows it down."

Horton shrugged.

Sebastian swerved around a small tan-and-white dog nosing something unidentifiable on the pavement. "I also had an interesting conversation with Margaret Jewell—or Meg, as she now calls herself."

"Ah, poor wee lass," said Horton with a sigh. "I hear she ain't been right since that night."

"I'm not sure any child could be after such an experience. She says one of the carpenters who worked on putting in Marr's bay window came into the shop the afternoon of the murders and asked them to look for his missing ripping chisel again."

"Aye. That was Cornelius Hart."

"You mentioned him as one of the men you thought might have been involved in the murders, but I don't recall you saying why."

Horton squinted up at the darker clouds beginning to bunch overhead. "I suppose part of it was because of the rippin' chisel—I never could see where it fit in the whole thing. But it was also because you could tell the man was hidin' something. He claimed he barely knew Williams, but then he sent his wife around to the Pear Tree askin' Mrs. Vermilloe if the lad had been arrested yet. Why would he do that?"

"Any other reason?"

Horton was silent for a moment. "It sounds kinda feeble when you say it like that, don't it? I reckon maybe the biggest reason I thought he was mixed up in it was because he was in tight with Billy Ablass, and I always figured if anybody else was involved, it was Long Billy."

"You said Hart is dead?"

"Aye. Found dead last summer, he was."

Sebastian looked over at him. "How did he die?"

"Stabbed in the back in an alley off Cinnamon Lane."

"Did they ever identify his killer?"

"No."

Sebastian pressed his lips into a tight line as he watched a drunken sailor stagger out of a nearby grogshop. He was beginning to realize that the true number of murders he was dealing with reached into the double digits. "How long was this before the seaman Hugo Reeves was murdered?"

"A month or two. Early August, I think."

"But Hart wasn't bludgeoned?"

"Nope. Just stabbed. Throat wasn't slit, neither."

"Was there any connection between Reeves and Hart? Or Reeves and Williams, for that matter?"

Horton thought about it a moment, his gaze on a ponderous old eighteenth-century carriage laboring up the lane toward them. "I suppose they could've been shipmates at one time, but if they were, I don't know about it."

"What about Timothy Marr and the publican of the King's Arms? Any connection there?"

"Not that I ever heard of. Old John and his wife ran that public house for fifteen years, whereas Timothy Marr opened up his linen draper's shop just months before he was killed."

"But Marr was originally from Wapping, wasn't he? His father was a haberdasher here."

"Aye. His brother still is."

"What about the women who were killed? Any connection between them?"

Horton looked thoughtful. "Not that I know of."

They paused at the corner as the air filled with the bleating of a herd of goats being driven down to the docks. Sebastian said, "I seem to remember you telling me you found the blood-covered shipwright's maul upstairs in the Marrs' bedroom."

"That's right. Why?"

"Because Margaret Jewell said she heard footsteps coming down from upstairs right before she heard the baby cry."

"Aye," said Horton, obviously not seeing where Sebastian was going with this. "I remember her sayin' it."

"Was anything taken from the bedroom or kitchen? Anything that could have been used to bash in a skull?"

"No. Asked Margaret about that specifically, I did. Nothing was taken from the house at all. She was sure of it."

"So if there was only one killer, and he left the maul he was using upstairs in the bedroom before he went down into the basement and killed the babe, what did he use to smash the baby's skull?"

Horton stared at him, and it was as if the sun-darkened skin were

suddenly stretched taut over the bones of his face. "Well, I'll be a s—"
He broke off, his lips parting as he drew a quick breath.

The last of the goats passed with a backward kick, and Sebastian
squinted down to where the river's forest of masts rocked back and forth
against the darkening clouds. At this point on the river, the tide could
rise and fall twenty feet in a day. It was rushing back in now, filling the
crisp air with the smell of the sea.

When Horton remained silent, Sebastian said, "I suppose one man
could have brought two heavy weapons with him, but I doubt it. We know
he also had a razor with him, and that ship's maul is massive. So why would
he burden himself with a third weapon? I think you were right when you
said there must have been more than one killer. One man brought the
maul, and a second man brought a different weapon he used to help his
partner kill the Marrs and their apprentice. I think the men then went upstairs looking for the Marrs' baby. They were up there when they heard
Margaret ringing the bell at the front of the shop. But rather than run, the
way a couple of thieves would surely have done, they left the maul upstairs
and then took the time—with Margaret now banging on the door—to go
down to the kitchen. With the maul upstairs, they used the second man's
weapon to murder the baby boy. And only then did they escape out the
back door. They didn't take the money from Marr's pocket or from his till
or even the hundred and fifty pounds in his bedroom drawer because they
weren't there to steal." Sebastian brought his gaze back to the former river
policeman's face. "I think they were there to kill—to kill them all. And
even with Margaret banging at the door, they didn't leave until everyone
was dead."

"Hell and the devil confound it," whispered Horton, swiping a meaty
hand down over his face. "Margaret Jewell told me that—and she said it
again at the inquest, about how she heard the footsteps comin' down the
stairs and *then* the babe's cry. But I never put it together with that maul
bein' left up in the bedroom like that. It was just sittin' there, too—

leaning against the chair. It wasn't like they'd got scared and dropped it; they left it there deliberately. Only, why would they do that?"

"Because they wanted it found," said Sebastian. "They were careful to take the second weapon—whatever it was they used to kill the baby—away with them because they wanted people to think there was only one killer. But they left the maul because they knew those initials would eventually lead the authorities to the Pear Tree."

Horton turned his face into the wind blowing up from the river, his eyes narrowing. "They set Johnny Williams up, didn't they? From the very beginning, they set that lad up. They got someone to lay information against him, and when he was taken into custody and thrown into that isolation cell up in Clerkenwell, they killed him." He drew a deep breath, then let it out. "But the murders stopped. Why would they stop?"

"Because the killings weren't random," said Sebastian. "Those two families were killed for a reason. It's just that no one has ever figured out what that reason was."

Painful shadows shifted in the old policeman's eyes. "But *why*? Why kill two entire families, including a wee innocent babe? Who would do something like that?"

Sebastian shook his head. "That's what I can't begin to fathom."

Horton chewed at his lower lip with his teeth. "And why has it started up again now?"

"I don't know that, either," said Sebastian, although that wasn't strictly true. He could think of several reasons why the killing of Pym and Cockerwell echoed the Ratcliffe Highway murders.

The problem was, if he was right, then Charlie Horton—the policeman who'd openly criticized the official explanation for the events of three years before and lost his position because of it—was right at the top of the list of suspects.

Chapter 42

$\mathcal{A}$s he drove away from Brewhouse Lane, Sebastian found himself adding up the uncounted victims. Johnny Williams, buried at the crossroads as a suicide. The turnkey from Coldbath Fields Prison, stabbed in the back. The ship's carpenter Cornelius Hart, who'd suffered a similar fate . . .

The brutal killing of two entire families in 1811 had captured the terrified city's imagination. But no one had noticed that men tangentially connected to the Ratcliffe Highway murders had continued to die suspicious deaths.

Turning up Old Gravel Lane, Sebastian reined in before the grim, soot-covered brick workhouse run by the parish of St. George's. The air here was so heavy with a foul stench that it was hard to breathe.

" 'Oly 'ell!" said Tom, his voice muffled by the hand he'd clapped over his nose. "What's that smell?"

Sebastian handed the boy the reins. "Something dead, I suspect—or, rather, someone dead."

Tucked away in a corner of the workhouse lay the parish's deadhouse, a tumbledown shack with a leaky roof. It was Sebastian's intention to ask there where he might find the local surgeon, Walt Salter. But a body had just been pulled from the river near Wapping New Stairs, and Salter himself was there to deal with it.

A paunchy older man with tightly curled salt-and-pepper hair that encircled his head like a dark halo, he had a jowly face, multiple chins, heavy bags under his eyes, and heavy eyebrows knotted as if in a perpetual frown. The frown deepened when Sebastian introduced himself.

"Yes, I did the postmortems on the original Ratcliffe Highway murder victims," growled the surgeon in a rough baritone, his attention all for the bloated, decaying corpse laid out on the slab before him. "What of it?"

The dead man must have been in the water at least a week, and Sebastian was trying hard not to look at him—or to breathe too deeply. "I understand you testified at the inquests that you thought five of the victims' throats had been cut with a razor."

"I didn't simply 'think' it. Their throats *were* cut with a razor. All I did was state the facts."

"You're certain?"

"Of course I'm certain. The cuts were made so deeply with one slice that the windpipes were severed. Nothing but a razor could do that without tearing and bruising the tissues, and there was none—no tearing or bruising at all. That wasn't simply a razor; it was a bloody sharp razor."

"I thought a knife was found that they linked to the killings?"

Salter gave a derisive snort. "Ah, yes, the 'bloodstained French knife' found a good month or two later at the back of a closet at the Pear Tree by some blackguard who swore he'd seen it in John Williams's possession but somehow forgot to mention it earlier despite having been repeatedly questioned by the authorities. Earned himself thirty pounds of reward money with that little maneuver, he did."

"You don't believe the knife had anything to do with the killings?"

The surgeon's lip curled with derision. "Of course it didn't. The various inhabitants of the Pear Tree were 'finding' everything from bloodstained trousers to muddy socks for months, with the authorities beyond credulous when it came to handing out rewards."

Either credulous or complicit, thought Sebastian. Aloud, he said, "Did you think Williams was the killer?"

Salter's expression shifted into something less confident, more troubled. "To be honest? No," he said on a long exhalation of breath. "He was such a slight young man, and far from athletic in his build. I suppose he might have been one of the killers, but no one will ever convince me that he acted alone. Groups of people don't simply stand around waiting to be killed when someone starts swinging a hammer and flashing a razor. They run. But judging from the way the bodies were found, there was no time for that. And that tells me there were at least two killers."

"Old John was found separate from the others, wasn't he? On the steps leading down to the pub's cellar?"

"He was. But the steps went down from the kitchen, where the two women were killed, and his tibia was broken. I suspect he fell down the stairs—or his body was pushed down after his throat was slit." The surgeon jerked his chin toward the bloated, disintegrating corpse on the slab between them. "Now go away and let me get to work before the stench from this fellow sickens everyone in the neighborhood."

Sebastian started to turn away, then paused to look back and say, "Did you by any chance do a postmortem on a sailmaker named Jack Harrison?"

"Who?"

"Jack Harrison. He was one of John Williams's roommates at the Pear Tree that December. Someone said he was killed this past summer."

"Oh, yes. Him. I did—late August, I believe it was. Why?"

"How was he killed?"

"Knifed in the back. Typical."

"Nothing else?"

"What else would you expect?"

Sebastian simply shook his head.

"Interesting that you should bring him up now," said the surgeon.

"Oh? Why's that?"

"He's the man who claimed to identify that bloody French knife as having belonged to Williams."

"He was?"

"He was. Now go away."

Why the difference? Sebastian wondered as he walked away from the dead-house.

Why quietly stick a knife in the backs of the turnkey Joseph Beckett, the sailmaker Jack Harrison, and the shipwright Cornelius Hart, but butcher Hugo Reeves, Sir Edwin Pym, and Nathan Cockerwell in a manner deliberately calculated to remind everyone of the Ratcliffe Highway murders? It made no sense unless he was dealing with two different killers. And yet that didn't really explain it, either.

Still pondering the possibilities, he drove to the Pear Tree, where he found Robert Vermilloe up on a step stool in the courtyard replacing a couple of rotted boards on the side of the inn's dilapidated privy.

"I understand you had a sailmaker staying here a few months ago," said Sebastian, standing as far back from the noxious fumes wafting from the privy as he could without having to shout. "A man by the name of Jack Harrison."

Vermilloe ripped a rotted board from the privy and tossed it aside with a clatter.

"We did. What of it?"

"He was a roommate of John Williams three years ago?"

Vermilloe tore off a second board and let it drop. "He was."

"So tell me about this knife he found and claimed belonged to Williams."

Vermilloe wrenched off another board. "He didn't find it. He described it and suggested the constables search the room. And then they found it. All covered in dried blood, it was."

"When was this?"

"I dunno. Maybe a month or so after the King's Arms killings."

"And in all that time, no one had thought to search the room of the man they'd decided was the murderer?"

"No. Why would they?"

Why, indeed? thought Sebastian.

"They emptied this here privy, though," said Vermilloe, climbing down to grab one of the new boards he had lying ready.

"Oh? And what did they find?"

"A pair of old blue seamen's trousers."

"They'd been shoved down into the privy?"

"They had. Covered in bloodstains, they were, too. Or leastways, it looked like bloodstains once the shit was washed off them."

"What size man would they have fit?"

Vermilloe looked at him blankly. "Not sure they ever figured that out. My Sarah always contended they couldn't have belonged to Williams— said he was such a fastidious fellow that he'd never wear anything so shabby. But now I ask you, who wears their best clothes to go committing murder? Hmm? You tell me that."

Sebastian watched the man step back up onto his stool with the board and a hammer in one hand. "So what did this knife look like?"

Vermilloe positioned the board in place and fumbled in his pocket for a nail. "Fancy thing, it was. French clasp knife with an ivory handle and a blade at least six inches long."

Sebastian waited while he hammered in his nail, then said, "How sharp was this knife?"

"Pretty sharp." Vermilloe fumbled for another nail.

"It wasn't rusted after lying there for a month covered in blood?"

"Not so much, no."

"And Jack Harrison swore it had belonged to Williams?"

"He did." Vermilloe pounded in the second nail. "Like I said, he'd described it before the constables found it in the closet."

"Perhaps because he put it there?" suggested Sebastian. "Thirty pounds strikes me as a powerful incentive for a man to become inventive."

Vermilloe paused, his face scrunching up. Then he climbed down for a second board.

Sebastian said, "According to your wife, Williams didn't get along well with either of his roommates."

"Nope," said Vermilloe, stepping back up. "There was a heap of sailors resented him because of what happened on the *Roxburgh Castle.*"

"Oh? Why was that?"

"There was a mutiny on that ship, you know, off Surinam. Left some bad blood."

"Williams was involved in this mutiny?"

"He was."

"Along with the man they call Long Billy Ablass?"

Vermilloe held the second board in place. It was too long, but he simply fished another nail out of his pocket and hammered it in anyway. "That's right. Ablass was the ringleader. He and Hart and some of the others got in trouble for it, but not Williams."

"Hart? You mean Cornelius Hart?"

"Aye."

"He was on the *Roxburgh Castle* when the crew mutinied?"

"Aye."

"So why didn't John Williams get in trouble?"

"Guess they reckoned he was just in the wrong place at the wrong time. Long Billy was always sorely aggrieved by it, the way Johnny got off so light." He hammered in a second nail, then paused as if choosing his words before saying, "Heard something interesting about Long Billy the other day."

"Oh? What's that?"

The innkeeper climbed back down and lowered his voice. "Folks

around here are pretty scared of Ablass, you know. He's an ugly customer. Very ugly customer."

"Not to mention large."

Vermilloe nodded. "Very large."

Sebastian waited, but then, when the man still hesitated, said, "What
did you hear?"

Vermilloe dropped his voice to a whisper. "Heard he was arguing
with Pym. Right before Pym was killed, this was."

Sebastian nodded. "I've heard that."

Vermilloe's face fell. "Did you hear what the argument was about?"

"No."

Vermilloe's lips twitched into a smile, quickly hidden. "The person I
heard this from—"

"Who was that?"

"Never you mind. She don't want it getting back to Ablass, you see?
She didn't hear everything, but she heard enough to get the gist of what
was going on."

"Oh? And what was 'going on'?"

"Ablass was trying to blackmail Pym, that's what!" He said it dramat-
ically, as if delivering a revelation before an audience.

Sebastian kept his voice level. "About what?"

Vermilloe's face fell again. "I told you, she couldn't hear that. But it
makes you think, don't it?"

"Think what?"

"Why, that it must've been Ablass who killed Pym, of course."

Sebastian studied the innkeeper's narrow, sharp-featured face. "Generally it's the person being blackmailed who kills his blackmailer, not the
other way around."

"Maybe. But Long Billy's got a temper, he has. Reckon he could've
killed Pym in a rage over being told no." Vermilloe licked his lips. "If it
turns out Ablass is the killer, you will remember who told you this when
it comes time to divide up the reward money, won't you?"

"Is that what this is? An attempt to earn some more reward money?"

"What?" Vermilloe jerked his head back as if he'd been slapped. "No! Doing my duty, I am, like a proper Englishman."

"Why didn't you tell me this before?"

"Hadn't heard about it then."

"You're certain your friend didn't hear anything else?"

"Nothing she told me about, leastways."

"Perhaps you could persuade her to remember more," said Sebastian.

"I can try."

"You do that." He started to turn away, then paused. "Was Billy Ablass staying here at the time of the Ratcliffe Highway murders?"

Vermilloe shook his head. "He had a room with some woman over in Shadwell. She's the one gave him his alibis both nights, although no one believed her."

"Do you remember her name?"

"Alice something. Doesn't matter; she's dead now."

"Since when?"

"Nearly three years. Wasn't too long after the Ratcliffe Highway killings they found her. Maybe a month or two after everything settle down."

"Oh? How did she die? A knife in the back?"

Vermilloe shook his head. "Strangled, she was."

"You seem to have a lot of murders around here."

"Only in the last three years or so," said Vermilloe, and nothing in his face revealed any awareness of the implications of what he'd just said.

Chapter 43

$\mathcal{H}$ero waited at the end of Hermitage Street, near a shop with a new bay window displaying brass sextants, compasses, and quadrants. The brisk wind off the river flapped an awning overhead and tugged at the brim of her midnight blue military-styled hat. It was still only midafternoon, but the public house across the way—a mean, low-roofed establishment with a peeling sign that proclaimed it the Jolly Tar—was already spilling drunken laughter and staggering seamen into the narrow, teeming street. A gray-and-pink parrot in a wooden cage hung before the pawnshop next door, the wind ruffling its feathers as it squawked, *"Ahoy, mate! Fifty lashes! Fifty lashes!"*

"You poor thing," said Hero, watching the bird shift on its perch and bob its head up and down. "You were born to fly free through some warm, sweetly scented jungle, and they bring you to . . . this."

She sucked in a deep breath heavy with the smell of rum and dead fish, her gaze searching the faces of the men and women pushing past—laundresses, butchers in bloodstained smocks, laborers with their skin dyed blue by indigo. All around her, ropes splashed; saws grated; men shouted, goats bleated. And from farther up the hill came the striking of the church bell.

Three o'clock. She'd arrived early and been here nearly two hours.

"Blast," she said softly under her breath. "Come on, Molly. Where are you?"

Molly never came.

Several hours later, dressed now in an elegant afternoon gown of heavy peach silk with chiné satin stripes, Hero arrived at her father's town house in Berkeley Square. A light rain had begun to fall, tapping on the leaves in the square and filling the air with the smell of wet pavement.

"Good afternoon, Grisham," she said with a smile when the butler opened the door for her.

He was a trim, dignified man somewhere in his fifties, with silvergray hair and an awe-inspiringly wooden countenance. But he allowed himself a faint smile at the sight of Hero. "Good afternoon, my lady," he said with a bow. "Mrs. Hart-Davis is awaiting you in the drawing room."

"And Papa?" asked Hero, handing him her wet umbrella and shaking out her skirts.

"Is expected at any moment, my lady."

"Ah."

As she climbed the stairs, Hero found herself noticing the new Persian carpet runner, the unfamiliar gold-framed landscapes on the landing. She'd called this house home for twenty-five years, but the sense of belonging here was slipping away from her. And she knew it had little to do with Persian carpets or Turner landscapes.

She found Victoria perched on one of the window seats overlooking the square and working on an embroidery frame. At the sight of Hero, she set her embroidery aside and came forward with both hands outstretched. "*Hero.* I'm so glad you could come. Jarvis promises he'll join us shortly, and I told him I intend to keep him to his word."

Barely five feet tall and delicately built, Victoria always made Hero feel like a hulking giant. She caught her cousin's hands and stooped awkwardly to kiss her cheek, then let Victoria draw her to the chairs by the fire.

"Dreadful day, is it not?" said Victoria. "I know it's October, but it's too early for winter, wouldn't you say?"

"At least it's not snowing. Yet."

Victoria let out a delighted peal of laughter. "Oh, hush! Don't even think it."

Raised in India the daughter of an officer in the East India Company, she'd lost her first husband to a fever in Maharashtra and the second to a French bullet before the walls of San Sebastián in Spain. But she was past the prescribed year of formal mourning and now wore a simple gown of corded muslin with a lilac satin shawl that accentuated the lovely blue of her eyes. She was an accomplished harpist and a brutal chess player, spoke French, Spanish, Portuguese, Italian, Urdu, and Farsi, and could read Greek and Latin as well as any Oxford don. Yet she hid it all behind a gay bubble of small talk and frothy laughter that was always pitch-perfect and, Hero suspected, utterly, utterly false.

Hero herself had always been the kind of woman who refused to hide either her intelligence or her accomplishments behind the mask of frailty their society expected of her sex. And it disconcerted her to realize that, despite her best intentions, a part of her both scorned and envied this woman.

In some ways she understood Jarvis's increasingly obvious infatuation with the pretty young widow, for his taste ran toward petite, fair-haired women. But he'd always claimed to have no use for either opinioned females or what he called overeducated bluestockings. And as much as Victoria hid her intelligence and steely strength from the world, she had never made any attempt to misrepresent herself in that way to Jarvis.

Somehow, Hero's cousin had known Hero's father better than Hero did herself, and that troubled her more than anything.

"He's closeted with a courier from Castlereagh," Victoria was saying. And something about her tone told Hero her cousin was more aware of the progress being made by Britain's diplomatic mission in Vienna than anyone besides Jarvis and the foreign minister himself.

"Have they formally convened yet?"

"Not yet, but it won't be long now. Seems everyone who is anyone is in either Vienna or Paris these days. Did you hear Kat Boleyn is abandoning us to spend the season appearing in Paris? I fear London theater will be sadly flat without her, don't you?"

Kat Boleyn wasn't simply the most celebrated actress of London's stage; she'd also at one time been Devlin's lover, and surely this astute, well-informed woman must know that. Hero searched her cousin's pleasantly smiling face, looking for a hint of malice, but found none.

"Undoubtedly," said Hero, keeping her own voice light. "Even Devlin's aunt Henrietta is making plans to visit Paris next month. And she always swore she'd never travel again."

Victoria laughed. Then her amusement faded and she tilted her head to one side, her normally smooth forehead puckering with a frown of concern. "Jarvis told me about last night's attack. How absolutely ghastly!"

"It was, yes," said Hero. "One presumes if Jarvis knew anything, he would have told Devlin?"

Victoria's eyes widened. "Good heavens, how can you think otherwise?"

A heavy tread sounded on the stairs, saving Hero from having to answer. A moment later, Jarvis himself entered the room. He went to stand behind Victoria's chair, his big hands resting on her frail shoulders, his gaze meeting his daughter's.

"So? Has she told you?" he said to Hero with a smile she'd never seen before.

"Told me what?" Hero somehow managed to say, although her throat felt as if it were closing.

Victoria smiled up at him and reached to lay one of her soft white hands over his. "Not yet."

Then she turned to Hero and said, "Jarvis has asked me to become his wife."

Chapter 44

That night, Hero stood at the bedroom window overlooking the wet, lamplit street below. A hard rain had begun to fall just after sunset, driven by a gusty wind that sent raindrops streaming down the windowpanes in quick flashing rivulets that caught the light from the oil lamps below. She was still trying to come to terms with what she'd learned that afternoon at Berkeley Square, but she wasn't making much progress.

"You suspected it was going to happen," said Devlin, coming up behind her to slip his arms around her waist and hold her close.

"Yes," she said, her gaze meeting his in their reflection in the window. She rested her hands on his at her waist. "But that doesn't make it any easier."

"No. I can see that."

She tipped her head back against his. "I keep telling myself that Cousin Victoria obviously makes Jarvis happy, so I should be happy for him—happy for them both. But it's not working, and I have the most lowering reflection that I may not be a very nice person."

He gave a soft laugh and pressed a kiss against the side of her head.

"I think it's because you love him and you don't trust her. But if any man can take care of himself, it's Jarvis."

"I suppose. It's just . . ." She let her voice trail away and shook her head. After a moment, she said, "I'm thinking I might go down to Hermitage Street in Wapping again tomorrow, when I can stay longer. Perhaps Molly couldn't come today for some reason. Or perhaps she was too frightened."

"And you think she might work up her courage by tomorrow? I suppose it's possible."

She watched a gentleman's carriage dash up the street, the spinning wheels throwing up a fine spray that caught the golden lamplight and shimmered against the blackness of the rain-drenched night. She thought about the unknown girl, Molly; about what she might have seen and the danger she might not even know she was in. "Do you think Vermilloe was telling the truth? What he told you about Ablass and Pym, I mean."

He touched the backs of his fingers to her cheek in a light caress. "I don't know. I'm inclined not to believe a word the man says. But Timothy Marr's brother also mentioned seeing Ablass and Pym together, so perhaps there's something to it after all."

"Seems an oddly public spot to choose to approach your local magistrate for blackmail."

She felt Devlin's breath flutter the curls beside her cheek. "You have a point there. It also begs the question, blackmail for what? For paying Ablass to murder John Williams in his cell? Or for paying the two of them to murder seven men, women, and children for reasons I can't begin to imagine?"

"Dear Lord. You think that could be true?"

"That Pym and Cockerwell were behind the Ratcliffe Highway murders? I haven't found anything to suggest it. But I think someone was directing those killers. I'm finding it more and more difficult to believe that two or three men invaded those homes simply to indulge a desire to kill. And they obviously weren't there to steal."

"They did take Old John's watch."

"Did they? It was the only thing said to be missing from either house. And there were so many people swarming over that tavern both the night of the killings and in the days afterward that anyone could have taken it."

She turned to face him. "But why would Pym and Cockerwell want to slaughter two entire families?"

He gave a faint shake of his head. "I've no idea. But the deaths of Ian Ryker's father and that member of Parliament who was threatening to investigate corruption in the East End suggest they weren't above murder. And men like that don't do their own killing."

The wind gusted up harder, peppering the window before them with rain. She said, "So why the differences in the manner of death? Why stab some victims in the back and not the others?"

"Well, a knife in the back is quick, quiet, and relatively easy compared to bashing someone's brains out and slitting their throat from ear to ear. It could simply be a matter of time and opportunity, although that wouldn't entirely explain it, either. Whoever killed Pym and Cockerwell wanted us to remember the Ratcliffe Highway murders. Maybe it's someone's way of saying, 'Look at these men. They were responsible.'"

"But why would Pym and Cockerwell want to kill a simple linen draper?"

"I could be wrong, but I think the key to it all is Long Billy. He's the only person connected to them all—the Marrs, Williams, Pym, and Cockerwell—and Cornelius Hart and Jack Harrison, too."

"Except Ablass didn't have any meaningful connection to Old John and his wife, did he? Was there anything to link him to the King's Arms?"

Devlin drew her closer and pressed his forehead to hers. "Not really. That's the one part that doesn't fit."

Saturday, 15 October

The next day dawned cold and windy but clear, with a cornflower blue sky slowly smudged to a smoky blue by the city's coal fires.

Sebastian spent the better part of the morning looking for Billy Ablass. He began at the Three Moons, where a sullen Christopher Bishop told him Ablass had already gone out for the day. He checked the docks, the Sun Tavern, and a string of other public houses before eventually circling back to Pope's Hill.

"He still ain't here," said Christopher Bishop when Sebastian walked into the taproom.

"Is your sister around?"

The lad looked at him through narrowed eyes. "Why you asking?"

"Is she around?"

Bishop hesitated, then jerked his head toward the door that led to the inn's small flagstoned yard. "She's out talking to the stable hand."

"Thank you."

The Three Moons' stable was small and ran along one short side of the yard. Hannah Bishop was just coming out of the tack room when Sebastian stepped into the sunny, windblown yard. She had a hand up to catch her hair, her thoughts obviously far away. Then she saw him and hesitated a moment before continuing toward him.

"Lord Devlin," she said, her gaze holding his, her features carefully schooled to give nothing away. "I heard you were asking for Billy again."

"Do you know where I might find him?"

She shook her head, and for a moment he saw her mask of self-control slip, saw the flare of panic in her eyes before she looked away. "No. Sorry."

He said, "Tell me why you let him stay here. And this time I want the real reason."

She sucked in a quick, frightened breath. She held herself very still for a moment, and he knew she was tempted to brazen it out. Knew, too, when she gave up the idea.

They sat on an old stone bench in the feeble sunshine, with the wind flapping the hem of her muslin gown and blowing her light brown hair around her face, her fingers twisting and untwisting the lacings that dangled from the neck of her dark green wool spencer.

"My mother buried three husbands," she said quietly, her gaze fixed straight ahead. "The first died in a fire that destroyed the original Three Moons Inn before I was born. It was just a few months later that she married my father, and he helped her rebuild. He was a good man, strong, gentle, and honorable." She paused, her head tipping back as she stared up at the cluster of smoking chimneys rising above the inn's slate roof. "He died when I was thirteen. I guess Mama didn't like being alone, because she married again right away. Her third husband was a big, handsome seaman with black hair and nearly black eyes. The family was originally from Danzig, but I don't think he'd lived there long himself. Ablass was his name. Peter Ablass."

Whatever Sebastian had been expecting, it wasn't this. "Billy Ablass is his brother?"

She nodded, her lips pressed tightly together.

"That's why he stays here?"

"Yes."

"Yet he wasn't here in 1811?"

"No. After you asked, I looked into it. He had some woman he was staying with then."

"Did you know the woman is now dead?"

She turned her head to stare at him, her eyes wide and liquid with fear. "Is she?"

"Someone strangled her nearly three years ago." He watched the color fade from her cheeks, then said, "I still don't understand why you let him stay here."

"It's . . . complicated."

"When did your stepfather die?"

"Two years ago."

"That's when you came back?"

"Yes."

The wind gusted up, banging a shutter somewhere and bringing them the smell of the river. "There's something you're still not telling me."

Her lips parted on a quiet breath. "There might have been ten years between them, but the two brothers were very close and very much the same. You've met Billy. Until his big brother died, Billy was used to treating this place as his own. You really think Christopher and I are going to tell him he can't stay here when he wants?"

"Do you think Billy killed Pym and Cockerwell?"

"I honestly don't know. If you're asking, do I think he could have done it? then the answer is yes; I think he's more than capable of doing something like that."

"What about the Ratcliffe Highway killings?"

She was silent a moment, her gaze shifting to the dark recesses of the stables, and he knew from the tension radiating from her that she had considered this possibility before. "I can see Billy killing like that out of rage or hate. But do I know of any quarrel he had with those two families? No."

"He was on a ship with Timothy Marr. And from the sound of things, he didn't like him."

"Was he? I didn't know that. After my mother married Peter Ablass, I left as soon as I could, and I didn't come back until he was dead."

"You said he died two years ago?"

"Yes."

"And your mother was still alive then?"

She nodded.

"Do you know if your stepfather had any argument with the publican of the King's Arms?"

"Not that I know of, no. But he might have. He was a quarrelsome man with an ugly temper."

"Did you know the man who was blamed for the Ratcliffe Highway murders—John Williams?"

"No. I left London when I was fourteen."

He studied her half-averted profile, noticing for the first time the faint sprinkling of freckles across the bridge of her nose. "Why come back?"

"After Peter Ablass died, Christopher needed me. And my mother, too, although I don't know if I'd have come back just for her sake."

Sebastian was aware of all the things left unsaid. The hatred and fear of a brutal, quick-tempered stepfather; the angry resentment of the weak mother who'd brought a dangerous man into her children's lives and then done nothing to protect them from his wrath. "You said Billy quarreled with Hugo Reeves. Do you know what that was about?"

"No. I don't know any more than what I've told you." She looked at him then, her eyes dark and hurting as she searched his face, her voice a hoarse whisper. "You think I'm not frightened? You think I don't know what Billy is capable of? You think I don't count the days until he sails again?"

"When does he sail?"

"It must be soon. He should be running out of money by now."

"Do you know of any connection between Billy and the Black Eagle's Buxton-Collins?"

The question seemed to confuse her. "No. Why?"

"Where does the Three Moons' beer come from?"

Something that might have been amusement flared in her eyes, then was gone. "This is Shadwell. Where do you think?"

Some minutes later Sebastian was drawing up outside the Pear Tree when he recognized the small man in spectacles and a heavy greatcoat climbing out of a hackney stopped nearby.

"Sir Henry?" said Sebastian.

Lovejoy gave a faint start and turned to walk toward him. "Lord Devlin. I didn't expect my message to reach you so soon."

Sebastian handed the reins to Tom and hopped down. "I haven't received a message. Why? What's happened?"

"Robert Vermilloe has been found dead."

Chapter 45

The dead man lay on his back in a corner of the Pear Tree's untidy yard, his arms crossed at his chest, his eyes open and staring. The only visible sign of violence was the faint trickle of blood that had dried at the corner of his sagging mouth.

"He was found here? Like this?" said Lovejoy, his hands thrust into the pockets of his greatcoat as he stared down at the innkeeper's pale corpse. The sun might have been shining, but the inn's yard lay in deep shadow, and the wind was cold.

"No, yer honor," said the bulky, graying constable standing nearby. "A couple of seamen found him in an alley off Prospect Row this morning and carried him here."

Sebastian studied the dried line of blood on the dead man's chin. "Did you look at his back yet?"

"Aye," said the constable on a harsh expulsion of breath. "Been stabbed, he has."

Lovejoy glanced up. "How many times?"

"Maybe three."

"And the knife?"

"Ain't seen it, yer honor. I suppose it could still be in the alley."

Sebastian shifted his gaze to the dead man's flat, lifeless eyes. "Any idea when he was last seen?"

"The old sodger behind the bar says he went out about eleven and never come back."

Lovejoy drew a handkerchief from his pocket and set about thoughtfully cleaning the lenses of his spectacles. "Did he say why Vermilloe went out?"

"Says he don't know."

Sebastian glanced toward the window of the Pear Tree's kitchen. "How is Mrs. Vermilloe?"

A look of sadness settled over the constable's homely features. "She's knittin'."

While Lovejoy set about organizing his constables for a search of the alley near Prospect Row, Sebastian went to settle on the trestle bench beside the kitchen fire. The dead man's wife didn't lift her gaze from her knitting—blue socks this time. Her face was puffy and mottled from her tears, her eyes red, her hands shaky, her stitches woefully uneven.

"How are you doing, Mrs. Vermilloe?" he asked softly.

She drew a deep breath and looked up at him, her soft brown eyes swimming with grief and pain. "To be honest, my lord, I didn't think it'd hit me as hard as it has." She gave her yarn a fierce tug, her fist clenching so tightly around the thread that her knuckles turned white. "I mean, he was a foolish old man, always full of big talk. But he was a loving husband for all his faults, and the thought of never seeing him again just breaks my heart."

"Do you have any idea who would want to kill him?"

"*No.*" Her voice cracked with a sob when she said it, and she squeezed her eyes shut and brought up a hand to press her fingers against her trembling lips. "No," she said again more calmly after a moment. "He was a silly old man. Why would anyone want to hurt him? Just a silly old man."

"Did he talk to you recently about the Ratcliffe Highway murders?"

"Just to say your lordship was here asking questions about that French knife they found in Johnny's room."

"Do you think the knife belonged to John Williams?"

"Could have." She sniffed and rested her knitting in her lap so she could bring up a handkerchief and blow her nose. "It was a pretty thing, and Johnny always liked pretty things. I've often thought Jack Harrison must've stole it out of Johnny's sea chest after he died. Then he got the bright idea later to hide it and tell the authorities about it."

"You think Jack Harrison is the one who hid the knife in the cupboard?"

"Of course he was. Otherwise why'd he wait a whole month before saying anything about a knife? I think he dipped it in sheep's blood, hid it in that cupboard, then went over to the Shadwell Public Office and told them about it so's he could get more of that reward money. They were like vultures around a dead lamb, that lot, all trying to get more money—and my Robert right in there with them. Up until they found the knife, the papers were saying the killer had used a razor. Then all of a sudden they were talking as if everyone thought it was a knife all along. You ask me, they latched onto that knife so excited-like because it'd always bothered them that Johnny didn't have a razor."

"He didn't?"

"No. He wore a beard."

Sebastian was aware of the sound of gruff voices in the yard outside raised in inquiry: the men from the deadhouse come to carry Vermilloe's body to Paul Gibson. "Williams had a beard?"

"Oh, yes," said Mrs. Vermilloe. "Well, he did up until a day or two before he was taken into custody. Had to go to the barber to get it shaved off because he didn't have a razor. Everybody knew that."

Through the window, Sebastian could see the men from the deadhouse lifting the innkeeper's body onto their shell. "Was your husband nervous about anything lately?"

"Nervous?" She picked up her knitting again, but simply sat holding it, not even trying to lay down stitches. "No. Why would he be nervous?"

"Did he talk to anyone unusual or go anywhere unusual lately?"

She thought about it a moment. "Well, he did go up to Meux's Horse Shoe Brewery."

Sebastian felt his interest quicken. "Do you know why?"

"No. He had no reason that I know of. Thought it odd, I did. But when I asked him, he just winked and told me to never mind."

"Where does the Pear Tree's beer come from?"

"Meux."

"Not the Black Eagle?"

She shrugged. "You want to have a pub in the Tower Hamlets, you get your beer from either the Black Eagle or Meux."

"When did Mr. Vermilloe go up to Meux?"

"Yesterday evening, right after your lordship left. He came in from fixing the privy, told me you were asking about the knife, then said he was going up to Meux's. I said, 'What on earth for?' and he just gave me that toothy smile of his and said, 'Never you mind. You'll be seeing.'"

"Did you talk to him after he came back?"

"Oh, yes. Ever so chipper, he was—like a cat who's stole a roast chicken off the spit. Then he went out just before eleven, and I never saw him again."

"You don't know where he went?"

"No." She wiped her eyes with her handkerchief. "Foolish, foolish old man. I don't know why I loved him so, but I did. And now he's gone, just like that." She looked at Sebastian, her face contorted with pain and confusion and all the fears of an aging woman left alone in a harsh world.

Chapter 46

Meux and Company's Horse Shoe Brewery lay in Bainbridge Street, just off Tottenham Court Road in the parish of St. Giles. It was a massive brick complex with decoratively arched windows and towering chimneys whose belching smoke mingled with the reek of hot, fermenting beer to smother the wretched, crowded, festering neighborhood of poor Irish immigrants that surrounded it.

The enterprise had several investors but was dominated by Henry Meux himself, who rejected the French pronunciation of his ancient family name and always loudly reminded anyone who erred that he and his beer were called "Mewks." In the five years since Meux bought the Horse Shoe, he'd taken the brewery from eleventh to sixth largest in London, installing huge fermentation vats that were larger even than those of the Black Eagle in Bethnal Green. It was there, in the cavernous brick brewhouse thick with the stench of hot porter, that Sebastian came upon him in conversation with a clerk, who bowed and moved away at Sebastian's approach.

"Yes, I saw Vermilloe yesterday," Meux replied in answer to Sebastian's question. The brewer was a small, stout man in his mid-forties with graying fair hair that contrasted sharply with his dark eyebrows and swooping side-whiskers. His cheeks were full, his nose long and hooked, his chin small but protruding, so that together they overshadowed a tiny mouth with a tendency to settle into a self-satisfied smirk. "Why do you ask?"

"Someone murdered him last night."

Meux stiffened, an exquisitely dressed gentleman standing in sharp contrast to the dirty, smoky, rusty, foul-smelling warehouse around him. "You don't say? How very distressing."

"Why was he here?"

"To talk about porter. We supply the Pear Tree, you know."

"I would have thought you've agents to handle such mundane inter-actions."

Meux's small, smirking mouth pursed. "Well, yes, of course. But I do like to keep abreast of things myself. And there's nothing like personal interaction to get a feel for how a business is running."

"You're saying that's all your meeting with Vermilloe was? Just you keeping a finger on the business's pulse?"

"You could say that, yes."

"Why was he here?"

"I told you: We supply the Pear Tree with porter."

"Yes, but why exactly did he come here yesterday? To reduce his supply? Increase it? Complain about its quality or cost?"

Meux's nostrils flared on a quickly indrawn breath. "Increase it, of course."

"Interesting." Sebastian craned back his head to stare up at the vast fermentation tanks, some of which rose more than twenty feet above them. At least seventy feet across, the vats were made of massive wooden staves encircled by dozens of iron hoops that he figured must weigh over a ton each. "Those are quite impressive."

"The largest in London, you know."

Sebastian nodded. "I assume you were acquainted with Sir Edwin

Pym and Nathan Cockerwell, the two magistrates recently murdered in Wapping?"

"I've met them, yes."

"You knew they were forcing Tower Hamlet publicans to buy their ale and porter from either you or the Black Eagle?"

Meux's lips twitched. "I don't know if I'd say the publicans are *forced*, exactly. They always have a choice."

"You mean, between selling your beer and closing?"

Meux waved one hand in a gesture that took in the rows and rows of towering vats, the building's twenty-five-foot-tall, thick brick walls, and heavy-beamed roof. "This is the future you're looking at. Large companies backed by greater and greater concentrations of capital. We provide this Kingdom with economic stability, greater efficiency, and lower prices. What's good for us is good for Britain, and the Regent and Parliament know it."

"If your prices are lower, why do you need to coerce publicans into buying your beer?"

Meux's smirk was still in place, but his eyes were narrowed and glittering. "Publicans in general are an ignorant lot, I'm afraid. They don't always know what's best for them."

"I see." Sebastian watched a workman pause beside one of the casks' massive valves. "Do you have any idea why someone would want to slit the throats of men such as Pym and Cockerwell?"

"No, but I assume you're looking for some disgruntled publican or other miscreant." Meux studied Sebastian with a speculative expression animating his scrunched face. "Why are you involving yourself in this, my lord? I know you have something of a reputation for investigating murders, but Wapping is a tad out of your way, wouldn't you say?"

"A tad," said Sebastian agreeably. "I'm curious: Given that you and the Black Eagle both make it a habit of coercing publicans into buying your beer, how do you decide which brewery gets which tavern?"

Meux's full cheeks had taken on a purplish hue. "We work it out."

"I see. Interesting." Sebastian touched one hand to his hat. "Thank you for your time."

"Of course. Glad to be of assistance, my lord."

It was when Sebastian was walking back to where he'd left his curricle on Tottenham Court that he noticed the red-bodied barouche and magnificent team of bays drawn up nearby.

"Did ye see 'im, then?" asked Tom as Sebastian hopped up to take his reins.

"See whom?"

"The cove what got out o' that barouche. It was Sampson Buxton-Collins hisself!"

Chapter 47

*H*ero arrived at Hermitage Street in Wapping shortly before one o'clock that afternoon. The sky was still gloriously sunny, the cold bite of the wind lessening as the day wore on, the nearby Hermitage Basin crowded with ships moving in and out of the massive, high-walled rectangular dock that had eaten much of what was once Old Wapping.

The pink-and-gray parrot was still in its cage outside the pawnbroker's shop, and Hero studied it with a sad, heavy heart. "I wish I could do something, but I don't think my big black cat would be pleased if I were to bring you home," she said.

The parrot bobbed up and down and squawked, *"Furl the mainsail! Step lively there, lads!"*

Hero smiled, then felt her smile fade as she turned to let her gaze drift over the squalid street. She didn't really expect the girl Molly to come today, but she felt she had to be here, just in case.

She was dressed in one of her plainest gowns, a soft gray wool walking dress with a high collar and a bodice decorated only with narrow pin tucks. After some forty-five minutes, the gown's high collar was beginning to feel too warm, and a pin holding her casquet hat in place was digging into her scalp unbearably. She was reaching up to reposition it when she became aware of a girl watching her from near the Jolly Tar on the far side of the traffic-choked street.

The girl couldn't have been more than fifteen or sixteen, with golden hair and a thin, wan face that might have been pretty if not stamped with the weight of habitual fear and despair and what looked very much like self-loathing. She wore a tattered yellow gown that hung on her underweight frame and a cheap chip hat that was beginning to unravel at the edge of the brim. Hero smiled at her, and the girl jerked her gaze away, her thin chest shuddering with a quickly indrawn breath.

Terrified of scaring her away, Hero watched the girl, unsure of what to do next. Stay here and wait for her to hopefully get up the courage to approach her? Walk across the street herself before the girl lost her nerve completely and left? Impossible to know which would work and which would be a disaster.

But after another ten minutes, Hero came to the conclusion the girl was never going to summon up the resolve necessary to come any closer. So with her features carefully schooled into a pleasant, friendly expression, her gaze not on the girl but on a point some feet over her head, Hero started across the street.

The girl stiffened.

Don't run. Hero repeated the thought over and over again as if she could somehow will the girl to trust her. *I'm not going to hurt you. Please don't run.*

By the time Hero stepped up onto the opposite pavement, the girl was trembling, her hands fisted in the skirt of her gown, ready to bolt.

"Please don't be afraid," said Hero, her voice soft and low. "You're Molly?"

The girl hesitated, then nodded. A faint bruise in the shape of a hand showed on her white cheek where someone had obviously slapped her hard—someone with a small hand.

Hero said, "Letitia told you about me?"

"Her name's not really Letitia," said Molly. "It's Anne."

And is your name really Molly? Hero wondered. But what she said was, "I think 'Letitia' suits her much better, wouldn't you say? 'Anne' is so staid and commonplace—everything Letitia most definitely is not."

She was rewarded with a faint gleam of amusement in the girl's soft blue eyes—amusement that faded to wistfulness. "I wish I could be more like her."

"How long have you been on the streets?"

"Three years."

Oh, no, thought Hero. *You poor thing.* Aloud she said, "Letitia told you I would pay you to talk to me about your experiences?"

Molly nodded. "She wanted me to come here with her yesterday, but I was too afraid. She got mad at me."

"And slapped you?"

Molly nodded again.

"You don't need to be afraid," said Hero. "I mean you no harm. Are you originally from Wapping?"

"No. We had a cottage down in Kent. But we lost it when the lord got his Act of Enclosure, so we come up to London. Da thought he could get work on the docks, and he did. But then a load of sugar fell on him."

"It killed him?"

"Not right away. But he couldn't work, and Mama was already so sick. She tried to get us into the parish poorhouse, but they said we weren't eligible because we weren't born here."

"So what did you do?"

The girl looked at her with wide, hurting eyes, her voice a shamed whisper. "What else could I do?"

Hero struggled to keep her own voice steady. "Are your parents still alive?"

Molly shook her head.

"And now you share a room with Letitia and some other girls?"

"Yes."

"So where do you take your customers?"

A hint of color rode high on the girl's cheekbones. "Some of the men'll pay for a room in a lodging house or a coffeehouse, but most of 'em just . . ." Her voice faded away and she twitched a shoulder.

Hero felt her stomach twist at the thought of all that statement implied. "Letitia said you saw the magistrate Sir Edwin Pym the night he was killed."

Molly took a step back, her eyes widening, her breath leaving her body as if she'd been punched. "She told you that!"

It hadn't occurred to Hero that Letitia might not have mentioned her interest in the magistrate to Molly. She studied the girl's wide, terrified eyes and knew that at another word about Pym, Molly would run. Hero said instead, "If you had a chance to leave the streets, to work in a shop or as a domestic, would you take it?"

Molly swallowed hard and scrubbed a hand across her watery eyes. "It hurts, you know, when men laugh at me, when they call me a whore and worse. I mean, it's what they made me, you know? I never thought this'd be the life I'd be living. I always thought I'd be somebody's wife and have a cottage and babies of my own someday. But look at me. Ain't no man's ever gonna marry me, and ain't nobody gonna hire me to do nothing but what I've been doin'."

"I'll hire you."

Molly might have been young, and she might have been born and raised in the gentle Kentish countryside, but she'd been on the streets of one of the roughest parishes of London for more than three years. She wasn't innocent anymore. She shook her head, her lips pressed into a tight line. "I've heard about women who approach poor girls just up from the country, who pretend they're going to help them, only to lure them into houses they then can't leave. If I'm gonna do what I'm doin', then I'm gonna do it on my own terms, not for somebody who makes me service ten or twenty men a night and then keeps all the money."

It took Hero a moment to realize the girl had mistaken her for a procuress. At a loss for words, she nodded to the carriage and team awaiting her across the street. "That's my carriage. See it?"

She watched Molly's face as the girl took in the magnificent barouche with the crest on the door, the four high-spirited, carefully matched black horses, the coachman and liveried footmen. Her breath left her body in a soft sigh. "That's yours?"

"It is. I'm Lady Devlin, and I promise I won't hurt you. I only want to help."

The girl's eyes narrowed. "Why? Why would you want to help me?"

Hero drew a painful breath. What could she say? *Because my life has always been so comfortable and easy that a part of me can't help but feel guilty for it? Because I feel partially responsible for the way life and my country have treated you? Because sometimes writing articles to stir the public conscience simply isn't enough?* But she couldn't say any of those things. So instead she said, "I need someone to take care of my parrot."

"You brought her here?" said Devlin.

They were in the drawing room, Hero seated in a chair near the bowed front window, a cup of tea in her hand. Devlin had only just come in and stood before the fire drinking a glass of wine. Simon played nearby, the cat curled up asleep beside him.

Hero took a sip of her tea. "I don't think she'd have agreed to talk about Pym any other way. She was too afraid, and I can't say I blame her. She's upstairs in the servants' quarters having a bath. Claire has taken charge of her."

"What are we going to do with her?"

"She says she wants to be a housemaid, but I told her that for the time being she can take care of the parrot."

Devlin choked on his wine. "The parrot? We've acquired a parrot?"

"Mmm. The pawnbroker said it's a galah from New South Wales. I was thinking I could perhaps send it home with someone sailing there, but he said it was stolen from a nest as a baby and probably wouldn't survive if let loose into the wild."

Devlin stared at her a moment, then threw back his head and laughed. "So did this Molly ever tell you about Sir Edwin Pym?"

"Yes," said Hero. "She did."

Chapter 48

*B*en Carter was drinking porter in a low tavern in Farthing Alley, not far from the church of St. George's, when Sebastian walked up to his table.

Like most night watchmen, Carter was old, a big, bulky man with shaggy gray hair, rounded shoulders, a short fat neck, and a lined, sagging face. He had his beefy hands clasped around a tankard of ale; his red nose and the enlarged pores on his face suggested he spent most of his off-hours in taprooms. When Sebastian introduced himself and asked if Carter had been on duty the night Sir Edwin Pym was killed, he took a deep drink, wiped the back of one hand across his wet lips, and said, "Aye."

"Mind if I sit?" asked Sebastian.

Carter looked at him with a puzzled frown. "If'n yer lordship wants."

Sebastian pulled out the chair opposite and sat. "Were there many people on the streets that night? The night Pym was killed, I mean."

"Nah. Fog was real thick that night, my lord. Most folks don't like being out in the stinkin' fog."

"Especially around midnight," said Sebastian. Thanks to Molly, they now had a much clearer idea of exactly when the magistrate had died.

Carter nodded. "That's true enough, my lord."

"So did you see anyone out around that time?"

"You thinkin' that's when Pym was killed? Midnight?"

"Thereabouts, yes."

Carter took another slurping drink. "Well, there was this strumpet. Don't know her name, but I've seen her before. Skinny little thing with yellow hair, cain't be more'n fifteen or sixteen."

"Where did you see her?"

"Not far from here. Had a couple of seamen, she did."

"Did you see Pym?"

"No. Never did. Not that night, leastways."

"Anyone else?"

Carter scrubbed a rough hand over his face, his eyes slipping out of focus as he fought to remember. "Let's see. . . . There was the girl, and the two seamen. And then there was an apprentice runnin' an errand for his master. That's about it."

"What apprentice?"

Carter stared at him with vaguely hostile, watery eyes. "Ye think I asked him?"

Sebastian rested his forearms on the table and leaned into them. "Who do you think killed Pym?"

"Reckon it was that strumpet."

"The girl?"

"Aye."

"What exactly did she look like?"

"Like I said, she's got yellow hair. Tiny little thing. Don't look like she gets enough t' eat—but then, most of 'em don't."

"How could a tiny little girl bash in a big man's head?"

"Reckon she lured Pym into that alley, and her flash man's the one who beat his head in."

"I suppose that could have happened," said Sebastian, although he thought no such thing. Molly's halting recital of that night's sequence of events dovetailed with Paul Gibson's findings. According to Molly, Pym had coupled with her at around half past eleven, pinning her against the base of one of the church's distinctive pepper-pot towers. He must then have walked south toward the river and away from his house for reasons Sebastian couldn't begin to guess. According to Molly, it was just past midnight when she'd literally fallen over his body in the alley off Nightingale Lane. Minutes later, Carter walked down the misty lane, iron lantern and rattle in hand . . .

And had obviously seen nothing.

Molly swore to Hero that she'd taken nothing except the magistrate's watch, and she'd done that only because he'd refused to pay her for that rough coupling.

"Did you sell it?" Hero had asked.

Molly had shaken her head, her voice a frightened whisper. "I didn't know who to take it to. I've never done anything like that before, I swear. And I was afraid if I tried to pawn it, someone would find out and think I was the one who killed him."

"So you still have it?"

"No. Somebody stole it. One of the other girls, I guess. And that scares me more'n anything, because what if she pawns it, and then the constables track her down and she says she got it from me? They'll hang me!"

"Although now that I think about it," Ben Carter was saying. "There was somebody else—and not too far from Nightingale Lane, too."

"Oh? Who's that?"

"Thief by the name of Faddy. Seamus Faddy."

"You're certain?" Sebastian's voice came out sharper than he'd intended.

"Oh, aye. Known Faddy since he was a wee tyke causin' trouble, I have. He was gone fer a while, but he's been back two or three years now." The night watchman's face darkened. "And up to no good, you can be sure of that."

Sebastian didn't find himself inclined to disagree with that summation. "Do you remember when Faddy moved back to Wapping after being gone?"

Carter brought up one blunt-fingered hand to rub the back of his neck. "Don't remember exactly, but I know it was before the Ratcliffe Highway murders."

"How can you be certain of that?"

" 'Cause I remember seein' him fer the first time in years at the King's Arms. He was there with everybody else, gawkin' at the bloody bodies. I told him he could just go back wherever he'd been, that we didn't need any more of his kind around Wapping."

"And what did he say?"

"He didn't say nothin'. Just tipped his hat and laughed in my face."

Sebastian found Grace Calhoun looking over a stall of dried herbs at a street market in Saffron Hill. She watched him walk toward her, then deliberately turned her back on him, her attention all for a bunch of sweet-smelling lavender.

"I need to talk to Seamus Faddy," he said, pausing beside her.

She didn't look up. "I take it something's made you suspect him again?"

"He lied to me."

"And you're surprised?"

"Not really. Where can I find him?

She moved on to the next stand, this one selling soft white cheeses that filled the air with an earthy, ripe scent. He thought for a moment that she wasn't going to answer him. Then she said, "There's a public house down by the river, in Wapping Wall. The Pelican, it's called."

"Thank you," said Sebastian.

She put out a hand, stopping him when he would have turned away. "You didn't get that from me."

He nodded, his gaze on her handsome, fine-boned face. "Jules said Seamus was orphaned when he was eight or nine."

"Thereabouts. Why?"

"What did his father do before he died?"

Something gleamed in her eyes, something that was there and then gone before he could identify it. "Danny was his name. Daniel Faddy. Kept a tavern in Halfpenny Court." She tilted her head to one side, her expression, as always, unreadable. "Reckon you can make of that what you will."

Chapter 49

*A*Stuart-era hostelry dating back to the first years of the sixteenth century, the Pelican rose three stories tall directly from the shores of the Thames. Built of yellow brick, with two wide bow windows recently added to its ground-floor entrance, the Pelican was known for attracting an unsavory mix of smugglers, bargers, seamen, cutthroats, and thieves. Before venturing into its ancient smoky depths, Sebastian swung by Brook Street to rub ashes into his clean face, disorder his hair, and change his well-tailored coat, fine buckskins, and gleaming Hessians for an unfashionable collection of secondhand clothes culled from the rag fair in Rosemary Lane.

It was only late afternoon, but the Pelican's taproom was already thick with a raucous, boisterous assortment of unshaven, unwashed men. Here by the waterfront, every other man was a stranger, and no one paid Sebastian much heed as he pushed through to the bar, ordered a pint, and let his gaze drift over the motley crowd. It wasn't simply a matter of wearing the right clothes. Sebastian had learned long ago that if he wished to pass unobserved, he needed to change his entire way of walking and standing, the way he looked at the world and expected the world to look at him. He couldn't see Seamus in the crowd. But one man—a short, gray-whiskered sailor Sebastian had never seen before—stared at him intently for a moment, then quietly left.

Sebastian was still at the bar, holding a pot of beer but not drinking it, when Seamus Faddy strolled into the taproom and came to stand nearby, his back to the bar, his elbows on the scarred counter, his hat tipped low over his eyes. He had his back teeth clenched on the long stem of a white clay pipe with a bowl decorated with a horse's head, his eyes narrowed against the rising smoke.

"I take it yer here lookin' fer me?" said Seamus.

Sebastian studied the river thief's youthful profile. "You were seen down by Nightingale Lane last Saturday night."

Seamus pursed his lips, a quiver of what might have been amusement tugging at his mouth. "Nah. 'Twas foggy that night. Weery foggy. Reckon a man could make a mistake, thinkin' 'e saw somebody 'e didn't."

"So you're denying it?"

Seamus turned his head to look directly at him. He was not smiling. "I am."

"I understand your father kept a tavern in the Tower Hamlets before he died."

The intelligent green eyes widened slightly. "The Turk's Head. What of it?"

"Halfpenny Court isn't that far from New Gravel Lane. He must have known Old John, the publican of the King's Arms."

"Reckon 'e did."

"When did your father die?"

Seamus cupped the bowl of his pipe in one hand, as if considering the question. "Nine years ago or thereabouts. Why?"

Sebastian was aware of the great age of the room around them, of the centuries-old heavy beams, the worn flagstone floor, the massive old-fashioned hearth. Nine years ago would put Seamus's father's death at around 1805, or six years before the Ratcliffe Highway killings. Was that significant?

Impossible to know.

Sebastian said, "Did your father have trouble with the magistrates on the Middlesex licensing committee?"

"Ye only have trouble if ye fight 'em."

"And was your father a fighter?"

Seamus sucked on his pipe for a moment. "Never thought 'e was. But sometimes folks can surprise ye."

Which wasn't exactly an answer, Sebastian thought. And yet in some ways, it was. Aloud he said, "How did he die?"

"Somebody stabbed 'im in the back."

Sebastian drew a sharp breath. "Did they ever find who did it?"

Seamus looked over at him. "What ye think?"

The blaze of combined intelligence and willpower in the man's eyes was impossible to miss. And Sebastian found himself thinking he could understand how Seamus came to command a crew on the river at such a young age.

"Did you know Timothy Marr?" said Sebastian.

"The linen draper? Nah."

"Why do you think the Marrs were killed?"

"How would I know?"

"I think you have an idea. You told me you hear things—that it's an important part of your business."

"Those murders had nothin' t' do with the docks or the shippin' on the river."

"No? Seems as if there were a lot of seafaring men involved."

Seamus lifted his shoulders in a dismissive shrug. "This is Wapping. What do ye expect?"

Sebastian rested his pot of beer on the counter. "You heard that the publican of the Pear Tree was found dead this morning?"

"I heard."

"I suppose you don't know anything about that, either?"

"If I did, ye don't think I'd tell ye?"

"Probably not."

Seamus surprised him by smiling and jerked his chin toward the crowded, noisy room. "One nod from me and half a dozen men 'ere would slit yer throat, no questions asked."

"Is that a threat?"

"A threat?" Seamus gave him a cocky wink. "Nah. That's jist an observation."

Sebastian found himself turning his conversation with Seamus over and over in his head as he drove toward Tower Hill. An idea was forming on the fringes of his consciousness. Faint and amorphous, it taunted him with hints of insight and clarity. Yet when he tried to grasp it, it skittered away.

He found Paul Gibson in the stone outbuilding at the base of his yard, the cadaver of a slim, dark-haired man on the slab before him. "If you're here to know more about that Wapping publican," said the surgeon, glancing up at him, "I haven't had a chance to look at him yet. A couple of doxies got into a knife fight over in St. Katharine's and needed to be stitched up. Then I had to cut the leg off a bricklayer who slipped off a scaffold and crushed his knee, and a kitchen maid scalded herself so bad she'll be lucky if she doesn't lose her arm. And that's not to mention this fellow who was brought in last night."

Sebastian felt his breath back up in his throat as he took a better look at the dead man between them, at the waxy olive skin, the hawklike nose, the thin, deeply incised line of bruising left around the neck by what looked like a garrote.

"A couple of watermen pulled him out of the Thames near the

Tower," Gibson was saying. "But he obviously didn't drown—not wearing a purple necklace like that. Looks a bit French, wouldn't you say? No one seems to know who he is."

"He is French," said Sebastian, his voice sounding odd even to his own ears. "His name is Labourne. Émile Labourne."

Chapter 50

$\mathcal{J}$arvis was coming through the neoclassical marble colonnade that screened Carlton House from Pall Mall when Devlin intercepted him. The last of the daylight was fading from the sky, the temperature plummeting, the flickering lamplight filling the air with the scent of hot oil.

"The body of a Frenchman by the name of Émile Labourne was fished from the Thames last night," said the Viscount without preamble. "You wouldn't know anything about that, would you?"

Jarvis paused, his gaze taking in his son-in-law's filthy face, the ragged, ill-cut coat and trousers, the scuffed boots, the black kerchief instead of a cravat. "Good God. I hope you weren't intending to try to enter the palace looking like that."

"Labourne. What do you know about him?"

"You can't seriously think I am to blame for every corpse that turns up in London?"

"Not all of them. But this one was garroted. Very professionally."

"Oh? And you say he was French?"

Devlin nodded, his lips pressed into a tight, angry line. "When I saw him a week ago, Labourne told me the Bourbons were following him. He was afraid they meant to kill him, and I'd say they have."

"Why would the Bourbons want to kill this . . . Labourne, did you say?"

"You know why. They've been racking up an impressive body count of late."

"He was antimonarchist?"

"I suppose you could say he was anti the restoration of the theory of the Divine Right of Kings."

"Well, then." Jarvis started to turn away, but Devlin shifted to cut him off.

"You know who their assassins are in London."

Jarvis drew up. "I know some of them, yes, but not all. And if you think I have any intention of giving any of them up to you, I fear you are sadly mistaken."

"If I find him, I can promise you he will not kill again."

Jarvis shrugged. Assassins were easy enough to replace. Aloud, he said, "This Labourne was a friend?"

Devlin hesitated a moment before answering. "He worked for me."

"Ah, I see." For a moment Jarvis's gaze met his son-in-law's, and an acknowledgment of all that could not be said, all that had never been and would never be said, passed between them.

Jarvis said, "I've heard she is in Vienna."

Devlin's breath came out in a hiss. "Do you know why?"

"That was not divulged to me. All I know is that she recently arrived there."

"With whom is she traveling?"

"That I don't know, either." Jarvis saw the doubt in Devlin's face. "I see you're not inclined to believe me, but it's true. If I knew, why would I conceal it?"

"I suppose that depends on why she is in Vienna."

Jarvis studied the younger man's tense, determined features. "You know that no good will come of this quest of yours. One man may already be dead because of it."

A feral gleam of interest shone in those unnatural yellow eyes. "So you do know something."

"I know she styles herself Dama Cappello these days, but that is all."

"Who told you this? Castlereagh?"

"As a matter of fact, yes. He saw her by chance in the Stephansplatz, thought he recognized her, and made some inquiries. It's said she lives in Paris."

"Do you know why Paris?"

"No."

Devlin obviously didn't believe him. "There are probably more English aristocrats in Paris at the moment than there are in London."

"Then perhaps you should direct your inquiries to any you consider your confidants. And now you must excuse me."

He thought the Viscount might detain him further, but he did not.

He simply stood beside one of the palace's soaring columns, a tall, raggedly dressed figure with the unmistakable air and self-possession of a lord's son.

Chapter 51

That night Sebastian lay with Hero snuggled in the crook of his arm, the fire crackling on the bedroom hearth, the house dark and quiet around them. In the distance he could hear a dog bark and, nearer, the rattle of a night-soil man's cart.

She said, "Labourne never sent you the names of possible replacements, did he?"

"No, but then he may not have had the chance to contact anyone. Gibson said he thought the man had been dead for a couple of days before the body was dumped in the river last night."

"My God," whispered Hero. She was silent for a moment, her hand coming up to rest lightly on his bare chest. "What are you going to do now?"

"About Labourne's killer, or about my mother?"

"Both."

"To be honest, I don't know where to begin looking for Labourne's assassin. And as for finding my mother . . ."

"Have you thought about going to Paris yourself?"

He drew a deep breath. "I've thought about it, but I doubt it will be a quick trip. Perhaps we could all go in the spring, when Simon's a bit older, so we can more easily take him along. I saw Paris as a boy, but never since." He shifted so that he could look down at her. "What about you?"

A smile curled her lips. "No. Never." She was silent for a moment, and he knew her thoughts had drifted. She said, "Do you really think Seamus Faddy could be behind these new killings?"

Sebastian ran his hand up and down her arm. "I think it's possible, yes, even if I don't understand yet why he'd choose to make these deaths look like the work of the Ratcliffe Highway murderer. It's all connected somehow—the new killings and the old. There's nothing random about any of this."

"Even the killings of three years ago? You don't think they were random?"

"Let's just say I doubt it."

"But what could possibly have connected that young linen draper and his family to an aged tavern keeper?"

He gathered her in his arms to shift her on top of him. "I don't know. But I suspect if we could find the answer to that, the events of both today and three years ago would suddenly become much clearer."

Sunday, 16 October

The next morning Sebastian was still at his breakfast table when Sir Henry Lovejoy came to see him.

"My apologies for troubling you at such an early hour, my lord," said the magistrate when Morey ushered him hat in hand into the dining room. "Especially on a Sunday. But I thought you'd like to know that some disturbing new evidence has turned up against the publican Ian Ryker."

"Please, have a seat and a cup of tea," said Sebastian. "And perhaps some toast?"

Sir Henry hesitated, then pulled out a nearby chair. "Some tea would be lovely, thank you."

Sebastian reached for the teapot. "What's been found?"

"We had some of the lads search the Black Devil in Bishopsgate last night, and they found a pair of blood-soaked trousers rolled up with a bloody shirt and waistcoat and stuffed behind a row of casks in the cellar."

Sebastian looked up from pouring the tea. "That sounds ominous. What does Ryker say?"

"He swears he knows nothing about it—insists that someone must have hidden the clothes there to implicate him. But the woman who does the tavern's laundry swears the clothes are his."

Ian Ryker's fetters clanked dully as he shuffled into the visitors' room in Coldbath Fields Prison. He was even more unkempt than before, his clothes torn and bloodstained, both eyes blackened, and his nostrils caked with dried blood. But his gaze was as defiant and hostile as ever.

"Who did this to you?" said Sebastian.

Ryker curled his split lip in a sneer. "Who you think? And if you was to guess some other guest of His Britannic Majesty, then you don't know much about prisons—especially not this hellhole."

Sebastian nodded toward the table and stools. "Please, sit."

Ryker stared back at him, blood-caked nostrils flaring with his breath. Sebastian wouldn't have been surprised if the man had simply continued to stare his defiance. Instead, his gaze broke away and he sat.

Sebastian sat opposite him. "Tell me about the bloodstained clothes Bow Street found in your cellar."

The publican leaned back on his stool, both hands pressed flat on the table before him. "You tell me. I don't know nothin' about 'em."

"Your laundress identified them as yours."

"Maybe. I still don't know nothin' about the blood or how they come to be in the cellar."

"You're suggesting Bow Street planted them?"

Ryker huffed something that wasn't quite a laugh. "You're the one so cozy with that bloody magistrate. You tell me."

"Sir Henry wouldn't do something like that."

"No? Well, then he ain't like any magistrate I ever tangled with."

Sebastian studied the ex-rifleman's mottled, bruised face. He had no doubt that Ian Ryker was more than capable of killing. But the man hadn't been in England three years ago, he'd been locked up when someone stuck a knife in Robert Vermilloe's back, and Sebastian was damned if he could see any reason for the ex-rifleman to be quietly eliminating everyone connected in any way with the old Ratcliffe Highway murders.

Sebastian said, "Did you know Timothy Marr?"

Ryker stared at him, his eyes flat. "Told you I didn't."

"What about his wife, Celia Marr? Did you know her?"

The prisoner rolled his shoulders in a dismissive shrug. "Knew her when she was Celia Nichols."

"When was this?"

"That I knew her? Growin' up. Her da owned the Bull and Bush in Pearl Street."

Sebastian felt a strange humming in his body, so intense his hands were tingling. "Celia Marr's father was a publican?"

"Aye. Heard he gave it up right after his daughter and grandson was murdered."

"Do you know where he is now?"

"No." Ryker swiped the back of his hand across a thin line of blood beginning to trickle from one nostril, his eyes never leaving Sebastian's face. "They're gonna hang me for this, ain't they?"

"It might help if you'd tell me everything you know. If you're innocent, I'm not your enemy."

Ryker stared at him, all of his animosity, all of his loathing, plain to read in his face. "Don't you understand? I don't know nothin'. Nothin'." He pushed to his feet. "We're through here."

Before leaving the prison, Sebastian stopped at the governor's comfortable residence and told the pompous little tyrant that if his prisoner suffered any further damage, Sebastian could guarantee he'd regret it.

"You can't talk to me like that!" snapped the governor, a small middle-aged man with slicked-back black hair and a thin, pointy nose.

Sebastian looked the man up and down, then said quietly, "I just did. Be wise and heed my warning."

He was coming out of the prison's looming, sinister front portico when he recognized the woman in a worn brown stuff pelisse walking toward him. She was young and comely, with dark hair and almond-shaped eyes, and she was carrying Knox's son on one hip.

He watched her face shrink when she saw him, watched her eyes flare with hatred and raging resentment.

Then she brushed past him without a word.

Chapter 52

The Bull and Bush turned out to be a small, well-kept tavern in Pearl Street, not far from the old Green Man in Rope Walk Lane. Sebastian reined in before the simple brick facade, then sat for a moment with his gaze on the snorting black bull on the pub's painted wooden sign.

The outlines of what he was dealing with were coming into sharper focus. It was a tale of ruthless greed and corruption that spanned decades. And now it seemed someone equally as ruthless and bloodthirsty had decided to put a stop to it. The question was, *Who?*

The Bull and Bush's new innkeeper, a young man with sandy hair and a serious face, told Sebastian that Frank Nichols was dead. "Died of grief, they say. His daughter and baby grandson was killed in the Ratcliffe Highway murders, you know." The innkeeper sucked in a deep breath and shook his head. "Terrible business, that."

"Is his widow still alive?" said Sebastian.

"Well, she was last I heard. I think maybe she's with one of his surviving daughters, but I couldn't say for certain. He had five daughters, I hear."

"Who do you think would know how I could get in touch with them?"

The publican thought a minute, then shook his head. "Can't say, really. You might try asking around."

Sebastian asked at the button shop next door, at the haberdasher beyond that, then at the chandler on the tavern's other side. He stopped a costermonger in the street, made inquiries at a ships' biscuit maker, a butcher's, and a tailor's. The day was clouding up again, the wind off the river cold, and his impatience rising. After another half an hour, he gave up and turned toward Stepney.

Sir Edwin Pym's daughter, Katie Ingram, was down on her knees in her garden, her hands deep in the earth, when the little girl Sebastian had seen before showed him outside to her mother.

"Oh, my lord!" said Katie, flustered and coloring as she pushed to her feet. "Oh, my goodness. *Sally!*"

"Don't blame her, Mrs. Ingram," said Sebastian. "I quite overcame her reluctance to show me out here."

She wiped her hands on the old apron she wore pinned over her dyed muslin gown. "What must you think of me?"

Sebastian smiled. "That you enjoy gardening. Please don't let me interrupt; I only want to ask if you knew a publican named Frank Nichols or his daughter Celia. He used to own the Bull and Bush in Pearl Street."

She thought about it a moment, then shook her head. "No, I don't believe so. Why?"

"Celia was Timothy Marr's wife."

"Oh." She twisted her hands in her apron, a haunted, frightened expression creeping into her face. "I heard what happened to that publican from the Pear Tree." She swallowed. "It's all tied together, isn't it? These new deaths and what happened three years ago."

"I believe so, yes."

The wind blew a loose strand of her pale, fine hair across her face, and she put up a hand to tuck it behind her ear. "I'm so grateful for all you've done. I haven't seen anyone watching the house since you posted the guards."

"Good," said Sebastian, although he wasn't entirely convinced the guards explained it. "When was the last time you saw him?"

She took a deep breath and let it out. "The night before Father was killed."

Sebastian nodded. "I thought so."

The two ex-cavalrymen weren't due to come on guard duty until dusk, but Sebastian found them easily enough at the coffeehouse in Westminster.

"No, we ain't seen nobody hanging around, Cap'n," said Adam Campbell when Sebastian asked. "Nobody at all. But we been talkin' t' folks in the neighborhood like ye suggested—them and others we see comin' through regular-like."

"And?"

"There's a few say they noticed a shabby-lookin' cove watching the house a week or so ago, but they ain't seen him lately."

"Anyone see him well enough to describe him?"

"Seems he pretty much kept to the shadows. But there's a few say they think he was a big man—tall, with wide shoulders and maybe a beard."

Sebastian felt his interest quicken. "A beard?"

"Well, that's what the lamplighter's boy said, although the lamplighter himself says he don't remember seein' no beard, and neither does the ostler at the stables down the street."

"How old is the ostler?"

"Fifty-five, maybe more."

"And the lamplighter?"

"A few years older."

"Then I think I trust the lad's eyes. Did the boy notice anything else?"

"Well, he claims the man had a long nose. But how could he see that in the dark?"

Sebastian went back to Wapping. Ignoring the cold drizzle that started up, he spent a lot of time talking to publicans and the neighbors of various publicans; he went to see the Reverend York again, then Charlie Horton, asking both men what they knew about Frank Nichols and carefully watching their faces as they replied. He drove through the rain to the Middlesex Sessions House and spoke to an old magistrate named Thompson who also served on the licensing committee. Then he drove home, stoked the library fire, poured himself a brandy, and sat down to think.

He was at his desk, rolling a pen back and forth between his fingers, a piece of paper on the desktop before him, when Hero came to stand in the doorway, her elbows cradled in her palms, and watched him.

"Figure it out yet?" she said softly.

Looking up, he set the pen aside and spun the paper around to face her. "Not entirely. But I'm definitely seeing a pattern. Look."

She came to pick up the page and run through the column of dates and names he'd listed. "Good heavens. That's a lot of deaths."

He nodded. "The Ratcliffe Highway murders and these new killings were brutal enough to stand out and attract attention. But people have been dying in the East End for years. The area has a bad reputation for a reason, although I'm beginning to suspect it's not for the reason most people think."

She read through the list again more slowly.

1805: Daniel Faddy, publican of the Turk's Head. Stabbed in the back.

7 December 1811: Timothy Marr, linen draper, and family. Beaten to death, two with throats cut. (Note: Celia Marr and baby Timothy were the daughter and grandson of Frank Nichols, publican of the Bull and Bush.)

19 December: Old John, publican of the King's Arms, his wife, and servant. Beaten to death and throats cut.

26 December: John Williams, seaman and suspect in Ratcliffe Highway murders. Found hanged in cell.

January 1812: Joseph Beckett, Coldbath Fields Prison turnkey. Stabbed in back.

Spring 1812: Alice, alibi of seaman and suspect Long Billy Ablass. Strangled.

June 1814: Ian Ryker, publican of the Green Man. Broken skull.

Early August 1814: Cornelius Hart, ship's carpenter and suspect in Ratcliffe Highway murders. Stabbed.

Late August 1814: Jack Harrison, sailmaker and John Williams's roommate. Stabbed.

September 1814: Hugo Reeves, seaman. Beaten to death, throat cut.

8 October 1814: Sir Edwin Pym, magistrate. Beaten to death, throat cut.

9 October 1814: Nathan Cockerwell, magistrate. Beaten to death, throat cut.

15 October 1814: Robert Vermilloe, John Williams's landlord at the Pear Tree. Stabbed.

At the bottom of the page was an asterisk, followed by: *MP for Devon, drowned. Date and place of death uncertain.*

She looked up. "There are an extraordinary number of publicans—or relatives of publicans—on this list."

"There are indeed. And everyone else on there is linked in some way to the 1811 Ratcliffe Highway killings, with the exception, as far as I can tell, of Hugo Reeves—and, I suppose, the MP from Devon."

"Daniel Faddy died way back in 1805. Why is he on here?"

"Because he's Seamus's father and because he's another murdered publican. It's the same reason Ian Ryker's father is there. I spent a lot of time today asking questions around Wapping and Shadwell, and with the exception of the men on this list, no other publican in the area has died violently for thirty years."

"And there are four here," said Hero, going through the list. "Five if you count Celia Marr's father."

Sebastian nodded. "According to the surgeon Walt Salter, only two of the four victims in the first Ratcliffe Highway killings had their throats slit: Celia and her son, Timothy."

Hero sank into a nearby chair, her gaze on the paper, her features crimped with the horror of it all. "I see the pattern, but I don't have the slightest idea what it means."

Sebastian pushed up from his desk and went to stand before the fire. "According to everything I'm hearing, Frank Nichols and Old John were highly respected publicans. Their houses were quiet and well run, and they were strong-minded, honorable, stubborn men. Both were fed up with the power of the big brewers and the corruption of Pym and Cockerwell, and they were organizing something of a revolt against them. There was even talk of the publicans banding together to start their own brewery. After the Ratcliffe Highway killings, that all went away."

Hero's eyes widened. "You think that's why the Marrs and Old John were killed? To stop the East End publicans from standing up against the magistrates and the brewers?"

"It fits, doesn't it? The elder Ian Ryker tried to fight them this year and he died. And while Seamus Faddy didn't come right out and say it, he suggested the same thing about his father. At first I couldn't figure out why the magistrates and brewers would go after Celia Marr rather than her father. But when I asked around more, I discovered he was a tall, burly man with a reputation for knocking heads together if he had to. I suspect Celia was simply an easier target."

"He doesn't sound like the kind of man who would let someone murder his daughter and grandson and get away with it."

"He might if his four other daughters and nine surviving grandchildren were threatened."

"Good Lord. Perhaps he's the new killer. You're certain he's dead?"

"I wondered about that, too. But he sold the Bull and Bush right after Celia and the baby were killed and died just a few months later. The Reverend York says he remembers burying him. But even after his friend gave up, Old John was still determined to get the other publicans to commit to starting their own brewery and fighting the magistrates."

"So they killed him, too," Hero said softly.

Sebastian drained the last of his brandy. "I talked to an elderly magistrate who's been on the Middlesex licensing committee for decades. He says Cockerwell and Pym ran it the way they wanted to, and everyone else basically went along with them. A few years ago a new magistrate was appointed who tried to stand up to them."

"Let me guess; he died?"

Sebastian nodded. "No one tried that again. I don't know exactly which of the two men—Pym or Cockerwell—ordered the Ratcliffe Highway murders, but I suspect both knew what was going on. And I wouldn't be surprised if Meux and Buxton-Collins did, as well."

"So who committed the actual murders?"

"My money's on Long Billy Ablass, along with one or more of his friends—probably Cornelius Hart, but possibly someone else, too. They deliberately set up John Williams by leaving that maul and crowbar, and then they strangled him in his prison cell so the government would close the investigation."

"And then killed the turnkey who let them do it," said Hero.

Sebastian nodded and went to pour himself another drink. "And because she knew he was out on the nights of the murders, Ablass also killed the woman he was living with who gave him an alibi."

Hero looked at the list again. "But that all happened almost three years ago. Why did the killings start up again now?"

He splashed more brandy into his glass, then set aside the carafe with a soft thump. "I suspect the elder Ryker was killed for the same reason as so many before him: because he was threatening to cause trouble for the magistrates and brewers. From what I was hearing today, he wasn't planning to go away quietly."

"And the others? The seamen like Hart and Harrison?"

"If my theory is right—and if they were feeling threatened for some reason—then I can see one or more of the men who originally ordered the Ratcliffe Highway murders setting Long Billy to eliminate anyone and everyone who knew what they'd done back in 1811."

"And the sailmaker Jack Harrison? You think he was the third Ratcliffe Highway killer?"

"He could have been. Or he could have been killed to cover up the fact that the 'discovery' of that bloody knife was simply a bid for more of the reward money—and to deepen the perception of Williams's guilt."

She was silent for a time, thinking. "I can see quietly eliminating Harrison and Hart. But why butcher Pym and Cockerwell in a way that immediately reminded everyone of the Ratcliffe Highway murders? And what about Hugo Reeves?"

"Reeves could have been one of the original Ratcliffe Highway killers—or at least, someone thinks he was." Sebastian came to sink into the other chair beside the fire and sit with his gaze on the flames, one hand slowly rolling the heavy amber liquid in his glass. "The only explanation I can come up with that makes sense is that these new deaths are the work of a different killer—a copyist who wants us to remember the Ratcliffe Highway murders. Someone who knows what Cockerwell and Pym—and maybe Reeves—got away with."

"But *who*?"

He shook his head. "Charlie Horton? Seamus Faddy? Ian Ryker? You could make an argument for any one of them doing it. Even Reverend York."

"So why kill Robert Vermilloe?"

Sebastian took a deep drink that burned all the way down. "I could be wrong, but I suspect Vermilloe fell victim to his own greed. I think he knew more about the conversation he overhead between Ablass and Pym than he was willing to admit, and made the mistake of trying to use it to get money out of Meux."

"That implies Meux was also involved in the Ratcliffe Highway murders. And had Vermilloe killed."

"Either Meux or Buxton-Collins. Buxton-Collins was up at the Horse Shoe Brewery visiting Meux right before Vermilloe was killed. He could have been the one to actually order it."

"It makes a horrible kind of sense, but it's all still just a theory. You can't prove any of it."

He turned his head to look at her. "Not yet."

Chapter 53

*T*hat night, the fog rolled in again from the Thames, smothering the city. In Wapping and Shadwell it brought with it the stink of the tanneries on the far side of the river, their pungent odors mixing with the ever-present stench of manure and urine and rot.

Sebastian stood in the shadows cast by the recessed doorway of a cooperage, his gaze on the mist-swirled facade of the inn across the lane. He watched a stream of men come and go, laborers and shopkeepers, tradesmen and apprentices, seamen and watermen, their numbers lessening as the fog thickened and awareness of the dangers of the night increased. He was waiting for one person in particular, and he'd about decided he wasn't coming when a tall bearded man with a rolling sailor's gait strolled up from the direction of the docks.

Billy Ablass was about to push open the door to the Three Moons' taproom when the sound of Sebastian's footsteps crossing the dew-slicked cobbled lane made him pause and glance around.

"Good evening," said Sebastian, one hand lingering significantly in the pocket of his greatcoat as he stepped into the feeble light cast by the oil lamps flickering on either side of the inn's door.

Billy Ablass swung to face him. "You? Wot ye want wit me again?"

"I'm wondering if you're nervous."

Something flickered in the man's hard eyes. "Me? Why would I be nervous?"

"Perhaps because everyone else who was associated in any way with the Ratcliffe Highway murders has died in the last five months. Hart. Harrison. Pym. Cockerwell. Even Vermilloe. That tells me we're looking at one of two possibilities. Either you're liable to be next and you've a good reason to be nervous. Or . . ." He paused.

"Or what?" growled Ablass.

"Or you're the killer."

Ablass snorted and started to turn away. "Yer daft. Why would I be doin' any o' this?"

"Oh, don't get me wrong. I don't think you killed Pym or Cockerwell—or Hugo Reeves, for whatever reason he figures into this. But the rest of them? I can see how the original Ratcliffe Highway murderer might think he had good reason to quietly eliminate them all. And—"

"I don't know wot yer talkin' about!"

"Don't you? Because now that I think about it, even if you did kill everyone from John Williams to Robert Vermilloe, you should still be nervous. It looks to me as if someone knows exactly what happened three years ago and why. They've obviously decided to take justice into their own hands, and I suspect you're next."

Ablass's lips peeled back from his teeth in a mean smile. "Don't know who ye been talkin' to, but they been spinnin' ye a tale, that's fer sure."

Sebastian shook his head. "The Sun Tavern was a stupid place to approach your former employer for a bit of blackmail. What were you threatening him with? Obviously you couldn't expose him for the part he played in ordering the Ratcliffe Highway murders, but you could threaten to kill his daughter and grandchildren the same vicious way, couldn't you? Is that why you were hanging around her house in Stepney? To frighten her and him so he'd pay up? I gather no one told you Pym declared ten years ago that his daughter was dead to him."

"I don't know wot yer talkin' about," said Ablass again.

Sebastian met the other man's glittering, angry gaze. "Yes, you do. At first I was thinking you must have killed Pym and Cockerwell the same way you killed the Marrs and Old John's family. But then I realized you're too smart to do something like that, aren't you? The Ratcliffe Highway killings were deliberately made gruesome and bloody because they were more than simple murders. They were a warning sent to every publican who ever thought about fighting back against the East End magistrates and the brewers. I can see you maybe deciding to kill the magistrates, but if it were you, you'd have done it the same way you killed Robert Vermilloe—quietly, with a knife in the back. Whoever killed Pym and Cockerwell didn't want their deaths to be written off as just another sad example of the violence that plagues the East End. No, whoever killed those two crooked magistrates wanted their deaths to remind everyone of the Ratcliffe Highway murders. And that tells me you're not the new Ratcliffe killer. That tells me you're probably the killer's next victim."

Ablass made a rough snorting sound, his nostrils turning white and pinched around the edges. "Yer mad. Ye hear me? Mad."

Sebastian gave another faint shake of his head. "No. And you know it. That's why you're scared. You're so scared I can smell it. And you know who else smells it? The killer. Tell me who you think is doing this; it's the only chance you have to survive."

Ablass sucked in a deep breath, the heavy moisture in the night air beading on the wild hairs of his long beard. "Ye don't care about me. Ye just want to see me hang."

"Was Hugo Reeves one of the killers, Billy?" said Sebastian, pressing him. "Is that why he was butchered the same way as Pym and Cockerwell? What about Buxton-Collins and Meux? Were they a party to what happened three years ago? Why are you protecting them? Because you're afraid they might send someone to quietly slip a knife in your back? They will, you know—if you let them. And if whoever butchered Pym and the others doesn't get to you first."

Ablass brought up one meaty hand to punch the air between them with a shaky finger. "Ye got nothin' on me, ye hear? Nothin'!"

He turned to fumble with the handle of the taproom's door. From somewhere in the distance came the howl of a dog and the rattle of cartwheels and, from nearer, the quiet *click* of a flintlock's hammer being pulled back.

"Look out!" shouted Sebastian, throwing himself flat as the night exploded with a roar of sulfurous flames.

Chapter 54

The bullet hit Ablass square in the chest with a dull *thwump*, expelling the air from his lungs and spinning him around. He wavered for a moment, staggering back against the brick wall behind him, his face slack with shock mingling slowly with the horror of comprehension.

Then his eyes rolled back in his head, and he fell.

"*Bloody hell,*" swore Sebastian, his gaze raking the misty darkness.

He could hear the sound of running feet receding fast into the distance, and the impulse to give chase was strong. He pushed it down. Keeping his head low in case there was a second shooter, he crawled across the glistening damp pavement to lift the seaman's head in his arms. He could hear the gurgle in Ablass's throat, knew the man was drowning in his own blood.

"Who did this?" Sebastian demanded, only dimly aware of people shouting, of the door from the taproom flying open to spill men into the street. "Tell me who shot you."

Ablass's tongue flicked out to wet his lips, sending a cascade of dark blood pouring down his face. "God rot ye," he whispered as Sebastian bent his head forward, trying to catch the cracked words. "Ye hear me? God rot ye."

"You think the killer was aiming at Ablass? Or you?" asked Sir Henry Lovejoy, the collar of his greatcoat turned up against the cold, damp night.

They stood together in the street before the Three Moons, the constables keeping back the nervous onlookers while they waited for the men from the deadhouse. At one point Sebastian had seen Hannah Bishop's pale face in the crowd, and for a brief moment their gazes met. Then she sucked in a deep breath and turned away.

"I could be wrong," Sebastian said now, "but I suspect the killer had more to fear from Ablass than from me. I might have a rough idea of what is happening, but I'll be damned if I can prove any of it."

Lovejoy peered over his spectacles at the dead man's blood-drenched chest. "Well, if Ablass was the intended target, then whoever did this is an extraordinarily good shot. A rifle, do you think?"

"Sounded like it."

"Anyone on your list of suspects a marksman?"

"Ian Ryker was a rifleman," said Sebastian. "But he's in prison, isn't he?" He thought a moment. "Sampson Buxton-Collins cultivates a reputation as a keen sportsman."

"Oh dear," said Lovejoy, turning his head to meet Sebastian's gaze. "Oh dear, oh dear."

"You're certain that bullet wasn't meant for you?" Hero said later as Sebastian bent over the basin in his dressing room and washed the dead man's splattered blood from his face.

"You sound like Lovejoy," he said.

"Well?"

Sebastian reached for a towel and looked over to where she stood beside the hearth, watching him. "With Ablass dead, who's left to implicate either Meux or Buxton-Collins in any of the murders?"

"You mean, if they were involved."

"They were involved—or at least one of them was." He set aside the towel and reached for a clean shirt. "Pym and Cockerwell might have been the ones who paid Ablass to quietly eliminate everyone from that Clerkenwell prison turnkey to the seamen Hart and Harrison. But Robert Vermilloe was stabbed sometime Friday night. And that means we're looking at either Meux or Buxton-Collins—or both, although my money is on Buxton-Collins."

"Rich men don't usually do their own killing."

He pulled the shirt over his head. "Not usually, although I can see one doing it if he's feeling threatened."

"But you've still no proof."

"Nope. None." He blew out a harsh breath and reached for a clean cravat. "I need to find Frank Nichols's widow."

"What do you think she can tell you?"

"I don't know. But if she can tell me anything, she's in danger." He kept his gaze on the mirror as he wound the cravat around his neck.

"You're going to confront Buxton-Collins again, aren't you?" she said, watching him. "Do you even know where he is tonight?"

He turned, his eyes meeting hers, and he smiled. "I hear Jarvis is having a dinner party."

He found Jarvis's town house ablaze with lights, the streets around the darkened square lined with gentlemen's carriages, the mist here no more than vague wisps that drifted through the shadowy trees and hugged the lamplit, rain-slick cobbles.

"Lord Devlin," said Grisham, his face wooden as he reluctantly opened the door to his master's son-in-law.

"Good evening, Grisham." Sebastian handed the butler his hat and walking stick as the sound of cultured voices, mostly male, spilled down the grand staircase to the entrance hall. "I assume they're in the drawing room?"

Grisham stared stiffly at the opposite wall. "Yes, my lord."

"Good." Sebastian turned toward the stairs, then paused to glance back and ask, "When did Buxton-Collins arrive?"

"A quarter of an hour ago, my lord."

Sebastian nodded. "Thank you."

He took the stairs rapidly, aware of the anger still surging through him. He found the drawing room crowded with a range of political and moneyed interests—everyone from Liverpool and his most important cabinet ministers to the heads of London's most prominent banking families. Sampson Buxton-Collins was standing near the hearth, a glass of wine in one hand, his face flushed with pleasure as he conversed with a petite, elegantly gowned woman Sebastian recognized as Victoria Hart-Davis.

Sebastian was halfway across the room toward them when Jarvis intercepted him.

"What the devil are you doing here?" he demanded in a low voice.

Sebastian was aware of the brewer raising his wineglass to his lips, his gaze meeting Sebastian's over the brim. "I've a message for one of your guests—Sampson Buxton-Collins, to be precise."

"The devil you say."

Sebastian brought his gaze back to his father-in-law's full, angry face. "If you'd prefer, you can deliver the message yourself. Tell him he can kill everyone from John Williams to Robert Vermilloe, but it won't make any difference. A man with his wealth and status might have nothing to fear from the public hangman, but this isn't about what passes for justice in the Kingdom of Great Britain. This is about retribution, and whoever butchered Pym and Cockerwell is coming for him next."

Jarvis let out a low hissing sound. "Are you mad? What the bloody hell are you accusing the man of now?"

Sebastian met his father-in-law's blazing eyes. "Ask him. And while you're at it, ask if he sent those men to break into my house last Thursday night. Then watch his face when he answers you."

"Are you quite through?"

Sebastian cast another glance toward the big, bulky brewer. "For now."

Chapter 55

Monday, 17 October

The next morning Sebastian stood at the corner of Cannon Street Road and Cable Lane, his gaze on the worn cobbles of the intersection before him, his thoughts on the skeleton that lay crumpled beneath the piles of reeking manure, beneath the endlessly passing cart and wagon wheels, the clattering hooves, the plodding feet.

The day was surprisingly sunny and warm, and Sebastian found his thoughts spinning away to another time, a time when a sixteen-year-old lad with sensitive features and a taste for fine clothes and good books had run off to sea, leaving an unknown home and an unknown family. And he wondered, *What drove you? A desire to see the world or the need to escape a father too handy with his belt and his fists? Where did you come from? Does anyone who once loved you know you're buried here? Or are you completely forgotten by all except those who still shudder at the mention of your name?*

Sebastian thought he understood now what had happened in that cold December of 1811. He understood the nexus between the rich brewers and the corrupt magistrates who'd treated the East End like a benighted medieval fiefdom. He understood, too, the angry determination of a handful of publicans pushed beyond the limits of endurance and compliance—those simple, hardworking men who'd fatally underestimated the ruthless fury of rich, powerful men so greedy they would protect their privileged position by ordering two entire families slaughtered—and then frame and murder a hapless seaman before quietly setting about eliminating everyone who'd made the mistake of cooperating with them.

Sebastian could never prove any of it, of course, and the frustration of that knowledge welled within him, bitter and painful. But the truth was known either in whole or at least in part by others. And one of those who knew—Charlie Horton, the Reverend York, Seamus Faddy, or perhaps someone Sebastian had yet to identify—was now wreaking his own revenge.

Sebastian had to acknowledge that a part of him sympathized with this new Ratcliffe Highway killer. He knew only too well that the wealthy and powerful rarely faced justice in this world, and he knew, too, how the need for justice could burn like a corrosive fire in a man's breast. For hadn't he himself succumbed to such temptations in the past?

And he was still paying for it.

He spent the next several hours walking the streets of Wapping, talking to a variety of shopkeepers and tradesmen. He was still looking for Frank Nichols's widow, but the entire family seemed to have abandoned the parish, and Sebastian had to admit he couldn't blame them.

In the end he left Tom to continue the search and drove back to Brook Street, frustrated and haunted by the certainty that the long string of violent deaths had not yet reached its end.

Several hours later he was drinking a pot of ale and staring at the map of London he'd spread across his library table when the front door slammed open and Tom's shout echoed around the entrance hall. *"I found 'er, gov'nor!"*

Looking around, Sebastian heard Morey's hiss and Tom's breathless "Where's 'e at?"

"The library," said Morey. "But you mustn't—"

Tom's booted feet were already pounding across the marble-tiled floor. Then the tiger burst into the room, bringing with him the smell of autumn sunshine and horses and hot boy and startling the big black cat that had been sleeping curled up in a chair by the front window. "I found yer widow woman!"

"Where?" said Sebastian.

"She's livin' with 'er middle daughter over in Lambeth. Leastways that's what the old groom in the stables o' that inn she used t' own says, and I reckon 'e oughta know."

"Does he know where in Lambeth?"

"Not exactly, but 'e says the daughter's married to an apothecary what's got a shop near the archbishop's palace, so I reckon it shouldn't be that hard to find."

The parish of Lambeth lay on the south side of the Thames, opposite the outer reaches of Westminster. Still fairly rural in character, Lambeth was dominated by the soaring fifteenth-century towers, venerable old hall, and crenellated redbrick Tudor gateway of the archbishop of Canterbury's ancient sprawling palace.

Sebastian found the nearby apothecary's easily enough, in a row of shops that faced onto Lambeth Butts just around the corner from the palace. An old sunlit orchard stretched out behind the shops, and it was to the orchard that the bespectacled middle-aged apothecary directed Sebastian.

"She took our lads there not half an hour ago," said the apothecary, displaying a complete lack of curiosity as to the reason for Sebastian's interest in his aged mother-in-law. "After all this rain, it's a lovely day, isn't it?"

Sebastian walked between the rows of gnarled pear and apple trees, the wind soft against his cheek, the air of the countryside tasting blessedly fresh as he drew it deep into his lungs. He could see her now, a woman somewhere in her sixties. She was perched on a milking stool beneath a spreading apple tree, a faint smile on her face as she watched her two small grandsons chase each other around the stout trunks of the old trees. She was a frail-looking woman, rail thin, her hair wispy white, her deeply lined face dragged down by the horror and soul-crushing sorrow of her life. For a moment Sebastian found himself reluctant to intrude on this moment of peace. Then she looked up and saw him, and he stepped forward to introduce himself and explain the reason for his visit.

"It's not easy, thinking about it, my lord," she said, her face taking on a pinched look as she stared up at him.

"I understand. I'm sorry, but it could be important."

She searched his face. "You think these new murders are connected to what happened three years ago?"

"Yes."

She nodded, then looked away. "I don't see how anything I have to say could be of any help to you, my lord. My Frank, he didn't talk to me much about what he and Old John were planning to do about the breweries and the magistrates. He knew I was against what they were up to, so he kept most of it to himself. And I was right." She looked down, her fingers alternately pleating and smoothing the sturdy cloth of her gown where it lay across her knees. Then she said it again, more softly: "I was right."

"Did you ever know a man named Billy Ablass?"

Her face twisted. "Ablass? He came into the taproom sometimes, but I never liked him." She gazed across the orchard to where the wind was gently rippling the long grass, and swallows darted around the eaves of a weathered shed. "They held him for a time, you know, thinking he might've been the killer—or at least one of them. But in the end they let him go."

"Do you think John Williams was really responsible for the murders?"

She brought her gaze back to his face. "Oh, no. He was such a kindly, considerate young man. No one will ever convince me he did such a thing."

"So you knew him?"

She nodded. "He used to come into the Bull and Bush and see me whenever he was ashore. I never had sons, you see, and he liked to say I reminded him of his mother."

Sebastian watched one of the little boys hunker down nearby, his hands on his thighs, his face serious as he watched a lizard scurry across a half-buried rock. "Did he ever talk about his family?"

"Some. I don't think Williams was his real name."

"Oh? What was?"

"That I couldn't tell you."

"I've heard people say he was Irish."

"*Ach*, no. The Irish are always good for blaming, aren't they? That's just people saying what they want to be true. Anybody who listened to him knew he was from London."

"He was?"

"Oh, yes. Nicely spoken, he was. Didn't talk like your typical seaman at all. Told me once his mother owned an inn, but she married some man from Germany who didn't treat them well. Used his fists on Johnny during the day and bothered his sister at night." She lowered her voice and leaned forward. "If you know what I mean."

Sebastian stared off across the rows of ancient fruit trees. He was intensely aware of the warmth of the afternoon sun on his face, of the clouds moving in from the south and the buzzing of bees in the scattered asters and silkweed blooming purple in the long grass. It was a moment before he could bring himself to say, "What happened to his sister? Do you know?"

"Not exactly. I gather they ran away at the same time, but then went their separate ways. She took off with some man she'd met. I remember Johnny saying they hated leaving their baby brother with their mother and that man, but in the end they decided they couldn't bear it anymore."

Sebastian could feel the veins throbbing in his forehead, feel his breath coming shallow and quick. "Did Johnny ever mention his sister's name?"

Mrs. Nichols looked thoughtful. "Emma, maybe? No, that doesn't sound right. Anna? No, that's not it, either. Let me think." She paused, then said, "Hannah!" and Sebastian's world spun around in a whirl of laughing children, blue sky, and dying leaves. "That's it. The sister was Hannah, and the little baby brother was Christopher."

Chapter 56

It's not far from Wapping to Shadwell. The two districts flow one into the next so seamlessly as to make the shift unnoticeable to those unfamiliar with the area. Less than two miles separated Pear Tree Alley from Pope's Hill. Yet they were in different worlds. The Pear Tree Inn stood just a few hundred feet from the Thames, where a man could hear the wind whistling through the rigging of the big ships riding at anchor out in the river and smell the sea in the air. It was a district dominated by sailors and watermen, lumpers and purlmen. But Pope's Hill lay at the top of the ridge looking down on what had once been marshland. It catered to tradesmen and shopkeepers rather than men whose livelihoods were intimately linked to the water.

As he stood in Pope's Hill, his arms crossed at his chest, his gaze on the neat brick facade of the Three Moons across the street, Sebastian found himself thinking about those differences. How many people on the docks of Wapping would recognize the studious, sensitive sixteen-year-old boy who'd once run away from a cruel Shadwell stepfather? How many would see the boy Johnny Bishop in the heavily bearded sailor "John Williams" had become?

Probably none.

But the man who'd called himself John Williams had shaved his beard just a few days before his arrest and death. Why? Had it been his intention to play the prodigal son and go home to see the mother and baby brother he'd once loved? To search for the sister who'd gone her own way? And because he was now clean-shaven, had someone in the silent crowd who'd watched the dead man's body trundle past in that long, drawn-out, degrading funeral procession recognized the boy in the man he'd become?

Perhaps.

And then there was the postmortem sketch drawn by Thomas Lawrence's skilled hand and made into a print that was reproduced and sold as a macabre souvenir by the thousands. Had Hannah Bishop at some point seen that haunting profile and recognized her brother? Surely she had. Would she have believed him guilty of all that he'd been accused of?

Sebastian doubted it.

I wasn't here then, she'd told Sebastian, and a few discreet questions directed at longtime residents around Pope's Hill elicited the information that she'd been in Kent. No one seemed to know exactly where or with whom, only that she'd reappeared a few weeks after her stepfather's death to help her widowed mother and younger brother with the inn. Yes, said the aged proprietor of a nearby coffeehouse in answer to Sebastian's query, there had been an older brother once. Johnny was his name, but he'd run off years before, around the time Hannah disappeared. The coffeehouse owner said everyone blamed Peter Ablass for it.

No one Sebastian spoke with seemed to regret the man's death.

So how and when had Hannah and Christopher Bishop learned the truth about the Ratcliffe Highway murders? Sebastian wondered. How had they pieced together the sordid, tangled tale of those events? From Long Billy's ramblings late one night when he was in his cups? Perhaps. And it occurred to Sebastian now, as he crossed the street toward the inn, that Billy Ablass must surely have known who John Williams really was. Long Billy, who'd served with Johnny on the *Roxburgh Castle*, must have recognized the well-spoken young sailor as his brother's stepson. Was that part of why Ablass had decided to set up "John Williams" to take the fall for the Ratcliffe Highway murders?

Probably.

So why, once they knew the truth and decided to take their own revenge, hadn't Johnny's sister and brother killed Long Billy first? Because someone as big and dangerous as Ablass would be difficult to kill? Is that why they began with Pym and Cockerwell and the seaman Hugo Reeves, whose involvement in all this Sebastian still didn't understand?

It made sense. And as he pushed open the door to the Three Moons' taproom, Sebastian was aware of a host of conflicting emotions. What would he himself do if he discovered his own brother had been killed and dumped in a suicide's grave while the rich, powerful men responsible both for his death and for a series of heinous murders were allowed to go on living their luxurious lives in comfort and safety?

What would he do?

He was afraid he knew only too well. And perhaps as a result he was not exactly disappointed to see that neither Hannah Bishop nor her brother was behind the bar.

"They went off maybe an hour ago," said the unfamiliar dark-haired barmaid in answer to his question.

"Any idea where they went?"

"They didn't say, but I heard 'em tell the hackney driver St. Giles—the Horse Shoe Brewery in St. Giles."

Chapter 57

The weak October sun was already slipping below the horizon, leaving the narrow, squalid lanes of the city in deep shadow as Sebastian headed toward St. Giles. He felt a sense of urgency that he could not explain, a cold sweat of foreboding that spurred him to drive his chestnuts faster than he should have.

He told himself there could be an innocent explanation, that Hannah Bishop and her brother might simply be exploring the possibility of shifting their supply source to Meux. But Sebastian knew in his gut that their mission wasn't harmless, knew that whatever they had planned would surely end in disaster for someone.

It was nearly dark by the time he drew up outside the brewery's tall, soot-stained brick walls in a narrow street that was beginning to fill with tired workmen dragging homeward. "Wait here," he told Tom, tossing the boy the reins.

He hit the pavement at a run, oblivious to the stares as he sprinted across the road to push his way through the crowd of grimy-faced workmen streaming out the gates. He could hear the roar of the brewery's steam engines, smell the pungent reek of the fermenting porter and vast stores of malt. Halfway across the lamplit courtyard, he intercepted a gawky, skinny young clerk carrying a leather-covered file under one arm and shouted at him, "Henry Meux's office—where is it?"

The clerk stared at him wide-eyed. "By the stables. But if you're looking for Mr. Meux, he's not there. A hoop's slipped off one of the vats, you see, and I—"

Sebastian had to stop himself from grabbing the man and shaking him. "Damn you, where's Meux?"

The clerk took a frightened step back. "Last I saw, he was talking to a young woman and a boy."

"Where? Where were they?"

"By the brewhouse." The clerk nodded toward the northwestern section of the complex. "It's behind the cooperage, by the—"

But Sebastian was already running.

The brewhouse lay dark and deserted, its filthy, steamy gloom relieved only here and there by the dim light of the lanterns that hung from brackets set high on the bare brick walls. As he slipped in through the open door, Sebastian was aware of the massive vats soaring twenty-five feet above him, of the roar of a steam engine, and of the powerful stench of a million or more gallons of fermenting beer.

He paused to allow his eyes to adjust to the near darkness, holding himself still as he listened for the least betraying sound. At first he heard nothing. Then he caught a metallic clang from somewhere in the depths of the chamber and the whisper of a voice too soft to be heard distinctly over the thunder of the engine.

The vats here, like those at the Black Eagle in Bethnal Green, stood in rows on iron foundations, edged by walkways accessed at intervals by skeletal iron staircases red with rust and grime. Sebastian crept forward, keeping to the darkest shadows of a row of enormous vats some sixty to seventy feet across. As he ventured deeper and deeper into the vast building, the hot vapors grew nearly smothering, the smell of rust and dirt and beer thick in his nostrils.

He could see them now, up on the walkway that ran along the next row of vats, where a lantern cast a faint light that caught the steam in a shimmering, ghostly glow. As he watched, the glow wavered, and Sebastian realized the light came from a lantern Hannah held for her brother, who was bent over doing something—something that involved a spanner. Then Sebastian heard a trickle of liquid hit the metal platform. The trickle grew stronger as he crept forward, and he knew what they were doing.

They were opening the valves on the vats.

There was no sign anywhere of Henry Meux, and he thought the brewer must be lying unconscious someplace.

Unconscious, or already dead.

The stream of porter from the open valve was gushing now, splashing down from the metal grating above to the flagged flooring, mixing with the rust and grime and oil as it flowed in all directions. Then the metal platform vibrated as brother and sister shifted to another vat.

Sebastian stepped out from beneath the shadowy foundations of a vat as high and wide as a barn and shouted, *"Don't do it!"*

His voice echoed and reechoed in the cavernous space. Brother and sister jerked around, their faces pale in the shimmering, vaporous light. Then Christopher threw the spanner at Sebastian's head and took off running.

"No!" screamed Hannah as Sebastian sidestepped the spanner and tore after him.

The boy was no more than twenty-five or thirty feet ahead, but he was running on the dry metal grating of the walkway, while Sebastian was slipping and sliding down below in a growing toxic mix of spilling beer and grime. He saw Christopher clatter down the last iron-framed staircase and turn to dart along the back of the building. It made no sense until Sebastian caught sight of the open door in the high brick wall and realized they'd had the forethought to break the lock that normally barred it and propped the door open as an escape route.

He saw the boy disappear through the doorway. Then he was through it himself, erupting into the cold night air to find himself at one end of a narrow, squalid street of wretched, tightly packed old houses flanking the yard of a mean tavern with a crumbling, vine-covered wall. He saw Christopher throw a quick glance over one shoulder, then swerve to leap up and grasp the top of the wall just as a rumble sounded from inside the depths of the massive brewhouse.

A thunderous explosion split the night, shaking the ground beneath them. Turning, Sebastian watched as a section of the twenty-five-foot-high back wall of the brewhouse collapsed in a roar of gushing hot porter and crashing bricks that sent great roofing timbers hurtling like sticks into the night.

Flinging up his arms to protect his head from the debris raining down around him, Sebastian felt the first wave of the dark, foaming river hit him, swirling up around his knees with a powerful force that nearly swept him off his feet. Then another explosion rocked the night, and another, and he realized that the cascading flood of beer and the flying pieces of shattered casks and massive iron hoops must have been breaking the other vats, one by one.

A second, higher wave slammed into his chest, lifting him off his feet to hurl him into the darkness. His shoulder smashed against a wall; something hard struck him in the ribs as the night around him filled with the crash of falling masonry, the groans of tearing timbers, the screams of terrified women and children.

Then a massive beam borne along on the crest of the flood raked across the side of his head, knocking him under the hot, foaming river. His sight dimmed; he breathed in porter and felt it fill his lungs. Choking, fighting blindly, he clawed up toward the surface and felt his hand brush against soft yielding flesh that was there and then gone.

Bursting into the cold night air, he gasped for breath and swung around, thrusting his hands into the steaming torrent again and again. He found the child's arm and grabbed it just as his head almost went under again. Scrabbling to keep upright, he yanked and hauled a little girl not much older than Simon out of the swirling flood.

"I've got you," he told the sobbing child as she frantically wrapped her arms around his neck. He hugged her tight. "It's all right. I've got you. I've got you."

The torrent was subsiding. He staggered to his feet, turned in a slow circle.

What had once been a mean, narrow lane of decrepit houses now looked like the artillery-blasted rubble of a war-ravaged village. He glanced back at the brewhouse and saw a gaping sixty- to seventy-five-foot hole that had been torn in its back wall. From all around him came cries for help, the wail of frightened children, the groans of those trapped beneath collapsed houses.

"I want my mama," whispered the little girl, wet and shivering in his arms.

Sebastian sucked in a deep breath that stank of porter and swiped with one crooked elbow at the mingling beer and blood running down the side of his face. "Let's go find her, shall we?"

They worked through the night, a motley collection of volunteers and frantic fathers, sons, and brothers. It soon became obvious that most of the victims were women and children, for the flood had struck at half past five, when the men were still at work or just heading home.

The first victim they found was a young girl of perhaps fourteen, crushed beneath the rubble of the tavern's collapsed wall. Then a child of three and an aged woman with gray hair and staring blue eyes.

Some were pulled out of collapsed houses grievously injured but alive. Every once in a while someone would hear a plaintive cry, and there would be calls for silence, the rescuers standing still, straining to catch the sounds of the living. At one point Henry Meux—quite alive and unharmed—appeared dressed in evening clothes and a silk cloak. He set guards around his shattered brewhouse to keep the riffraff from trying to steal any of his remaining beer, then left.

Sebastian chose that moment to slip away from the search long enough to find his tiger and send the lad home with a message for Hero.

Tom was obviously fretting that his responsibility to the horses was keeping him from pitching in. "I want to help," he insisted.

Sebastian studied the boy's freckled, earnest face and thought about the shattered body of the tiny boy he'd just pulled from a flooded basement. "It's ugly."

"Ye think I can't take it?"

"No," said Sebastian. "I know what you're made of. Carry the message to Lady Devlin, then catch a hackney back up here. But best grab something to eat first. It's going to be a long night."

Working side by side, he and Tom found Christopher Bishop just before two in the morning, pinned beneath the rubble of a collapsed wall. He was still alive when they dug him out, but it was obvious he wouldn't be for long.

"Hannah," said the boy with a gasp when his eyes focused on Sebastian's face leaning over him. "Where's Hannah? Did she get out?"

"She's fine," lied Sebastian. Hannah's body had been found shortly before midnight, floating amongst the butts in the brewhouse.

The boy struggled to draw breath, his face contorting with a grimace. "Don't understand . . . what happened. Didn't mean . . . to do this. Just wanted to let out some of the bastard's porter . . . make a mess of that brewhouse he's so proud of."

"It's all right," said Sebastian, gripping the boy's thin shoulder. "Don't try to talk."

"No." The boy flung up a bloody hand to grab Sebastian's arm. "It was my idea, you know. All of it. After we heard Long Billy talking to Reeves that night about what they'd done—about what Pym and Cockerwell and the brewer had them do . . . Hannah wanted to go to the authorities, but I said . . . I said, 'They *are* the authorities. Nobody's ever gonna hold them accountable for what they did to Johnny . . . to that baby. . . .'"

"*The* brewer?" said Sebastian. "Only one? So it was Meux and not Buxton-Collins?"

Christopher's head shifted restlessly against the wet, beer-drenched earth. "Billy didn't say which. I wanted to kill them both, but Hannah . . . she said . . . wouldn't be right, because we didn't know."

A new spasm of pain convulsed Christopher's features. And by the time it had passed, the boy was dead.

Chapter 58

*S*ebastian left St. Giles midway through the afternoon on Tuesday, stopped by Bow Street briefly to see Lovejoy, then went home to wash the stink of beer from his aching body, choke down a few spoonfuls of soup, and collapse into bed to sleep the clock around.

"I don't think you've broken anything," said Gibson when he stopped by on Wednesday morning to see him. "But you're going to hurt for a while."

"Hurt? You think I hurt?"

But Gibson only laughed, put sticking plaster on the worst of the cuts on Sebastian's face, fashioned a sling for his left arm to take some of the strain off his shoulder, and went away again.

Downstairs, Sebastian found Hero in the drawing room with the pink-and-gray parrot in its cage. Their big black cat was sitting in the middle of the floor, its bushy tail swishing back and forth as it stared at the bird.

"*Baak*," squawked the galah. "Step lively there, ye bloody bastards. *Baak*."

"As you can see," said Hero with a soft smile, "the parrot not only talks like a sailor; he also swears like one."

Sebastian started to laugh, but broke off to press a hand to his bruised ribs. "Oh, that hurts." Then his gaze fell to the newspaper lying on a nearby end table, and he lost all desire to laugh. "Jesus," he whispered. "Nine dead."

She came to stand beside him. "And with the exception of Christopher Bishop, all were women and children."

"Christopher was only fifteen years old."

"It's hard to think of him as a child, after what he did."

"But he was."

She was silent for a moment, her gaze still on the newspaper. "Jarvis was here earlier."

He heard the strain in her voice. "And?"

"He says they've decided the best way to handle the situation is to blame the magistrates' murders on the three killers who broke into our house last week. The deaths of Reeves, Ablass, and Vermilloe will be portrayed as typical of the violence that plagues the docks."

"And 'the brewer'? Does Jarvis seriously think I'll simply walk away and let Buxton-Collins or Meux or whoever it is get away with everything he's done?"

She looked up then, an expression he couldn't quite read in her eyes. "It seems Mr. Buxton-Collins suffered a fatal fall from his horse while out riding yesterday evening. He appears to have struck his head on something, although rather oddly they haven't found anything in the immediate vicinity that might have caused the rather extensive damage to his skull."

Sebastian felt a grim kind of satisfaction wash through him. Short of murdering the man himself, he didn't see how he could have managed to bring down such a rich, powerful man. But Jarvis had never had any such scruples. "Jarvis found out Buxton-Collins was behind the attack on our house, did he?"

"He didn't elaborate, although one assumes. Arrogance can tempt men into dangerous foolishness, and Buxton-Collins was nothing if not arrogant."

"And Meux?"

"Under what I gather was considerable pressure from some of Jarvis's men, Meux confessed to telling Buxton-Collins about the visit from Vermilloe. But he swears he had no idea Buxton-Collins intended to kill the man, and that he was completely ignorant of the involvement of Buxton-Collins, Pym, and Cockerwell in the Ratcliffe Highway murders."

"And Jarvis believes him?"

"For now. I suspect he will press the man further when he and Victoria return from their honeymoon."

Sebastian understood then the unusual tension he could hear in her voice. "They've married?"

She tightened her lips, her nostrils flaring with a deep breath. And everything she couldn't bring herself to put into words showed in her face. "Last night. By special license."

That evening, Sir Henry Lovejoy came to sit beside the fire in the library and drink a cup of tea while Sebastian sipped a brandy.

"Some interesting information has emerged from a preliminary investigation into what happened at the Meux brewhouse," said Lovejoy. "Seems one of the seven-hundred-pound iron hoops near the bottom of their hundred-thousand-gallon vat was found to have slipped off Monday afternoon. A clerk by the name of Clik reported to Meux at around half past four that the rivets had rusted away, allowing it to fall. Meux says it happens two or three times a year, so he wasn't overly concerned, especially since there were still twenty-seven other hoops on the vat. He sent the clerk off to write a report, while Meux himself went home to dress for dinner. Then the vat burst."

Sebastian stared at him. "They're quite certain?"

"Oh yes, although of course that was only the beginning. The broken staves from the burst twenty-two-foot-tall vat crashed onto the adjoining vats, shattering some and knocking the valves off others. Meux estimates they lost well over three hundred thousand gallons altogether, in addition to the damage to the brewhouse."

"Not to mention all the houses that were destroyed on George Street."

"Yes, well, he's pressuring the authorities to declare the accident 'an act of God.'"

Sebastian took a slow swallow of his brandy. "God wasn't the one who neglected to watch for rusting rivets."

"Nevertheless, I suspect he'll get the verdict he desires." Lovejoy cleared his throat. "Meux reports that the valve on one of the vats at some distance from the site of the explosion was also found to be opened, although the assumption is that flying debris must have knocked it."

Sebastian was silent for a moment, his gaze on the flames leaping on the hearth. "So the Bishops had nothing to do with the beer flood at all."

"Well, they didn't cause it, at any rate—although I suppose one could say they did in some small measure add to it." Lovejoy sipped his tea in silence for a moment, then said, "It seems almost irrelevant at this point, but the Admiralty finally located the crew manifest from the *Roxburgh Castle*'s 1810–11 voyage."

"And?"

"Hugo Reeves's name was on it. According to the notations found along with it, he was one of the principal leaders of the mutiny—he, Billy Ablass, and Cornelius Hart."

Sebastian took a long drink of his brandy. "And then they got together again to butcher two entire families."

"At the behest of two magistrates." Lovejoy drained his teacup and set it aside, his features troubled. "There's no denying their deaths were shockingly brutal, and yet it's difficult not to feel a measure of grim satisfaction in knowing that justice has to a certain extent been served."

"To a certain extent," said Sebastian.

After Sir Henry left, Sebastian stood for a time with his gaze on the fire, a heaviness in his heart that he recognized as sadness for a deadly but troubled young woman and her brother, and for an innocent man whose body would forever lie in disgrace beneath a Wapping crossroads.

He heard a soft step behind him, then felt Hero's hand rest lightly on his back. "They knew the risks they were taking when they decided to avenge their brother's murder," she said, somehow understanding where his thoughts lay. "And they succeeded in what they set out to do; everyone responsible for what was done to John Williams has paid."

"Except that now they're dead. Whatever life Christopher and Hannah Bishop might once have gone on to live will now never be. And the only reason any of this happened is because our society is so bloody corrupt. That hasn't changed, and I'm not sure it ever will—or even could."

"That doesn't mean we don't keep fighting for it."

His gaze met hers, and he found himself reluctantly smiling. Then he drew her into his arms and held her. Simply held her.

Monday, 14 November

Early one morning in mid-November, Sebastian was walking down Brook Street when he noticed a hackney carriage pulling up outside his house, the horse's hooves clattering on the frosted cobbles. The air was crisp, the sky above heavy with the promise of snow. A woman dressed in a warm red cloak hopped down, then turned to reach back into the carriage and take a sleeping child from the arms of a man who stayed within.

As Sebastian watched, the woman clutched the child to her for a moment, her eyes squeezing shut. Then she sucked in a quick, shallow breath and turned toward the front steps.

"May I help you?" said Sebastian.

Jamie Knox's Pippa swung to face him. He could see that she was crying, her cheeks wet, her eyes red and swollen. She stared at him for a moment, her throat working as she swallowed.

Then she said, "Ye told me once that if I needed anythin'—anythin' at all for the boy, all I had t' do is ask ye."

"Yes," said Sebastian, not knowing where she was going with this.

"Jamie—" Her voice broke so that she had to start over. "Jamie always said he thought ye were his half brother."

"I think it very likely, yes."

She gave a nod. "Then that would make Jamie's son yer nephew."

"Yes."

She glanced toward the carriage and the shadowy outline of the man within. "Ian says he don't want to live in England no more. So we sold the Black Devil and we're off to America. He . . . he says we need to start over fresh, and he reckons the voyage'll be hard on the boy, so—" She broke off and sucked in another quick, high breath before saying in a rush, "Will ye take him?"

Sebastian stared at her. "You mean, keep him? Raise him as my own?"

Her voice hardened. "Ye did say—"

"Yes, and I meant it." He reached out. Her arms spasmed around the child, but after a moment she let Sebastian take him from her. The boy stirred, then sighed and snuggled against Sebastian. He realized she must have drugged the child with laudanum to make him sleep so soundly, and his heart ached for the boy, who would awaken amidst strangers in an unfamiliar house to find his mother gone forever.

Sebastian looked up, his arms tightening around Jamie's son, holding him close. "What's his name?"

Pippa was already turning away, but she paused with one hand on the hackney door to look back at him. "Patrick. His name is Patrick."

Author's Note

The Ratcliffe Highway murders of December 1811 terrified Regency London at least as much as Jack the Ripper panicked Victorian London decades later. Whereas the Ripper targeted marginalized women walking the streets at night, the Ratcliffe Highway killer struck "respectable" families, brutally slaughtering them in the supposed safety of their own homes. The killings exposed the unprofessionalism and woeful inadequacy of London's archaic law enforcement system, which was ridiculously fragmented between the medieval parish vestries and a handful of undermanned and underfunded public offices. There were loud calls to create a centralized, trained police force, and although the idea was resisted for years, it finally led to Robert Peel's Metropolitan Police Act of 1829.

I have tried to be faithful to what is known about the original killings, their bungled investigations, and the death of John Williams. The depositions of evidence taken before the magistrates did in fact disappear in early 1812, leaving only the inadequate and often inaccurate reports in the newspapers. Because so many of the people involved were named John or William/Williams/Williamson, I have at times used nicknames in an effort to lessen confusion ("Jake" for John Turner, "Old John" for the publican John Williamson, "Jack" for John Harrison, etc.).

The Home Secretary at the time, Richard Ryder, did task Bow Street magistrate Aaron Graham with trying to coordinate the investigation; within a year his health had indeed seriously deteriorated. The magistrate of the Thames River Police Office, John Harriott, also played an important part, but he is not mentioned in this story because the last thing we needed was *another* John. Both Graham and Harriott typically took active roles in their investigations and helped inspire my character Sir Henry Lovejoy.

So what is complete fiction? If you read surgeon Walt Salter's testimony at the inquest, Celia Marr's throat was definitely cut, although most later writers seem to have missed that. However, to my knowledge her father was not a publican, and the Nichols family is my invention. Charles Horton was the Thames River policeman first called to the site of the Marr killings; he investigated the scene, found the bloody maul, etc., but to my knowledge he did not later lose his position or open a slopshop. Timothy Marr did sue his only brother, who was held for a time as a suspect, but the reason for the lawsuit is not recorded, and their father was still alive at the time of the killings. "Long Billy" Ablass and Cornelius Hart were considered prime suspects and continued to be held after the death of John Williams. They were ordered released by the Home Office (which was indeed anxious to quiet public fears), but their ultimate fates are unknown. The story about the sailmaker John Harrison and the French knife is real, but to my knowledge Harrison was not later murdered.

The proprietors of the Pear Tree, Sarah and Robert Vermilloe, were much as depicted here, but to my knowledge Vermilloe was not murdered. Ian Ryker, Hugo Reeves, Hannah and Christopher Bishop, and the Reverend York are completely fictional. Wendell Flood is a composite; what he tells Sebastian about the night of Williams's hanging is taken from the testimony of several different men. To my knowledge, the turnkey responsible was not later found murdered.

Thomas Lawrence did sketch a portrait of John Williams after his death. Some writers have assumed that because the maul and other tools associated with the murders were displayed on the cart with John Williams's corpse, they must have been thrown into the hole with him. They were not. They were sent to Bow Street but have since been lost.

The events surrounding the detention, death, and burial of John Williams were essentially as described here, although his origins remain completely unknown. He did wear a beard that he shaved off right before his arrest; Mrs. Vermilloe testified that he did not own a razor and had to use a barber. There was speculation at the time that Williams was not his real name, but attempts to paint him as Irish are attributable to the anti-Irish prejudices rife at the time. Do I think he was one of the Ratcliffe Highway killers? I seriously doubt it. Do I think he was framed? The use and deliberate abandonment of a weapon as easily traceable as the maul, plus the anonymous informant and Hart's inquiries into whether Williams had been arrested "yet," suggest it. Billy Ablass did harbor a grudge against Williams dating to the mutiny Ablass led on the *Roxburgh Castle*. Do I think John Williams was murdered in prison? Yes. So did Bow Street magistrate Aaron Graham, who did indeed order a watch kept on Ablass and Hart to prevent them from suffering the same fate while they were in Coldbath Fields Prison. But I have no idea why the Marrs and Williamsons were actually murdered. It seems almost certain that more than one killer was involved, and robbery was obviously not the motive.

The Ratcliffe Highway murder victims were indeed laid on their beds and left on display so the people of London could traipse through their houses and gawk at the mutilated bodies and blood-splattered walls and floors. The same thing happened decades later with the victims of Jack the Ripper.

Much of the information on the Ratcliffe Highway killings is available online. There is also a 1971 true crime book *The Maul and the Pear Tree* by T. A. Critchley and P. D. James (yes, that P. D. James). Thomas

De Quincey (of *Confessions of an English Opium-Eater* fame) wrote a fanciful essay on the Ratcliffe Highway killings, but much of what it contains is either inaccurate or pure fiction. For example, he describes Williams as "wiry" and "muscular," whereas multiple witnesses at the time described him as slight, nonathletic, and "effeminate"; De Quincey is also the only source for the strange hair color he describes.

The magistrates Sir Edwin Pym and Nathan Cockerwell are fictional, but inspired by the very real Joseph Merceron, who was even more corrupt, nasty, and vindictive than they could hope to be (see Julian Woodford's *The Boss of Bethnal Green*). The Middlesex magistrates and big brewers did indeed cooperate to bleed and coerce the East End publicans, and yes, they really did cooperate with the Home Office to force publicans to spy on their customers and report any murmurs of unrest. Several publicans did try to rebel and set up their own brewery; the venture failed.

The history of the Bloomsbury Foundling Hospital is essentially as described here. They did at one time take in fifteen thousand babies in four years. The original building was torn down in the mid-twentieth century, but a smaller building near the site now houses a museum. Their collection of tokens left by mothers forced for financial reasons to give up their babies, and the letters that often accompanied them, are heartbreaking. The Foundling Hospital did have its own art gallery, but one could not see the rope walks from its windows.

Sampson Buxton-Collins was inspired by the historical Sampson Hanbury, who was a close associate of the nasty Joseph Merceron referenced above but was not killed by Jarvis.

The Great Beer Flood of October 1814 was much as described here, although there was no sign of any sabotage. The flood occured at half past five, when the factory was closing and most men were just getting off work. The laboring poor of early nineteenth-century England put in long hours in the summer, and domestic servants slaved endlessly. But in the days before gaslight or electricity, much work ceased at sundown, so days ended earlier in autumn and winter. Eight (the number is sometimes given as nine) poor women and children were killed. The body of a woman was found floating amongst the vats, but her name was Ann Saville. The Meux brewery did successfully pressure the courts into declaring the disaster an "act of God" rather than the result of negligence, thus avoiding any monetary responsibility for the deaths, injuries, and massive destruction they'd caused.

The Pelican public house still stands beside the Pelican Stairs on the banks of the Thames; its name was changed to the Prospect of Whitby early in the nineteenth century. Many of the streets that play a part in this story have been renamed. Ratcliffe Highway became, first, St. George's Street East, then simply the Highway. New Gravel Lane is now Garnet Street. The parish church of St. George's-in-the-East was bombed during World War II and the interior destroyed by fire; the walls and towers survived and have been given a new, modern interior. The great warehouses and docklands of nineteenth-century Wapping were abandoned in the late twentieth century and lay derelict for a time; the area is now dominated by luxury condos popular with Russian and Chinese oligarchs. And, in a bizarre footnote, workmen laying pipes at the intersection of Cannon Street Road and Cable Street in the late nineteenth century uncovered the skeleton of a young man with a stake through his heart. For a time the skull was kept on display at the nearby Crown and Dolphin. It has since been lost.

Read on for an excerpt from C. S. Harris's
next Sebastian St. Cyr Mystery,

WHEN BLOOD LIES

Available from Berkley

Chapter 1

Paris, France
Thursday, 2 March 1815

*O*ne more day, he thought; *one more day, perhaps two, and then . . .*

And then what?

Sebastian St. Cyr, Viscount Devlin, walked the dark, misty banks of the Seine. He was a tall man in his early thirties, lean and dark haired, with the carriage of the cavalry captain he'd once been. For two weeks now he'd been renting a narrow house on the Place Dauphine in Paris, near the tip of the Île de la Cité. He was here on a personal quest, await-ing the return to the city of his mother, who had abandoned her family more than twenty years before.

Waiting to ask for answers he wasn't sure he was ready to hear.

The night air felt cold against his face, and he thrust his hands deeper into the pockets of his caped greatcoat, his gaze on the row of fog-shrouded *lanternes* that ran along the quai des Tuileries before him. The great ancient city of Paris stretched out around him in a sea of winking candles and the dull yellow glow of countless oil lamps. He could hear the river slapping against the stones of the embankment beside him and the creak of an oar somewhere in the night, but much was hidden by the mist.

Ironic, he thought, how a man could strive for years to achieve a goal and then, once it was almost within his grasp, find himself shaken by misgivings and doubts and something else. Something he suspected was fear.

He turned away from the dark, silent waters of the river and climbed the steps to what had been called the Place Louis XV before it was renamed the Place de la Révolution. It was here that the guillotine had done some of its deadliest work, whacking off well over a thousand heads in a matter of months. The blood had run so thick and noisome that in the heat of summer the people who lived nearby complained of the smell. Not about the roaring crowds or the haunting pall of death that even today seemed to hang over the enormous open space, but about the smell.

Pausing at the top of the steps, he stared across the vast lantern-lit intersection, still surrounded by the stone facades of its once-grand pre-revolutionary buildings. Even at this hour the place was crowded, the air ringing with the clatter of iron-rimmed wheels on damp paving stones, the clip-clop of horses' hooves, the shouts of frustrated drivers mingling with the cries of street vendors selling everything from sweet-smelling pastries to pungent medical potions. The guillotine was no longer here, of course. At the end of the Reign of Terror, they'd rechristened the space the Place de la Concorde—the place of harmony and peace. But with the fall of Napoléon and the return of the Bourbon dynasty, the sign plaques had been changed back to "Place Louis XV." He'd heard there was talk of renaming it once more, this time to Place Louis XVI in honor of the king who'd lost his head here.

So much for harmony and reconciliation.

It was a drift of thought that brought him back, inevitably, to his mother. She had lived in this city off and on for over ten years—the estranged wife of an English earl turned mistress to one of Napoléon's most trusted generals. Why? It was one of the many questions he wanted to ask her.

Why, why, why?

The church bells of the city—those that hadn't been melted down to forge cannons—began to chime the hour, and he turned his steps back toward the Pont Neuf. It wasn't a stylish place to stay, the Île de la Cité. The British aristocrats who'd flocked to Paris since the restoration of the Bourbons tended to take houses in the Marais district or the newer neighborhoods such as the Faubourgs Saint-Germain and Saint-Honoré. But it was on this elongated ancient island in the middle of the Seine that Paris had begun, and it called to his wife, Hero, for reasons she couldn't quite define but he thought he understood.

He could feel the cold wind picking up as he stepped out onto the historic bridge that cut across the western tip of the island. It was still called the Pont Neuf, the New Bridge, even though it dated back to the sixteenth century and there were now much newer bridges over the river. Built of a deep golden stone with rows of semicircular bastions, it consisted of two separate spans: a longer series of seven arches leading from the Right Bank to the island, and another five arches that joined the island to the Left Bank. In the center, where the bridge touched the Île de la Cité, stood a large square platform that had once featured a bronze equestrian statue of Henri IV but now held only an empty pedestal.

Earlier in the evening he'd noticed a painfully thin *fille publique* soliciting customers beside the old statue base. But the ragged young prostitute was gone now, the platform deserted, and he paused there to look out over the ill-kept stretch of sand, grass, and overgrown plane trees that formed the end of the island. The gusting wind shifted the mist to show, here and there, a patch of black water, a weedy gravel path, the bare skeletal outlines of branches just beginning to come into leaf. Something caught his attention, a quick glimpse of what looked like an out-flung arm and delicately curled, still fingers that were there and then gone, lost in the swirling fog.

His fists clenched on the stone parapet before him as he sucked in a quick breath of cold air heavily tinged with woodsmoke and damp earth and the smell of the river. His imagination?

No, there it was again.

He bolted down the flight of old stone steps that led to the water's edge. A tall, slim woman lay motionless on her side in the grass near the northern span's heavy stone abutment. This was no wretched prostitute. Her exquisitely cut pelisse was of a rich sapphire blue wool accented with dark velvet at the cuffs and collar; her blood-soaked hat was of the same velvet, trimmed with a jaunty plume; the gloves on her motionless hands were of the finest leather. Her face was turned away from him, her cheek pale in the dim light and smeared with more blood.

Then she moaned, her head shifting, her eyes opening briefly to look up into his. She sucked in a jagged breath. "Sebastian," she whispered, her eyes widening before sliding closed again.

Recognition slammed into him. He fell to his knees beside her, his hands trembling as he reached out to her, his aching gaze drifting over the familiar planes of her face—the straight patrician nose, the high cheekbones, the strong jaw. Features subtly changed by the passage of years but still recognizable, still so beloved.

It was his mother, Sophia, the errant Countess of Hendon.

Chapter 2

*I*n Sebastian's happiest memories, his mother was always laughing.

A beautiful woman with golden hair, sparkling blue-green eyes, and a brilliant smile, Sophia Hendon—Sophie to her friends and loved ones—had charmed everyone who knew her . . . everyone except her own husband, Alistair St. Cyr, the Fifth Earl of Hendon.

Even as a young child, Sebastian had been painfully aware of the tensions between his mother and the man he'd believed to be his father. As he grew, the brittle silences became longer, the inevitable scenes uglier. Those were the memories he tried to forget: Sophie's tearful pleadings; the Earl's angry voice echoing along the ancient paneled corridors of Hendon Hall; the clatter of galloping hooves as Hendon drove off to London while Sophie wept someplace alone and out of sight.

Four children had been born to that troubled marriage: first a girl, Amanda, followed by three healthy sons. But then the eldest son, Richard, drowned in a rocky Cornish cove. And four years later, in the blistering heat of a brutally hot summer when their mother had defied the Earl and taken them to Brighton, the second son, Cecil, died of fever.

The marriage ruptured. Sebastian could remember his eleven-year-old self sitting on the floor in a corner of his room, his legs drawn up to his chest, his arms wrapped around his head as he tried not to listen to the furious accusations and threats the grieving parents hurled at each other. But afterward, he wished he had listened. For just a few days later his mother sailed away with friends for what was supposed to be a pleasant day's outing.

She'd kissed him that morning, the day she sailed away, and laughed when he ducked her embrace in that way of all eleven-year-old boys. But the pain in her eyes had been there for him to see, even if he hadn't understood it.

Lost at sea, they'd said.

He'd refused to believe it. Every day of what was left of that miserable hot summer he'd spent standing on the cliffs outside of Brighton, his nostrils filled with the smell of brine and sun-blasted rocks, his eyes painfully dry as he stared out to sea, watching for her, waiting for her to come sailing back. Steadfastly, he continued to insist that she must be alive, refused to believe he'd never see her again. But eventually acceptance had come.

He didn't discover it was all a lie for another twenty years.

Chapter 3

A single branch of candles lit the small old-fashioned room, its golden light flickering over the pale face of the woman who lay motionless in the bed, her eyes closed.

Hero Devlin sat beside her, a bowl of water on a nearby chest, a bloodstained cloth in her hand, her gaze on the motionless features of her husband's infamous mother. Until today, Hero had never met—had never even seen—this woman. This woman who had caused her son the kind of damage that was difficult to forgive.

Hero had seen portraits of the Countess in her youth. She'd been so beautiful, her smile wide and infectious, her eyes thickly lashed and sultry. She was still beautiful even in her sixties, with classical bone structure, smooth skin, and an aura of gentle vulnerability that might or might not be deceptive. But Hero was having a hard time tamping down the anger she'd long nourished toward the notorious Countess, for she knew only too well what Devlin's discovery of his mother's betrayal had done to him. How does any man recover from the knowledge that his mother played her husband false, then staged her own death to run off with her latest lover, never to return?

Since learning the truth, Devlin had been quietly searching for her across Europe. As long as the war between France and Britain raged, it hadn't been easy. But the coming of peace brought reports that the Countess lived here, in Paris, although she traveled frequently—sometimes to Vienna, sometimes to other destinations that proved surprisingly difficult to uncover. In the end they'd decided simply to join the horde of British aristocrats flocking to Paris and wait there for her to return. She had been expected back sometime in the coming week, but not today. Not yet.

"I don't understand what she's doing here," said Hero, leaning forward to gently wipe away a trickle of blood that rolled down the side of Sophia's temple. She kept her voice low, although she was afraid Sophie Hendon was beyond hearing anything. "She wasn't supposed to be in Paris."

Devlin stood with his back pressed against the nearest wall, his gaze on the pale woman in the bed, his face a mask of control that carefully hid every emotion, every thought, every betraying trace of pain. A streak of his mother's blood showed on one lean cheek; more of her blood stained his waistcoat and the cuffs of his shirt. Uncertain of the extent of her injuries and afraid to move her himself, he'd found a couple of street porters with a board to carry her up the stairs and across the bridge to the house on the Place Dauphine. They'd sent for a physician, but the man hadn't arrived yet and Hero was afraid there wasn't much he'd be able to do anyway.

"I don't know," said Devlin, his voice carrying a strange inflection that Hero had never heard in their nearly three years of marriage. Then he swung his head away to stare at the blackness beyond the window, his nostrils flaring as he sucked in a deep breath. *"Where is that damned doctor?"*

Hero set aside the bloodstained cloth and reached to take one of the Countess's limp hands in her own. It was a strong hand, aged and fine boned but not delicate. Beneath her fingertips Hero could feel the woman's pulse, erratic and faint. So faint. She lifted her gaze to study again that pale still face, tracing there the ways Sophie was like her son and the ways in which they differed. "Do you think she fell from the bridge?"

Sebastian shook his head. "How do you fall from a bridge with a high stone parapet?"

"Was thrown, then. If she fell from that height, there could be other injuries. Internal injuries we can't see . . ."

Hero's voice trailed off, for the wounds they could see on the Countess's head were bad enough. Her breathing was becoming as erratic as her pulse. *Please,* thought Hero, her throat so tight it hurt. *Please don't die. He's fought so hard to find you. Please, please, please . . .*

But the pulse beneath Hero's fingers grew ever fainter, then skipped, skipped, and was no more. The Countess's shallow, ragged breath stilled.

Hero leaned forward. *Breathe!* she was silently screaming, her fist tightening around that limp hand. *Please breathe!*

Then she heard Devlin say, his voice sounding as if it came from a long way off, "She's gone."

he physician arrived some ten minutes later.

They were still seated beside the Countess's deathbed when a house-maid brought word of Dr. Pelletan's arrival. A small fire crackled on the hearth, but the bedroom was in heavy shadow, and for one long moment, Sebastian could only stare at the servant. He felt numb inside, so numb he wondered if he'd ever feel anything again. A part of him knew that somewhere beneath the numbness must, surely, lie pain and grief.

Surely?

He felt Hero's hand touch his arm, heard her say to him quietly, "Would you like me to go down to thank him and tell him he's no longer needed?"

"No." Sebastian pushed to his feet. He had the strangest sensation, as if he were moving through someone else's life, or as if he were outside of himself, watching his own actions with a wooden sense of detach-ment. "No. I'll see him."

He found Philippe-Jean Pelletan standing near the window at the front of the house's small salon, his gaze on the darkly shifting, wind-tossed trees beyond. The physician was a slim man of just above average height, his thick dark hair mingled with gray, his long, thin face dominated by a prominent jaw, his dark eyes deeply set. Although Sebastian knew the man must be somewhere in his sixties, he looked and seemed younger, his movements quick and energetic.

"Monsieur le vicomte," said the doctor, turning from the window with a bow, "I came as soon as I could. Is the patient—"

"She's dead."

Pelletan was silent for a moment, his gaze on Sebastian's face in a way that made Sebastian wonder what the physician saw there. He had met the Frenchman the week before in a courtesy call, for Pelletan's daughter now lived in London and was known to Sebastian. But that had been a social occasion, whereas this was a professional visit and therefore quite different.

"It's a pity. You know this woman?" said Pelletan.

Sebastian walked over to where a decanter and collection of crystal glasses stood on a tray. "May I offer you a drink?"

"Thank you, but no."

Sebastian splashed a hefty measure of brandy into a glass. "I hope you don't object if I have one?"

Pelletan shook his head.

Sebastian replaced the stopper in the decanter with studied care. "For some years now she has called herself *Dama* Cappello. But her real name is the Countess of Hendon." He paused, then looked over at the French doctor. "She is—was—my mother."

Pelletan pursed his lips, his brows lowering in a way that suggested *Dama* Cappello was not unknown to him, at least by reputation. "Please accept my sincere condolences on your loss, *monsieur.*"

"Thank you." The brandy glass cradled in one hand, Sebastian went to stand at the window, his gaze on the small triangular-shaped Renaissance-era square below. For one shuddering moment, the physical ache of his grief was almost unbearable, so that he had to force himself to go on. "The circumstances surrounding her death are . . . confused. I would like to ask you to examine the body, perhaps give us some idea as to the cause and circumstances of her death. She was found lying in the grass beneath Pont Neuf in a way that suggests she might have fallen from above. There are significant head wounds, but I don't know if they are the result of the fall or if she was perhaps struck before being thrown from the bridge."

Pelletan stared at him. "You're asking me to perform an autopsy? Here? Now?"

"Not an autopsy precisely. More along the lines of a preliminary examination and analysis." He hesitated and, when the doctor still looked reluctant, added, "If you would be so kind?"

In France a man could be both a physician and a surgeon, for the professions were not separated here the way they were in England by centuries of custom and prejudice. Thus Dr. Pelletan was both a longtime professor at the Faculté de Médecine de Paris and chief surgeon at the ancient hospital known as the Hôtel-Dieu, positions he'd held for the past twenty years. And it occurred to Sebastian as he watched Pelletan consider his request that the man was both a respected professional and a consummate survivor, for he'd somehow managed to maintain his places despite the Restoration, despite having served as consultant-surgeon to the Emperor Napoléon, despite having once performed the autopsy on the body of the ten-year-old uncrowned boy king, Louis XVII.

Pelletan thoughtfully swiped one long, fine-boned hand down over his mouth and chin, his palm rasping against the blue shadow of his day's growth of beard. "Very well. Perhaps you could send Lady Devlin's abigail to assist if there is a need to remove her ladyship's clothing?"

Sebastian sucked in a deep breath. "Yes, of course."

It was more than an hour before Pelletan came back down the stairs from the guest bedroom, his features grim. He was in his shirtsleeves and waistcoat, for he'd stripped off his coat, and he apologized to Hero for forgetting and moved quickly to draw it on again as he entered the salon.

"There's no doubt she fell from a great height," he said, adjusting the collar of his coat. "Presumably, as you suggest, from the bridge near which she was found. Her right femur and right humerus are broken, along with several ribs and perhaps several vertebrae. I presume there is also considerable internal damage, although without a more invasive examination there's no way to know for certain."

Sebastian held himself quite still. "And the blows to her head?"

"The injury to her right temple is, I believe, a result of the fall. It's difficult to be certain about the more severe blow to the back of the head. But the knife wound in her back was obviously not caused by the fall."

"She was stabbed?" How could he have missed that?

"She was, yes. By a stiletto, most likely. It's a small but deep wound that bled very little, at least on the outside. I suspect the internal damage was considerably more severe."

"She was stabbed only the once?" said Hero.

Pelletan glanced toward her. Another man in his position might have resented being questioned by a woman. But Pelletan's own daughter had studied to become a physician in Italy, and he answered without hesitation. "Just the once, yes, my lady."

"Would a more invasive examination provide any additional insights?" asked Sebastian.

"Probably not." Pelletan paused, his gaze on the cuffs of his shirt, which Sebastian now noticed were stained with blood. "But I did notice one other thing. . . ."

"Yes?" prompted Sebastian when the physician's voice trailed off.

"There are bruises on her arms that were not caused by the fall."

"Show me," said Sebastian.

She looked so small lying in the center of the heavy old-fashioned bed, the white coverlet drawn up over her chest, her bare arms resting outside the covers and straight down at her sides. A delicate gold chain with a single pearl pendant lay around her neck; in her earlobes were simple pearl drops. Her eyes were closed, her features composed, almost at peace. With the help of Hero's abigail, Pelletan had removed and set aside her clothing and washed the worst of the blood from her face and head. In the dim light cast by the flickering candles, she might have been sleeping.

Might have been.

"If you look at the bruising here, on her forearm," said Pelletan, going to lift one arm gently and turn the delicate inner flesh to the light, "and there, on the other"—he paused to nod to where her right arm still rested at her side—"you can see quite clearly the marks left by a man's fingers digging into the flesh. The bruises are not old; they were made essentially at the same time as her other injuries, within an hour or so of death. Going by these marks, I'd say it's highly probable someone stabbed her in the back, either before or after possibly striking her on the back of the head. He then left these bruises while lifting her up to throw her over the bridge's parapet."

Sebastian stood with his arms crossed at his chest, his breath backing up tight and painful in his throat. The dark purple oval-shaped bruises showed quite clearly against Sophie's pale skin, and he felt a rush of rage so hot and powerful that he was shaking with it.

Pelletan laid her arm down and said quietly, "Have you notified the police?"

Sebastian cleared his throat and somehow managed to say, "Yes. But we haven't heard from them yet."

Pelletan nodded as if he found this unsurprising. "How much do you know about Sophia Cappello?"

Sebastian felt himself stiffen. "Why do you ask?"

"She was . . ." The Frenchman hesitated as if searching for a delicate way to phrase it, then settled on "quite close to General McClellan, one of Napoléon's marshals."

"So I've been told," said Sebastian.

Alexandre McClellan was something of a legend. The descendant of a proud old Scottish Jacobite family that had taken refuge in France after the disaster of 'forty-five, he'd long been considered one of Napoléon's most brilliant generals.

"Like most of the former Emperor's marshals, McClellan has now sworn allegiance to the Bourbons," Pelletan was saying. "I believe he's in Vienna, working with Talleyrand to secure the best possible terms for France from the Congress."

Sebastian studied the French doctor's solemn profile. "What exactly are you suggesting?"

Pelletan snapped his bag closed and turned to face him. "I'm saying there may be more to this death than a simple robbery somehow gone terribly wrong. It's not easy to unite a country again after so many years of trauma and bloodshed. In the past quarter century, France has seen half a dozen different governments come and go—absolute monarchy, constitutional monarchy, republic, directorate, consulate, empire. Now here we are once again, back to monarchy. In the past eleven months, we've torn down the tricolor and raised the white Bourbon flag, chipped the Emperor's bees and eagles off our buildings, renamed squares and bridges, and replaced the prints of Napoléon in our shopwindows with those of Louis XVIII. Such external changes are easy. But beneath it all, resentments and hatreds linger. Fester. And unfortunately, certain powerful people are far more interested in retribution than in reconciliation."

There was no need for him to mention any names. The newly restored King Louis XVIII might be genuinely interested in compromise, but he was lazy and weak. The real power in the family lay with the King's younger brother and heir presumptive to the throne, Charles, the comte d'Artois, and with their niece, Marie-Thérèse, the only surviving child of Louis XVI and Marie Antoinette. Both were filled with bitterness and wrath and an unquenchable thirst for revenge.

"What does any of this have to do with my mother's death?" asked Sebastian.

"I don't know that it does. But . . . I would advise you to be careful, my lord. Be careful what questions you ask and be very careful whom you trust." He reached for the hat he'd set on a nearby bureau. "There. I've probably said more than I should have. Good luck to you, *monsieur*. You're going to need it."

Photograph by Samantha Brown

C. S. Harris is the *USA Today* bestselling author of more than two dozen novels, including the Sebastian St. Cyr Mysteries; as C. S. Graham, a thriller series coauthored with former intelligence officer Steven Harris; and seven award-winning historical romances written under the name Candice Proctor. A respected scholar with a PhD in nineteenth-century European history, she is also the author of a nonfiction historical study of the French Revolution. She lives in New Orleans with her husband and has two grown daughters.

CONNECT ONLINE

CSHarris.net
 CSHarrisAuthor

Ready to find
your next great read?

Let us help.

Visit prh.com/nextread

Penguin
Random
House